Nathan Adler

A. n.
1. A joint connecting the hand with the forearm.
2. An effect achieved in fencing, baseball, or sleight-of-hand, etc., by working of the hand from the wrist alone. Hence craftsmanship, 'its all in the ~', 'wonderful ~work', and 'that was all ~'. A symbolic intermediary bridging the gap between the hand and the brain [From the Middle High German, and Old Norse word 'rist,' and probably from the Old English word 'wraesta' or 'writhan,' for wrest and writhe]

Wrist© Nathan Adler, 2016

Published by Kegedonce Press
11 Park Road
Neyaashiinigmiing, Ontario N0H 2T0
www.kegedonce.com
Administration Office/Book Orders
RR7 Owen Sound, ON N4K 6V5

Printed in Canada by Sunville Printco
Cover Art: Adrian Nadjiwon
Design: Eric Abram
Editor: Kateri Akiwenzie-Damm

Library and Archives Canada Cataloguing in Publication

Adler, Nathan Niigan Noodin, author
    Wrist / Nathan Niigan Noodin Adler. -- First edition.

ISBN 978-1-928120-05-6 (paperback)

    I. Title.

PS8601.D554W75 2016   C813.6   C2016-902965-4

Sales: mandagroup.com
Distribution: litdistco.ca
Customer Service/orders: Tel 1-800-591-6250 / Fax 1-800-591-6251
LitDistCo c/o Fraser Direct
8300 Lawson Rd.
Milton ON L9T 0A4
orders@litdistco.ca

We acknowledge the support of the Canada Council for the Arts which last year invested
$20.1 million in writing and publishing throughout Canada.

The Canada Council | Le Conseil des Arts
FOR THE ARTS | DU CANADA
SINCE 1957 | DEPUIS 1957

ONTARIO ARTS COUNCIL
CONSEIL DES ARTS DE L'ONTARIO
50 YEARS OF ONTARIO GOVERNMENT SUPPORT OF THE ARTS
50 ANS DE SOUTIEN DU GOUVERNEMENT DE L'ONTARIO AUX ARTS

We would like to acknowledge funding support from the Ontario Arts Council, an agency of the
Government of Ontario.

For Mae and Marion,

PART I

WIINDIGO

"Often we are driven to eat to fill other hungers that can't be filled with food...Loneliness, sadness, trauma. An emotional hollowness."

~Paraphrase of Lionel Shriver on CBC Radio

"Life is a series of natural and spontaneous changes. Don't resist them—that only creates sorrow. Let reality be reality. Let things flow naturally forward in whatever way they like."

~Lao Tzu

"Do not go gentle into that good night. Rage rage against the dying of the light"

~Dylan Thomas

It started with a joke. A dirty joke.

"If it wasn't for that joke, none of us would be alive." Day said, her words punctuated by the sound of cold water dripping into pots. The tin roof leaked every time there was rain.

"Great-grandmother was visited by Wiindigo during the lean winter months, and Gaawiin would have been eaten too, if it were not for the fact that she knew how to distract the creature—pay attention Church." Day looked at him over the edge of her glasses. "This works for both men and women."

"Gaawiin took off her clothes. Because of the joke that Wiindigo's hunger can be diverted. It also happens to be true. When her husband returned from hunting, and found Wiindigo in the midst of gratifying its hungers, Osedjig attacked the monster and was killed. This might have saved her life, because after contenting itself with her sexually, it slowly ate Osedjig—but left Gaawiin alive."

As Church listened to his grandmother's voice, he fell into the rhythms of the story as easily as the plot of a movie, his imagination helping to construct the events. Day's voice was like the light which passes through film in a projector, composing the images on-screen but rarely the subject of examination.

The Death Scene: a long shot of their cabin overlooking Ghost Lake. The camera zooms in, agonizingly slow. A Finnish-style lob-and-daub structure. The door hangs open on its hinges. Closer and closer, fine details begin to resolve themselves. Blood stains, like the marks a hand—or a claw—would make, scrambling for purchase across the heavy oak.

A man's scream rips through the silence.

It goes on and on before, abruptly, it comes to an end. Soft whimpering can be heard inside the cabin. The snuffling of an animal. A woman is crying. Grunting and meaty tearing. The slow zoom brings us through the entryway, and for a moment the screen goes black as the camera takes a moment to adjust to the dim interior. Pan to the left, taking in the sparsely furnished room and a large oak table. Pan to the right, taking in a fireplace dominating one entire wall, where a woman—Gaawiin—is crouched in a corner of the cold hearth, quietly sobbing amongst the charcoal and ash. The whites of her eyes show, pupils rolling up and away from something. Something else in the room with her.

Cut to: her husband's mangled body, limbs twisted at impossible angles. One arm is missing, torn out of its socket at the shoulder, gristle glistening white where the clavicle meets scapula. The initial spray of blood has slowed to a dribble, and only sluggishly pumps.

Something obstructs her sight-line to Osedjig's carcass, blocking the view for a moment, before it is removed. Meaty tearing sounds, animal grunting. The sight-line is obstructed again, but this time her eyes focus on the object. It is Osedjig's missing limb. The arm is raised, and the man-creature-thing takes a bite, teeth sinking into the raw human meat, rending flesh from bone. Just the creature's hand and part of its lipless mouth are visible within the frame of the shot. Wet chewing and saliva sounds.

Cut to: an extreme close-up of Gaawiin. Only her eyes are lit in a non-diegetic beam of light, like a film-noir star. A contrast of shadows, darkness and light. Cut back to the beast: a worm's-eye point of view. This is what Gaawiin sees. The ulna bone is cracked open with a snap, and the marrow inside is sucked out. Slurping-grunting sounds.

Shot of the mangled body. It twitches and moans. Osedjig is still alive, even as his arm is being eaten. Extreme close-up as Wiindigo tears off hunks of flesh, teeth scraping against bone, consuming him in exactly the same way one would eat the flesh of an animal.

Not much is revealed of the monster's physiology: only skeletal hands, and teeth uncovered by a lipless mouth, like the fleshless grin of a skull. The violence that happens outside the frame leaves one to imagine something more terrifying than special effects could ever hope to replicate. As he envisioned the sequence of events, Church decided to leave that part blank, not wanting to fill in the details. He would rather wait until they could meet in person. If it was still alive. Church had already begun to formulate a plan.

He also shied away from other details, like Gaawiin's choice to offer her body in sacrifice. Focusing instead on those details surrounding the cannibalism of Osedjig. But if the Wiindigo wasn't human, was it accurate to call it cannibalism? Church wondered.

Certainly the Wiindigo wouldn't appear human. Maybe it would manifest as the stories claimed, as a spirit in the aspect of howling wind, a man screaming and a baby crying. In physical form, it was often portrayed as a giant, without any lips— because he had eaten those parts of himself—with eyes like an owl, and a starvation thin, emaciated body.

The Wiindigo tears off one of the hunter's legs at the knee with a crunch and pop, twisting and turning the limb to loosen the ligaments and connective tissue. Osedjig screams. Miraculously he is still alive, though his scream is short-lived, as the fire of life leaves his body. Red droplets fly through the air speckling the lens as the beast brandishes the leg like a drum-stick, raising fibula to maw. Main arteries are torn, but there isn't enough blood pressure for his veins to spurt, his heart has stopped beating, so the blood leaks lethargically from Osedjig's thigh.

The Wiindigo turns to Gaawiin, to continue where it had left off, before the interruption. The smell of her husband's blood fills the room, strong on the monster's breath. It tears off great hunks of meat from the fibula gripped in its fist. She waits for her turn, for the Wiindigo to tear her apart while she is still alive, so that she too, can watch herself being devoured as she bleeds out.

But this does not happen.

The Wiindigo goes back and forth, from her body to what is left of her husband, periodically consuming Osedjig's flesh. Sating itself with one meal, even as it sates itself with her. When it is done, nothing remains of her husband except a pile of gleaming bones.

Cut to black.

The scene opens, with Gaawiin lying in bed. Her twin brother, Goshko, tries to spoon-feed her a watery broth, but the thought of eating anything after watching what the creature has done, repulses her.

"Giin-noonde-wiisinid gegoonzhishan." You have to eat something, her brother insists. "Gaawiin-giishpin-siinh maa mwetch giin-dibinawe, dash wiin maajitaa maa mwetch binoojiinsag." If not for yourself: then for the babies. The words fill her, and she gasps, choking.

"Bizzzaan." Shhh. "They are Osedjig's children." Goshko says to calm her. "You must believe that." With care and patience, he nurses her battered body back to health, though there is little he can do for her mind.

"Binoojiinsag" Goshko had said. Babies plural, because she is pregnant with twins. Niizhoodenyag. She refuses to drink the concoction of Pennyroyal and Deadly Nightshade he prepares. Why would she need the concoction, if he truly believed they were Osedjig's?

She rested her hand on her abdomen and wondered what was forming inside her, and whether they would be normal babies. Would they eat their way out of her body, or would they be born in the usual way? Even if they did turn out to be the offspring of a Wiindigo, Gaawiin was not going to abort the fetuses. They couldn't help being monsters.

Gaawiin carried the babies to term and noticed nothing out-of-the-ordinary about the pregnancy, except the way she always seemed to be hungry. But many women found themselves having strange . . . cravings when they were pregnant.

When the baby came there was a lot of blood. Too much blood. And Gaawiin died shortly after giving birth. Only one baby was born alive. There were tiny teeth marks on the remains of the dead fetus, as if something had been gnawing on it in-vitro. Goshko felt the baby's gums with a finger, where he found little teeth, hidden under the thin membrane of her gums, but sharp. Otherwise the baby appeared perfectly healthy, and normal.

She is only a baby, Goshko thought, she can't be blamed for this.

He quickly burried what was left of the other twin, as was their custom, in the trees, along with the body of Gaawiin. Wrapped tightly in a shroud like a tikinagan, they were held up high in the outstretched branches, limbs offering up their burdens to the sky so that the scavengers couldn't feast on the mouldering bones.

He was left with only one niece whom he loved like his own daughter. Goshko named her: Bagonegiizhig, a Hole-In-The-Day.

Magic

After the story, Church and Inri retreated to the second floor landing of the fire escape to sneak a few cigarettes. Cigarettes are an appetite suppressant, and in their family—to a greater or lesser extent, they all smoked—though Day did not approve of her grandson smoking. Marie smoked constantly, lighting one menthol-cigarette off the other between her shaking fingers. Mukade-wiiyas preferred her tobacco in a pipe.

Mukade-wiiyas and Church occupied two of the three small bedrooms on the second floor. Day's Daughter, who they called "Day" for short, and Marie shared the front room on the first floor. The third guest bedroom upstairs remained empty, for when Inri or Peter came to visit. (They never visited at the same time because they disliked each other).

It was damp out, but the rain had stopped.

"Gaawiin was being punished." Inri brushed a lock of hair out of his wolfish eyes. It like he was wearing a pair of contact lenses, though Church knew this wasn't a special effect; they were real.

"What for?" Church leaned in to the flame, ember glowing as he inhaled and the tobacco caught.

"She and Osedjig were converted to Christianity by a missionary. Gaawiin was the first to willingly leave the old ways, and abandon the protection of her manitous. Maybe without those guardians, she was vulnerable. Hunger came to take her. But Gaawiin found a way to escape."

Inri's eyes drifted down to the cross-hatching of hesitation marks—and one lengthwise scar—decorating each of his forearms, from elbow to wrist. "There's always a way out. It just depends on how desperate you are to escape. And whether or not you're willing to pay the price."

When Church was twelve Inri slit his wrists. He'd finally overcome the test scratches and dug in deep enough to hit an artery. They barely sewed him up fast enough before he bled out. Inri was lucky to have survived.

All Church had to do was look at the cross-hatching of blue-green veins on his forearms to see that he always had a way out. Inri had taught him that. It was a relief to know that freedom was so close. He imagined what this liberation must have felt like for Inri, right before the end, when the freedom finally overtook him, bursting from his ulna in a red streak. s

Sometimes, Inri wore baggy clothes that hid his body. Sometimes, he did everything he could to efface his gender. Negate it. Hooded sweatshirts and baggy jeans. And other times he wore tight, form-fitting clothes, or skin-tight dresses. Opposite extremes. But no matter what he wore, Inri couldn't completely disguise himself. His lips were large and full, and his face was round and heart-shaped, like a bruised supermodel. He was the male version of his twin sister. He viciously and compulsively tore out his eyelashes.

They took turns taking drags on the cigarette, and Inri told him about magic.

"All magic is just sleight-of-hand. Distraction and misdirection. The only real magic left in the world is the kind you can steal. Something from nothing."

Then he showed Church how to read the future.

"Give me your hand."

Inri hunched over his palm, trying to decipher the lines hidden there. In contrast to his own—Inri's long lacquered nails were painted with denatonium benzoate in a hue of dried-blood—the black on Church's nails was chipped and bitten to the quick. Inri's traced the lines of life, and love. A long, sideways slash bisected his palm, fate cutting across the lines of the head and the heart.

"Sometimes there isn't much of a difference between magic and staying alive, between sleight-of-hand and breathing. Distract, misdirect, and a coin or a knife can appear. Like magic. Distract, misdirect, and other things can disappear just as easily—your wallet, or your heart."

"What do you see?" Church asked.

"Trouble." Inri predicted. "But I wouldn't take it personally. Most of us have very little wiggle room. You can't change the future any more than you can change the past. The dice will fall as they are cast. There's no such thing as free will."

Church knew about misdirection. Peter used his "help" on occasion because Church's smaller frame was able to sqeeze through tight spaces, and his hands were light and quick. Peter said he was "too young to go to jail." Stealing was second nature, like breathing in his sleep. It was all in the wrist.

"One day you will show someone your scars." The words hung in the air. Bleeding. "One day, you might even let someone make a few of their own." Inri was fond of inventing provocative little statements, accumulating sayings the way some people collected baseball cards, philosophical observations, or Buddhist koans. They always stuck around in his head long after.

Church already had scars, he hardly needed any more, and the idea of showing someone seemed wrong. He spent so much effort trying to keep them hidden. The only thing worse than revealing your scars, would be to allow someone to make new ones. Inri displayed his scars openly, anyone could see the damage decorating his body.

"Let them stare," Inri held his nose high in the air. "They'd stare anyway."

Inri introduced Church to Simone, a knife. He'd named it Simone, "because she sings. But only I can hear it." Something delicate and deadly, Simone kept Inri safe.

"I got something for you," Inri handed him a box wrapped in a red silk ribbon, menthol cigarette held to his lipsticked lips, shoulders hunched under muskrat-trimmed stole.

If his life were a movie, this would be the part where everything froze, and angels sang. The part where the character encounters something significant with a capital "S," an earth-shattering, life-changing, never-be-the-same-again, remember-this-because-it's-going-to-become-important-for-the-plot-later kind of moments.

Church pulled the drawstrings on the ribbon like the knot on a shoelace, and lifted the lid on the box. The bone hilt of a knife was just visible above a leather sheathe; the sharp blade catching and reflecting the light.

"What are you going to name it?" Inri asked. "A blade needs a name."

He'd call it Religion.

"Religion." Church said, and Inri smiled.

"Why are you giving this to me?" Church asked.

"I wish I hadn't been born," Inri said as if that were an answer to his question, "or at least that I'd been born really, really ugly. But sometimes even being ugly isn't enough. You're only safe when you're dead." And then: "If you were going to kill yourself, how would you do it?"

Church shrugged, not knowing whether he should confess to his uncle exactly how he would do it. Not knowing if he should reveal how meticulously he had planned it out, if he were going to do it.

"If I was going to kill myself, this is the place where I'd do it," Inri said, showing him the place on his arm where he would slit his wrists. Cigarette held daintily between the fingers of his left hand as he indicated the blank space between two scars that he'd made on a previous attempt.

"This is my way out," Inri exhaled smoke. ". . . It's like, when things get too fucked up, I always know that I have a way out. I can walk through the walls. I can leave anytime I want. It's a get-out-of-jail-free card. Religion will keep you safe, just like my Simone."

"Is this because you saw something in my future?" Church asked.

"No one should know their own future," Inri's eyes were unfocused as he stared at something in the near-distance, not really answering the question. Then he showed Church how to strap the blade to his ankle, so that the cuff-leg of his jeans hid the blade.

"Now you'll never have to be alone."

"Sometimes it feels as if the philosophers were wrong, and that the earth is not round. It is flat. I'm close to the edge and don't even realize that at any moment I might step off of it . . ."

~Excerpt from the field notes of Harker Lockwood.

York, Upper Canada. June 1st 1872,

Dear William James,

You have my eternal gratitude for making the introductions! Othniel Marsh has agreed to take me on, as a member of his field expedition. I will not have to travel the distance from the northern terminus of the Ontario-Simcoe & Huron Railway on my own, and I shall have the company of another scholar. I leave on the train towards Sydenham—the tracks being so recently extended—almost the entire way—on the 3rd of June to meet with M. Marsh. From the halfway distance between Sydenham and Owen Sound, we shall set out by coach to that riotous port town—"The Dirty"—as it is jovially referred to, where we will meet with the rest of the crew, and thence travel by steamer to the Twin Cities. And yet still our journey will not be complete. From the Twin Cities we shall travel by canoe and portage with the aide of our Indians-guides. By the grace of their aid, we shall reach our unlikely destination.

It is fortunate that a person of such high scientific esteem is engaging in this journey, when I myself am also looking to make just such a pilgrimage, and that he would be so generous as to take me on as a member of his party. I expect to observe first-hand these queer instances of the phenomena known as 'Wiindigo Psychosis.' This illness that you have set in my sights is surely one worthy of studying, and this research trip shall undoubtedly provide much fodder for my dissertation.

Thank you for your assistance & warmest regards,

Your colleague,

Harker Lockwood

Black Hole: is a region of space-time from which
nothing, not even light, can escape. The theory
of general relativity predicts that a sufficiently
compact mass will deform space-time to form
a black hole. Around a black hole there is a
mathematically defined surface called an event
horizon that marks the point of no return. It is
called "black" because it absorbs all the light
that hits the horizon, reflecting nothing.

The death of a black hole

A galaxy is a swirling cluster of stars. A black hole is a swirling
cluster of darkness. A darkness that eats stars, a darkness that
eats entire galaxies. In its hunger a galaxy of darkness can never
be full, it is an insatiable funnel siphoning all light, swallowing
stars whole. The more it eats, the greater its hunger, and the
greater its hunger, the more it can eat. And eat. And eat. And
eat. And eat. Except, the thing about a galaxy of darkness: it
is invisible and swallows all light, but it will still devour you,
even if you don't believe. Things that are real don't need you to
believe in them, they'll consume you just the same. That's why,
to her uncle, the medicine man who named her, she appeared as
a gap to his eyes.

Goshko could sense her presence with his djiiban, his sixth-
sense; that invisible ability of perception, as an absence. So
he called her Bagonegiizhig, a Hole-In-The-Day, after the
Ojibwe constellation, also known as the madoodoowasiniig,
the sweating stones, after the seven stones used in sweat lodge,
and after the seven poles used in the shaking tent, and the seven
Grandfathers and their seven Teachings, and the seven brightest
stars in the winter constellation also known as the Pleiades,
that rises in the East during binaakwiiwi-giizis, leaves-falling-
moon, travels across the sky during those cold moons of winter,
and sets in the west during aandego-giizis, the crow-moon. He

named her after that distant progress of the stars, from east to west, the same direction the dead travel on their journey to the spirit world. Goshko named her after the doorway between this world and the next, and the darkness between stars.

When she looked at her great-grandson, Bagonegiizhig could feel the age in her creaking limbs. Church's youth was like a blue smear obscuring her vision with thoughts of Ghost Lake, where the bodies of her relations rested in the trees, laid out like ghoulish ornaments. She had no peers, all were dead: friends, enemies—she had outlived them all. All she had left were her descendants. Sometimes she felt like a tightly wound spring, containing force, motion, and kinetic energy. She wondered how much longer she could endure? Her life was grueling; day after day, starvation ate at her like a burning ember. She was the first of her kind, if you believed the story of her birth.

For Church, Hole-In-The-Day was a bit scary, even as an old woman, a frail, skinny-to-the-point-of emaciation, old crone of a woman. She was almost as dark as some Africans, the people Anishinaabe called Mukade-wiiyaas, or Black-meat. This was, in fact, what most people called her, though it was not her original name. Mukade-wiiyaas: hard as bone, like opaque glass, reflecting nothing. In his recollections of her, she was a buzzing, barely contained hive of electricity, sitting on a nest of bees but holding back her screams. Church always worried she would shatter. Bagonegiizhig, Hole-In-The-Day. She unnerved him until the day she died, choking on a turkey bone in the Christmas stuffing. The Last Supper:

Mukade-wiiyas sat in the place of honour, at the head of the table. In one of his rare appearances, Inri had made it home for the holidays, and he sat to the left. Day's Daughter sat to the right, in the empty spot reserved for her. There was always a missing chair, so there would be enough space for her wheelchair. Marie sat beside Inri, distant and silent as always.

The only time she could pull herself away from her dreams, was when they were about to eat. Church sat across from Marie, and beside his grandmother.

The scraped and scarred oak table was laden and creaking under the weight of the food. It was at least as old as Mukade-wiiyas herself, if not older, and it had been in their family for as long as Church could remember. Generations. Generations of wiindigowak had sat around that old table and eaten, like some sort of spiritual ritual, and maybe for them, it was.

It was a feast fit for a kingdom, or in this case, one wiindigo family.

There was no grace, though Day's Daughter had gone to a Roman Catholic Residential School, and Mari and Inri had both gone to a Presbyterian one. Mukade-wiiyas had gone to none, and refused to worship foreign gods, or even Anishinaabe manitous. She had no need for them. Mukade-wiiyas and her progeny were themselves spirits out of legend, what need did they have for prayers to their peers or competitors?

When everyone had found their appropriate places, there was a moment of acknowledgement as they surveyed the abundance arrayed before them: poultry, pork, beef, fish, turnip, beets, pie, carrots, turkey, stuffing, corn, gravy, squash, potatoes and yams. And then. They began to eat.

Black holes are a creative force in the universe. This may seem counter-intuitive, but it is believed that they exist at the centre of most galaxies, including our own. They are the dark heart that forms galaxies even as they destroy them; creation and destruction are two sides of the same coin. This is difficult to understand when you are the one being devoured, but true just the same. They are the engine that drives the universe.

But black holes can also die. Not with a bang or an explosion, but a slow steady decline as particles evaporate and the gravity well slowly shrinks over time. In the natural scheme of things, such a death would happen on a scale that makes geological time seem juvenile. Ancient beings that are for all intents and purposes immortal, or as immortal as anything truly can be. Luckily for Bagonegiizhig, she didn't have to wait an eternity for her hunger to end.

It happened like this:

The bone lodged in her throat and pierced her esophagus, every spasm of muscle as she coughed driving it deeper as the lump of half-chewed food above the bone caught in the Y of the wish. Her airflow clogged, and the need to breathe increased as panic sent her heart rate thumping, adrenaline coursing, lungs burning, brain screaming. Blotches of darkness crowded at the edges of her vision like brown clouds coalescing. No amount of coughing could dislodge the netting of bone piercing her throat, and blocking access to the air.

Sound of chair legs screeching, clunking as they fell to the floor, pushed aside by the back of the knee as everyone stood up, one long drawn out moment of oh-no what-should-we-do? A frozen tableau, before the chaos of movement returned, Day crying out and struggling to free her chair from under the confines of the table, Inri and Church rushing to Black-meat's side, Marie's eyes gone wide tracking the sudden movements, not understanding the actions taking place before her, frantic telephone calls, and finally, stillness.

Even black holes can die. Eventually.

Black-meat seemed to collapse in on herself, until there was nothing left except skin and bones. The gravity well of her presence was gone, and they were left suddenly adrift, like asteroids without an orbit. Flung careening out into space. An orbit is just a controlled fall, and this was the inverse of that controlled fall. At one-hundred-and-nine years old—her official age on paper, though they all suspected that in reality she was much older—she was only the second person he had ever seen die. In his head, Church hadn't even started counting yet. She was Number Two: Bagonegiizhig. Hole-In-The-Day. Mukade-wiiyas. Black-meat. The Wiindigo's daughter.

Ghost particles: A description of neutrinos, subatomic particles so small, that solid objects are as wide as empty space; they pass right through. They have very little mass, and travel at speeds close to the speed of light. Each neutrino is associated with a corresponding anti-neutrino, an identical particle with symmetrical mass.

Thirteen Moons

"A woman's body follows the phases of the moon. Each time the earth rotates around the sun, the moon rotates around the earth thirteen times, thirteen cycles of 28 days, thirteen phases of blood."

"There are thirteen moons in the Anishinaabe calendar. You count the months by the phases of the moon, and you count the years by the winter. One winter, is one year, because winters can be harsh, and not everyone always manages to live through them. And the days are counted by the night. The night, rather than the day, is given the place of importance in organizing the week. Nights. Moons. Winters. This is the way that the Anishinaabek organize their time—and even though we are wiindigo, our family is no different."

If anything, they felt a certain kinship with the night, the phases of the moon, and the cold depth of the white beast called winter. These were the things that occupied their thoughts; not the days of sun, but the dark depths of the night, the winter, and the frost that was said to grip their hearts. They had, so the stories said, hearts made of ice. But Church's heart still beat, even if it was cold. Maybe wiindigo were just cold-blooded? Church wondered. Maybe that's what distinguished them from the rest of humanity? Church wasn't a biologist, he only knew that he was different, no matter how much Day insisted that he try to be human. He wasn't.

At least—not entirely.

"Long ago," Day's Daughter told him, "they used to tell stories in the winter, during those long nights when winter was at the height of its power. When the days were so brief, they seemed a mere lightening of the sky, then darkness; the wind would pull at your cabin, like long fingers prying at the chinks in your shelter, a mad beast, hungry for the warmth of your fire, your hearth, and the heart that beats in your chest. During the shortest days of the year, this is when they'd tell the best stories. The adsookan. The sacred stories, the legends. They were different from the dibaajimowinan of summer. The adsookan tell the story of how the West Wind impregnated Sky Woman, or how Nanabozhoo burned his ass. Stories of creation or destruction, stories to lighten the mood and stories to make the time pass, and ward off the darkness of the day."

"Winter, is the time for stories."

And with this preface, Day would begin to tell a tale. For a while it would hold both Church and Inri spellbound as she weaved a web, to the sound of Mukade-wiiyas cooking in the kitchen, clattering pots and pans and running water.

The Wiindigo's Daughter

Inri, Marie, Day, and Mukade-wiiyas. They all had the same tattoo. It was a narrow blue line that ran from the lower lip, to the tip of the chin. Gaawiin had once had the same tattoo, as did her mother before her. Mukade-wiiyas had decided to carry on the tradition as a connection to the woman who had given birth to her. A mark of beauty, and a rite of passage from childhood to adulthood.

Gaawiin had been born first. Premature. She was slimy and covered in blood and vaginal fluid like something half-formed. Her twin brother was born three weeks later. Delayed interval pregnancy. He was a surprise, and something of a miracle. There was a running joke that she came out too early, so they named her Gaawiin-giizha-noode, Not-fully-cooked. They named the boy, Goshko-waagooshens, Little fox surprise.

Unlike her mother, who had been born too early, Bagonegiizhig the Wiindigo's daughter, had been born too late. Burnt instead of being raw. Although most people called her Mukade-wiiyas, Black-meat. Born from death, and the bleeding chrysalis of her mother's body.

Bagonegiizhig couldn't help blaming herself. If she hadn't been wiindigo, would her mother still be alive? Was it her fault? Had she been so greedy, even in the womb? Her uncle never held her responsible. Goshko raised her as his own daughter. She was all he had left of his twin-sister.

As she grew, Bagonegiizhig attempted to fit in with the rest of her uncle's family, her cross-cousins. But her appetites were too large. And her uncle's family too soft hearted. When she cried for food, they fed her. If there wasn't enough, Goshko would go hungry, rather than see his niece suffer.

But as she grew, so did her appetite. It grew out of all proportion to the size of her body, and even though she ate more than any of the strongest men of Ghost Lake, her diminutive stature was unaffected. In outward appearance she was only a young girl, but all the Elders looked upon her with worry, as other members of the community donated resources to support Goshko's family.

When Bagonegiizhig was nearing the end of childhood, she looked upon the skinny faces of her cross-cousins, and knew what she had to do. She could no longer live with her family. They were starving, and she feared that they wouldn't be able to keep her sated for much longer.

She was still a girl when she left. She hadn't even bled yet. She didn't tell anyone where she was going or why. Leaving without saying good-bye was the most merciful thing she could do. They could feel relieved that she was gone without feeling guilty for secretly wishing her away.

They were too generous, too willing to give. Goshko's wife— Giizhaate, and his step-children, also claimed a mythical lineage, deriving ancestry from mitigo-naabe—a tree-spirit. It was in their nature to give, even to give portions of their body. If it hadn't been for the unique ability to partially subsist on light, Bagonegiizhig suspected they wouldn't have survived.

It wasn't good for her to be near them. A Wiindigo's daughter. Though her uncle tried to keep this knowledge from her, he couldn't keep it a secret. The circumstances of her birth. She was Wiindigo. It was what the people called her, in whispers, just below the range of hearing.

Wiindigo.

Softly spoken, like the sighing of the wind through the trees, winter branches clacking together. It was omnipresent, this word.

Wiindigo.

She knew what it meant. She wasn't entirely human. She was a monster though Goshko would never admit it.

Driven by hunger, she ate Deadly Night Shade berries. She knew they were poisonous, but couldn't resist the temptation. Dark as fresh blood, leaves filled with holes as if corroded by acid, and delicate purple flowers, yellow anther stamens perched on filament tendrils. They were juicy and sweet! They made her stomach ache, but she suffered no other ill effects. She became immune, or maybe she always had been. Just because the birds ate them, did not mean they were fit for human consumption. But she wasn't entirely human.

She was grateful her uncle taught her how to survive. He'd insisted that she learn, even more than he taught his step-children. Had he known she would leave? She became skilled at hunting, fishing, and trapping, building on the knowledge Goshko imparted, learning which roots were good to eat, and how to use each plant in the forest. Even those plants most considered noxious.

" . . . And—for the most part—Mukade-wiiyas learned how to dull her appetites, without causing harm to others."

This is where Day would finish the story.

Church asked Inri to fill in the rest.

"Your grandmother won't speak of this." The fire escape rattled as Inri brushed a strand of hair behind his ear. "It had been an unusually long, cold winter. People say Day and Mukade-wiiyas resorted to cannibalism when they ran out of food. But desperate actions in a desperate situation doesn't make them monsters. They did what was necessary." Inri never spoke like this without reminding Church that his grandmother was "delusional."

"It's not her fault. Day's getting older, and sometimes when people get older they get things mixed up in their head. I don't want you listening to her stories as if they're plain truth. Anyway, this is the way the rest of the story goes . . ."

As Church listened, the individual words that made up the narrative shimmered and vanished like a hot-day black-top mirage, or barbeque-heat visual distortion. He fell into the rhythms of the story easily, his imagination helping construct the events.

It was mid-winter, and they had not laid by enough preserves to keep themselves fed for the winter. Whereas a few mouthfuls of food could keep Wabitii alive, Day and Mukade-wiiyas required much more. And Wabitii suspected that his wife was pregnant. Each night they would go out to scour the snow-swept land for sustenance, and each day they would return with their hands, empty. The winter had been particularly harsh and unseasonably cold, even the coyotes and wolves, who are excellent at scavenging, were beginning to starve. You had to be careful with them around small children. Under normal circumstances they would have posed little threat, but starvation drove everyone to desperate actions.

The dam had blocked up the river, raised the level of the lake, flooded the wild rice beds, upset the natural rhythms of flora, fauna and fowl, the wild game, the trapping lines, the low-lying gardens. The water even unearthed bodies from their graves, at least the new ones; the ones who had chosen to be buried in the

Christian way, into the arms of eshkaakimikwe, their mother earth, instead of being interred in the proper way of scaffold, or tree burial, safe in the outstretched arms of the poplar trees, which hold the shrouded bodies up to their grandfather and grandmother in the sky like an offering.

The people of Ghost Lake went to their relatives in neighbouring communities, into Sterling or the Twin Cities, swallowed up by the towns. Only a few stayed, those who had somehow managed to avoid being devoured by their schools, those who still lived in the traditional way, or those too old or too stubborn to contemplate living in any other place.

Wabitii looked into the eyes of his wife and realized that if she didn't get anything to eat, she and his unborn children weren't going to survive the winter. Day wasn't as hardy as ninzigozis, his mother-in-law, who he had no doubt, would weather the storm like an old piece of leather. As the winter wore on, the kernel of an idea slowly formed. A way he could ensure his wife's survival.

Wabitii derived part of his ancestry from a white-tailed deer. He didn't hunt or eat the flesh of deer, because it was too much like cannibalism. During The Time When Animals Spoke to Humans, it was not uncommon to go and live as the animal people did, taking a beaver or deer for a husband or wife. This could be done if they gave up their human life; but some of the children from this union would inevitably grow up curious about their lineage and choose to return to the human way of life, marrying human people and growing up to have human children closely connected to their animal ancestors.

Anishinaabe stories are filled with such intersections, across species, across-states of being, between animate objects; like the girl who fell in love with anang, a star, or Nanaboozhoo, son of an Anishinaabe woman who was impregnated by the West Wind, and grandson of the moon.

Day was dying. Even though Wabitii gave up his rations to sustain her, it was clear she wasn't going to make it through the winter. Each night that she left to scour the land, she came back more frail, her body wasting as her muscles and other tissues were broken down to keep her heart pumping, brain functioning. The basic definition of starvation is an imbalance between energy intake and energy expenditure, and a Wiindigo is by definition always hungry, always starving. Day being part-wiindigo, needed more energy under the best circumstances. And right now, they were all starving.

So one evening, after his ninzigozis had already left to scour the land for food (Day being too weak, at this point, to scavenge anything), Wabitii kissed his beautiful young wife, fed her both their remaining rations, and then took his shotgun out into the snow, and shot himself in the head.

Shooting himself in the head would preserve most of the meat.

The gun-shot echoed around for miles in every direction, reverberating off of the hills, the snow-swept landscape, and the branches of the poplar trees reaching up to the sky world. Wabitii had known that Hole-In-The-Day would hear it, and that the scavenging wolves and coyotes wouldn't be able to find his body before his wife and mother-in-law got to it.

Mukade-wiiyas's ghost.

It was a custom amongst the Ghost Lake Anishinaabe, not to name children until after they were born. Just in case. And so, Bagonegiizhig's twin sister was never given a name, because she had never been born. Except that Bagonegiizhig knew her sister's name, because her sister had told it to her, herself. Her name was Zhii-bzii-awaag. Tough-meat.

Names have power. There is a proverb against saying the names of the recently departed, and risk drawing their spirits back to earth. Some Anishinaabek won't say "wiindigo," for fear of conjuring hunger's presence. Their very name is a curse. Something unlucky, like saying the name of the Scottish play aloud.

But if it wasn't for her twin sister, Bagonegiizhig wouldn't have had any playmates as a child—even her cross-cousins were leery of spending time with her. She always had Zhii-bizii-awaag though, and this also, other children found unsettling. Not only was she wiindigo, she was also haunted. Gzhaate and Goshko chose to regard the spirit as an imaginary friend.

Bagonegiizhig threw a stone across Ghost Lake, and to her amusement, Zhii-bizii-awaag made it fly, skipping across the water in an arch, continuing onto the land in a circle, back onto the water, back onto the land, before finally losing steam and sputtering out in the lake.

Her young cousin Dedenaan, named Grandfather even as a child, witnessed the trick. He stared at her with wide eyes, then went off to play with his brothers, who were probably bathing somewhere, basking in the sun like rattlesnakes on the rocks. Her cross-cousins were so much like their mother.

Gzhaate. Silent as trees that have seen moons pass beyond the memory of living memory, and in their wisdom, would see more moons pass if they were patient, and hardy enough. Like the gnarled evergreens that cling to the edges of the cliff face, safe from the ravages of forest fires, above and below, and the browsing antlers of the moose and deer. Gzhaate had outlived her first husband, and then another, before marrying Goshko, and bringing with her a brood of radiant children. Maybe they'd be unlucky, and get swept away by the flames. Seedlings really didn't have much choice in where they became rooted; their range of movement limited to tracking the progress of the sun across the sky.

Gzhaate's children were not the most active lot, happy to sit in one place, as long as there was plenty of sunlight and fresh water. They didn't engage in play like other children mimicking the occupations of their elders.

Bagonegiizhig didn't blame them. Why bother hunting for food when they could simply absorb sustenance from the sun? And with such little effort? Bagonegiizhig was envious. She wished she too, could eat sunlight—but found photons too thin a soup. When her cousins became cranky and dormant over the long winter months, Bagonegiizhig felt at her most alert.

A forest doesn't know what the future holds, but it is patient. Larger than the sum of its parts, the roots knot together underground to form one rhizome, if you cut down one tree, it doesn't destroy the whole. Pitted with muskeg, swamp, and areas of badland, the forests around Ghost Lake would be alive long after people were gone. The pace of mortals in comparison, were like the blip of spark-bugs in the night; here one moment, gone the next. Bagonegiizhig didn't know how long a wiindigo could live, but figured she would find out—eventually. Is it better to burn out, or fade away? She wondered.

Watching her adopted step-cousins, she knew if you waited long enough in one spot, what you needed would come to you. But this strategy didn't suit her. Bagonegiizhig didn't have the patience to wait that long.

When she mastered control of her hunger, Bagonegiizhig returned to Ghost Lake. Four winters after leaving Goshko, his radiant wife, and his radiant stepchildren. She returned to where the story began.

The cabin had been boarded up and shunned, a place of maji-mashkiki, bad medicine. Gaawiin and Osedjig had constructed it in the manner of the Finnnish settlers, logs stacked and slathered with mud like a beaver's lodge to chink the gaps in the timber. Here, her mother had been beset, Osedjig had been murdered, and Mukade-wiiyas and Zhii-bizii-awaag conceived in blood, death, and cannibalism. She claimed it as her home—no one else would have it, and it was hers by right; as Gaawiin's only living descendant.

"Zhii-bizii-awaag."

Whenever a fork fell off the counter, or a casserole dish flew across the kitchen to smash into a wall, "Zhii-bizii-awaag" they'd say, "tough meat," or "she's in a cranky mood today," and then leave an offering to shrivel and rot on the window sill. In death, everything that is destroyed is made whole.

And even in death—or pre-life—since she had never lived to take a single breath outside of their mother's womb, Bagonegiizhig's twin sister was hungry. The ghost of an infant wiindigo. Zhii-bizii-awaag coveted the pleasure of flesh and bone, and the process of blunting the sharp angles of hunger. Initially her growth kept pace, and she appeared to grow older as Bagonegiizhig grew older, as if the vestiges of life kept working for a brief time even after death, or maybe she was merely imitating her sister, simulating growth as she was drawn along in her sister's wake for a short way, before falling off and being left behind.

She could only keep pace so far.

Zhii-bizii-awaag would never grow up, her development was frozen in death. She only appeared in the form of a young girl, even as Bagonegiizhig kept maturing, and growing older, and older, and older. She was Mukade-wiiyas's shadow, the un-living disembodied childhood mirror that would always be with her, throughout her long wiindigo life, her childhood imaginary friend. She had never once been alone, in fact, she didn't know how that would feel, she always knew her sister wasn't far, and being truly alone was one of only a few thoughts that scared her. Zhii-bizii-awaag. Mukade-wiiyas's twin sister. Mukade-wiiyas's ghost.

"This is my account, being the journal of Harker Lockwood, of the events I have been a witness to at Ghost Lake, Ojibwe Indian Territory, located in the heart of Rupert's Land, Hudson Bay country."

~Harker Lockwood

Exerpts from: the field notes, diary entries & letters, of Harker Lockwood, MB BS, Ph.D.

June 3rd 1872, Upper Canada,

The train is soothing. The rocking motion puts me at my ease. The country and surrounding wilderness is filled with beauty and mystery and I am looking forward to this expedition.

I have come a long way since I first began studying to become a physician at Guy's Hospital on the Banks of the Thames, and even further now that I've left Harvard far behind on the banks of the Charles. We are now passing through a small area of badlands at the Forks of the Credit where the Mississauga Indians come to trade. It is ironic that since deciding to study the ailments of the mind, rather than the ailments of the body, I seem to retreat further and further from civilized society as I trek into this Canadian wilderness. Though I have lived for some time in the New World, I realize now that I have not yet experienced one tenth of its vastness.

The hills and valleys envelope us in their embrace. The greens and blues of a Renaissance painting, rolling country here and there interrupted by a rocky promontory, or the cliff-face bluffs of the escarpment. Birch trees cavorting like skeletons amidst the living greenery. The land rises steadily, and we seem to climb higher with every fathom's distance further away from the city of York. We have yet to pass through the townships of Mono, Mulmur, Melancthon and Grey.

June 5th, 1872,

I did not sleep well, in anticipation of what is to come. My meeting with Marsh and his crew-men, and this endless country, fills me with a restless anxiety. Despite my fatigue, I remain hopefully optimistic. I am looking forward to understanding this strange illness that afflicts the Indigenous inhabitants. It is so little examined, any study of it, can not help but to yield rich discoveries. The implications for the field of psychiatry are illimitable.

I'm already weary of the train. It stops so frequently, either from distruptions on the newly laid track, or some mechanical failures. We've spent more time sitting on the tracks, than we have moving along them. I am ready to get on with the next portion of my travels.

My restless anxiety has given way to chills. I fear I am unwell but hope to make a speedy recovery. I stay in my cabin, wrapped in a blanket, and go out only sparingly to the dining cart for refreshments.

I meet with M. Marsh on the morrow.

June 6th 1872, Thornbury

The first meeting with M. Marsh did not go as well as I had expected. I am not even sure what I expected,; a man of some repute, a scholar, a man interested in discovery, certainly, but . . . he is not as I imagined.

I disembarked from the train near the town of Thornbury, the rails on the last leg of the journey between York and Sydenham having not yet been laid, and where it had been arranged, I was to meet Marsh at the end of the line.

His expression on our first meeting was sour, he had a scowl upon his face, an admirably strong hand shake, and then my luggage was bundled roughly into the storage compartment of the stagecoach by his half-breed servant, and we departed at a brisk trot along the Sydenham road, with barely more than the few gravelly words spoken in greeting.

The escarpment rose to our left, blotting out a portion of the sky, while to the right, we had views of the bay as we followed the curve of the lake. Othniel appeared disinterested and insensible of appreciating anything that passed outside the dappled windows of our carriage.

I attempted to engage Othniel in conversation.

"Do you hope to make any specific discoveries?" I asked, and then mentioned how grateful I was that it had pleased him to do this favour to his colleague, William James, and how lucky for me that they were such good friends. To both attempts at discourse I received but two word responses, "We'll see" and "That's so." He might as well have said, to the deuce between gritted teeth, and in just that manner.

Marsh pulled his cap down and was soon fast asleep without even making an excuse of weariness. Seeing that he had seen fit to please himself, I was heartened that we were not going to stand on ceremony. Aren't we a suitable pair to divide the desolation between us!

I made myself comfortable on my side of the coach, and tried to sleep. I was actually pleased to do away with the niceties that would be expected under normal social circumstances, as I was still feeling slightly feverish. The rocking motion of the carriage occurred with greater ferocity than the steam-train, and I found it difficult to understand, not without some envy, how Marsh could lapse so easily into slumber.

I slept only fitfully, waking with a start every few moments at some jostle. When I did sleep, I was plagued with troublesome dreams, whose shadowy presences disappeared upon waking, melting away from my mind like mist, before I had a chance to grasp what it was that had so disturbed me. To say I passed the night in some discomfort would be an understatement.

June 7th 1872, On the Sydenham road

I woke to the rocking of the carriage, and sunlight streaming in, feeling tired and wan, a blasting heat on one side of my face, where, having finally settled into a restful sleep at dawn, my fair skin proceeded to burn. Like an ant under a magnifying glass, the dappled texture of the spun-glass window had no doubt focused the rays of the sun—the day apparently having dawned bright and clear. My face, neck, ears and lips were already blistered, though I was rested, and the fever seemed to have fled from the heat, leaving only a crimp in my neck, a lingering queasiness, and my cooked, tender, skin. All in all, it was a worthwhile trade for the benefit of a restful sleep. Though I felt some feelings of recrimination towards my travelling companion.

I squinted at Marsh, wondering why he hadn't seen fit to wake me, or at least to close the drapes. He couldn't have failed to see my head bobbing with the restless carriage as we passed through the townships of Grey and Bruce, my face slowly broiling in the heat of the sun until well past mid-day. Rather than get off on the wrong foot, I thought it best to ignore the oversight. Marsh is a scientist, and certainly he has more important things on his mind than babysitting his fellow travelers. Whatever the case I chose not to address it, commenting instead on the remarkable distance we had covered, and the quality of the air.

Marsh remained taciturn and incommunicative, though I noticed he had a satisfied grin that my imagination couldn't help but attribute to the occasion of my burned skin. It was this incident that made me wonder what relation Marsh had with my friend James, whether it was on amiable terms, or if there might be some system of debt and repayment that made my presence on this journey, not particularly welcome, but merely part of some exchange.

The wave-particle duality: is a central concept of quantum mechanics which states that all matter can exist, and behave as, both a particle and a wave.

Shirly

Her Christian name was Shirly. This was not the name she had been given when she was born, but the name she'd been given at that school because her real name had been 'unpronounceable.' Bagonegiizhig O'daanis. The daughter of Hole-In-The-Day. Most people called her Day or Day's Daughter, but after the "accident," she went back to using the name "Shirly," instead of "Day."

Her first husband was gone. Though he was never far. He would be a part of her forever. And now her second husband had left her. She was now alone, and Owanii was long gone. So were three photographs from her album, their shapes forming pale shadows, like ghosts where the people used to be.

Baby Inri cried for milk, but she had nothing to give him. Her breasts had stopped lactating, her greedy wiindigo body unwilling to give up its sustenance. They had run out of food days earlier, and Inri wouldn't stop crying. He kept crying and crying. Shirly wasn't sure what to do. They were down to drinking spiced water, but it barely eased the ache of need burning in her. The scent of cinnamon and cloves filled the air like an empty promise. Like an exclamation mark that emphasized the end of a sentence, it punctuated their need, and their hunger, underscoring the emptiness of their bellies and the barrenness of their cupboards. What had been intended to offer respite to their suffering was an additional torment.

Shirly gave baby Inri a bottle of the lukewarm tea to drink, and for a few brief moments there was blessed silence. Then he realized that it wasn't milk, only more disguised water. The bottle clunked to the floor, and Inri opened his mouth to scream.

A fine network of feathery veins branching out around her eyes, strained and stood out in relief as she prepared herself for the wave of sound that was about to come crashing around her. A twist in the set of her lips. Shirly knew her husband wasn't coming home. Owanii couldn't deal with being married to a wiindigo, let alone a cripple. She didn't blame him. She didn't even mourn his absence really, only the inconvenience of his loss, and the catastrophe of their lives, left drifting in his wake. Maybe she should have taken a page from the life of Wabitii, and put her second husband to better use. Owanii could fill their bellies, if not her bed or their hearts. After all, that was why she had married him, so he could put food on the table. It had been, for her at least, a marriage of necessity.

Shirly knew how to use a rifle, and how to tie the knots to snare rabbits. If she hadn't been confined to a wheel-chair, she could have put food on the table herself. The growling hunger clawed at her stomach, a pulsing counter-point to Inri's screams. He kept screaming and screaming and screaming. His screams filled the house like a rising symphony, their waves lapping at the walls, searching for some escape. Inri's twin sister, Marie, hadn't made a peep, for what seemed like days. Marie's silence made Shirly's scalp tingle. She had to do something.

Taking out a knife, Shirly made an incision lengthwise across her thumb deep enough to draw blood, and then pressed the gash to Baby Inri's lips before he could draw in another breath to scream. The pigment of her skin was splotchy in places, as if the light and the dark were trying escape from each other, dappling her hands with leopard-like spots. Baby Inri's mouth closed around the wound, and he drank intently with a suction motion; maybe this will quiet him, she thought. It was better than the water at least. He was part-wiindigo after all. Baby Inri drank enthusiastically, and when he started to fidget, Shirly squeezed the gash open again, and he seemed contented.

Shirly wasn't sure what more she could do for her children. They couldn't subsist on her blood alone, there wasn't enough of it to go around. And Baby Inri wasn't going to stay soothed forever. He would be hungry again. Soon.

The Indian Agent had been coming around—she knew what he wanted—he wanted her children. Each time she had sent the man packing—but she had no choice. She was going to have to send them to the Residential School, though she knew there wouldn't be enough to eat there either. Even the human children at the school Shirly had been forced to attend, had gone hungry. She remembered digging tunnels under the storage building to eat the raw onions. Inri, Marie and the other children would be together in their hunger. But at least they wouldn't starve. And right now, they were starving. She could only hope that this wasn't the best that could be said about the residential school: her children wouldn't starve.

"**Wiindigo Psychosis:** A rarely diagnosed psychological disorder specific only to those cultures in which the wiindigo were believed to exist, entailing the fear of turning into a wiindigo, and an intense craving for human flesh.

Causes, incidences, & risk factors: People from an Indigenous background, specifically of the Algonquian language group, those who have lived through periods of starvation, those who have engaged in acts of cannibalism due to starvation, those who have encountered a wiindigo, had dreams of a wiindigo, or are convinced that they have been cursed.

Symptoms: Extreme hunger, craving for human flesh, eating parts of one's own body (lips, fingers, fingernails, hair etc.), delusional belief in possession or the existence of wiindigo-monster spirits, fear of turning into a wiindigo oneself, grief and anxiety.

Treatment: historically incidences of windiigo psychosis have been dealt with by Indigenous Spiritualists and healers, as well as priests, and in rare cases victims have been executed."

~Excerpt from Wiindigo Culture Amongst the Northern Ojibwe, Ph.D. Dissertation 1875, by Harker Lockwood.

Denatonium benzoate

"LIKE SANDS THROUGH THE HOUR-GLASS, SO ARE THE DAYS OF OUR LIVES," said an authoratative sounding voice on Marie's TV, the image of a slowly revolving hourglass and the slow chiming build-up to a sappy-sounding musical crescendo.

The omnipresent sound of The Soaps, was like background static to the normal soundtrack of their home—the closing and opening of cupboards, the clap-clap-clap of chopping vegetables on the cutting board, and the clatter of cutlery being removed from a drawer.

Marie sat ensconced in one corner of the kitchen, with her TV, her radio, her paperback novels and her magazines. Hunger hid in the whorls and interstices of her mind, constructing vast landscapes of other worlds, other lives, other possibilities, more real to her than her own. She lived these lives with a fixed intensity of focus as she devoured the images, the words, and the songs. Her wolf-like eyes tracked the lines of text on the page, the newest paperback clutched in her hand, nails painted a deep shade of red like talons dipped in blood. Her eyes drifted up to scan the glowing smears of shifting colour on-screen, head tilted to catch some stray bit of song playing quietly on the radio; the centre of a small tornado of light, energy, and noise.

Church was never supposed to disturb her, but every once in a while he would sit with her, and watch her eyes scanning the page. He'd tug at her sleeve, scream directly into her ears, ask questions, demand answers, but she would only frown, as if he were another input of media she couldn't properly consume or understand.

"Life is suffering, then you die." Inri said.

Much to Day's irritation, Inri was a practitioner of Buddhism and meditation. "What kind of Indian is that?"

In some ways they were all seeking the middle path, but true moderation was something none of them could ever achieve—not until they were dead; and maybe not even then. Zhii-bizii-awaag was dead, and she was still hungry. They were wiindigo. And wiindigo, are by definition, hungry.

For them life wasn't suffering, it was hunger. To seek the cessation of hunger was to seek oblivion. Inri might have a death wish, but he wasn't ready to die yet. His antic energy only flat-lined—for a moment—before jumping again into the steady beat of life, the hectic chaos of creation. Their bimaadizin, the best way of life, was to walk the path of moderation as best they could manage, negotiating the landmines of excess, and asceticism, carefully balanced between nourishment and starvation.

Inri would burn sage and sit for hours in complete stillness—Church suspected he was trying to understand Marie better—but it never lasted long. Stillness was not a natural state for him, the way that it was for his twin sister. Though he might strive for it, stillness could only elude him. Impermanence and flux; this was a fact of existence that Inri seemed to embody well. He would be gone the next day; temporary tranquility followed by flight. He could never stay in one place for very long.

"Movement is life and stillness is death." Inri said, one of his many abstract, philosophical sayings.

Sometimes Church would try to short-circuit his hunger by overloading his senses. It was a trick that he had learned from his mother. He would simult-aneously listen to the radio, watch television, and read a novel. Sight and sound would swirl around, siphoning into him like light descending into a black hole. Eating only made the hole bigger, but at least this repast was insubstantial, and he found ingesting so many sources of information somehow soothing. This sort of consumption didn't ease his hunger, but at least it hit some sort of plateau.

They'd all learned tricks to subsume or expend their hunger in various forms of dissolution. All except Mukade-wiiyas who didn't seem to need any; all she did was garden and cook. Although Church supposed that anything compulsive could become a form of escape. The phrase getting lost in your work came to mind. Marie had her somnambulism, her T.V, and her cigarettes. Inri had his meditation and ceaseless motion. And Day had moss tea, and her stories. Church borrowed tactics from all three—and sometimes he drew pictures.

Drawing made the hunger retreat to the background static of a storm, sound and fury unable to reach him when he was sheltered in the play of angles and lines, the shadows and contradictions of perspective, the physicality of pen on paper, the soft scritch of graphite or the pen nib on the grain.

Church drew Mukade-wiiyas, withered and frail-seeming but with a strength that belied her advanced age. He drew Day; and her wheelchair, empty, her face floating next to her mother's rifle. He drew Marie and Inri; so alike in form and feature. He drew Peter; sour and grizzled, with the tattoo of his numbers showing prominently on his left forearm, and written top-to-bottom and bottom-to-top on either side of the page like the mirror-image lettering decorating a joker card.

Maybe Inri was right. He could see the future after all. Maybe Church was going to be an artist. Church couldn't imagine anyone being interested in the little drawings that populated the pages of his sketchbooks, like a zoological fantasmagoria of mythical creatures, real and imagined. But they all had their own little coping strategies—their own mechanisms for survival.

Day's Daughter, Inri, Marie, and even Church wore nail polish mixed with denatonium benzoate, a foul tasting substance, like sulfur, or rotten eggs, only worse. What was left of his fingernails was often bitten to the quick, despite the taste he'd chew on them until his fingers bled.

Day's Daughter and Marie also had a habit of chewing on their own lips, so they always wore lipstick as a deterrent. Marie smoked long slim menthol cigarettes, one after the other. Every butt in the ashtray kissed with the red outline of her lips, which Day's Daughter was constantly applying and re-applying. Church wondered how much of the lipstick Marie ate, and how much of the lipstick ended up on the filters on the end of her cigarettes.

Day's Daughter would spend hours fussing over Marie's hair and nails, applying denatonium benzoate to her long nails in a shade of fire-engine-red. "Marie does not have the strength to resist the urges of her nature. She can only subsume them, dissipating them in lesser hungers."

For Marie, these "lesser hungers" were sated by a constant flow of Soap Operas, trashy novels, and top 40 songs. She built elaborate fantasies to imprison her instincts, and she became a prisoner of those dreams, less mobile than Day's Daughter confined to a wheelchair.

"Something happened to her in that Residential School," Inri gestured towards his unmoving twin, "something that left her like this. She's never recovered. Her mental state is very delicate. You must never disturb her."

"To do so is to risk her sanity, and put yourself in peril." Inri said in a Transylvanian accent. Inri always did tend to have a flare for the dramatic. In the movie version of their life, Bill Merasty could play the role of Inri.

He wasn't sure who could play Marie. Maybe Angelina Jolie?

From within the vortex between her and the rest of the world, Marie watched her son grow. She watched her mother rear Church the same way she herself had been raised. Memory of Day wiping the snot and tears from his face after a fall as a toddler, shouting after him to make sure he didn't forget his lunch on his way to school—and if the stories of their family were true, this was something that could prove to be a disaster for a boy raised in a family of wiindigowak.

Eating either too much, or too little—both posed a potential risk. They were always tight-rope-walking a fine line, where to either side lay a chasm with stalagmites like sharp teeth waiting at the bottom to chew them up and spit them out, mangled and unrecognizable on the other side. The hunger was something that could devour you, if you were weak enough to let it. But who knows what was true? Marie already knew she was crazy. For her, there wasn't much division between fact and fiction. Her dreams and fictional worlds were more real to her than the one she hid from.

Once the benzodiazepines and anti-psychotics had sufficiently loosened her tongue, Marie had been diagnosed with a mixture of catatonia, oneirophrenia, and Wiindigo Psychosis. Catatonia happened all the time on the soap operas she watched. Why should it not happen to her?

It was usually caused by some terrible trauma, followed by the resulting mute scar of silence that formed a chrysalis, while the skin underneath healed. If something had occurred to necessitate the construction of a cocoon, it was hidden so deep inside herself, not even she was aware of where it was hidden. She'd learned that "wiindigo psychosis" was a rarely diagnosed and little known psychological disorder specific only to those cultures in which the wiindigo were believed to exist, entailing both the "fear of turning into a wiindigo" and an intense "craving for human flesh." Marie's doctors had been very pleased with their diagnosis, and she had briefly become the object of intense scrutiny.

Church had been her saving grace, her coup de grâce; her great escape. Like Houdini, chained upside down from his ankles, suspended above a shark tank, and escaping from a straight jacket. She knew, if it hadn't been for her unexpected pregnancy and the threat of litigation, the white doctors would never have let her leave that place. For a short time her psychiatrists had become enamored with the idea of making a name for themselves in the little-explored field of para-psychiatry, documenting and studying an actual case of "Wiindigo Psychosis."

But not even the pills could rouse her from stupor for long. Who knew if she'd ever crawl out again? She watched the phases of the moon, and the passing of winter upon winter, unable to feel much of anything in her trance-like state. A sense of relief that her son hadn't turned out like her; present but absent.

When Church looked at his mother, he often took her presence for granted. Mute, frail, beauty. Hair like black glass. She never left the house, and she rarely spoke, a hermit amidst their lives. Everyone tiptoed around her lest her delicate castles of sand come crashing down. Her radio and television, a murmuring presence in the background. She couldn't really be a part of their lives, because she wasn't really alive. More like a coma victim planted in one corner of their kitchen, unable to speak or respond, a living example for WHY IT WAS SO IMPORTANT not to let the hunger take control.

"Noon-des-kaa-taay," it said, voice gravelly. A theatrical monster's voice. "Noon-des-kaa-taay," it whispered. I'm hungry. Please feed me. Please fill me up. But it could never be filled or fulfilled; it was a well with no bottom, a bucket with a hole, incapable of being sated. The murmur of Bakade's voice was unceasing—Hunger—was his constant companion.

Church didn't know why Marie woke up for long enough to conceive, he only knew that it had happened, because he was the living product of it. Not even a Wiindigo could have a virgin birth—could they? But the story of his conception was not one that he had been told.

Not even Inri had told him this story.

Inri had finally convinced his mother that Marie should be admitted to a Mental Institution for an evaluation. "Maybe they can help her?" he had said at the time. "They have drugs these days, new forms of treatment, they can do something!"

The Stering Shores Mental Institution was a large, sprawling, three-storey red brick Victorian structure that wouldn't have been out of place in a horror movie like The Shining, or Dream Warriors: A Nightmare on Elm Street III. With 118 feet of full lake frontage it was originally built as a luxury hotel in the

1850s, and later converted into an "Asylum for Idiots," then a "Hospital for the Mentally Insane," and finally as it is known today, simply, "The Sterling Shores Hospital."

Church's father had been working as an orderly, and doubling as a security guard, walking the dead of night, halls polished to such a high gloss, you could see your own reflection. Peter wore the pastel scrubs of a nurse, the same uniform all the staff wore to designate themselves as sane. Keys jangling at his waist he strode the halls, listening to the occasional screams or cries. He was the night-watch man. He wasn't a nurse, his actual title was "Health Care worker," and his job was to keep the inmates under control during the night, while most of the staff slept soundly in their own beds. He had only acquired the job a few months earlier, and it wasn't a bad gig, sedating the occasional nut-job. Sending up the odd red flag if things got out of control, or if one of the patients tried to set the place on fire.

Marie had not eaten as much she was accustomed to for many days. She ate the same portion-controlled cafeteria-style diet as the rest of the patients, no exceptions. The flickering images on screen in the day-room offered her a means of escape, as did the bland magazines and tasteless meals. The faded walls were as grey as her faded soul, but she found it difficult to efface herself, to disappear; there was nothing here substantial enough to fill up the hole. She ate the serene blue of the walls, she ate the television volume set down low, she ate the drivel of same-old magazines. Her only sanctuary was in the plentiful supply of cigarettes. They were doled out like medicine, and they stained her fingers yellow with nicotine. They were the only thing that kept her from ripping the face off of her psych-analyst with her teeth, and digging in like some 2-4-5 Trioxin zombie from

Return of the Living Dead Part II. Part II because she hadn't seen Part I, and O'Bannon's zombies craved brains, and she imagined the smart brain of a doctor must taste better.

This fact made her hands shake.

The cigarettes wouldn't stave her off for much longer.

The hunger wouldn't let her sleep, prowling like a black jaguar locked behind the pearl bars of her bones. Her body was the cage, and Bakade—Hunger—waited with the patience of a predator ready to strike. The only movement was the lonely security guard in his pale scrubs, walking the halls on his rounds. What was more troubling to her: he was starting to look good. Really. Really. Good. She began to salivate each time he passed by her room, like a conditioned Pavlovian response to a bell. Marie knew the story of Gaawiin, and how her grandmother had survived the Wiindigo. And so she knew how to appease the monster, when nothing else was at hand. The hunger shifted in her soul like a great beast, stretching and yawning, and testing the strength of the bars holding it prisoner, squirming with frustration when the bars held against the momentary pressure, and then settling down to wait and endure.

At two o'clock in the morning, Peter peeked in through the door to check up on her. The patient was awake he saw, sitting as immobile as always, with a cool kind of beauty. He stared at her breasts through the thin medical gown they gave the women for a night-dress. She didn't acknowledge his presence or his gaze, she didn't even move, she scarcely seemed to breathe! She's a looker, he thought, that's for sure! Too bad she's as whacko as the rest of these nut-jobs. It was a real shame, a shame he couldn't screw her! Ha-ha ha-ha ha-ha-ha!

Peter moved on down the hall, whistling quietly into the silence, keys rustling as he peered into the rooms. Each door had a window, although none of the doors were locked. The patients on this floor were not considered a danger to themselves or to others, and most of them were given a handful of pills to make them more tractable, like that girl in room number 2233.

Marie's body moved before she consciously made the decision, she was already moving. Her body had its own mind, its own will, its own goals, its own desires, its own control. She was no longer in control - the beast would have its way. She stalked the man down the hall, a ghost on whispery bare feet, like the Sarah Connor escape scene in Terminator II. She shadowed him through the building, into the dingy staff room with the stained coffee machine, small kitchenette, and a few yellow flower-patterned couches.

The beast tackled him from behind, the wind knocked out of him before he could draw in breath to cry out. With his arms pinned under him, he couldn't reach his pepper spray. And then her mouth was on his, sucking at his lips like a she-devil. It was the raven-haired girl from room 2233. Her lithe arms had more strength than he would have believed possible, and he was helpless at first to disentangle himself from the knot of their limbs. She seemed determined to tangle them.

Fuck it, he thought, I'm not getting paid enough for this. He found himself returning the kiss, feeling her body through the thin material of her gown. Why should he say no? Because he was supposed to be sane? That was laughable.

It wasn't like he was taking advantage of her. She had bloody tackled him! The girl knew what she wanted, there was no one innocent here, just passionate need. Maybe she was a

Nymphomaniac? And what a wild-cat! He couldn't believe his luck! He wasn't the sort of old guy beautiful young women went after. There had to be some perks to this job.

After.

He returned Marie to her room, and she went calmly, no sign of the wild-cat lurking behind her skinny-girl frame. That was fucking wild, he thought, and went back to walking his rounds, shaking his head and smiling ruefully every few minutes when he thought about what he had done. He could get fired! But, who cared! It wasn't as if this job was all that precious to him. He had a good thing going, and he wasn't going to stop unless he got caught.

After that first time, they met almost every night. He'd step into her room, locking the door quietly behind him and drawing the little curtain across the window for privacy, in case one of the other orderlies walked by. She'd look up from her trance, and it was like she was a different person from the zombie he saw in the day-room when he was covering a shift. In the day-room she didn't acknowledge his presence in any way. You would never guess they were anything but strangers.

She never spoke, there was only the fire between them; the lust, and he knew he was probably taking advantage of a deranged mind, but he didn't care. And neither did she, she had found something to placate the hunger, without needing to leave her chrysalis, that mute scar of silence.

When she began to show, one of the female nurses noticed first, and there was a kafuffle: "Doctor! You'd better come in here and take a look at this!" How had she gotten pregnant? Was it one of the other inmates? She was in an all-female ward. The only men were staff members! The Bagonegiizhig family was disgruntled, and invariably suspicion landed on the night staff orderlies.

And more specifically: on Peter.

Peter was the newest member of the staff. Marie's room was along the circuitous route of the rounds he was to pace multiple times per night, and also, he was guilty. It was no surprise to anyone when he was fired, and it went some length in appeasing the family, they agreed not to sue the hospital. Several of the doctors were sorely disappointed that they had lost the opportunity to study an actual patient suffering from the almost unheard of—in modern day practice—culture-bound disorder "Wiindigo Psychosis." But the decision came from the higher-ups in the hospital administration; they didn't want the bad press.

Day knew it wasn't the orderlies' fault. No mere man would have been able to force himself on Marie. She was wiindigo. Day suspected, that in truth, he was the victim, but she was happy to have her daughter returned home, whatever the reason. She never should have acceded to Inri's wishes in the first place. He didn't always know what was best for his twin sister.

But to Day's surprise "the orderly" didn't go away. The man kept tabs on the woman he had impregnated, and Peter would drop in on the family to visit Marie during the pregnancy, and later to visit his son.

I'll visit my son, Peter thought, no matter what that crazy crippled woman says. The mother was as crazy as the daughter, always talking about wiindigo, threatening to eat him for Christ sakes! Like out of some sort of Brothers Grimm tale. But against all odds the child seemed normal enough, though it was a miracle considering the atmosphere he was growing up in, but God knows he wasn't built to be any kind of father. The kid was better off where he was—even given the environment—Church was still better off with them, than with him, that was for damn sure!

Heterochromia Iridis: is a difference in coloration of the eyes, where one iris is a different colour from the other due to an excess, or lack of melanin. This is a result of genetics, disease or injury.

Shit

Church wondered what strange things lurked in his genes. What things might he have inherited from his ancestors, from his father, or his father's father? He knew about the appetites he had inherited from his mother, but what sorts of things had he inherited from his father? What kinds of disease might be lurking within his cells like a ticking time bomb waiting for the perfect moment to jump out and say "boo!" An aneurysm exploding inside his head.

"What were your parents like?" Church's graphite pencil never stopped working as he sketched out Peter's features from the unformed blankness of the page. He heard many stories from Day and Inri, and even Mukade-wiiyas, but his father never talked about the past, his presence was marked by a conspicuous absence—as if he existed in a perpetual void. There were no stories; no dalliances between semi-divine beings or demi-gods and a mortal—no stories at all. The only thing Church knew, was that Peter had been named after his grandfather, so he would be hidden from the Angel of Death.

Peter squinted at him, one eye green-brown, and the other steel-grey. This gave him a constant, manic expression. Peter always looked crazy. But he looked even-more crazy now with the skin around his cheekbones tight, and his jaw clenched. Church immediately regretted asking the question.

"For fuck's sake!" Peter's gaze was unwavering, "Why would you want to know something like that?"

Church's pencil stilled.

"Listen to me," Peter pointed two fingers at Church's dark brown eyes, and then to his own blue-grey and hazel-green—like the don't mess with the bull scene in The Breakfast Club. "You come from a long line of shit. You were born from shit and you'll die in shit. And that's all you need to know about where you come from. We're all shit." Peter picked up the Sterling Rag and went back to his newspaper. This was the extent of the family history that Peter imparted.

There was more to the story—Peter had numbers tattooed on his arm, and Church didn't think that they were a rite of passage—but he knew better than to hazard more questions. For Peter, the past was past—and better left that way. It certainly wasn't worth talking about. Maybe he was afraid that by talking about it, his words would breathe new life into it.

Peter

The doctor in the white lab coat injected him with a green liquid. There was a sharp pain of the insertion, as he poked around digging for a vein. Sometimes children had small veins, and it made them harder to find. Petyr barely even flinched, they'd withdrawn so many viles of blood, he was almost used to it now. Sometimes injections, and sometimes extractions. Some of the kids got sick after they got an injection, and then it was off to the infirmary, and later the gas chambers, and after that the ovens.

The air was thick with the smell of their bodies. It was inescapable. That smell. Like burnt hair, only a million times worse. Sometimes Petyr hated even to breathe, imagining the infinitesimal particles of ash filtering their way through his lungs. Pieces of the dead becoming a part of his being.

The kids who were sent to the infirmary never recovered, it was merely a place to track the progress of whichever disease they'd been injected with, and then both twins were doomed, because once one died, the other was no longer useful for Mengele's experiments.

The doctors spent hours each day measuring the width of his skull and then comparing it to Pavels; measuring the length of their arms, from elbow to wrist; the thickness of the bridge of their nose; the distance from shoulder blade to shoulder blade, and from ear to ear, making small notations in the books; all the minutiae of their symmetry and asymmetry, the exactness of their similarity and the width of their divergence. Chronicling the secrets of their sameness.

Pavel lay on a bed opposite from his own, connected by an intricate network of tubes, snaking from his arm up to a plastic bag suspended from a metal stand, down into a machine with valves like an accordion, then out and up to another stand, another tube coming out from the plastic bag, and down to Petyr's own arm, where one of the clear plastic tubes had been inserted into his flesh through an incision. Pavel's anxious blue-and-brown eyes stared into his own brown-and-blue, Pavel's left-eye-blue and right-eye-brown, to his own left-eye-brown and right-eye-blue. Like mirror images of each other, what was left on Petyr, was right on Pavel, and what was right on Petyr, was left on Pavel. But all this had been chronicled.

Every mole and whorl. Their mirror imagery had fascinated Megele, especially their "heterochromia iridum," their dual-coloured eyes. Petyr suspected, that they were given better treatment than even some of the other twins. More care had been expended in maintaining their body and souls together.

But with every day that passed, their chances of survival grew increasingly slim. As Mengele's twins, they were afforded some measure of protection, but that protection came with a price, and it wouldn't last forever, and it wouldn't save them. Mengele's "protection" was not any better than the alternative. They might be better off dead. The tests some of the twins had been forced to undergo had been unspeakable, worse than any conducted in fiction he'd read, like Doctor Frankenstein. Petyr and Pavel both knew they probably weren't going to survive, and that this could be the experiment that killed them.

Mengele indicated that the procedure should begin, and a doctor in a white coat flipped a switch on the machinery. The accordion bellows on either side of the machinery began pumping like arms, and the blood began to flow into the clear tube from his arm, being drawn up like fruit punch through a curly straw and into the plastic bag suspended above, and from there flowing down into the machine, before coming out the other side, and crossing paths with the stream of blood being drawn out of Pavels arm and up to a corresponding bag suspended above, until the entire length of clear tubing had been stained claret, a solid red line connecting Petyr to his brother. Petyr gasped as he felt the first intrusion of Pavel's blood into his arm, the circuit was complete, and he heard Pavel's gasp, almost simultaneously as his own blood finally reached Pavel's left arm, through the intricate network of tubes connecting him to his brother.

The blood had chilled on its journey through the bendy-straw tubing, and he felt a strange, sharp, painful pressure as it entered his left arm, replacing the blood that continued to be drawn out his right. Petyr squeezed his eyes shut tight, feeling his tears dampen his cheek, as he tried to remain calm, stay silent, ride out the pain as the procedure continued, until all of his blood· had been cycled out though the machine and into Pavel, and all of Pavel's blood had been cycled out through the machine and into him; until all of their blood that had been exchanged, was back where it had started, pumping out into the tubes with every breathe that passed, fuelled as equally by the bellows of their hearts, as by the bellows of the machinery, they were for a short time, one being again, as they shared for a space of time, the same circulatory system. After what seemed like an eternity, the procedure came to an end, the machinery with its' accordion-like arms was switched off, the tubes were removed. And they were still alive! At least for the moment.

Petyr didn't know it then, but they were lucky they were identical twins and shared the same bloodtype. Petyr looked at his brother Pavel, and Pavel smiled weakly, attempting to comfort him, but not managing much more than a slight upturning to his lips. More the ghost of a smile, than an actual smile.

After some time, Mengele tired of swapping out their blood, one-twin-to-the-other, and they were sent to the death wards. The death ward was a special, hospital-like room, with many beds, where the children waited their turn to be killed and then brought back to life. These barracks weren't only for twins, they housed many children, although there were a few other sets of complete twins, and a few who'd come back to life, only to find that their brother or sister hadn't made it back from their most recent return-trip into death. Some died many times, and were brought back to life, and some didn't survive the first death, and only got the chance to die once. There was no predicting how many times one would last. Some of the weakest looking children seemed to cling to life, living and dead, living and dead, living and dead, weathering the passage from life to death, and from death to life, time after time after time, while other more hardy-looking children failed to return from their first trip into non-life. There seemed to be no reason or rhyme to it, and survival was left up to the roll of the dice.

Petyr and Pavel shared their own bed, and they were given medical frocks to wear instead of their own grimy clothes. The atmosphere in the ward was subtly different from the other barracks where they'd been stationed. There didn't seem to be the same . . . atmosphere of dread. These children knew they were already dead. They had all died at least once already.

Death had already happened. Every last one of them knew where they were going. They'd already gone there. They were going to die. Again. Soon.

"It's not so bad." The girl in the bed next to theirs said. "The Doctor gave me a piece of chocolate last time!"

Petyr looked at his twin brother, and saw his own reaction reflected in his dual-coloured eyes. This place wasn't any better. But at least when they where dead, Mengele wouldn't be able to experiment on them anymore.

When they said anything at all, the children in the death ward only seemed to have the same converstion, asking the same two questions: 1. "How many times have you died?" and, 2. "What did you see when you were dead?"

"I saw a bright light," said the boy in the bed on the other side of theirs. He had a distant, far-away look in his eyes, as if he were still seeing, now, the light he had seen when he was dead.

"I didn't see anything," the girl in the bed next to theirs said, shrugging and twirling her short-cropped hair. One of the privileges of being a Mengele guinea pig, was that they didn't get their heads shaved quite as short as the rest of the inmates of Berkenau.

"I saw my mother!" Another boy piped up, a goofy smile on his face. "I can't wait for my turn to come again. Next time, I'm not coming back."

"I don't go anywhere" another girl said, "I just kind of hover around, and I watch the doctors as they work for a while. I only stay dead long enough to get my chocolate, then I come back. They don't like it if I don't stay dead long enough, but if I stay dead too long, I'm worried I won't get any candy."

"That's stupid," another boy said. "You should come back as soon as you can! I see a tunnel when I die, and I travel through the tunnel . . . towards something. But I always wake up before I get to the end."

"That's Navarska," the girl in the bed next to theirs said, "He's been here for a long time. He's died like seven times!"

"How many times have you died?" Pavel asked.

"Only twice—so far."

"How many times can you die?" Petyr asked. And the girl next to their bed shrugged.

"I dunno. Navarska? What's the most times you've seen someone die?"

"Troyska lasted a while. Nine, maybe ten times?"

"Minerva lasted thirteen times!" The other girl piped up, peaking out from underneath her blankets so you could only see her eyes.

"There you have it." Their neighbour said, "Thirteen times."

A small sharp pain as the hollow-tipped hyperdermic needle punctured the inside curve of his elbow, creating another star in the galaxy of track marks on his arms. The plunger was slowly depressed, and there was a new pressure as the mysterious substance was injected into his arm.

Petyr let his head flop to the side as he felt a growing weight in all his extremities, and a strange heat suffusing itself outwards from his chest. The doctor in his white lab-coat stepped outside of his field of vision, no longer obstructing the view of his brother, laying on the gurney next to his, lethargic as the drugs took hold. "Good-bye" Pavel's eyes said. He didn't need to speak, Petyr understood. He was saying good-bye too. "If I don't make it, don't die too! Come back if you can! Don't stay dead just for me, live if you can!" A frantic last minute alarm of communication before the sound of his heartbeat overtook all sensation, and his vision went dark.

All he could hear was the beating of his own heart, growing louder and louder in his ears as it sluggishly beat, slower and slower, louder and louder, as the weight of his limbs seemed to grow heavier and heavier, as if his bones were slowly being replaced by lead weights. THUMP-THUMP, THUMP-THUMP THUMP-THUMP. The sound of his heartbeat loud in his ears. THUMP-THUMP. THUMP-THUMP. All-encompassing in the darkness. THUMP. THUMP. Radiating outwards, filling the blackness of space like its own tiny universe, grown suddenly huge, the closer he got to the sound. THUUMP. Like a warm, heavy, blanket draped over top of him, smothering out consciousness, self-awareness, and awareness of the world outside himself, a slowly retreating speck of light, as the warmth and the heartbeat overtook him. THUUUUUUMP. Darkness. Warmth. Silence.

--THUUUUUUMP--

Darkness.

--THHHHUUUUUUUUUMMMMMMMPPPP--

Nothingness.

The speck of light was back. A small pin-prick of light in the nothingness. Except instead of retreating, it was getting closer. Coming forward like a swiftly approaching train, growing larger and larger, and accelerating faster and faster the closer it came, growing so large it became a tunnel of light as it surrounded him, filling the universe of nothingness, but now the light was all around him, surrounding him, and he travelled through it, the way a train travels through a tunnel. Except the tunnel was made of light instead of darkness.

And then Petyr gasped for breath as his eyes dialed open, shocked violently back to life and consciousness, as his body was dropped unceremoniously into a tub of ice cold water, his heart beating in his chest like a mad, frantic creature trapped in the cage of his ribs, trying to escape. Pavel sat in an ice-cold bath, in a metal tub set next to his own, his skinny arms and legs sticking out over the sides, his head draped. Motionless.

Petyr was left to sit in the tub until his lips and the tips of his fingers turned blue, his teeth chattered, and his limbs began to shiver with such violence, the ice-cold water sloshed out of the tub. He hugged himself for warmth and stared at his twin brother's motionless body, waiting for the cold water to revive him too, but he just lay there like an abandoned marionette, the strings of life that animated the puppet, snipped. He tried to recall the last look in Pavel's eyes, imploring him to keep living, even if he didn't survive.

Each time they killed him it was the same. The heartbeat. The darkness. Then nothing. The pinprick of light as he returned to consciousness and life, like a tunnel to another world, or merely a return trip to this one? In and out of the tunnel of death, darkness and light, and the THUMP-THUMP of his slowing pulse, and then the sudden shock of the chilling ice water. His heart jump-started like the frantic beating of a hummingbird's wings. He almost lost track of how many times he died, but the other children in his barracks wouldn't let him lose count. There was such a high turnover, and there were always new children to kill. Not many survived very long, and each time Petyr died he thought it would be his last, but he kept coming back, through the darkness, through that tunnel of light, his returning heartbeat pounding away in his chest, until all the children who had been in their ward when Petyr and Pavel first arrived, had been replaced by new children, like Pavel's blood that had cycled through his veins.

As long as Petyr was still alive, part of Pavel would always be living. Petyr didn't want to let Pavel down, his unspoken promise, the last request that he saw every time he closed his eyes. Pavel don't give up. Keep on living. Even if I don't survive.

--"How many times have you died?" the children would ask amongst themselves.

--"Five."

--"Three times"

--"Petyr?"

--"Thirteen," Petyr answered, though he didn't want to keep track. He knew, no one had ever survived being killed more than thirteen times. The next time, he was certain, would be his last.

--"No way! Thirteen times?"

--"It's true!" One boy said, "He's been here the longest."

--"There was that one girl! Minerva. She made it to thirteen!"

--"No Minerva died the thirteenth time! Petyr has gone past Minerva!"

 --"I didn't think anyone could make it further than Minerva!"

--"Well, we'll all be dead soon anyway."

--"It's better than being here."

A Family of Wiindigowak

Day's Daughter is fat for a wiindigo—which meant she wasn't really fat at all, but somehow it seemed she was able to retain a little more meat on her bones than the rest of them, though it is likely this quality was simply more psychological, than physical. Day was fat for a wiindigo. She never leaves her wheelchair. Every month she receives a disability check, which barely provides the day-to-day funds necessary for the operation of their household. Mukade-wiiyas also had her own mysterious source of funds; she never seemed to lack for money.

Day shares a bedroom with her daughter Marie toward the front of the house, at the end of the long hallway. The windowless hallway is dark because the glass globe explodes every time they put a bulb in the socket. The front steps are crumbling, and blockaded from use by two two-by-fours nailed in a cross formation—they would have been useless to Day even if they had been in good repair—so the entire family enters and exits their home through the steep ramp at the back, off a small enclosed mudroom that opens onto the kitchen.

The kitchen is a large room, a later addition to the original red-bricked Victorian structure, and it is the true heart of their household. Outside, a narrow flagstone walkway leads down the side of the house, below the metal fire escape where Church and

Inri share smokes. The back yard is dominated by the remains of a large, skeletal cherry tree. There is a ramshackle doghouse, a small, illegal chicken coop, and an extensive Victory garden that Mukade-wiiyas maintains. Plunging the silver spade of a shovel into the earth, over and over again, aerating the soil in the fall, legs disappearing into the wells of two large black rubber boots.

A small TV set sits on the windowsill in the kitchen. It is always left on, flickering quietly in one corner to keep Marie company. She reminded Church of the gnome-like creature in The Dark Crystal, transfixed by a beam of light so the skeksis could drink her essence and live forever. She spent most of her hours staring at the colourful screen, her gaze unflinching, and unseeing. Shifting light and sound without story or meaning.

Their home was cluttered with cookbooks, some of them yellowed with age, stacked up in piles, in corners, and cramming every available inch of space on their book shelves. In the hallway to his Nokomis' bedroom, the walls were lined with books, so that she could barely scrape past in her wheelchair.

In the kitchen recipes from newspaper and magazine clippings were tacked up onto the fridge with magnets, glued to the walls, layered one over top of the other like papier-mâché wallpaper. Directions, ingredients, and photos of chicken fried steak, okra, three-cheese pizzas, peanut-butter fudge, bacon and eggs with hash-browns, coco with whipped-cream, apple pie, chocolate cake with cherries, sugar free-pecan pie, lobster tail, butterfly shrimp, strawberry cheese-cake, strawberry ice-cream, chicken cacciatore, pork chops, pickled cucumbers, lemon meringue pie, chocolate ice-cream, garlic bread, onion rings, peach pie, linguini with white clam sauce, black-eyed peas, tomato salad with egg and french dressing, vanilla ice-cream, peach pie, spaghetti with meatballs, pasta marinara . . .

. . . it was like they were all living inside of a giant stomach. They would always have pictures of food to keep them company, even when the cabinets were empty.

They supplemented their diet in many ways. Mukade-wiiyas maintained her Victory Garden in the backyard. They foraged for wild edibles in the surrounding wilderness. Day grew spices on the window-sills, and made snares to catch rabbits. A large percentage of their time was dedicated to acquiring and cooking the food necessary to sustain themselves. They were wiindigo, and food dominated their lives. The hunger never really went away, but it got worse if they ate nothing, too much, or not enough, one miss-step could send the hunger snowballing out of control. It was a delicate balance—like dancing on the edge of a knife.

Mukade-wiiyas and Day were always cooking.

Day sat in one corner of the kitchen directing the orchestration of meals from her wheelchair like a maestro leading a symphony. Their kitchen wasn't 100% wheel-chair accessible, so Day needed someone to stir the larger pots (and some of their pots were very large), and to reach the items on the higher shelves, though they made do by organizing the shelves most-to-least important, bottom-to-top.

Day instructed him when to stir, how often, when to rotate the various pots simmering on the stove, and when to add ingredients. Day was a master at juggling eight or nine different culinary enterprises at the same time, so that while three dishes with short cooking spans were being prepared, four other dishes with longer cooking times were in separate stages of completion, boiling, broiling or roasting, while another two were cooling or being put into the fridge.

Church would chop endless amounts of carrots, onions, garlic, and potatoes. He was an expert. The point of his knife stayed on the cutting board, and he raised the handle and brought it down in a quick succession, curling his fingers back from the blade, creating perfectly uniform horseshoes of celery or cubes of raw turnip. He rarely sliced any of his fingers along the serrated edge, the bright red of his blood dripping amongst the stray peelings on the floor.

He put the finger to his lips to prevent any more from going to waste, sucking on the wound and tasting the metallic tang of his own blood. Cannibalism, Church thought, and tastes good. The knife felt like an extension of his hand.

Day would be gutting a fish, boiling water, exchanging one pot for another, stirring, mixing, measuring and kneading while she called out instructions, one cupful of this, six handfuls of that, nine pinches of this, two sprinkles of that. Recipes were usually altered by improvisations, especially since they didn't usually call for the sheer quantity of food they regularly produced.

While most recipes serve 4-6, Day and Mukade-wiiyas prepared quantities in the range of 12-16 even though there were usually only four people in their household. Mukade-wiiyas, Day, and Marie had by far the greater appetites, but Church figured that he must eat at least four times as much as other kids his own age, probably equaled by only the most obese of children. Except Church was skinny skinny skinny: the bones of his ribs protruding through the skin.

In Church's household, food wasn't just something they ate to refuel. It was respected as something hard-earned and valuable because it was so often scarce. Everyone knew how much work went into growing, scavenging, acquiring and preparing their meals, so nothing was wasted, even the peelings from carrots and onions were saved and used for soup stock. Food was both their obsession and their curse.

In the backyard the Victory Garden was slowly over-taking the lawn. Mukade-wiiyas grew three sisters, and a brother: squash, beans, corn and potatoes, as well as whatever else they could manage to coerce from the earth to supplement their diet; tomatoes, pumpkins, chives, onions, rhubarb. Something was always being harvested, early spring to late fall.

Mukade-wiiyas often wore old-fashioned dresses. Day helped her mother lace up the whalebone, like drawstrings on a shoe, pulling the chords taut to create an hourglass figure out of her boney, stick frame. The corset flared out at the hips to create the illusion of bulk that did not exist in nature, and to create curves where there were no curves. Her waist was already narrow, so it was the flair of the peaks, rather than the hollow of the valleys, which were artificial. Her withered shoulders adorned with puffs of moth-eaten lace. Her legs disappearing into a pair of black rubber gardening boots.

Day's Daughter didn't like it when her mother wore these old dresses not just decades, but almost a century out of date, and insisted she wear something more modern when they left the house. "Ningaashi, this isn't the 19th century anymore," she said as a joke. But the best jokes always have an edge of truth. Mukade-wiiyas was old. Not just old. Ancient. She was the oldest person Church had ever met, and this no doubt accounted for her taste, as she imitated the women at the height of fashion in the books and magazines of her youth. Though she remained as hale as a much younger woman, these dresses, more than her wrinkles—and slow, careful movements—gave away her truly, advanced age.

Mukade-wiiyas often played records on the old gramophone. Records so ancient, that the records were not even records— they were cylinders. Playing old songs for Marie to listen to, humming softly to herself and swaying to the rhythm as she recited the words to the songs, and moving about the kitchen, cooking and preparing a meal. The small, scratchy voices of the singers emerged as if from out of a long, dark tunnel, sifting down like pollen from the brass, flower-shaped bloom.

This also, gave away her truly advanced age.

"Aadikwe'an!" was a frequent command heard in their household. It was an imperative usually issued by Mukade-wiiyas or Day after dinner was served when Church, Inri, Marie or even Day herself, showed too much enthusiasm—because they all lived by Mukade-wiiyas's eighth rule.

Seven is an important number for Anishinaabek. There are seven original clans, seven directions, and seven grandfather teachings; debwewin, dibaadendiziwin, gwekwaadiziwin, aakwa'ode'win, minaadendmowin, zaagi'idiwin, nbwaakaawin. Truth, humility, honesty, bravery, respect, love, wisdom. These are like the Ten Commandments, except the "thou shall nots," are "thou shalls." But for their wiindigo family there were really eight rules. They had an extra, golden rule, more important than all the rest, the one rule to rule them all: aadikwe'igewin. Control. "Aadikwe'an!" meant "stay in control!" Church was expected to maintain control over his hunger at all times.

Even when they were eating—especially when they were eating. They did not eat quickly. They ate slowly, and methodically, and voraciously, though they did not rush. Rushing a meal was against Mukade-wiiyas's rule, because this precaution allowed them to survive. It was too easy to get caught up in the hunger—even if for only a moment—in the act of consuming (because moments after a morsel was swallowed, the hunger returned). Restraint was key.

The business of eating a meal was serious, and they did so carefully, and with great patience. It was a necessity that could easily turn to tragedy, either from the ever-present hazard of choking on your own half-chewed food, or from losing contol and going full-wiindigo. You bucked the system at your own peril, something that quickly became apparent the moment Church deviated from the path laid out for him by his great grandmother's tenets. Her rules had evolved over the years, been shaped by experience, and tempered in the furnace of time— and they worked. Their continued survival proved that they were effective. So they ate slowly, methodically, and voraciously.

Moss tea

Day's Daughter took a sip of moss tea. Day, Mukade-wiiyas, and Inri were constantly boiling water for this tea, and drinking it in huge quantities. Even Marie drank it. Sometimes Day wouldn't even bother making the tea and would simply eat the dried green stuff from which the tea was made. Moss tea was an ever-present facet of their lives in the same way, he imagined, coffee was in the lives of other people. Church was encouraged to drink the tea as well. It tasted like warm dirt, leaves, and sticks. He didn't know why everyone drank so much moss tea, and it had never really struck him as odd, until one day he asked his grandmother, "What are you drinking?"

Day's Daughter looked at him as if he had gone mad, or sprouted a second head. An alien from outer space had just appeared in her kitchen. "Moss tea of course, it's what we always drink. You know that."

"But what is it made from?" Church asked.

"Moss," she said, her voice pitched high as if Church were being incredibly dense. Where had Church been for his entire life that he hadn't ever noticed that she drank moss tea? "You must have seen me harvest it a million times."

"Oh," Church said, he'd never really thought about it before. He'd always assumed that it was just a name, like a brand, divorced from any meaning outside its own history. "But why would you want to drink moss?" he asked.

"For the same reason I'm always trying to get you to drink it. It's good for you. And it keeps you regular." Oh, Church thought. But he suspected that Day wasn't telling him everything, and that there was more to it than that.

Church asked Inri the same question. "Inri, why are you always drinking moss tea?" His answer was different.

"In the old days, when hunters went out on a long hunting trip and ran out of supplies, they would eat this moss." Inri held the dried moss up to his face, examining it like an artifact from the past. The moss looked more like some sort of animal fur more than it did dried leaves. "It grows everywhere, it's edible. It will keep you alive, and it will put something in your belly besides hunger." Then almost as an afterthought, he added, "it is also an appetite suppressant."

So, it was good for you, and an appetite suppressant.

parallax, n. from para, "among", and allos,
"other". Is the difference in the position of an
object, along two different lines of sight. This
can be used to determine distances. Human eyes
have overlapping visual fields that use parallax
for depth perception.

Harvest

Church pushed Day's wheelchair through the snarl of tree
roots that invaded the path and the ruts made by bicycle tires.
He had grown strong from pushing his grandmother over the
pitted ground. The trail snaked through the city of Sterling
where fragmented bits of wilderness still maintained a foothold;
along streams, railroads, and parkland, connecting with a larger
network that riddled the surrounding hills and valleys. There
were dirt bikes in the summer, and Ski-Doos in the winter.
There were hikers, bikers, bird watchers and nature enthusiasts .
. . and sometimes, one or two hungry wiindigo.

Every weekend Day's Daughter and Church went out to forage
and snare rabbits. They looked for morel mushrooms, sumac
berries, fiddleheads, crab- apples—whatever was edible and in
season. Day would select the best place to set up a snare, spitting
out seeds as they went, "so that one day, the plants will grow,
and there will be more for us to eat."

The best time to harvest morels and fiddleheads is after the
first thunderstorms while there is still electricity on the air, and
while the ferns are still tightly coiled in on themselves. But they
harvested edible plants throughout the summer; bishiiminag,
crab apples, ozagadibaweg, burdock, joojooshaaboo-jiibik,
dandelions, ozhaashijiibik, fireweed, gaagaagiwaandagominan,
juniper-berries, giizhikag, cedar, waabiziipin ojiibik, arrowhead

root, oziban zhingobiig, the inner bark of the balsam fir, gaawaandagoog bigiinsag, white-spruce gum, mazaanaatig, thistles, gezibinashk, horsetail, and of course asaakamigoon, the edible moss they used as tea-leaves, while waiting for the berry picking season to start in the fall. Apaakwaanaatig miinensan, sumac berries, that grew on the shrub-like tree with feathery leaves and the sour red seeds that grew in fuzzy, cone-shaped clusters, ininiminan, blueberries, and even niiboowini-dibik-aagawaate-miinan, the berries of the deadly nightshade that so often liked to grow side-by-side, blood red next to their darker cousins.

During the months of spring, summer and fall, it was rare for them to come home empty handed. And throughout the week, it was Church's job to follow the paths they'd walked, checking the snares for rabbits along the trap-lines they'd laid out. After discovering a patch of wild rhubarb, cattails, or berries, they would fill their baskets and put down semaa. Tobacco. They might be wiindigo, but they still followed protocol.

"When you take something from the earth, you give something back," Day told him, sprinkling semaa from her outstretched hands like she was feeding bread crumbs to the pigeons. The way Church understood it, tobacco operated like a kind of karmic currency. Not exactly payment, but covering all their bases spiritually. It was grown in the Victory Garden in their backyard, specifically for this purpose, and for Mukade-wiiyas's pipe.*

"Mukade-wiiyas knows every edible thing that has ever lived or moved in the forest," Inri once bragged. And rightfully so, for although she was now too frail to be much good at foraging, Mukade-wiiyas had insured that all her children and grandchildren knew the skills they needed for their survival. She now spent most of her time cooking and gardening to feed the appetites of their family.

"Gchi-nokomis, gi-gii-gego-wiika na zhagaji-jaabaakwaadang?" Church once asked his great-grandmother. Don't you ever get tired of cooking?

"Gaawiin." Mukade-wiiyas said, "Ninendamowin jiibaakwewinan azhese." – No. I find the process of preparing a meal soothing.

When they finally came home at the end of a long trek, Day's wheelchair would be caked with mud. Church would wipe the tires down while Mukade-wiiyas peeled the hide off the rabbit, turning it inside out so only its eyes stayed right-side out. Stirring the meat into a concoction with a large bone.

"That dinosaur bone really adds flavour." Day licked her lips.

"Do not cross her, or you will find out what fate awaits her enemies." Inri spoke with a Transylvanian accent, like Dracula. Joking that the bone was human. Here again was Inri's flair for the dramatic. Church thought he would be a great actor, if he ever stuck around long enough to make it past the first rehearsal.

Sometimes Church doubted they were the descendants of Wiindigo. Sometimes he thought that Inri was right, and that Day was mad. Maybe the scarcity she had experienced as a child had driven her insane, and she was now obsessed with food security. It was possible that they were only psychologically scarred, passing on the trauma of deprivation from one generation to the next.

"She's not right in the head," Inri told him. "Don't contradict her delusions, it won't accomplish anything, but I don't want you encouraging her either. You're old enough to know better by now."

Mukade-wiiyas never spoke of a husband. Maybe she never had one. No one knows for sure—not even Inri. It was a mystery among mysteries. Church asked Inri, because he was too intimidated to ask Mukade-wiiyas himself. And Day didn't want him to go around dredging up old wounds.

"What's the point?" Day asked. "It won't solve anything, it won't heal the hurt, and you can't go back in time and change things." What was she talking about? Was she talking about herself, Church wondered, or her mother?

They let sleeping dogs lie, or in this case, a bestial old woman with a furnace-blast temper. It was best not to raise her ire, and face the lashing of her quiet words distorting the very air, as if the vibrating molecules that conducted the vowels were traumatized by the transmission of sound. She never raised her voice, in fact she rarely raised her voice above that of a whisper—she didn't need to. Volume wasn't required to add emphasis to her words.

"She probably ate him," Inri mused—outside of Mukade-wiiyas's hearing of course—although Church knew he was only joking. Inri didn't really believe. Though Church thought it was at least plausible.

After all, it was the same end to which Day's first husband had fallen—albeit in a period of starvation and famine that resulted in an act of sacrificial-suicide-cannibalism. But it was, nevertheless, cannibalism. If Day's Daughter and Mukade-wiiyas had fallen prey to the necessities of hunger once, who was to say it hadn't happened before? Bagonegiizhig was, after all, the matriarch of their family, the daughter of the wiindigo monster who was the father of them all.

Mukade-wiiyas never gave any indication that she'd ever had a nbaazgim—a sweetheart—or a lover. And maybe she never had one. She was the least human of them all—maybe sex was unnecessary for reproduction? Black widow spiders only needed to mate once, and then they could reproduce whenever they chose. Many things were possible in the kingdom of non-human species.

Like so much else, Church was left groping for answers, trying to reassemble the puzzle of their lives, and the past that always seemed to be shrouded in mystery. Even the stories meant to explain the mystery of their existence raised more questions than they answered.

Were they really wiindigo? Or were these yarns meant to make sense of a senseless world? There were no monsters, and these stories were just ways of understanding things too hard for the human mind to adequately imagine or explain. Maybe they were metaphors? They weren't real in any literal sense, and only had a deeper symbolic meaning.

A burning question

It was a passing comment, in a moment of frustration, which had at first awakened his curiousity. "I married a White man and see where it left me!" Day's Daughter said, gesturing down to her crippled legs and the wheelchair encasing her body, as if that were somehow her second husband's fault—and maybe it was— Church didn't know. Day's Daughter had been sitting in that chair for his whole life—and as far as he knew, she always had. But, apparently, this was not the way things had always been. His grandmother had once been able to walk.

The revelation was jarring.

Church had never spent much time considering his grandmother's disability, he'd simply accepted it as a reality. Now he knew this had not always been the case, and he had no idea what trauma had caused her disability. Church had no doubt that it was some trauma which had left her crippled; he had never once seen anyone in his wiindigo family catch so much as a cold, let alone suffer from a prolonged illness. They ate so much maybe they had too many vitamins flowing through their veins. It must have been something bad. Really bad.

He was impatient to discover what tragedy had befallen his grandmother. Church was determined to unravel this one mystery—among so many others—which he lived with on a day-to-day basis.

"Ask a burning question, get a burning answer." Church heard Inri's voice echoing in his head, reciting one of the many quotations from his collection of invented and memorized phrases.

When Church learned how Day's Daughter came to be disabled—when he finally had his burning question answered—he was not surprised that no one had told him. Mukade-wiiyas, Day's Daughter, Inri—none of them had been willing to answer his questions.

"Stop being a nuisance, Church," Day's Daughter reached up to tack another recipe on the wall, flattening the glossy paper with the heel of her palm.

"Don't be a pest," Inri exhaled a stream of blue-grey smoke from the menthol cigarette. Standing on the landing of the second-floor fire escape, Inri didn't turn from his contemplation of the stark, dead cherry tree in their backyard, the twisted branches reaching ominously towards the sky. His back irises bleeding to a pale blue at the edges where corneal rings met sclera, like the eyes of a husky.

"You little jeet."

"Hrrmpphh," Mukade-wiiyas grunted non-commitantly as she continued stirring her soup. She lifted the ivory-coloured spoon to her ruined purple lips, blowing briefly on the scalding liquid before slurping the tiniest possible sip, and then swallowing audibly. Part of her upper lip was missing, so he could see her two front teeth, white and glistening.

Eventually, the information Church sought came from an unforeseen source—his father. It was Peter who finally explained how Day's Daughter got her wheels. Church shouldn't have been so surprised. After all, Peter had known their family since before he had been born.

The burning answer:

"I'll be honest—I never wanted children. I'm not fit to be a parent. You know it, I know it, God knows it. But I keep comin' back because I'm the most sane person you've got in your entire godforsaken life. And that's truly pathetic because it's not saying a lot." This was an unusual moment. Peter was rarely forthcoming with his own feelings, or his take on things.

"Black-meat shot your grandmother. Your crazy wiindigo family, they're not all there," Peter pointed at his head, slowly rotating his finger. "They're all crazy. Why do you think I keep coming back?"

"Why, would Mukade-wiiyas shoot Day?" Church frowned.

"You"ll have to ask her." Peter shook his head. "But Black-meat did it. Black-meat shot your grandmother." Church was left to imagine the rest, to visualize, down to the smallest detail, how it had happened. Though he had no evidence that this was how the events had played out, he knew, with an absolute certainty that this, this was how it had happened:

Day

Day was pregnant. She could feel the life growing inside of her, and the smaller plural hungers of the fetuses. She was eating for three now. Goshko predicted she was going to have two hungry children to feed, and they would have no father. So Day's Daughter re-married in the traditional way, which is to say, there was no ceremony. She was still in mourning when she entered into the new arrangement. The customary grieving period of thirteen moons had not passed, and in fact, she had re-wed almost immediately.

Those residents of Ghost Lake who gossiped about the family of wiindigo had more fuel with which to feed their condemnation. It was cruel for Day's Daughter to shack up so soon after her husband's death, they whispered. It demonstrated that she had never truly cared for Wabitii. It proved her heart was frozen. They were wiindigo, what else could you expect from monsters?

To add insult to injury, she did not marry a relative of her husband or even a member of his clan: but a White man. Day's Daughter did not keep Wabitii's ghost for thirteen moons. She did not assemble those personal objects that were of importance to him, wrapping them together in a grieving bundle—she gave these things away. She had no need to keep his ghost. He would always be with her.

Day's Daughter hoped that her new husband Owanii'igeg, a white fur trapper and good hunter, would be a good provider. And because he was White: he did not believe the rumours whispered about their family.

There is no such thing as a wiindigo.

She had thought Owanii could help feed them through the long, cold, hard winters. But she was wrong. He wasn't as good at hunting as she had hoped, though this was being uncharitable, as no one was a good hunter that winter; it was too cold. The animals stayed hidden in their burrows. Even Mukade-wiiyas—an experienced hunter, and half-wiindigo besides—came back with empty hands. It was a repetition of the year before.

Nine months after her first husband's death, Day's two small babies—Inri and Marie—were born. The Great Spirit had cursed her with fertility. Twins, a symbol of abundance, were a counterpoint to an endless hunger that could never be filled. Prosperity and desperation—like two sides of the same coin.

Little wiindigo babies with empty bellies made crabby little things. Crabby loud little things. Three months old, and they could already scream. And they did what all babies do when they are hungry, they cried, and they were always hungry, so they never seemed to stop crying, except for when they ate or slept.

Even though she was already pregnant when Owanii took up with her, Day's Daughter was still beautiful. More than beautiful, she was exquisite, and one of the most beautiful women Owanii had ever seen. This, more than anything, swayed his decision. He was not the sort of man that women normally chased after, but he was a good hunter. And Day's Daughter hoped he would be a good provider for her hungry children.

So much drama had taken place at the door of their cabin. A year had passed—a full thirteen moons—since her first husband's death. Since Wabitii had sacrificed his own body to feed his family. And it was on the very anniversary of his passing that another tragedy would befall her.

The winter had been unseasonably cold, in fact, the past three winters had been unseasonably cold, seeming to grow colder with each passing year, the mercury dropping to fifty below. Not even the smallest animals could be found walking the earth; they all seemed to be hunkered down somewhere, or hibernating, waiting for the worst of the chill to pass, before they would emerge, blinking, from their dens. The residents of Ghost Lake—including the shunned family of wiindigowak— huddled in their shelters for warmth, unwilling to leave the comfort of their homes.

It happened in December, late in the month of Manitou-giizis, the Spirit-moon, when the high noon sun appeared at its lowest declination, casting long shadows as sunlight forked through the trees. Fingers laced together; like flesh stitched across the sky. The shortest day and the longest night, this was when their wiindigo nature was at its strongest, and their humanity, weakest.

Their resources had dwindled, despite all their preparation, bringing with it another dilemma. Day was out of her mind with hunger. Though hunger is too paltry a word to describe the madness that had engulfed her. This was need, necessity, desire, desperation, demand without denial, a vacuum consuming itself, like a star collapsing. She tore out her own hair and ate it, ripping out her own fingernails, and sucking on her own blood. She was crazed by hunger; hunger filling her whole world, hunger filling her whole mind, hunger occupying her entire being. There was no more room for "I", for individuality, for the woman called Day. There was only one thing: Hunger. She was hunger personified.

She remembered this loss of identity, abstractly, like watching the actions of someone else on a screen, it wasn't her teeth gnawing on her own fingers, it wasn't her fingers tearing out her own long hair, and greedily stuffing the locks into her mouth, chewing and swallowing the bundled-together strands, it wasn't her, it was Hunger, for that's who she had become. She was Hunger itself, if Hunger could transform into flesh, the smaller part of a much larger whole.

She ran out of their cabin, hell bent on . . . doing what? She could not remember. Hunger must be fed. Then there was the sharp crack of a rifle being fired, pain like a burning hot coal embedding itself into her spine, sending lava coursing through her extremities. Had she been struck by a bolt of lightning?

No, this was no lightning, only a small wedge of metal driven into her back, and an electric fire, fire, fire searing her from the inside, live-wire ants crawling underneath her skin.

Numbness.

Immobility.

And then, blessed darkness.

Bagonegiizhig

Bagonegiizhig watched her daughter descend into madness. And she watched Day's new husband, Owanii, slowly come to realize the monsters that they truly were. The trapper watched helplessly as his bride tore out her long, beautiful black hair, her warm brown irises swallowed by mydriasis, pupils grown large and dark as if possessed by a demon. Hugely dilated, the better to gather in light, hugely dilated the better to zero-in on, and pinpoint potential prey—flashing like the reflective eyes of a cat in the darkness.

Only there was no demon possessing her, she was the demon herself. Set free from the chains of self-possession, nothing except.

Thankfully, Day still had enough presence of mind not to attack those around her, though it was only a matter of time.

Day finally broke and fled for the door. She ran because what was left of her restraint was all but gone. If she didn't leave, she would turn on her loved ones. She would fall upon anything and anyone in her path. Tormented by the presence of living flesh, fresh human meat, she had to run.

The newborn twins—Inri and Marie—cried incessantly, their tiny lungs working like bellows fueling an audible blaze that swept over all who heard it. The twins cried with hunger and fear, because even they could sense that something was wrong. Their little tongues moved like frantic slugs as their mouths fell open to wail.

Hbabies Owanii screamed as he—foolishly—tried to hold his wife back from the door. Day scraped and clawed at his face and eyes, caring for nothing except her desperate need to escape before her hunger took over completely. The babies' cries grew louder. Her clothing tore, the door was ripped open, and the minus fifty-degree chill rushed in. The sound of Hunger: babies' crying, a man screaming, and the wind howling.

Bagonegiizhig had been unable to prevent her beloved daughter from descending into madness. Over the course of that long, dead winter, Day had gradually lost restraint. No longer able to curb her wiindigo nature, she devolved into her mythical self, leaving her humanity, and her mother, far behind.

Day did not have the iron will—which Mukade-wiiyas possessed. Her child was weak. She could not stand the thought of losing her only daughter. She knew that if Day reached the darkness of the forest, Day would never come back. There would be no return once hunger got its grip on her entire mind and soul. Day had neither the strength nor the discipline to save herself.

While Owanii was still rolling around on the floor uselessly, screaming and clutching at his bleeding eyes, Bagonegiizhig became filled with the necessity to act. She grabbed her rifle and followed Day to the door of the cabin. She did the only thing she could think to do; she took sight down the barrel of her gun, squinting against the glare of the setting sun. As the winter progressed, the trunks of the trees acted like sundials, tracking the progress of the sun across the horizon, the azimuth shifting so that the light of the setting sun fell full across the front door.

Bagonegiizhig could sense her father in the stillness of the forest, watching, and waiting to welcome his granddaughter. So they could be together in their hunger—except she refused to allow this.

From forty feet away, she waited until the last moment to pull the trigger, wishing she could reverse the flow of time. Wishing that her daughter would come back to herself, and she wouldn't have to shoot.

The wail struggling to escape somewhere inside did not affect her aim: she had too much mastery over herself to miss. She had never let her own hunger win; she wouldn't let her daughter's hunger win now. Day's life was at stake, and accuracy was required. A few inches to the left or right could prove fatal if the bullet were to hit a vital organ: her heart, her pancreas, her kidneys, her liver, her lungs, and maybe other mysterious wiindigo organs that have no counterpart in the natural world. Mukade-wiiyas wanted to avoid hitting all of these, but Day was a moving target. She took aim. Held her breath.

Thankfully, she didn't miss.

Mukade-wiiyas had spent her entire life hunting, she knew how to fire a rifle, how to take aim, and how to fire with accuracy. The instant Day's foot stepped into the darkness of the waiting trees, Mukade-wiiyas squeezed, and the bullet rocketed from the chamber. It was a precision shot to Day's lower spine, immobilizing her legs, permanently disabling her.

A grazing wound would not be sufficient to stop her—Day was going full wiindigo, and would merely brush off any wound, even an egregious one, as inconsequential. The only thing that would halt Day was the injury Mukade-wiiyas inflicted: the one that took away Day's ability to walk, and the wound that preserved her humanity.

Owanii

His wife ran for the cover of the woods, lost in some insanity that afflicted her, eating her own hair, barely clothed, the cloth having torn as she wrenched free of his grasp, fleeing into the frozen wastes. She wasn't right in the head. Some madness had touched her. Some hysteria. He needed to protect her from herself. But then his mother-in-law, in some fit of madness of her own, picked up her rifle and fired before he had the chance to intervene. The bullet hit Day in the lower back, and she pitched forward at the edges of the dark forest, waiting to welcome her into a shadowy embrace. Owanii wished that Day had been able to make it into the trees before Mukade-wiiyas pulled the trigger. Maybe then, things could have been different.

His wife survived, recovering miraculously quickly from the gunshot wound, and from her bout of hysteria, without the aide of doctors or medicine, although she would never walk again. She was paralyzed from the waist down, and he now had three mouths to feed, his wife, and her twin babies. They moved into town, and bought a house, a two storey, red-brick Victorian, far away from Day's crazy wiindigo-mother, though Day refused get the RCMP involved, or to lay charges against her mother. Day wouldn't hear of it.

"She saved my life," she insisted.

Though how that was possible, Owanii couldn't fathom. Owanii wasn't his real name, his real name was Owen, but the Ojibwe nickname stuck, and it was what everyone called him. He'd spent so many years living in the bush, he even thought of himself as Owanii now. Day's Daughter, he was beginning to learn, was just as crazy as her mother, and he wished he had listened to those ridiculous, superstitious rumours. Though they might not have been wiindigo, they were definitely, and certifiably, crazy. And though he cared for them, the twins were not his children, and his wife, though beautiful, was crippled and insane besides. This was not the way he had imagined his married life would be. So after seeing to Day's recovery, and setting her up in her own home in the city, he left her.

She was on her own.

Day

Day's Daughter hadn't always been confined to a wheelchair. That's how she viewed it, as a confinement, but it was better than crawling around on the floor with her arms. Day sometimes longed to be free from the anchor of meat below her waist. It weighed down the upper portion of her body like dead flesh, like a WWII soldier, foot slowly rotting away from the muddy trenches. Other times, she dreamed that the power to walk was returned to her.

It was a reocurring nightmare: she ran through the woods, tree branches lashing at her, whipping at her face, at her arms, at her eyes, ripping out great hanks of scalp along with her dark tresses—thigh muscles standing out in relief as they carried her through tangled briars, through tightly knit stands of spruce, nettles and thorns tearing at her clothes, tearing at her flesh, tearing her apart. The thrill and exhiliration of movement ruined by the slashing-slicing brambles, her skin bursting open like ripe fruit. Her legs could move again, but they still would not respond to the commands of her mind. Her feet pounded the earth no matter what obstacles confronted her, no matter how her lungs burned and her heart pounded inside her chest, threatening to explode.

She would wake up slick, not with blood, but with sweat, and she would remember the sensation of movement accompanied by a pervasive sense of loss for a faculty she knew she would never regain. She would rather forget that she had ever had the capacity to walk, than to be plagued with impossibilities. In waking life, she had her chair, and her increasingly muscular arms, and they now carried her almost everywhere she had to go.

She'd never thought her arms could grow so strong.

It had all happened so many years ago, when her twins were still babies. She was so used to her wheelchair now, she rarely thought of the events that had led her to her disability. It was a fact, and facts couldn't be changed. There was no use dwelling on unalterable truths.

At times, she felt the original shock of the hunting-callibre bullet snapping her spine, the numbness, and the instantaneous loss of motor control below her waist. Her legs collapsed beneath her as she ran, and she fell face-first to the forest floor, legs unresponsive. The slug lodged somewhere in her back, where it would stay, nestled against her spine. Wiindigo did not go to doctors. Wiindigo did not get sick, so what need did they have for medicine? Scar tissue grew, encapsulating what her body could not absorb.

She still heard the gunshot, the bang of the explosive force as the projectile left the barrel, reverberating throughout the forest like the sinew twang of a released arrow. And this arrow had found its mark, altering her life forever. It was amazing that a little piece of metal could change so much.

It did prove one thing. Wiindigo were not immortal. Wiindigo could be killed, and it didn't require a silver bullet. Though they didn't get sick, they did age, and though they might be long-lived (her mother, Mukade-wiiyas, was ancient by anyone's standards) they could be injured. Whether the same was true for her grandfather, that original Wiindigo spirit that had impregnated Gaawiin, Day's Daughter didn't know. She suspected that he was not as bound to the flesh as his offspring, and so was not as accordingly vulnerable. It was a double-edged sword; whatever powers were gained from their wiindigo nature, were offset by drawbacks in equal measure.

In her weaker moments, Day's Daughter resented her humanity knowing it held her from true recovery. If she gave herself up to her monstrous nature, even now she might regain the ability to walk. In her nightmares, she ran across the clearing outside their cabin, seeing again the face of her grandfather, for the first and last time. It was the face of Hunger, stretched and inhumanly elongated, crouching in the shadows at the edge of the forest, with a predatory stillness, waiting to welcome her home.

This is what haunted her, the knowledge that if she gave up her humanity, she might regain her mobility. She knew her grandfather was alive. She'd seen him with her own eyes. Wiindigo were very long-lived, if not immortal. All she had to do was let go, stop fighting, and she could be with him. She could be a monster too.

At first, Day's Daughter felt hostile toward her mother, but came to understand why Mukade-wiiyas had been forced to act. In reality, Day had always known, but she needed to feel angry with someone, and her mother was the obvious candidate. Though she knew, in fact, her mother had saved her life. When she was able to overcome the anger at her new way of life, she was able to overcome the anger she felt towards her mother. But first she needed someone—anyone to blame. Sometimes, she couldn't help blaming Christ, the European man-god— something vile always seemed to happen around the little shit's birthday. Maybe he envied other pagan Gods and demi-gods— maybe he waged war against them all? Their wiindigo family had emerged with the arrival of Christianity. Maybe he had wished this drama upon them?

An entire year would pass before Day's Daughter spoke to her mother again—a full thirteen moons— since that long night in December, Manitoo-giizis, the Spirit moon. And still she felt nothing but resentment, though she knew why Mukade-wiiyas had done it.

But by then, it was already too late. The Indian Agent had come and taken away her children. She couldn't take care of them by herself, without Owanii. She had no choice. She'd let them be taken away to the residential school, where at least they'd get something to eat. Not enough, she knew from personal experience, but more than she herself could provide. The guilt ate at her, even as the twin screams faded from the range of her hearing, their fear and confusion echoing through her mind long after they were gone, leaving behind another dark stain on her soul. She hung on for a few weeks, before realizing she couldn't even take care of herself. She went home, returning to Ghost Lake to forgive her mother.

Forgiveness was the only choice she had left.

June 8th 1872, Sydenham,

After a long journey by coach, we have finally arrived at the town of Sydenham, where we will henceforth be travelling not by land, but by water. I look forward to leaving the lurching carriage behind, for the more comfortable accommodations that will no doubt be afforded to us aboard passenger ship. It appears that Aabitiba—for that is his name—the half-breed servant Othniel has employed in his service, has driven the entire way, apparently without rest, as we drove through the day and night.

While waiting for Marsh to secure our passage aboard the steamer, the half-breed Indian began unloading our luggage and supplies. "You must be very tired," I remarked, to which he responded that Marsh was very insistent that they arrive "as soon as humanly possible," and that he would "permit no delays."

Ah-bit-too-yah'iing, he tells me, is the proper pronunciation of his name. In his Ojibwe language it means 'half', to reflect his mixed-blood heritage. Half white, and half Indian. From our brief exchange, I come away with nothing except a positive impression of the industrious fellow. Othniel soon returned, and we made our way up the gangplank, Aabitiba following with the luggage.

As we made our way up the gangplank we were met by Brennen, Marsh's assistant, whom I believe is also one of his former students at Yale. "The others have already boarded and are settled in." Brennen said, "But I still don't know if it was wise to split up our party like this."

"I left Hoppin, Russell, and MacNaughton under the chaperone of Jesse Lee and his Ninth Infantry—he's no Wild Bill but they'll be perfectly safe in my absence. I can't ignore this find and leave it all to Jones. It has too much potential."

"You know," Brennen said. "This expedition could turn out to be nothing but a wild goose chase."

"It had better not," Marsh said, shooting Aabitiba a curious look that I can only describe as black-hearted. "But that is exactly why I split up the party. If this turns out to be a fool's errand, at least the season won't be a complete loss. As far as anyone is concerned, we are still out digging in Hell's Half Acre."

"At least, it should offer some misdirection or camouflage for this enterprise," Brennen said, "If Jones or some other interested party is keeping tabs on your movements."

"Exactly what I was thinking," Marsh said.

After this cryptic exhange, we boarded ship. It was a relief to finally be free of the shaking and bumping of the stagecoach. Moreso, to have free reign to perambulate about the deck of the Harbinger and stretch my legs on our journey, instead of being confined to the enclosed space of a carriage.

The air aboard ship is bracing.

June 12th 1872, The Harbinger,

My initial delight at being able to amble about the deck of the ship, has given way to sea sickness, the bumps of the carriage, having simply been replaced with the ceaseless motion of the ship. I've spent the last few days in agony, shut up in my cabin, or retching over the side, as I've been unable to keep down any of my meals. I feel my fever beginning to return.

I fear I am not made for extended journeys. Now I long for the jolts and bumps of the carriage that I had so derided—anything would be preferable to this persistant, stomach-churning movement. It is odd, that I have never before been afflicted, beyond a mild nausea, on any of my other journeys, even across the Great Divide. On this crossing, my symptoms seem to have been magnified, probably owing to my recent fever.

As of yet, I have seen neither hide nor tail of Aabitiba and Othniel, though I have met Brennen and the other Yale-men in the refectory. The ship is not so large, and it is odd that I have not yet encountered them, either on the deck, or in the mess hall. Maybe they too, are holed up in their respective cabins, overcome with seasickness.

June 17th 1872, The Harbinger

My nausea seems to have subsided as my constitution acclimatized to the restless motion. I am no longer in misery, shut up in my cabin day and night, and I can now walk about the deck of the ship. I have resolved to finally begin to enjoy this journey. It was evening when my sickness finally broke and I felt well enough to emerge from my cabin, like a badger emerging from its den. The stars were already out, scattered across the sky like a thousand sparkling snow crystals. I found Othniel on deck, leaning over the railing of the ship, contemplating the distance of the stars and the roiling black waters lapping at the hull of the ship.

"Here you are Othniel! I haven't seen you at all since we disembarked. I have been locked in my cabin with seasickness for the duration."

"I prefer the solitude of the water that can only be found at night." Othniel said, "The day is too filled with the chatter of travelers, too willing to talk of their own concerns."

"So you've become nocturnal?" I smiled at him.

"For the most part, yes. It's the only way for me to gain the solitude I seek." Marsh glanced side-long in my direction.

Knowing when to take a hint, I took my leave, and left Marsh to the contemplation of the dark waters, and found my own vantage point from which to observe our passage. The waters were calm, reflecting the stars, so that it seemed almost as if our ship was passing through the ether of the spheres, disturbed only by the gentle crest and bob where the prow sliced through the waves, parting to break against the breast of the ship. The deck was deserted, except for the still form of Marsh observing the night from his side of the boat, and me on mine.

The stars were brighter than I had ever seen them. The entire stretch of the Milky Way was visible as a clearly defined arch, bending across the sky, each individual star suspended in space as if held there by some viscous, invisible fluid. They seemed to be so much closer than they had ever been, almost as if I could reach out and gather them. It made me feel as if I were a part of the universe, instead of being a separate part within it.

After observing the sky for some time, I made my way below deck retiring to my cabin. There is only so much insignificance I can take. Leaving to the solitary figure of Marsh, entire possession of the ship.

Where Aabitiba passed the remainder of the journey aboard ship I do not know, reappearing only as we came within sight of the Twin Cities to dock. I saw Othniel only at night, like Lord Ruthven—rising in the evening as the sun sank in the west, a dark figure at the stern, staring into even darker water. What thoughts he mulled over, I do not know, but I left him to his silence, and solitary company, knowing how he valued that solitude. I would not impress upon him the offence of my society, should he not seek it out.

I.N.R.I. Abbrv. Latin. 1. Is an acronym for the phrase "Iesus Nazarenus, Rex Ivdaeorvm", or Jesus the Nazarene, King of the Jews. 2. Is the inscription placed above Jesus on the cross, Latin was used because it was the language of the Roman Empire, during which Crucifixions were a common form of punishment. 3. The Titulus Cruces was a sign hung above crucified people, detailing their crimes.

There was a rustle at the door and Day wheeled her way over to answer it. A few of the recipes lining the walls became dislodged with the movement of air at her passing, and shifted to the floor like fallen leaves.

Church already knew who it was by the electric chill in the air. Like before a thunderstorm. It was his uncle, Inri. Inri liked to wear a dress, nail polish, and gold bangles in his ear. But even though he dressed like a woman sometimes, there was nothing feminine about him. And even though he wore men's clothing sometimes, there was nothing masculine about him. Inri said he wore women's clothing to reflect his "other-worldly nature," his "more-than-dual inclinations," for he was "neither man nor woman nor some combination of both or somewhere in between". He was something else entirely.

You only had to look into his eyes to see.

It felt more like looking into the eyes of a wolf, or some dangerous predator, inhabiting the body of a man, than like looking into the eyes of a human being, and whether that predator was male or female meant very little when it was about to eat you. And whether that predator's gender was at all equivalent to the closest human counterpart was another question entirely.

When he turned his head, the golden glitter on his eyelids would sparkle and the bangles would jingle. He radiated an aura of just-suppressed energy, like a tightly wound spring. The molecules in the air around him were super-charged and frantic, like running your feet barefoot over carpet you could get zapped just by sitting next to him. He felt dangerous.

"It doesn't take much force to snap a man's spine if you know how to do it correctly," Inri told him. Inri was filled with these useful bits of wisdom. He gave off a faint whiff of perfume, and something darker, more metallic, something that implied beauty and promised pain, simultaneously delicate and deadly.

At an early age, Inri had been given a taste for blood, and he had more scars than anyone else Church knew, and he wore them openly. There was a story for every scar and every mark on his body was a symbol of his strength, his ability to survive. So many scars gouged into his flesh for the shame of being alive, for the price of defiance.

Broken bones, insults, and racial slurs . . . .

"See this one here?" Inri said, pointing with all five fingers to a large half-moon scar on his temple, "This one almost killed me! This macho-fuck kicked me in the head, I was lying on his couch for days hemorrhaging internally . . ." he laughed as he told the story, " . . . and the guy kept on telling me that if I died, he was going to dump my body into the river because he didn't want to have to explain how a dead transvestite came to be decomposing on his sofa." And then he laughed, as if it was the funniest story.

Inri told him about Os Tich and Ozaawendib, Yellow Head, about ogchi-daakwe, warrior-women, and powerful mashkikii-nini, medicine men, and the Anishinaabek who had been erased from history. Inri had collected stories from across Turtle Island, mikinaakominis, literally the land that used to be a turtle, from the far north of the Arctic all the way down to the Isthmus of Panama.

Inri told Church how "all Medicine Men" used to be powerful like he was, or dual-natured like the Agwe-kwe, the And-woman, "Or at least all the really good ones were." And he told Church about Morrisseau, and how "All great Anishinaabe artists can see with X-Ray Vision, because you have to be able to see from a different angle in order to be visionary."

"I'm telling you this, because you too, are going to be a great artist one day," Inri said with conviction, as if he knew for certain that it would come true. The sound of water dripping into pots punctuated his words. "I can see this."

Their kitchen was built as an addition onto the original structure of the building, and the tin-roof leaked, pots and pans were left scattered around to catch the rainwater. You could count the seconds between the raindrops, waiting for the spaces between to lengthen, so they knew when the storm had let up. Every few minutes Day or Mukade-wiiyas would fling a bucket of water out the window, like some nineteenth-century chambermaid emptying pots onto the streets.

It was on this occasion that his Uncle had told him the story of their ancestors Aanzinaago and Kakiigan, and how the blood of a great warrior had come to flow through their veins. Inri claimed that Kakiigan's blood let him see visions, and that sometimes, he could even see the future. As the storm let up, the expanding spaces between drips formed a backdrop for the telling of the story.

The sound of cold water, dripping into pots.

The Raw-meat widow

Aanzinaago, or ashkami-zhiigaawikwe the Raw-meat widow, as the Anishinaabek of Ghost Lake had began calling her, bound her breasts and donned the clothes of her gaa-nibodjig onabeman, her deceased husband, taking care to make sure that her throat was covered. If the illusion wasn't perfect Kakiigan would see through the deception. If she were to leave her throat bared, the lack of a bikagondaagan, an Adam's apple, would show to anyone who cared to look that she was, in fact, not a man, no matter what she appeared. The voice was a man's gift, just as blood was a woman's.

Aanzinaago separated her hair into two braids, because, if she were to leave it flowing long and free, no one would believe that she was a man even if she wore men's clothing. Her face was almost too soft, too feminine to pass for a man's, and so she rubbed ashes from the cold fire-pit into her skin so that her complexion would not be so flawless—few men were so beautiful. There was nothing she could do about the tattoo on her chin. It was permanent. Stitched through the skin with sinew and a caribou-bone-needle dipped in pitch, the marking didn't just go into her body, if she had one, it went into her soul. She could only hope that it wouldn't be recognized. It was a dead-give-away; but as few Anishinaabek seemed to understand its meaning, she still felt fairly confident.

Aanzinaago finished dressing and slipped silently from the roundhouse and out into the night where the stars were glowing brightly, like a thousand jewels strewn carelessly across the sky. She stepped lightly past other sleeping wigwams and made her way to Kakiigan's camp. She had spent time learning how to walk like a man, practicing, and studying the swagger of the men in the village and comparing it to the way of the women.

The men seemed to take up more space, and the women seemed to sway more. Aanzinaago suspected it had something to do with the fact that women had childbearing hips.

Aanzinaago hadn't been able to conceive with her husband, so after Mskwaa-mkwaa died, Aanzinaago searched for someone that could give her strong children. Many of the Jiibay Zaaga'igan nini, Ghost Lake men, seemed strong, but her husband had also been strong. And she wanted children who could survive anything from war, to famine, to whatever diseases the zhaaganaashiwag brought with them. No matter what the future held, she wanted her children to have a fighting chance.

By far the most famous and well-known Jiibay Zaaga'igan nini, was Kakiigan, a great warrior, a magician, a priest and a prophet. The reports of his exploits were known far and wide, though he rarely returned to the place of his birth. Now was her chance. Men and women would go to Kakiigan and try to seduce him, hoping that some of that power would rub off him and onto them. It was said that men who had lain with him had become hunters of unparalleled skill, and that men who had lain with him before battle had become great warriors, or seen great and terrifying visions. All the women had been rejected.

If Kakiigan preferred men, Aanzinaago thought, she would just have to become a man. She wasn't going to let a small thing like that get in the way of her and her future children. If all it took was one night spent with Kakiigan to become a great warrior, then just think what one night could do for her if all she wanted was strong children! Aanzinaago was willing to bet that Kakiigan could give her the children she longed for. There was just the matter of her gender.

Aanzinaago slipped into Kakiigan's tent and was happy to find that he was still awake, and that he knew what she had come for. Kakiigan took one look at her and said, "Giiwenaazha' gwiizenzhish! Niin gego gwech nbishigwaadizi-ziinh shkiniigish, gego nwiikoshkaa-ziinh gwiizensag! Nwiikoshkaa gchi-niniiwag eta! "Go home boy! I do not lust after boys! I prefer my men fully grown!" And for a moment, Aanzinaago thought he had somehow deciphered her real reasons for coming, but then realized he had called her a boy! Gwiizens.

In reality, Kakiigan was not much older than Aanzinaago herself, but she realized she must look more like an adolescent boy than a grown man. She had donned the disguise at the trading post to see if she could pass for a man, and when she had been addressed as "shkiniigish," a young man, she had assumed that her deception would work. But now that she could pass for a man it was no longer her gender that was the problem, it was her youth! She looked too young.

Aanzinaago put a disrespectful sneer on her face and half-turned away as if to leave, remembering to modulate her voice and speak in a lower octave. "Maanoo akiwenzi, misawaaj nminjinawezi." Never mind old man, I'm disappointed anyway. She spoke in Indian, because Kakiigan spoke no English. She had a naturally husky, throaty sounding voice, and there was nothing about it that gave her away as being female. "Inakaag aajimookaanan gimashkawiziiwiniwaa minjim gii-gimino-ayaa nibaaganing, amiiwag gichi-onzaamaajimo, debwewinan gikendaagozi apiich dago-gichigikaam." Rumours of your prowess and virility have been greatly exaggerated and fade in the face of your advancing age.

She decided that the easiest way to provoke him would be to insult his manhood and insinuate that he was not up to the task, while at the same time suggesting that, it was not her that was too young, but he that was too old. This would make Kakiigan want to prove that his abilities were not waning, which was exactly what Aanzinaago wanted. His proof.

It was obvious that Kakiigan wasn't accustomed to people speaking to him in such a manner. They probably had better sense, and knew when to show respect. The magician's eyes went wide, his nostrils flared, and his face turned a darker shade in anger. Which was what Aanzinaago had been counting on. When people are angry they don't think as clearly. That would be to her advantage.

Kakiigan stepped forward as if to strike her, but Aanzinaago had anticipated the attack, he was a warrior after all, and predicted where it would land. It was a back handed slap aimed at her face, suitable for an arrogant boy who needed to be put in his place—she caught his arm before the blow could land.

And then, holding Kakiigan's arm, Aanzinaago began to laugh, amused at her own ability to manipulate the warrior, letting Kakiigan know that just because he was a powerful magician, didn't mean that he was infallible. Aanzinaago the Boy had bested Kakiigan the Warrior.

Kakiigan studied Aanzinaago as she laughed, for the first time noticing how beautiful he was for a boy, and how smooth his skin was, even with all that black grime smeared on his face. The boy was not as young as he had at first presumed either, the way he held himself was too certain, too self-assured, and he was very pretty.

"Aaniish ezhinikaazyin?" What's your name? Kakiigan asked her, and Aanzinaago had to grope around for a more manly sounding alias, and came up with the name "Waagoshens" or Little-fox.

"Aahaaw, Waag-goosh-sheennss," Kakiigan said in a lower, gravelly tone of voice, "debi'ezhinikaadeg ganage." Well, Little-fox, at least you have an appropriate name. And she could sense the shifting of his interest, his growing curiosity, and Aanzinaago knew; she had him. Now for the tricky part, she thought.

Kakiigan kissed her, and his hands began to stray, exploring the terrain of her body, but she couldn't let him find her breasts, or the vegetable she'd stuffed into her aapizhaan, the breechcloth between her legs. But, she was supposed to be a man now wasn't she? When she had been with Mskwaa-mkwaa, he had always taken the role of intitiating, but she couldn't let Kakiigan do that now, she needed to be the one in control. Aanzinaago pushed Kakiigan down onto his apishimon, and pinned his hands above his head so that he couldn't touch her. He resisted, but she wasn't weak, and though he wanted to continue his own campaign, Kakiigan let Goshko have his way, because he thought that it too, might be pleasant. Kakiigan was usually the one to press ahead when it suited him, or to simply refuse, maybe it would be nice to be submissive for once?

Aanzinaago kissed Kakiigan. She didn't give him a chance to breathe as she unfastened the important bits of clothing standing between them. She didn't even bother removing their bashkegino-midaasan, their leather leggings, as she used all her weight to pin Kakiigan's hands down above his head. The less clothing she had to remove—the better. He was straining against her, and it was almost more than she could manage with only one arm. Aanzinaago teased him, and when she felt that Kakiigan was ready, guided him into her, and brought herself down upon him, kissing him, trying to distract him from what was taking place down there. Lucky for her, she'd always enjoyed sex, and had had lots of practice with with her onabeman before he passed; she knew her way around a cock. And she needed Kakiigan to come as soon as possible, so that he wouldn't have a chance to question the physics of what was actually taking place—Aanzinaago squeezed, and as she hoped Kakiigan came, almost involuntarily.

Aanzinaago held him down for another moment and then she was off of him, re-fastening her clothes and gone before he had a chance to blink, leaving Kakiigan too bewildered and confused to be certain of what had happened.

"Aapiish gdzhaamin?" Kakiigan asked. Where are you going? But she was already out the door before he had even sat up. The next morning, Kakiigan could find no trace of the man, and no one at Jiibay Zaaga'iganing had ever heard of a young man named Waagoshens. He almost believed it had been some Manitou that had come to visit him in the night, and not a human being at all. He'd heard stories about those foxes and coyotes.

Eight moons later, ashkami-zhiigaawikwe, the Raw-meat widow, gave birth pre-mature, noonde-nitaawigiwin, to a beautiful baby girl, and a few weeks later, unexpectedly, to a beautiful baby boy, on-time, but a surprise. Aanzinaago had chosen wisely; Kakiigan had given her nizhoodenyag! Twins!

It was something of a miracle. The beating of two-hearts in-vitro had gone undetected. Niizh-ode, after all, means two-hearts. And to have such a long delay in-between births, was also a rare thing. Only a few wise getaadizidjig, old people, counted the months back and connected her aanjigowinan, her pregnancy, to Kakiigan's visit. A full moon longer than it would have been conceivable for the twins to belong to her onabeman. The first child, perhaps—but Goshko, the surprise? Such long pregnancies weren't possible for bemaadizidjig, people.

There were whispers. Could she have been impregnated twice? By two separate fathers? There were stories of such things occuring, though no one had encountered such a thing in their own experience, or could even point to a specific historical instance. The binoojiinyag were so unlike, so dissimilar from each other, it was hard to believe they had shared the same womb, let alone shared the same father.

And so it was that the Raw-meat widow named her premature daughter, Gaawiin-giizha-noode, Raw or not—by anticipation—fully cooked, because she looked so small, bloody and unfinished, and of course she named the boy Goshko-waagoshens. Surprise-littlefox.

Oh, great! Church thought as he listened to the story, he already had to worry about sometimes eating people running in his family, now he had to worry about being a homo too? He wondered what else he had to worry about? What genetically inherited surprises lurked in his veins? What other secrets hid in his blood and in his brain, waiting to leap out at him at an inopportune moment, like a hungry tiger lying in wait? Congenital heart disease? Polio? Diabetes? Madness? If his grandmother was any kind of yardstick by which to measure, he suspected that sanity only had a passing glimpse of their family. Peter's psychoses were a mystery, Day's Daughter had always shown signs of instability, and Marie was certifiably crazy, incarcerated as he had been, in Sterling Shores.

Maybe a sudden brain aneurysm would explode inside his head and put him out of his misery? There probably wasn't anything to worry about once you were dead. Although, he'd never seen Mukade-wiiyas, Day's Daughter, Inri or Marie ever get sick. Not ever. He'd never seen any of them so much as catch a cold, let alone become ill from anything. Maybe wiindigo were immune? Maybe they ate so much; they had too many vitamins coursing through their veins?

And if Inri was correct, they might also have a pre-disposition for psychic ability. That was possible, given the powerful figures that occupied the cast of their family tree. Church only hoped that he didn't take after his father, and that drinking and gambling weren't genetic. Maybe it skipped a generation, like twins?

`Cryptophasia,` n. A secret language that develops between twins or close siblings. The language usually evolves prior to, or alongside, the children's mother tongue, and is usually forgotten as the speech of the surrounding world takes precedence.

Inri and Marie

Inri looked at his twin sister. They were so alike, and yet so dissimilar. If he had been born a woman, they easily could have been confused one for the other. Same eyes, same lips, the same bone structure. Except, there was some trauma hidden inside her skull, something that made her retreat from the world, while he was out exploring every corner of it. Inri had been to every continent except Australia and the Arctic, while Marie sat in a corner of the kitchen, wearing her dreams like armour, like castle walls so high no knight could scale them.

Inri gave his twin sister a kiss on her forehead. Poor Marie. "I miss you baby-sister."—She was younger by twenty minutes— "One day maybe you'll come back to us." There was a slight upturn to her lips, and for a moment her eyes stopped scanning the page, to flick up to his face before returning to their ceaseless roving. Inri and Marie. Even their names were similar. Similar, and yet so different.

They had been taken very young—surrendered to the residential school like unwanted puppies. Those first few years, Shirly didn't even like to think about what she'd been forced to feed them. It was better for them there. They'd be together with the human children in their hunger.

Even as a child Inri couldn't sit still, and the school staff couldn't keep him captive for long before he ran away, and was then captured, ran away, and was re-captured. The police charged seven cents a mile, by dog-sled and automobile, which fact alone, made him smile. But Marie had no appetite for adventure, only their eventual return, and stillness. Her heart wasn't in the escape.

Each time Inri ran away the length of time before his capture lengthened. He only returned to visit his sister. As androgynous children they were interchangeable. Dolls, whose only mark of difference was the shape of their clothing. They would often swap uniforms and trade dorms and class-rooms, Marie going with the boys, and Inri going with the girls. The staff could never tell the difference, although the other children always knew.

Marie rarely spoke except in the language that was all their own, a secret tongue, which only they knew. It wasn't English, it wasn't Anishinaabemowin, and it wasn't some conglomeration of both. It wasn't a language that anyone had ever before heard spoken on Earth, until Marie and Inri invented it. But as Inri's nature drove him to leave, Marie became more hushed and more silent. Inri spent more and more time away, and they spoke less and less in their own patterns of speech, until they no longer remembered their own secret, whispery, slithery, sibilant, babyish words.

And then something dark and awful happened to Marie in that school, and she stopped speaking altogether. Not even Inri knew what happened. Marie retreated from the world, while Inri ceaselessly explored it.

The First Law of Newtonian Physics: An object in motion tends to stay in motion, and an object at rest tends to stay at rest, unless some force is impressed upon it.

The Second Law of Newtonian Physics: The greater the mass of an object the more force that is needed to move that object.

The Third Law of Newtonian Physics: For every action, there is an equal and opposite reaction.

Inri

When Inri looked at his nephew, he could see a spark; a small ember, bright with possibility, bright with potential. Church wasn't mute like his mother—thank the Wiindigo! But neither did he seem to be born with any of their afflictions: Day's Daughter crippled and half-mad with stories of their own family mythology—Inri wouldn't say history, because to say history would be to lend too much credence to their veracity—and his poor baby-twin-sister, wrapped in a cocoon of scar-tissue, who knew what horrors she had experienced that made such a thing necessary?

And poor Mukade-wiiyas, his ancient, withered grandmother. She was barely human. He hoped never to live so long. He never wanted that much wisdom. He'd paid a high enough price for the knowledge he did have; and he'd had enough blood and suffering in his life already. He prayed for no more wisdom.

And Inri had his own . . . fixations. He was omnivorous when it came to sex. Both men and women suited his desires, and he was always filled with desire. He was consumed by a constant need to be on the move. If he stayed in one place for too long, he would be tormented by claustrophobia. He needed to stay in motion. Movement is life, and stillness is death. It was a law of nature; objects in motion tend to stay in motion, unless something got in the way, and nothing had yet dared to get in his way.

Inri knew he wasn't exactly a great role model—he couldn't sit still long enough. And every time he returned after a whirlwind trip, his mother Day seemed ever more adamant that her stories weren't myths or legends; they were history, and their family were wiindigo.

"Screw Nanaboozhoo!" Day said, "Nanabush's got nothing on us wiindigowak." As a joke, Inri had the words "Screw Nanabush" silk-screened, white block letters on a black t-shirt. Except the printer misspelled the word "Screw." Day wore the shirt anyway. "There is no 'r' in Anishinaabe," She said.

Day's Daughter

Both her children were weak. Marie and Inri. The Twins. They
were both slaves to their hunger; they let it consume them
instead of learning how to subsume it. They were both less
powerful than her, less wiindigo, less monstrous. They should
have had it easier than she did. But they also had less strength,
were less determined. They lacked the strength of will required
to subdue her, him, it; the growling beast of December, when
stores of food ran low and you needed to ration what was left
to make it through the winter. They fell victim to its howls and
were forced to endlessly feed, but never fill it.

Marie: lost. Beauty like on the cover of a magazine. So thin.
All elbows. Limbs. Full lips. Useless. Fading away behind her
screen of fulfillment.

Inri: so strange. So different. So other. Animal-gendered
spirit, confused by human limits. Sexual appetite and ceaseless
movement. Flitting from one place to the other, always in
search of the next conquest.

Church: weakest of the weak. Least monstrous of them all, but
with a strength of will to rival her own, or that of her mother,
Mukade-wiiyas. Day still had hope for her grandson.

Cryptozoology, n. the study of animals whose
existence has not yet been proven. This includes
animals that are considered extinct, such
as dinosaurs; animals whose existence lacks
physical evidence but which appear in myths
and legends, or are reported, such as Bigfoot
and the Loch Ness Monster; and wild animals
dramatically outside their normal geographic
ranges. Cryptozoology is not a recognized branch
of zoology or a discipline of science. It is
an example of pseudoscience because it relies
heavily upon anecdotal evidence, stories and
alleged sightings.

Jiibay Zaa'igaaning, the Ghost Lake Reserve:

Church's family would often stay out on the Ghost Lake reserve, dividing half their time to their home in Sterling, and the other half to "the Chee-bye." Mukade-wiiyas, Inri, or Peter drove. It took two hours to get out to the lake. There were no roads on the reserve, so they had to take ATVs down the path along the Jiibay River. Then boat out to the north shore.

The cabin had been standing for over a century. Osedjig had built it well. Day preferred living in town where there was lots of concrete, but sometimes even she needed to escape the bustle of so many bodies congested together like so much human meat, it wasn't natural. "Anishinaabe prefer having their space," she said, "Elbow room is traditional."

Few souls lived on the lake, and those who did were crazy. No running water, no electricity, and no indoor plumbing. The only buildings on the reserve were the ones that happened to have been built on higher ground, and had managed to escape being flooded, or sinking into the ground when the land turned to swamp. Most of the Indians had long ago moved to neighbouring communities, and Band Members were discouraged from building homes on the reserve by Chief and Council.

"I was born here," his Nokomis would say, "Your mother was born here. This is our home, Council has no right to tell me I can't bring my family here." Not that anyone on Council would complain in anything above a whisper. Everyone had heard the stories about their family. People were either superstitious, or respectful, and knew when to leave well enough alone.

When they arrived there would be a layer of dust settled over everything. "The cobwebs are the glue which holds this place together," Day brandished a colourful feathered duster for tackling the silken strands. "Without them, it would have fallen apart long ago. Like so much else."

Church went out to chop firewood while Day and Mukade-wiiyas set about cleaning. Marie sat, watching the hummingbirds feed like a living documentary out their window. Wings beating the air like the electric blur of helicopter blades, too quick to see. Shifting from side to side with pneumatic speed as they maneuvered for space amongst the brightly coloured bird feeders. Speaking in tiny, inhuman voices.

After splitting logs, Church took off up the shoreline to explore, reciting the names of the larger rocks dotting the coast according to their shape, and size. One looked like a post-armageddon map of the United States. It had a crack down the centre from an earthquake, and Florida had sunk into the sea. If it had been a road map, the highways would have been marked in red, and zigzag across the land, like the curly cued and many-fingered veins of a blood vessel. This was one of Church's favourite places to read; the waves of Ghost Lake lapping at his feet, drowning parts of Arizona, Texas, California and New Mexico.

Church sat looking out at the lake, imagining the shore of the Niobraran, a vast inland sea that had once divided North America during the Cretaceous. Shallow, semi-tropical, and filled with ammonite cephalopods; prehistoric fish like gillicus, aspoplexia, bananogmius, and xiphactinus at eighteen feet long - the largest predatory fish ever; six foot tall hesperornis like giant cormorants, pterodons ruling the skies; prehistoric sharks, cretoxyrhina, squalicorax, and ptychodus; six and ten foot long prehistoric turtles, toxochelyids, and protostegids; mosasaurs, the largest lizards ever at fifty feet long, and the elasmosaurus platyurus cope, at forty feet, resembling nothing if not the Loch Ness monster—the lush, diverse ecosystem of the Niobroran, teeming with life and sea monsters.

He passed the rock that looked like Saskatchewan, narrow and flat, and the one that looked like Quebec, the misshapen flaming paw of a lion. Then the jigsaw rocks all cracked and broken. The pieces fit together seamlessly, like tiles or a map of the world, water rushing in to fill the broken fragments of continental drift, wresting apart what had once been whole.

Most of the rocks on the reserve were shale and sedimentary instead of the volcanic-igneous and metamorphic rock which comprised the surrounding Canadian Shield. This is an important fact. The Ghost Lake reserve had a secret. And the fewer people who know a secret, the easier it is to keep. That's why Council used their authority to deter Band Members from living on the land, and barred outsiders from visiting.

It was a quirk of geological fate, happenstance, or luck that had left this particular section of the Canadian Shield untouched by the passing of glaciers, and the ravages of erosion. Somehow, their reserve had managed to avoid much of the processes by which the fossil record could have been obscured. A confluence of natural forces had conspired to preserve this place from the weathering and metamorphosis that had transformed so much else.

Ice ages came and went, massive shelves of ice three kilometres deep passed over the surface of the land, leaving deep gouges in the earth, while leaving other areas miraculously unscarred. The Ghost Lake reserve was located in a goldilocks zone, like "the lee of the stone" in The Rats of NIMH, untouched by the passing of the plow. Some places managed to escape unscathed. Church would have liked to see a fast-forward CGI special-effects version of the millennia-long process, if such a thing existed, but made do with his imagination.

He picked his way along the water's edge, turning into the forest at a spot with no marker, but it might as well have had a glowing X. He knew the route well. A few steps into the trees, the underbrush closed around him, obscuring time and distance. It could have been the Cretaceous. It was darker under the trees, like being in another world or under water. Light penetrated the canopy in dappled patches, painting everything with the same mottled brush.

And rising from the leaf-strewn forest floor, were the bones of an ancient creature, protruding up from the ground like the rotted skeletal carcass of a beached whale. No meat remained on these bones. He sat gingerly beneath the brittle remains, closing around him like the jaws of some great beast.

The ribs were a defence mechanism, a cage of organic armour that evolved around vital organs, the heart and the lungs. The design hasn't changed much over the course of millennia. Humans share this morphology; bilateral symmetry along a sagittal plane, mirror-image halves and frontwards cephalization of sensory organs facing forward to the direction of movement. Dinosaurs also had protective scales, thick hide, horns, barbs, spikes, bristles tooth and claw.

People wear their armour on the inside, Church thought.He pulled a book out of the pocket of his jeans and sat reading amidst the expanse of exposed ribs jutting up from the ground. The paperback was called All About Dinosaurs, and it was filled with the sort of information he usually devoured.

The chapter he was reading was about Othniel Charles Marsh and Edward Drinker Cope, two competitors whose greed and insanity ended in 'ruin' and 'despair':

> *In the 1800s, two rival scientists sparked a gold-rush-like quest for the lost bones of dinosaurs in the New World. Othniel Charles Marsh and Edward Drinker Cope competed to see who could dig up and discover the greatest number of previously undiscovered species. They wanted their names written into history books so that they too wouldn't go extinct, forgotten like the dinosaurs they hunted.*

> *Although Othniel Charles Marsh discovered more previously un-documented species, neither one can truly be considered 'the winner,' because their rivalry verged on madness, ending in bankruptcy, despair and ruin. Both scientists are now regarded as important pioneers in the field of paleontology.*

Their dispute apparently stemmed from a mistake. A mistake Cope made when he placed the skull of an Elasmosaurus, on the wrong end! When Marsh pointed out the error, Cope held a grudge.

Church thought Cope would be happy to know that Marsh was later to make a similar mistake, naming a dinosaur apatosaurus, and a later find of the same species brontosaurus, but also placing onto the reconstructed skeleton, the wrong skull; the head of a camarasaurus!

If Marsh knew, he'd be rolling in his grave, and Cope would be filled with glee at the karma of history. The moral of the story, Church figured, was that you never knew how you would be remembered, or what errors would come to light posthumously.

There was a black and white photo of Marsh and his dinosaur hunters. They wear old-fashioned clothing, rifles rest between their legs, the butt of a gun on the ground, and the barrel pointing in a diagonal sweep into the sky, hands gripped loosely about the shaft like the neck of a guitar. They hold their guns casually—as if they are used to danger—but in reality, Church knew, they were all Yale men and probably unused to holding guns at all.

And all of them, all of them, look straight into the eye of the camera.

A caption under the photograph proclaims the guns were used to ward off "hostile Indians."

Most dinosaur bones are found in badlands, like Hell's Half-Acre in Wyoming or Drumheller in Alberta. Think of Area 51, Wile E. Coyote and the Road Runner, the area in the Mohave Desert called Dreamland where classic Hollywood movies were filmed. Westerns. Sci-fi. Horror. Titles like: The Mummy,

Rocketship X-M, or The Thing from Outer Space. They tested
nuclear experiments there, detonations drawing in sand and
raining molten glass down onto the dessert floor.

Though the topography of Ghost Lake was different, if you
knew where to look, you could find bones protruding from the
shale and phanerozoic strata. These were not the carcasses of
beached whales. Though at one time, the ocean had been much
closer.

Ghost Lake was likely the site of an ancient river system
that flowed into the Niobraran, an ancient inland sea. Most
Bone Beds were formed in this way with layers of silt burying
creatures in sedimentary rock, skeletons slowly mineralizing to
create fossils. The Canadian Shield was mostly Precambrian,
metamorphic, volcanic, igneous rock, much older than that of
the Mesozoic. Any reports of the existence of dinosaur fossils
here, would have been discounted, simply due to the unlikely
location. This probably accounted for their continued obscurity.

Though, long ago, someone had began the work of excavation,
only to abandon the labour halfway through, leaving the
marrow half-born from their resting places, emerging jaggedly
from the ground, to clash in a layered pattern with the growing
tangle of organic growth.

In the mid 20th century, the construction of a dam at the
outflow of Ghost Lake raised the water level, and caused
flooding. Maybe this eroded the sediment where the dinosaurs
lay entombed, so that when the water receded, the bones were
left exposed—like the scaffolding of a canoe, and the pockets
of badland were quickly hidden again beneath the underbrush
growing along the shore.

The Anishinaabek passed down stories about the ghosts of extinct species, awakened from their long sleep. Some things were meant to come to light, other things were meant to stay in the ground. Bad things happened, when you messed with the dead, or their resting places. No one wanted to make the spirit of a twelve-ton monster, angry.

Maybe these beliefs helped keep the bones in the ground? Some argued these ideas were outdated, and the Band should capitalize on their history. They could build their own museum. Bring in those tourist dollars. Start up the community again. Move back home. Others feared the repercussions of such actions, remembering the long-ago war between two paleontologists, and the disaster of their presence.

Church wondered what happened to the spirits of extinct species, whether they faded away, or if their spirits still roamed the earth, restless. Creatures with no physical link to the world in the form of living descendants—although he supposed, all forms of life that came after, were their descendants.

Human brains were probably still constructed a lot like lizards. Like the scene in Fear and Loathing in Las Vegas where all the people turn into reptiles, and they fight and rut together in the muck of their primordial ooze.

Dinosaurs had once walked this land . . .

On some nights, Church thought he could hear the ghost of a wayward Tyrannosaurus Rex, roaring like the last scene in Jurassic Park where the amusement park is destroyed, all the dinosaurs are set free, and a single torn banner flutters down amidst the chaos. Even in the city of Sterling, Church could hear the spirits of extinct species, like distant sounds of the train. He imagined them like Calvin and Hobbes in the comic strip, stomping on the buildings and toy cars, gobbling up children on the playground. On nights like these, people would curl up in their beds and pull the blankets tighter without knowing why.

Dinosaurs had once walked the earth.

Dino-saur means "terrible-lizard", deinos from the Greek word meaning "terrible" and sauros from the Greek word for "lizard." Names are important. In the Anishinaabe language, names mean something. They are more than just a series of syllables strung together. Names have power. Names have the power to heal or to wound; the power to change the course of one's life; the power to change history, or fate itself. Names define the things they name, and determine the meaning of the things they name, even as they name. Like the lines drawn on a map, they demarcate where one thing ends, and another begins.

"Gtchi-gete-kaadi-gnebig,'", Mukade-wiiyas called them, or "Shkode-bisiwashkoon." Gnebig means snake, kaadi means leg, gete means ancient, and gtchi means great or big. Shkode-bisiwashk translates closer as dragon.

Either terrible, meaning "bad," or great, meaning "good" or "big," the search for bones of extinct species was ongoing. Paleontology may have changed over the last hundred years, or maybe paleontologists would come like Cope and Marsh bearing guns in the name of science. Science is objective. You can't argue with what is objective because it means "right," "good" and "impartial." From the stories Church had heard, Marsh and Cope were none of these things, pursuing their goals at all costs - personal, spiritual and monetary.

He sometimes wondered why his ancestors had chosen this area of land as a home site for their community, long before it had become designated as reserve land. They had always known about the dinosaurs.

Amongst the bones, Church dozed off, paperback crushed beneath him. The historical figures he'd been reading about, that had so captured his imagination, had also apparently captured his subconscious, given life and form, peopling the landscape of his mind. He began to dream. Even of people he hadn't read about. Like a glimpse of what had been, more than what could have been.

Fact rather than fiction. This was his dream:

Othneil Charles Marsh rolled up his sleeves, set down the rifle, and then stroked his mustache as he crouched down in the dusty earth, examining the exposed section of ribs sticking up from the dirt. "Dead Dog!" he eventually announced, smacking the digger who had blown the whistle on the back of the head as he rose.

"Everybody back to work!" he yelled. "It was just a false alarm! Nothing to see here. Back to work. Back to work," he said, shewing the crew who had already begun to mill around as soon as the whistle had been blown. He surveyed the crew of Yale students who formed the expedition as he picked his way through the various craters that made up the excavation site, and made his way to a brown canvas tent

He was Othniel Marsh, born Charles Othniel Marsh, but he disliked the name Charles, and so instead went by the name Othniel. So far, the newest excavation site had proven less than fruitful, and this leg of the expedition had unearthed nothing except the run-of-the-mill items: arrow heads, broken shards of pottery, an ornately carved pipe, human remains and a few dead dogs. They should have stayed in Kansas—Wyoming was a disaster.

He exhaled a sigh of frustration, filling a metal cup from a canteen of water outside his tent, squinting in the glare from the sunlight as he took his first sip. The water was more than lukewarm. He could feel grit from the sand as he ground his teeth. The taste of sweat, dust, and sunlight. He splashed some water on his face, arms and chest, trying to clean off the muck of the place, then drying himself on a filthy towel before lifting the flap and entering his tent. The base of operations.

Sunlight gave the interior a soft buttery glow, offering shade, but little relief to the sweltering heat. Most of the tent was occupied by a large table strewn with maps rolled up and spread out with chunks of amber and bone weighting down the corners. It was so hard to find good, reliable maps. Detailed maps that resembled the layout of the land, let alone maps that accurately represented it, were worth more than gold. Much of the area he studied was still "Indian Territory" even if it was technically under the control of the United States. Swaths of the Frontier were still uncolonized, and filled with Indians. Everyone in his crew carried guns; no one was left unarmed. The lines separating the civilized from the uncivilized world encroached further each year, and the Indians mostly had bigger worries on their hands than a group of white men digging in the dirt. Truth to tell, the weapons were as much for warding off hostile Indians as they were for warding off the threat of competing teams.

"Damnit!" he swore, scrutinizing the yellowing paper for some hint of what lay hidden beneath the surface. He couldn't let that Quaker bastard be the one to stake out and claim the next big find. That pretentious hack: Edward Drinker Cope.

Othniel looked up from the map as two people barged into his tent; his assistant, Brennen, his second-in-command and overseer of "the troops"; and another man, unknown to him and with the mottled complexion of a half-breed.

"Yes?" Othniel asked, arching one eyebrow as if to say, what-the-hell-do-you- want-can't-you-see-that-I'm-busy? "Can I help you?"

"Um. Yes. This is Aabitiba, the man you asked for," his second said nervously. When his employer failed to respond, except to glower, he added, "you know, the one who has been talking to Cope."

Othniel's eyes widened. "Oh, yes," Marsh responded, raising his hand to offer the half-breed a chair. "Please, have a seat." When the man failed to sit down, he said "make yourself comfortable." Marsh sat down and poured himself a glass of Rusty Bourbon before offering one to the half-breed, who accepted.

"Now then," Othniel said, "I've been given to understand you've been providing my colleague with certain information, regarding the location of bones–"

"Sir," interrupted the half-breed, "if we could first discuss the matter of my fee, I would be happy to provide you with whatever assistance I could." His English was unbroken and impeccable, with only the trace of an accent to give away the fact that he had once spoken, solely, another language. "You are a wealthy man, and I came here at great personal risk to be of some service to you. I would not have come at all had I not intended to help you." That said, the half-breed was silent.

"Name your price," Marsh said simply.

He did, and to his credit, Marsh barely even blinked at the sum. This season had not been going as well as he had expected. And it had only been getting worse. The sum Aabitiba named was extortionate, but if the information proved to be true, it would be worth it. He had nothing to gain by remaining here, and so he had nothing to lose. It was a gamble he was willing to take.

"Agreed." March said, raising a finger, "On one condition. I want you to be my guide. And I want you to come work for me. I don't want you selling any more information to Cope. Understood?"

Aabitiba nodded his assent.

"Now, on to the next order of business." With a glimmer of eager, red hunger in his eyes, "Tell me everything that you told Cope."

"Very well," said the half-breed, finally pulling out the chair and rather stiffly taking a seat. "When I was a child, my grandfather told me a story, a legend really, of great creatures which had once ruled the earth, and then been wiped out; a race of giants. When I didn't believe him, my grandfather told me that he could prove it. He said that he knew where the bones of these great creatures lay. And that they were in fact all around us, buried under the earth where they'd died, so long ago that only the trees still remembered. He had seen them himself, with his own eyes. He knew that they were real, and the legend was true.'" With that he was silent.

"That's it?" Marsh asked.

The half-breed inclined his head slightly in a nod of assent.

"Can you show me where they are on this map?" Marsh asked, his lips pulled back from his gritted teeth, an almost feverish sheen to the intensity of his steel-blue eyes.

The half-breed pointed. Far to the North, in Ojibwe territory, on the shores of a distant lake. Othniel smiled. His current position was closer to the distant lake than that of his rival Edward Drinker Cope. He could stake his claim while Drinker was still fumbling around through the wilds of the uncharted West.

Church woke up. His head was resting in the crook of his arm, and his cheek and arm were covered with drool, his limbs stiff and aching from resting in such an awkward position for so long. He got to his feet carefully, ducking under the arch of bones, and set off further into the woods, trying to clear the lingering remnants of the vivid dream from his head.

The path was barely decipherable, but he already knew the way.

Church stepped carefully through the trees, dreading the sound of a single small *snap* like a gunshot echoing in the strange silence. Forests were not usually quiet places. Not really. If you stopped to think about it, forests were alive with sound, forests were living! So they couldn't be silent, not really. No more than you could still the beating of your own heart. You could. But then you'd be dead. Only dead things could ever truly be silent.

The shshshshshshsh of air molecules passing through the needles of a million evergreens, the small rustling noises of a small wesiinh in the dried-out husks of fallen leaves, birds calling to one another in the canopy. These were not quiet places, they were alive with sound, like voices speaking disparate parts to every other part incestuously. But this place. This place was quiet. This place was hushed. It was a place of death.

Church stopped. He looked up and saw bodies decorating the canopy like ghastly Christmas decorations. The corpses slowly decomposing and disintegrating, the leather wrapped shrouds giving way and ancient yellowed bones protruding. This was the graveyard where the people used to bury the dead in the traditional "proper way," his Nokomis would say. Branches like hands offering up their remains to the creator.

Beneath the scaffolding of poplars, grew atropa belladonna, deadly night shade, the winding tendrils curling like vines, winding themselves around the stilted coffins like houses for the dead, acid corroded leaves, purple flowers, yellow anther stamen, and succulent poisonous berries. The berries were considered a delicacy in his family. Before Church knew what he had done, he'd picked some, and popped them in his mouth, before considering the ground from which they grew. The grittiness of seeds ground between his teeth, and his mouth was filled with the sweet, bitter taste. He imagined the roots, entwining with the rotted limbs that had fallen from some of the older graves, entwining with the bones under the earth the same way the tendrils entwined around the stilts.

Wiindigo, Church thought, and he suddenly felt spooked, feeling the age of the burial grounds pressing close, and the weight of years for all those ancestors who rested here, their lives no longer felt so distant, and relegated to the past. Instead they felt much closer, they felt present.

Church ate a few more of the red berries before taking his leave of the place—he couldn't help himself, not really—even if it was as close to true cannibalism as he'd ever come; he was a wiindigo after all. He was sure his ancestors would forgive him. Before making his way back up the shoreline to Marie, Day, and Mukade-wiiyas setting up camp in Osedjig's Cabin.

Peter's tricks

Day's Daughter and Mukade-wiiyas were Church's primary
guardians, raising him, and seeing to his day-to-day needs.
Mukade-wiiyas spent her time cooking and tending to the
garden, listening to her ancient records, so old that they
had been recorded on wax cylinders by musicians no one
remembered. Day's Daughter spent her time caring for her
somnambulant daughter, taking Church out to forage, snare
rabbits, and telling stories to curb his appetite. If Church didn't
behave, an Ooghoul might spirit him away and drink the
marrow from his bones—because "disobedient children taste
better. Everyone knows that."

Or if he wandered too far, the Memegwezhiag might spirit
him away, and turn him into an image in stone. "It's happened
before," Day told him, "It could happen again." Church had
seen the carving in his wanderings. He had felt the terrain of
peaks and valleys under his fingers, the shape of their canoe,
and the lines that made-up what was left of their earthly bodies,
rock; worn-smooth by the elements. The graven image of two
headless boys, their torsos like the writing on a headstone—only
their severed heads had been found. Their bodies had never
been recovered. And only their image in the stone was left to
mark their passing.

Some people said that the Memegwezhiag are benevolent
spirits, some said that they are malevolent; but Church
thought the truth was much greyer; that they are neither good
nor bad, but like a force of nature—like thunderstorms—or
lightning, they don't care about the plants they water, the
life they give, or the life they take. Nature isn't cruel or kind,
just necessary. Human concepts of kindness and cruelty don't
factor into the equation.

Inri dropped in as infrequently as his father, like a brief whirlwind touching down just long enough to break up the normal operation of their household, taking Church to see a play or an opera at the theatre, and then he was gone.

Peter preferred to take him to see horror movies, rated R, and laugh in all the inappropriate places. He would drop by unannounced after an absence of several months, for one of their father-son field trips. Day thought it was important for him to spend time with his father, so Peter could teach her grandson how to be more human. Even if he was a dead beat, she saw it as an opportunity none of the rest of them had been given.

Church's dad knew more ways to scam people, weasel out of paying a bill, or fake an injury than Church would have thought possible if he hadn't seen it first hand. Peter would rack up a bill at a restaurant and get out of paying by pulling a broken piece of glass out of his mouth as the waitress walked by.

A little bit of blood never hurt either. As soon as they saw blood, even if it was only a few small drops, management would be tripping over each other, apologizing and praying that they wouldn't be sued. When he was younger, Church had thought Peter's acting skills were entertaining, but as he got older they became more and more tiresome.

Peter did a lot of traveling, and he didn't visit very often. He was "nomadic" he said, like certain "Indian tribes who travelled around so they didn't exhaust their food supply." Except that he hunted a different sort of prey. He had a string of girl-friends who never seemed to last very long.

Peter taught Church how you could walk into a store, pick up something, and simply, non-nonchalantly walk out the front doors because everyone would assume that because you weren't running, you had already paid for it. "Never run," his father told him, "running only makes you look guilty."

Peter would even enlist the aide of uniformed employees to help him carry out his "purchases" to the car. Instructing the minimum wage employee on how to load the item into the back of the van without displacing his other belongings or scratching the paint job. Peter seemed to take a perverse amount of joy in convincing others to steal for him.

Peter didn't like stealing. That is not to say that he was opposed to stealing, or that he did not steal often. He would only steal when there were likely to be no consequences for his actions, or in situations where he felt confident he could bullshit his way out if he got caught. Other times he stole for practice, to keep from becoming "too rusty." But he preferred to get things for free, and he often had Church steal for him.

Most people didn't even look at children, and Church was great at pick pocketing. Peter would distract them, and Church would pull the bills out of their wallet. If Church got caught, no one would call the cops, because people left the discipline of children to their parents, not to the police. Church was a curious child, and his father would scold him for "snooping." That's what robbery was called for children—snooping, not theft.

"How many times have I told you not to go through other peoples' things?" His father mock-chastised him in front of the woman who had caught Church with his hand in her purse when she had unexpectedly reached back for something. The woman laughed and didn't even seem upset—she was too busy flirting.

When Church had "done good," Peter would give him one of his hand-rolled Heller cigarettes or a sip of C-Six whiskey from his flask as a reward. Peter had pressed Church into service so often, he could turn the waterworks on-and-off as easily as a faucet. It was a trick he had perfected at a very early age. In seconds Church's face could be red, streaked with tears, and covered in snot. His tantrums had gotten Peter out of paying for all sorts of things, taxies, hotels bills, toothbrushes, cigarettes . . . the list was long and varied. On principle Peter never paid for anything unless it was already stolen or illegal. Even when he had money Peter didn't like paying.

Although there were perks to having a 'dead-beat' for a dad. Like being allowed to see R rated movies—Church loved watching a gory horror flick. He watched enthralled as the fictional blood splattered across the white screen—this movie definitely wasn't PG—though he was slightly uneasy that he kept sympathizing with the monster, instead of its victims.

When they went to the concession stand, Peter ordered a pop and a bag of popcorn that he handed off to his son like a football, and as instructed, Church took off with the goodies. When Peter pulled out his wallet, he pretended to be surprised that it was empty, and with a hangdog expression, turned and offered to go, "chase him down," to return the merchandise that he was unable to pay for. Anyone who didn't want to make the guy look bad in front of his son, and disappoint a little kid, would let it slide.

Peter had once asked Church to lie down behind the back of a car with a bike as the car was backing up out of its parking space. His dad yelled angrily at the driver as Church turned on the waterworks. Church didn't know what kind of dirt the man had against Peter, but no money ever exchanged hands.

After, Peter had said that Church had "done good," and that, "the bugger is now too afraid to even shit in my direction." Church was given a mickey of C-Six, and one of Peter's hand-rolled Heller's as his prize. Peter was big on bribery, or "positive reinforcement" as he liked to call it. At some point, he must have read a terrible self-help book on parenting—or a dog-training manual, he wasn't sure which.

When Church was young, these sorts of tricks were fun because Peter made them into a kind of game, winking at him as he screamed, but as he grew older, it became increasingly clear that these sorts of games were not games; they were cons. And Peter wasn't playing for fun. Peter was using him.

Wherever they went Peter looked into the car windows of every vehicle they passed, looking for unlocked doors. And if there was anything that caught his eye, he would casually open the door, take what he wanted, and they'd be off again with an extra a pack of cigarettes, a pair of sunglasses, or some spare change. For Peter, there was no scam too small, as long as he came out ahead. And as long as he could get away with it.

The Sterling Standard, June 12th 199-

Search and rescue teams made a grisly discovery today. The partially eaten bodies of two missing prospectors working for Magnon Inc., an oil and resource extraction company, have been found. The bodies were recovered from a ravine in the Ghost Lake region of the county.

The two workers were reported missing last week and a search and rescue campaign was launched to try to find the missing technicians. Initial hopes of recovering the men alive have been dashed by the gruesome discovery.

It is not yet known what kind of animal attacked them, or whether some other fatal accident occurred to cause their deaths, followed by a natural predation by scavengers. Specialists have been brought in to examine the scene, and determine what went wrong for the two unfortunate employees.

Bagonegiizhig

"Ah-nah-may-guh-mick," Mukade-wiiyas said to Church, "Nandawenim ayaangwaamizikandaw wemichigoozhi." I want you to be careful around that man. "Naanawenim nini. Gaawiin apiitenimsii nini." I don't like him. I don't trust him. "Gtchi-kiwenzii, niin gegaadawi wiiji-apiitaadiziim." He is an old man, almost as old as me. "Basabaagise daabishkooj wazush-gwaajime." Slimy as a blood-sucker.

"Kaawiin migoshkaadendamsii gchi-nokomis." Don't worry great-grandmother, Church said. "Nayaangwaamizikandaw noyoosimaa." I will be careful around my father.

"Anami-gamig nandawendan gikinawaabi nitaa-aya'aawi," Day's Daughter said. "Nindawaa banaabeg!" He needs to learn how to be human, instead of banaabeg. Quasi-anishinaabek. Quasi human. "Gikinawaabi." He needs to learn by observation.

"Gaawiin gikinawaabisii, ashowizhag wiindigoowag." He can't learn, by watching us. "Anami-gamig nandawendan wiisookaw goosan." Church needs to spend time with his father.

Church was sure that Day wasn't aware of what Peter was teaching him, because he knew that she would not approve of any of Peter's 'lessons.' He also knew that Peter would not be pleased if he squealed. And Church was worried about the repercussions if he spoke up, so he kept his mouth shut, about the thievery, and the bribery, the Heller cigarettes and the mickey of C-Six.

The Sterling Standard, June 17th 199-

A mountain lion is now believed to be responsible for the attack on two prospectors working for Magnon Inc. after their bodies were discovered in a ravine in the Ghost Lake region last week.

"The bite marks of the jaw are consistent with a cougar attack," says Brawn Neilson a mountain lion expert, and an experienced tracker and forest guide who works for National Parks Canada.

Though the risks are said to be low, nearby residents in the sparsely populated region of the county are being warned to stay alert, and not to leave young children playing outside unattended, at least until the large animal can be found and destroyed.

Experts say to be cautious, but that the risk of another freak attack such as this is very unlikely as fatal encounters with wild animals are a relatively rare occurrence.

`Cryptobiosis, n.` Is a period of dormancy during extreme environmental conditions such as drought, extreme cold, lack of oxygen or toxic contamination. In this state, all metabolic processes come to a halt, and an organism can virtually live for an indefinite amount of time, until the environment returns to a hospitable state.

Gone Like Nanabush

"What ever happened to him?" Church asked. They were standing on the small second floor landing of the fire escape. Inri was smoking some menthol's he'd palmed from his twin sister. Church had some hand-rolled Hellers he'd borrowed from Peter's tin.

"Who?" Inri wanted to know.

"You know. Bakadewinan. Is he still alive?"

Inri considered his answer for a moment before responding. "Of course not Church," Inri said, his breath exhaling like smoke on the cold air, the lapels on his fur-coat brushing against his cheeks like the feathers on a boa, wrapped tightly around his stick-thin frame. It's only a story, it's not real."

Church wasn't so sure. When he asked Day, he got a different answer.

"Come here," Inri said, digging in his purse. Church stepped forward and Inri pulled out a tin of mascara, smearing his thumb into the black gunk. "Look up," he said, Marie's menthol hanging from one corner of his lips, as he intently applied his thumb to the bones of his cheeks. Church looked up, exposing the white sclera of his eyes. Soft whisper of flesh on architecture of bone.

"Now you're a real wiindigo." Inri laughed. "You'll make a good monster one day." Predators grew dark smudges under their eyes to cut down on the glare from the sun. Baseball players wore dark smudges under their eyes for the same reason, except with different ends and aims. Players wanted to win. Predators wanted to eat. Humans had their dark inventions, adaptations and technology making them worse than any monster. Better even. More inhuman.

Day's answer:

"Who knows?" Day said, awkwardly sweeping up the latest light bulb explosion of shattered glass from the outlet in the now darkened hall. Church didn't even know why they bothered replacing it, it would just shatter again; a delicate iridescent soap-bubble bursting into jagged crystalline shards, falling to the hall floor amidst the sound of breaking glass and an explosion of sparks from the outlet like droplets of mist raining down. "Something must be protecting that land. It's stayed nearly empty ever since the flooding. Not even the zhaaganaashiwag go there. People go missing. They say it's cursed. I don't think that it is."

"We still go there," Church pointed out.

"Were family." Day said, leaning dangerously forward in her wheel chair, so that Church feared she might topple out as she used the dustpan affixed to a piece of dowelling and a broom to sweep up the mess. The thinly curved frosted glass crunching under the hard rubber soles of her wheels.

"Some people say he's gone. Gone like Nanabush. Some people say he's just sleeping, or hibernating like a bear. That one day he'll wake up, and you can be sure, that when he does, he'll be hungry."

The Sterling Standard, June 22nd 199-

The mountain lion believed to be responsible for the recent attack on two prospectors working for Magnon Inc. has now been tracked down and euthanized. Officials are saying that the danger has now passed, and the episode is unlikely to reoccur.

Predation may have played a part in the death of the two men, as the feline was an unusually large example of its species, and it may have had difficulty finding enough food to sustain itself. It is also possible that the men could have stumbled upon the animal's young—though no indication of offspring has yet been found—this would explain a mother's behaviour if it had felt threatened.

It has also been suggested that the mountain lion may have crossbred with another species—possibly a jaguar—making it more fearless. Cross-breeding between closely related species has been blamed in other cases of animal predation on humans, especially in animals that don't often attack people. Normal behaviour is altered by interbreeding, which could also explain the cougar's exceptional size, and why it would have behaved in such an uncharacteristic manner.

"It's not all that surprising that this sort of cross-breeding should occur when you consider the recent changes in climate, and the expansion of their natural habitats." Though such hybridization may have become more common, this sort of attack is still considered very rare. "Once an animal begins to view humans as potential prey," Neilson went on to explain, "they lose their fear of man and can become a dangerous threat."

Experts say euthanizing the animal was necessary in order to prevent these sorts of attacks from happening again, and that most interactions with wildlife do not end in disaster, as it did in this fateful encounter. Locals and nature enthusiasts can now rest easy, knowing that the man-eater is no longer on the loose.

Revelations

"I know what you're thinking." Day said. "And it's too dangerous."

"Why can't I?" Church asked, even though he already knew the answer.

"Fasting would awake the hunger in you . . . and you wouldn't like the visions that you might see, or the spirits that might decide to visit you." She stared out the window at the hummingbird feeders as she spoke, the little birds flitting between the brightly coloured urns like small winged spirits, but her eyes didn't track their zipping movements; they saw something else entirely. A something else she wasn't sharing. For a moment, she looked like Marie. "Booni' iw booshke'iniwe awenesh nawanj-aya'aag nawanj-giindiwa, nbanaabegoom nimishenh." Leave that for those who are more human than one such as you, my quasi-human grandson.

"If you starve yourself for days, what do you expect to see?" Inri scoffed dismissively from where he sat reading a paperback novel, reclining on the sofa as if it were a 19th century recamier. "Of course you're going to see visions." Inri believed that any manitous or insights that might come while in such a deprived state were merely products of a "nutrient-starved brain," and that this, therefore, somehow invalidated the experience. But maybe that just happened to be the best state in which to talk to spirits—half-starved, and closer to death?

"Nimishhenh. Naaniizaanendam." It's too dangerous Mukade-wiiyas said, her voice whispery and soft. Carrying from the kitchen where she stood over a large vat, stirring, stirring the pot with a withered bone that almost looked as ancient as she was. "Apane gegiinawind gii'igwishimoowin; apane gegiinawind bakade." We are always fasting; we are always hungry. "Gaawiin-wiikaa-waasasiinh bawewinan miina waaseyaabindamowinan gandawenjigewinan." The dreams and visions you seek are never far. "Miina gaawiin minwenim-siinh waaseyaa-bindamowinan odishiwe'iw." And you might not like the visions that come. Mukade-wiiyas feared losing her great-grandson to the hunger, as she had once lost her daughter. She didn't want to let that happen again.

"Mniidook gaawiin-wiikaa-waasasiinh." The spirits are never far. "Gaawiin naandaawenim-siinh gdizhaa makadekewin waabam wiinawaa." You don't need to go on a vision quest to find them.

"Ninisidotam." Church told Inri and his grandmothers. I understand. But in his heart, he was already plotting how he could put his plan into action. He wanted answers. He wanted these mysteries solved. And how else could he learn to be a human? It was a right of passage. It was part of being human, not numsookan. Not a monster. How could they understand?

In the end it was easy.

He chose the place known as the Burnt Grounds to wait, a place of black rock and black earth that looked, well . . . burnt. A piece of land in contrast to the Drowned Lands, full of dead grey trees standing in puddles of water up to their knees, their skeletal fingers stabbing into the sky.

The burnt grounds were occupied primarily by black rocks of all shapes and sizes, from grains of sand to large monolithic-sized boulders. Very few people came to the Burnt Grounds. It was a place that had always been shown respect and avoided. Everyone agreed: something terrible had happened there. No one knew what had damaged the earth so badly that it never recovered, even after so many years, for the damage had been there since before the great migration, since before the great megis shell had told the Anishinaabek to come to this land; what the archaeologists called the time of the Clovis people.

There were many stories about the Burnt Grounds. It was supposed to be a place of death, a place of death in the world of life, a place where the afterworld existed among the living. Only the crazy or desperate went there, and not everyone came back. But Church went anyway. He wanted to meet his grandfather. So he waited. And waited. Growing hungrier by the hour, growing hungrier by the minute, growing hungrier by the second. Until his hunger felt like something outside of himself, like a facet of the weather; cold when it was night and warm when it was day, wet when it started to rain. Hunger was the constant.

He had never been on a fast before, and had only rarely skipped a meal, so there was no preparation for his mind or body for the real deal. Not even a practice run. Fasting was not allowed. It was too dangerous.

Church always had to keep his appetite on a tight leash. He was never allowed to give in to his ceaseless hunger and feed it-feed-it-feed-it-feed-it, endlessly trying to satisfy the unsatisfiable hunger, or to starve it, as if by refusing to feed it at all, his hunger would dwindle away. This didn't work. Not eating at all made the hunger more unrelenting, and impossible to ignore, ballooning out of all proportion to the size of his body . . . But Church didn't like to dwell on the feeling of emptiness in the pit of his soul. An emptiness the size of the whole universe, an emptiness that could never be filled. Regular, structured allotments of measured portions: this was the time-tested management solution. No spikes or sudden dips in blood-sugar. No curve balls. No fouls. No fails. No droughts nor downpours. Only steady increments for the beast.

Intentionally starving the beast was dangerous. This is stupid, Church thought, wrestling with the numbness. The numbness of cold after you could no longer feel the cold and the cold started to feel warm—except the cold he felt was hunger. And the hunger was starting to feel like a blanket. "Just go to sleep" the snowdrift said, all soft and white and inviting. (That's not a bad idea at all. No, not at all. Yeah right!)

Church was hungry. He felt as if he could reach out, and eat the stuff of his surroundings. Everything shifted colour, casting odd shadows. His stomach churned. He ate some of the black dirt at his feet to quell the hunger. Put a small stone under his tongue. Even swallowed one.

It is said that whistling brings the wiindigo. Day always warned Church against whistling. "You never know who, or what, might be listening." Church didn't know what she was so worried about; they were already wiindigo. Maybe she wanted Church to stay human, because being human was easier than being a monster.

To pass the time, Church practiced how to whistle. He'd never really learned how to whistle properly before. And it gave him something to do, something to focus on besides his growing hunger.

When his grandfather finally appeared, the Wiindigo wore the face of hunger, like a deer's skull, narrow and elongated. Like nothing human. Like nothing real, like no animal he'd ever seen or heard of, not even an extinct animal. He could see the Wiindigo's ribs sticking through its flesh like the bleached bones of a whale. On his head grew great antlers, too large for the weight of a human frame to bear. It stepped carefully, tentatively through the forest like a deer. His face was painted with mud like a pow-wow dancer, an old-time warrior, a

Marilyn Manson demon. Lips that were half eaten and tangled hair matted into dread-locks that fell down his back like the creature from Predator.

Everything felt colder, as if the temperature had dropped ten degrees. Church could see his breath when he exhaled. Classic horror movie ploys. Was this real? Or had he conjured this dream from his own starvation-deprived mind? The Wiindigo tilted its head, like an ornithropod, the aperture of its eyes focusing on him like a bird of prey laying its sights on dinner. The large black pupils of its eyes shifting with the precision of a cameras lens. It was unsettling to be viewed with such indifference; such cold, cruel dispassion. It saw only a meal. Its eyes seemed to weigh him, calculating how much of a fight he might put up, how swift he would be, and with how much speed it should descend.

Church didn't move. He remained perfectly still.

"Never run," his father had once told him, "it just makes you look guilty. If you have to get away, walk quickly." Running, Church reflected, also made you look like prey, because things that run, are a meal. The situation was different, but the advice was sound. If Church didn't behave like a meal, he might not get eaten.

Feeling his great-grandfather's gaze upon him, Church wondered if this was how he made other people feel. It was unsettling. But Church was hungry, too. And at this point, he felt as if he could eat anything. Even the sky looked lustrous. He felt downright predatory himself. Church smiled, and his grandfather's whole posture seemed to change, one moment predatory and fluid, now cautious and curious. Something in his bearing seemed to suggest—Church felt certain—recognition. The Wiindigo hesitated, waited a moment, tilted its head as if straining to catch some stray bit of song, to catch the slightest sound. Looking at him, just looking. The moment seemed to stretch into an eternity under that unearthly gaze, and then it was gone. He was gone within seconds.

His movements were strange and disjointed, like the uneven breaks between stop-animation, as if some of the frames had been deleted. He moved back into the forest like he were travelling through strobe lights on a dance floor, chunks of his presence through space non-existent, somehow exempt from the rules that required normal beings to occupy the space between two intervening points.

Church let out the breath that he'd been holding. The fog of his breath dissipating. He'd seen enough visions. He was certain that he'd come close to being eaten by his own grandfather. And there was something slightly incestuous about the thought, something un-kosher about being eaten by someone to whom he was so closely related. If they had been strangers, it wouldn't have been so bad.

It was time to go home. He was going to have a hell of a time getting his appetite to shrink back down to anything close to what resembled a human's. His grandmothers were going to be pissed.

And he decided that he didn't care what Inri thought: it didn't matter whether the visions that came during a fast were due to the spirit-world, or to deprivation. Church would take his insights from wherever they could be found. Church knew what he had seen. Even if it was just a delusion brought on by hunger and expectation, it was real in every sense that mattered.

Church had met Bakade, Hunger, the Wiindigo.

June 29th 1872,

I will not task myself by recounting the tiring journey of our canoe and portage routes, from the Twin Cities, with a brief stop-over in the town of Sterling to stock up on supplies before moving on to Ghost Lake. I will only mention one curious incident that occurred during our voyage.

En-route to Ghost Lake, my colleague thought it would interest me to stop at the home of a certain Medicine woman, or "charlatan" as he called her, who was well known in the area as a powerful witch. Dibikiziwinan-gashkii-dibik-ayaa, which is a long sounding name that translates as "Darkness-dark-as-night."

When we entered her home, she was making the chairs dance. Her hair was black, shot through with grey, bushy and rather untamed, her teeth broken and crooked. In one word, she was odd. I have seen other such gypsies and con men, magicians, psychics, and illusionists at fairs, plying their witchcraft on susceptible tourists. Preying on the foolish and the desperate.

The Ojibwe sorceress was, no doubt, one of these charlatans, but I have to admit, she was convincing. Something about the set of her eyes, the dark gleam of light reflecting at the corner of her pupils, the mad, frantic delight as her hands weaved and waved in sympathy with the chairs jerking violently in space, circling, scraping against the floor, wooden rungs clacking against the wooden rungs, some mysterious churning pattern of intricate and hypnotizing design, almost comprehensible, but chaotic and frightening. Having it almost meaning something, but not being able to quite grasp that meaning, was bothersome to the mind. Milling stew-pot conflagration of movement and noise. The woman cackling hysterically, like every storybook witch.

It made my hackles rise, although I know it was only a parlour trick, some subtle contraption of hidden wires, mirrors and displaced light. They were the kind of theatrics that might have fooled the gullible savages who were already predisposed towards a belief in the "supernatural." It was, nevertheless, unsettling.

After viewing the old woman making chairs dance around the room of her cabin like a maestro directing some unseen forces, we left. I had to wonder why Marsh wanted me to see this woman—whether it was his intention to shock or entertain. Regardless, Marsh made no attempts to disguise his amusement, the devil. He stood back to watch my reaction, rather than to watch the display of chaotic chairs, and took a perverse delight in my confusion.

The more I get to know the man, the less impressed I am with his character.

July 1st 1872, Ghost Lake,

These are the facts I have managed to glean, from speaking with the various Yale men aboard ship, and during our portage from Sterling. Somehow, Marsh's apparent rival—Drinker Cope—whom he refers to with the epithet of Jones, had managed to beat him to the chase. Cope has already begun excavations in the vicinity of Ghost Lake, having made arrangements with the local tribe of Ojibwes, both for permission to dig in their territory, and the most promising sites for his quarries. Marsh is at a loss to explain how Cope managed to out-manoeuvre him given their respective positions in the field, other than to conclude that his facts must have been in error.

Marsh is beginning his enterprise from a position of disadvantage, and has had to negotiate with the Indian Tribe, who have already made concessions to his adversary. I do not know what promises Othniel has made to the Ojibwes, or what payment Marsh has extended in exchange for his continued presence on their lands, but Mookman— their Head-man—had agreed to allow this venture to proceed.

Now that our party has joined the rest of Marsh's advance crew, whose encampment is already well established, the men have begun setting up their own tents, to add to those already erected. Yale men as well as Ghost Lake Indians hired as part of Marsh's bargain with Mookman. Upon learning how much progress Cope had managed to achieve in his absence, Marsh was furious.

He has been quiet and irritable during our entire trek, and now he is like a simmering kettle, his anger ready to boil over. The veins in his forehead stand out in relief as he gives orders to his men to set up camp in the area he negotiated for his operations. They are like a frantic hive of ants, clearing rocks, setting up tents and cook-fires, cutting down trees—and adding their numbers to the advance party that has already begun digging at their appointed excavation site. All the men in Marsh's employment sense his abysmal mood and are quick to heel—no one wants to draw his wrath. Marsh has lost no time getting the work under way, and I have no doubt he will have caught up with Cope's head-start in no time.

July 7th 1872, Ghost Lake,

The man who has fallen ill—Ogimaa, is a member of the local tribe of Indians. Ogimaa was hired by Othniel to be one of his diggers, and had been staying in the workers' encampment. He is the second man to have fallen ill in so many months. The first had been raving and beginning to scare the other workers, so he had been sent to the Sterling Asylum.

In this second instance, the sickness seems to be more subdued and the nature of the illness has been kept hidden. In order to breed good will and reassurance amongst his diggers, Marsh has let it be known that the man was injured during his labours, and is being well taken care of during his convalescence. Didn't he even enlist the aide of the white doctor from the south for medical assistance?

Upon entering the cabin, I was overwhelmed by the scent of sickness,; a stale, musty-sour smell. All the windows were fastened shut. I inquired why no one had opened them. Aabitiba, who has become like my shadow, following me wherever I go, translated for me, and I was told that the cool air would exacerbate the man's condition.

Upon entering the room where the "wiindigo" lay, two men sat, beating steadily upon drums, singing prayers to their "kitchi-manitou" for healing, and to drive out the spirit that had infected him. I waited until the Indians had finished their songs, and burning of strange, pungent herbs over his body. The acrid smell was overpowering in the small room, but much preferable to the damp-mould smell that permeated the air.

One of the men is Goshko, a well-known and respected medicine man, to whom most turn for aide should anyone fall sick, or be in need of cures. I'm told his folk remedies are often effective. The other man is Mookman, the rather elderly leader of the local tribe of Ojibwes who call Ghost Lake their home. Having finished their superstitious ministrations, the old men nodded to me with worried expressions, as if to say from one practitioner of healing to another, 'he's all yours', and left the room.

I sat in the chair beside the patient's bed. Ogimaa seemed to be asleep, his breaths coming in an even, steady rhythm. Thick blankets were heaped on top of him, a fire burned in the hearth next to him, and yet when I placed my hand on his forehead, it was cool to the touch.

"Do you know who I am?" I asked him quietly, not really expecting a response.

--"Gigikenimaa na zhaagaanash mashkikii-nini iw eyaa?"--

"Eeennnhhhyaanh." Ogimaa said. And I flinched, startled that he spoke. I hadn't really been expecting a response. "Mashkikiiwinini zhaagaanash bi-nanaa'itooyamban nide.'" Ogimaa spoke without opening his eyes or changing the rhythm of his breath. I could have sworn he was asleep.

--*"You're the White doctor come to fix my heart."*

Aabitiba stood in the corner, translating. The rhythms of his voice filling the air, as he spoke first my words, softly to the patient in Ojibwe, and then translating Ogimaa's responses to me in perfectly enunciated English. Their was a delay each time, as he had to first listen, translate my words, listen for a response, and then translate Ogimaa's words back to me.

"Your heart? What do you think is wrong with your heart?" I asked.

--*"Gide'? Wegonesh na maaminonendan machi-gide'eyaa?"*--

"Gssssiiinnnaaaahhh. Gchi-ningiikaj."

--*"It's cold. So cold."-- Aabitiba translated quietly.*

"Cold?" I asked.

--*"Gdakamanji'o na?"*--

"Enhyanh, indigo wii-gchi-mashkawaakwadin mii dash ishwaade'e aazha gegaa. Ninzegiz apii-ishwaade'e apii-nwii-wiindigo!"

--*"Yes, like it's going to freeze solid and stop beating soon. I fear what will happen when it stops beating for then I will truly be a wiindigo."*--

"Tell me. When did you first begin to feel unwell?" I asked him.

--*"Dibaadodan. Aaniish apii akawe-maajine?"*—

"Bangiiwagad gaa-dwaateg. Ngii-anokiitamaw Zhaagaanosh Cope nwii-waanike azhishkiing mii dash ngiidayekos, ngii-maaminonendan ganabatch ngii-bangishin. Gaawiin daa-nibaasiinh-dibik. Apane Ngiiwanaadingwaam, ngii-zegiz giiwe wii-nibaayaan, mii-dash gaawiin ngii-doodamsiinh.

--"A few weeks ago. I was digging in the dirt for the Zhaagaanosh
Cope, and I was so tired, I think I must have collapsed. I couldn't
sleep at night. I kept having disturbing dreams, I was afraid to go
back to sleep, so I didn't."--

"What were these dreams that kept you from sleep?" I asked.

--"Aaniish gaa-onoweniwanbawaajiganan awe onji-ayaa gaa-
nibaa?"—

"Maji-achaag gii-izhaa-min niin, gii-gagaanzom niin, gii-biizikaw
odengwaaning o-ayaa'aa-iman indigo biiskoojigan, wiikwaji'o
miikinji' niin."

--"The devil came to me, taunting me, wearing someone else's face like
a mask, trying to trick me. He offered me human flesh in a bowl made
of ice."--

"Someone else's face?" I asked, leaning in close to hear his quiet words,
though I did not know their meaning, until Aabitiba had related it to
me.

--"O-yaa'aa-iman odengway na?--

"Maaji-aya'aa gii-biizikaw o-niikaanenh-iman oshkatay-odengway,
indigo asekaade jiishaakwa'ang waawaashkeshiwayaan, eta go
gaawiin bapaabi oshkiinzhigong-bagwegak, aandi o-niikaanenh-
iman oshkiinshigong daa-gi-gii-ayaa, idash nwii-nindizhinan
iniw gaawiin dibendaagwak-siinh odengwaan-siinh. Noonishkaw
oziigazhage-biiskoojigan inagoojin geshawi-eyaa odaamikaning,
gaawiin giizhagomo-siinh izhi-agoojiwanaan-ing minawaa giiyaasing
zhiibaaya'ii."

--"He wore the skin of my brothers' face, like the scraped and tanned
hide of a deer, looking out through the eyeholes, where my brother's
eyes should have been, but I could tell that the face was not his. The
mask was wrinkled and ill fitting, and hanging loosely from his chin,
unanchored to the armature and ligaments beneath."--

"And it was this dream that made you frightened to fall asleep?"

--"Minawaa onowe gii-bawaajiganan iw izhi-gi-gchi-zegizi gawingwashi?"--

"Eeennhyaanhh."

--"Yes."--

"When is the last time that you've had a restful sleep?"

--"Aaniish apii gaa-ishkwaaj iw gi-gii-zoongingwashi?"--

"Gaawiin gego ako-dabwaa-ningiiwanaadingwaam."

--"Not since before I had the dream."--

I nodded, writing down notes in my journal. It seemed clear to me that whatever the man's symptoms were, they were probably caused by his insomnia. Simple rest should take care of his ailments.

I prescribed him a tincture of laudanum. Distilled from fermented opium, it should provide the patient with the rest he requires, and also prevent the interruption of dreams. Dreamless sleep, in the short-term, would provide relief from his symptoms, if not a solution to the greater disturbance to his mind. After administering the proper dosage, I took my leave, promising to return the next day to check on his condition. During this whole inter-change, the so-called 'wiindigo' remained in his reclined position, eyes closed, breathing steadily.

I am not convinced that this is a case of "wiindigo psychosis," but instead a simple case of mental exhaustion, insomnia, and neurasthenia, caged in superstitious fears and anxiety.

I am sorry to have missed the chance to observe the first patient, whose symptoms seem to have followed closely the pattern set by other cases of the peculiar psychosis. I am unwilling to make the journey back towards Sterling; the other victim is probably in good care at the Sterling Asylum, and my current patient has yet to make a recovery.

PART II

"An apple cleft in two, is not more twin/Than these two creatures"

~ Twelfth Night, Shakespeare

"Contrary to popular belief, a vacuum is not devoid of material but in fact fizzles with tiny mysterious particles that pop in and out of existence, but at speeds so fast that no one has been able to prove they exist."

~Richard Gray

"Arbeit macht frei." Labour makes you free.

~ A sign placed above the entrance to Auschwitz.

wrest, v. **1.** To forcibly pull, wrench or twist something away; to take power or control; to distort the meaning of, or interpret something, to suit one's own interests; to do someone an evil turn, or trick. **2.** n. A tuning-key for wire-stringed instruments like a harp or a piano [from the Old English word 'wraesta', to 'twist' or 'tighten']

The Neck

Church monitored his thought processes to see if he could catch himself craving human flesh, but he never seemed to find himself looking at another person as a meal. He wasn't wiindigo enough for that. His blood had been diluted through generations of intermingling with humans. All he felt was a lingering hunger, which never seemed to leave him. Hunger was his constant companion.

He had so few other friends.

Most of the kids at school avoided him. Even the goth-kids that he sometimes hung out with, Tiffany and Jason and that gang, weren't really his friends, they only grudgingly accepted him into their circle. He was too strange even for them. They preferred their monsters on the page, or on the screen, in fiction and not in fact. He had trouble fitting in at school, not being entirely human and all.

So Church cultivated his talent for being invisible. He could stay absolutely still for hours on end, with a patience that bordered on the supernatural, or at least the inhuman. Only certain animals—predators—had this kind of patience. When your next meal depended on being unseen, you learned how to stay still, or you grew camouflage. A bit of camouflage never hurt.

Church always wore grey. Not black. Grey. The grey of the pavement, the grey of the sidewalk, the grey of a cement wall. Black was too severe, too dramatic. Grey made it easier to blend in, to fade into the background. To disappear.

This ability might not have been supernatural, but it was just one more thing that differentiated him from other kids his own age. He would have stood out, if it had not been for his ability blend in, to become like his hunger;, the dream dog growling around the edges of his vision, his constant companion. Some days, he never left the grey fog of his invisibility, walking to school in the morning, walking home from school, sitting at his desk at the back of the classroom, grey clothes blending into the grey walls, grey sidewalks, grey roads.

At school one day a new boy walked into the classroom. Late. Everyone else had already taken seats. Geoff Suture scanned the desks lined up like the crosses of World War II vets, and his eyes came to rest on the seat beside Church. There were no other empty seats.

Geoff wore a white dress-shirt with the cuffs rolled up. The collar revealed his most striking feature: his neck. Sternocleidomastoid muscles showed prominently like ropy vines drawing nutrients from the soil of his body; like Michelangelo's Adam on the roof of the Sistine Chapel. Church knew the good guys in horror and science-fiction movies always had sterno-mastoids, a classic creature-design ploy (his Goth friend Jason, always kept his tree house well-stocked with Fangoria magazines). They were solely an adaptation by warm-blooded vertebrates—mammals. It made what was different and other, more palatable and familiar. Cheap tricks.

Church's stomach made a grumbling sound. Like always, he was hungry. The Neck looked in his direction to see what had made the sound, and Church slumped farther down in his chair. He chewed on the inside of his lip, hoping that his stomach would stay silent. He made himself a smaller target by hunching down and did his best to think grey thoughts. He preferred being invisible.

Wiibidaang, teeth

Later that day, Church was sitting on top of a pile of tables
folded and stacked in one corner of the cafeteria. Lunch at the
school always made him uncomfortable, with so many humans
crammed together for the purpose of eating, like one beast
with a thousand mouths, a thousand tongues, a thousand teeth.
Chewing. Chewing. Chewing, like masticating cows with
their cud, and seven-fold stomachs working away in unison.
A cafeteria monitor walked between the rows like a sheep dog
keeping the flock in check.

Church watched the other kids and he thought about the
sharpness of teeth. You could tell a lot about a dinosaur, or any
other kind of animal, by looking at their teeth; you could tell
whether they were a herbivore or a carnivore, predator or prey.

Hadrosaurids had flat teeth good for chewing vegetation, and
tyrannosaurids had blade-like fangs shaped to slice through
meat. Humans were somewhere in-between cud chewing
and flesh tearing, with flat pointy teeth configured for eating
everything. People were omnivores, because if they were hungry
or desperate enough, they would eat anything.

He thought of Gericault's painting, The Raft of the Medusa.
Jumbled, bodies in a heap, the moment of hope, limbs extended,
waving down a distant ship unseen outside the frame of the
painting. That painting, he'd learned in art class, was about
a sinking ship, and a life raft lost at sea, and the survival-
cannibalism which the victims had resorted to in order to
survive.

Church ran his tongue along his teeth trying to decide whether
they were sharper than they were flat, or flatter than they were
sharp. He smiled at a passing student and the kid tripped over

his own feet and dropped his tray. The kid pushed his glasses back onto his nose with one finger, and then hurried away. It confirmed a theory he had about the smile as a defence mechanism, evolving like claws or thick skin.

A smile displayed your teeth, your fearlessness, and could intimidate potential predators by warning them you wouldn't be taken down so easily. Look how pointy my teeth are, how dangerous. It was a promise and a threat. Humans were more like wolves in sheep's clothing, Church thought, than they were sheep.

Maybe laughter, by extension, was also a defence mechanism?

"What are you glowering about?" The new boy, Geoff Suture, asked. Church hadn't been aware that he had been 'glowering.'

"You're sitting here by yourself, and glowering at everyone. You're a real freak you know that?" For some reason, the Neck seemed to have taken an instant dislike to him. Or maybe he took an instant dislike to everyone?

"You're one to talk," Church said, smiling. Geoff Suture wore black, his hair in wrought iron spikes, staples imbedded into the rubber soles of his boots like claws.

"I heard you carry a knife." Geoff said, smiling too, showing off his set of even, pearlescent teeth.

"Sometimes," Church said. But in his head, he thought always. Inri had given the knife to him as a gift, "because sooner or later," he said, "you're gunna need it."

"Everyone is afraid of you," Geoff said. "But I bet if I kicked the shit out of you, they'd be afraid me instead." That might work, Church thought, but he didn't want to get beat up. At least the hostility wasn't senseless. Geoff was like a gun-fighter in an old cowboy movie. He wanted to get famous by killing an infamous gunslinger—or something like that—and Church happened to be that infamous gunslinger.

Geoff grabbed Church by what would be the lapels—if he had lapels on the front of his shirt—pulled him forward, and then slammed him against the wall. Hard. For a moment his vision was blurred by a sheen of glistening tears.

Maybe this would be a good time to practice my smile, Church thought, it worked before. Maybe it would again. Smile— you're weak and worthless. Smile—this is a threat, so back off. Smile—or I might just eat you. Teeth, so pointy they could have been filed down to razor sharpness. He knew a Goth kid that had filed down two eyeteeth for vampire sharpness, but Church's teeth were naturally intimidating. The gesture was so threatening and unexpected from the grey figure that the Neck immediately took a step back. Geoff let go of Church's non-existent lapels, a strange expression on his face—his top lip curled—and then he walked away without another word. The kids who had stopped eating to watch this confrontation were disappointed. The bully that had been terrorizing the schoolyard for the past week had surprisingly backed down. They'd been expecting a fight.

Once they realized there wasn't going to be a fight, the kids went back to their lunches, as if the brief interruption had never occurred. A threat of violence among so many others.

July 8th 1872, Ghost Lake, Ogimaa's Examination,

I came the next day to visit my patient, Ogimaa, and perform a more detailed examination. I had him sit up and take off his shirt. His limbs appeared puffy and enlarged as if he were having some kind of allergic reaction, or swelling from a wound. His whole body seemed larger. I am at a loss as to explain this sort of physical change. It is obvious to me, that whatever sickness of the mind from which this man suffers, there is also some bodily ailment involved, whether as a result of his severe conviction that he is in fact turning into a monster—the power of the mind to influence physical changes in the body— or merely some, as of yet, undetermined cause for his symptoms.

It could be that this disease of the body is exacerbating beliefs rooted in a spiritual explanation, thereby creating a sort of mirroring effect, like two images in the glass facing each other, and reflecting endlessly. Because he is physically sick, and experiencing certain changes and mental compulsions for which wiindigo-transformation is believed to be the explanation, his belief alone is encouraging the very symptoms that give rise to his belief.

I asked Ogimaa to lie down, and placing my ear next to the patient's abdomen, I tapped the middle finger of my left hand with the middle finger of my right, and listened to the sound this produced.

"What are you doing?" Aabitiba asked, frowning.

"This, my friend," I said, as I continued tapping the man's flesh, "is called percussion. It is a diagnostic technique introduced by Dr. Leopold Auenbrugger. It was originally used to test the level of wine casks in his father's cellar. He injected liquid into the pleural cavity of corpses to prove it was possible to determine the presence of fluid build up inside the body."

Aabitiba's expression didn't improve, if anything his frown seemed to have deepened. "Do you think that's what's causing the swelling?" He asked.

"No," I said. "There is only normal resonance. But see these striae? These stretch -marks? They are scars, usually the result of rapid growth during pregnancy."

"So he's pregnant?" Aabitiba asked.

"It's not very likely, no. But striae are also seen during periods of rapid growth during adolescence, and during rapid weight gain."

"Ogimaa is thirty," Aabitiba said.

"I know," I said, flipping through the pages of Ogimaa's medical chart, and writing down a few notes as to his medical condition. "It's possible he's recently gone through a late growth spurt."

Gently, I pinched Ogimaa's arm to test responsiveness and sensitivity to pain. When he made no comment, I pinched harder. "Does this hurt?" I asked him.

"Kaa! Gaawiin." He said.

I was certain I had pinched him hard enough that it should have hurt. This suggests there is some numbness, loss of tactile feeling, or otherwise some psychological reason that makes Ogimaa deny feeling pain, or even prevents his conscious awareness of the discomfort.

I pressed the stethoscope to Ogimaa's bare chest, counting the pulse in the radial artery at his wrist with two fingers, index and middle, as I listened for a heartbeat. At first, I couldn't find a heartbeat. I tried the left side of his chest, and there was nothing. I tried the right—nothing.

I placed the cold metal instrument against my own chest, to test whether the apparatus was functioning properly, and was greeted by the steady rhythm of my own heart beating: lub-dub. Lub-dub. Lub-dub. Lub-dub. Lub-dub . . .

"That's odd," I said, frowning. He should be dead, not sitting upright and talking. I placed the stethoscope directly above where the heart should be inside its cage of ribs, and finally heard the first murmur. There was one heartbeat. Lub-dub. Delayed and slow like he was in a very deep sleep, or a coma, though he was wide awake, blinking, and watching me as I listened, searching for a heartbeat. Lub-dub—one, two, three, four, five, six—lub-dub—counting the seconds between heart beats—Lub-dub—one, two, three, four—lub-dub. Lub-dub—one, two, three, four, five, six—lub-dub. Lub-dub—one, two, three, four—lub-dub. There was a heartbeat, although it was incredibly slow and irregular. I wasn't sure what to make of it, only that the patient's continued insistence that his heart was frozen inside his chest indicated that he himself was aware that something was not right. His own ideas about what was happening inside his body, though outlandish, were consistent with my own observations.

His heart might not be frozen, but it definitely wasn't beating correctly.

I moved the stethoscope around, listening, counting out the beats, frowning, listening as his heart gradually took on a more usual, rhythmic heart rate. The irregularities desisted, as if they had never occurred. Lub-dub—one two— lub-dub—one two. Lub-dub—one two—lub-dub—one two. Lub-dub—one two—lub-dub—one two. And I could perceive no more irregularities. I shook my head, inspected the stethoscope, and chalked it up to my imagination, or some unknown heart condition.

Up to this point, Ogimaa had remained quite compliant and tractable, remaining silent as I proceeded with the examination, pressing the cold stethoscope to his chest, feeling the pulse at his wrist, and conducting percussion sounding on his flesh. I wanted to see the range of movement in his limbs, bending his arms and checking for sensitivity and range of movement. But as I examined him, he began talking, slowly at first, but keeping up a steady stream in the Ojibwe language, which Aabitiba translated for me. He became increasingly upset, saying that he was going crazy, that every person he saw appeared like the deer it was customary for him to hunt, that every person looked good enough to eat and he couldn't stop imagining the way their flesh would taste. A torrent of words, flowing out of him so fast, Aabitiba had difficulty translating them all.

And then Ogimaa started thrashing with such violence at the horror of his own confession, I was worried he would cause injury to himself or others, so I was forced to strap him down to the bed frame. Once he was secured and unable to flail himself about in a frenzy, he seemed to calm down, secure in the knowledge that he was now restrained, and, therefore, unable to act upon his morbid impulses.

He said that he feared the mad Medicine woman had cursed him. The same Ojibwe witch—Dibikiziwinan— to whom Marsh had brought me on our way to Ghost Lake; the charlatan that had made the chairs dance, and then follow her about the room like a pack of trained dogs. For those who pay tribute to her, she makes bundles of leather filled with medicine, charms and talismans meant to accomplish all manner of tasks and cures. Ogimaa fears that he has in some way offended her, and that this sickness is her revenge.

I do not believe that this explanation for his madness has any measure of validity. There seems to be more anxiety in him at the thought of being a cannibal, than one would expect from a 'wiindigo monster.' A monster wouldn't care if he ate human flesh, the fact that this preoccupation is a prospect of disgust, and shame, demonstrates that he is not, in fact, a wiindigo. Or so I told him, speaking calmly and rationally, asking Aabitiba to translate my sentiments so it would be easier for him to understand. "You are assuredly not turning into a wiindigo," I told him. There is a medical explanation for his disorder, even if it has as of yet to be identified.

"I will cure you," I told him, with more confidence than I feel. I am less than certain that I will be able to restore him to health, although I intend to try.

I administered a tincture of laudanum, and prescribed rest—as much rest as he was able to bear—and to avoid anything that could possibly offer a disturbance to his mind.

Archimedes Law: the volume displaced by an object in water, is equal to the volume of the object, and with a buoyancy equal to the weight of the displaced water.

The missing potato salad

Church was pushing his grandmother's wheelchair along the sidewalk. Day said "Boozhoo" to a pretty Anishinaabe woman passing on the street. The woman looked up with startled-bird eyes behind thick spectacles like two magnifying glasses that enlarged her eyes to the size of fat marbles, exaggerating her expression of surprise. She reacted as if a wolf in sheep's clothing had said "Hi!"

"Boozhoo," she stuttered politely, with the greeting of respect due to someone her elder, her green cardigan sparking with electrostatic as she scurried away. This reaction wasn't unusual. Many of the Anishinaabek in Sterling knew the rumours and wouldn't associate with the family of wiindigowag.

His Nokomis never seemed to let it bother her. She attended many of the Native community functions, the potlucks and the social events, even if they were afraid of her. The other kids were discouraged from speaking to him. No one was ever rude. They were meticulously polite. Too polite.

If Day's Daughter baked a cake to bring to a feast, no one would eat it. Later it would be scraped into the trash, as if it were contaminated with an invisible layer of Ghost Buster's ectoplasm. Or worse. Chopped up bits of human flesh that would have them all turn wiindigo, with a craving for human meat, and they'd turn on one another like mad starving beasts.

Mukade-wiiyas avoided all crowded events, Inri's presence was scarce, and Church was forced to attend because someone had to push his grandmother's wheelchair. Church always hated these events. Even if there was food, he wasn't allowed to eat it.

Not in public. It was one of the rules. He must always restrict himself to eating "strictly human proportions." Always forced to attend, but never partake or take part. Church thought it must be her pride. Day wanted to display her supreme level of control, as if to prove they weren't the monsters they were said to be, and her grace and dignity in continuing to attend. Even though they weren't exactly made welcome, she insisted that they have a seat at the table.

No one was going to disagree.

"She does it for you, you know?" Inri told him. Ghost of a smile. Exhaled cloud of menthol scented cigarette smoke like car exhaust.

"What do you mean?" Church asked.

"She's trying to teach you to be more human." Inri told him. "So that one day you can survive on your own. She's trying to give you wings."

"Oh." Church said, for the first time realizing why Day went to these events. She was trying to teach him lessons in self -control, and social interaction. Like Mukade-wiiyas, Day also had hope for Church. Least monstrous of them all, he had a better chance of fitting in.

A chance to be human.

At the community events they attended, there was always a lot of food. His grandmother prepared a bowl of potato salad to bring for the next social, sprinkled with paprika. Small by their standards, it was one of the larger bowls at the table.

Conversations came to a halt as people recognized them. There were a few stray whispers and murmurs from groups of people milling around the large space, and the occasional heads nodded in greeting as they passed. An old woman even inquired into Day's health, and recommended something to help with her non-existent-arthritis. Day didn't have any problem with her bones.

Once everyone became adjusted to their presence, the business of laughter and talk resumed, as if nothing had interrupted it. Like a body gingerly immersed into lukewarm water, there were only a few ripples and swirls to disturb the surface, but plenty of room left to accommodate the rise in water.

Those who were friendly towards them were either band members of Ghost Lake or didn't believe in those sorts of things anymore, although—he noticed—everyone was careful to maintain a polite distance.

A few minutes later, something strange happened. Church felt something, and there was a slight adjustment in the room as newcomers arrived. There were more whispers and murmurs. A few people actually left the room. Water sloshed over the lip of the tub.

An old man came in with his grandson slowly trailing behind. His eyes swept through the crowd as if he knew everyone in the room, and who their great-grandparents had been. When the old man's eyes came to rest on Church and his grandmother, they remained for a moment longer than they had on anyone else, before they flicked away to continue their surveillance of the room. Church understood why people had reacted. He could feel the strength radiating from the man, a slight pressure behind his forehead.

Whoever he was, he had power.

Church bent down so his grandmother could whisper something into his ear. "That's Gzhaate's great-grandson," Day told him. "He is named Dedenaan after his grandfather—some people say he is his own grandfather—reborn. They are our adopted cross-cousins."

Church had a hard time keeping all the names and degrees of separation and connection straight in his head. Cousins, was a word he understood. Cross-cousins meant that they weren't related from a traditional perspective of the Anishinaabe clan system, and adopted meant they weren't really related by any regular interpretation of the word—though their families shared many of the same stories—and that was as good as the real thing. Church still found them interesting, even if they weren't blood related. He had met so few of his non-wiindigo relatives. And if you believed the story of their ancestry, Gzhaate and her children weren't entirely human either.

The feast got under way, and everybody adjusted to the new presences, just as they had for Church and Day's Daughter. The bathtub had not overflowed. Yet. Talking and laughter, and the whisper of gossip, resumed.

Once almost everyone else had served themselves, Church lined up at the table, carrying an extra plate to bring back for his Nokomis. It was an exercise to prove they weren't mad creatures, though he wasn't sure anyone bought it. He piled up as much food as the flimsy paper-plates could hold. Wild rice with dried cranberries, moose-meat stew, trout, scones, and pies. He froze when he saw that a serving or two was missing from the bowl of potato salad.

The dusting of paprika kissing the surface was clearly smudged, and two scoops were definitely missing. Some brave souls had dared try a wiindigo's cooking!

As Church made his way back to their table, he made a quick survey of paper plates as he crossed the room. He wasn't surprised to discover the missing servings on the plates belonging to Dedenaan and his grandson. And he was surprised to discover that he recognized the grandson. It was Geoff Suture, the boy with a reputation for violence. Church hadn't known their families shared some of the same stories. Geoff was mechanically shoveling the potato salad into his mouth, oblivious and, for some reason, clearly miserable.

Church returned to the table, and set down the paper plates, one for him, and one for his grandmother. He didn't mention the potato salad. In a grey fog, he went back to get their second serving, doing his best to blend in with the floor under his feet, and walked right into the tough kid, who stood scooping potato salad onto his plate. Just because no one could see him didn't mean that he ceased to exist. It only meant that most people wouldn't take any particular notice of him, unless he was dumb enough to walk right into them.

"Watch what you're doing!" Geoff said, shoving him. Claw-like staples embedded into his black sneakers. Hair shaped into spikes with white school glue, stiffening the strands into a punk-rock crustiness. Geoff didn't wear grey; he wore black.

Church mumbled an apology and moved to step around the boy with a limp indifference, but it was too late. Church was no longer invisible.

"Is there something wrong with the potato salad?" Geoff asked. "No one's eating it. Is it poisoned or something?"

"They're just afraid of our cooking," Church said.

"Yeah, I've heard about you. You're wiindigo," Geoff said with a twist of his lips, "But I'm not afraid of you. You're not even Native."

"I know who I am," Church said, giving Geoff a shove to the centre of his chest. Geoff took a small step back, but managed to keep the mountain on his plate from flopping over onto the floor. With his free hand, Geoff shoved back. Church smashed into the fold-up table that had been set up for the food to be laid out on, it wobbled, and all the dishes on the table quaked, red-jello mould quivering.

Church barred his teeth and went for the other boy's throat. The potato salad went flying, Geoff crashed onto the fold-up table, which collapsed under their weight, spilling its contents onto the floor with a crash as the various dishes and stews were strewn across the floor.

Everyone turned too see the potluck table collapsed, and the two boys fighting in the mess, fists flying and arms pulled back. A tangle of limbs and swear words. Adults quickly stepped in and broke up the fight before they could do too much damage, and they were quickly separated, covered in what was left of various bits of the meal. Day was not impressed with his behaviour.

"That boy is Dedenaan's grandson." Day told him when they got home, "Everyone thought the old man would die the moment the boy was conceived, but he just kept on living. His parents are both wild. I want you to stay away from that boy. They're nothing but trouble."

She didn't have to tell him twice. Church could only agree. But at the same time, he couldn't help but to wonder; what could be so bad, that even Day doesn't want me to hang around them?

July 9th 1872, Ghost Lake,

I came today to find Ogimaa's chamber in a mess, anything that could have been torn up or destroyed, was, and had been piled up in one corner, his bed was flipped over, his mattress flopped on its side and propped up, altogether creating a little nest out of the jumble of bedding and linen. He lay naked under his disarrayed furniture, like a muskrat in its den, his clothes strewn about the floor. The old man—Mookman—tells me, they had simply locked the door and let his nephew rage, tiring him-self out, rather than forcing a direct confrontation. The hearth has long since grown cold, and not even an ember of warmth remained, throbbing with light to heat the chamber.

Ogimaa lay unconscious in his cave, apparently dead to the world after his strenuous exertions. And together with the old chief, we set set about putting the room to rights. Standing up upended chairs, flipping over the bedframe, and reinstating the mattress. As we removed more of the wreckage covering Ogimaa's body, he whimpered and complained that he was too hot. He was burning up. He needed to go outside where it was cold, gsinaa gojing. But when I held my hand to his forehead, he was still, cool to the touch. His core body temperature was if anything, lower than it had been before. He did not have a fever.

I can only suppose, much like a fever—when ones body temperature rises, one feels cold, the surrounding air feeling chilly in comparison to one's own heat—and so the opposite should also be true. Ogimaa's core body temperature being abnormally low, he feels hot, and the surrounding air too warm, though more warmth is exactly what he needs, not less.

It is after this outburst that we again decided to restrain him, for his own safety more than anything else. Mookman fears he will walk off, naked and raving into the night, which can still become quite cool, even in the summer. This paradoxical undressing is similar to accounts of hypothermia, where victims are found frozen to death. Lost in some barren wasteland, they must become confused, having removed their own clothing as if to hasten their own passage from this world to next, even in cases where the victim's tracks prove they had trudged for miles, or even days, by every indication, determined to survive. These are not suicides—no! The hypothermia victim feels too warm, as if they are burning to death.

Except Ogimaa's chamber is not cold enough to bring about hypothermia. I begin to suspect it must be some hypothermia of the mind, rather than of the body, which afflicts my patient.

I have devised a simple to test to perform on Ogimaa. The erecter pili are small muscles attached to hair follicles, and my experiment will seek to induce a cold response—shivering or goosebumps. When the body is subject to cool temperatures these small hairs stand on end to create a layer of insulation, the same way a bird fluffs up its feathers to preserve heat.

The test was quite simple.

Taking a bucket of ice-cold water, I submerged Ogimaa's hand in the pail and waited. After five minutes, he still showed no response to the cold. I had tested the water myself by submerging my own hand, the aching cold infiltrating all the way down to the bone, so cold that it was painful, and I withdrew after only a few moments, thirty seconds at the most. It was that cold.

After ten minutes, Ogimaa still showed no homeostatic response, neither complaining of discomfort, nor showing any physiological response to the cold, such as shivering or goosebumps. He didn't even flinch when I placed his hand in the water! Even if he were masking his true psychological response for some reason, he should not have been able to entirely prevent a physiological one. I don't think anyone could be that deceitful. The body betrays us all.

This leads me to the conclusion that he felt very little discomfort on exposure to sub-zero temperatures that would have had, any man of normal health and psyche, shivering uncontrollably. I am still pondering why this might be the case. Shivering increases heat production, but it also increases respiration and energy consumption—which I hypothesize, is the reason these responses are absent. These are the later stage symptoms consistent with hypothermia. If only hypothermia were a psychological disorder, I would already have my diagnosis.

Food, like wood that fuels a fire, is used to generate a steady body heat, and only a small portion of that energy is converted into body mass. If the wiindigo patient doesn't require as much heat, the question becomes, why do they hunger? Why do they crave food energy if it isn't for maintaining the warmth of their blood like mammals? They crave flesh the way a starved animal would, yet they refuse to eat what is readily available. What advantage could human flesh have, over other sorts of meat?

I am afraid I am stretching the limits of credibility with my wild, strange musings. Ogimaa is still human after all. And biology can only offer so much insight into the disturbed mind.

Godzilla Manitou

Church wanted a dog, but he was rarely allowed to have pets. There was always a danger they would . . . run away. His little wiindigo family was predisposed more to raising livestock, than to having pets. One was a necessity, the other was a luxury. It was too painful when his pets died.

"You remember how much you cried when Godzilla ran away, don't you?" his grandmother asked. "It's better this way."

When he showed up after school with the stray dog at his heaels, and begged to keep him, his Nokomis had grudgingly relented. Church needed to learn his own lessons, Day thought. I can't protect him forever.

"He'll be a good guard dog," Church insisted, trying to make his case.

"We don't need protecting," his grandmother said, her red-smeared lipstick-lips compressed into a thin line. Pain is instructive, Day thought philosophically. And pain can be a great motivator; it helps you learn faster, quicker, keeps you from making the same mistakes again and again. Church had to learn on his own. He had to be allowed the space to make his own mistakes.

Godzilla was a large dog, a black Doberman/Bull Terrier mix with pointed bat-like ears, lots of teeth, and a three-inch spiked metal collar Church had bought to make him look even more ferocious. Godzilla was chained up to the cherry -tree in their backyard. The tree produced a small, reliable crop of tart berries with juicy red-black flesh, sweeter than any cherries from the store. Staining his lips the colour of dried blood when he ate too many.

"It'd be a skinny dog that lives off of our scraps." Inri said, "Dogs don't like living with us." And so Church's hopes had been dashed. But inexplicably, Day gave her assent. He could still see the ring around the tree where the chain had rubbed off the bark. It made him feel sad. After the dog . . . ran away . . . the tree refused to grow another batch of cherries, the branches remained stark and dead.

Church still saw him there sometimes, digging the ruts deeper as he paced the ground restlessly. That's why the tree never bore fruit. His ghost had never really left. Haunting the cherry tree in their yard. Godzilla manitou.

But before Godzilla ran away, something terrible happened.

In a glass cage, Church also had a pet mouse, albino-white with red, vampire eyes. The mouse gave birth to a huge litter of baby mice. They were born blind and furless, wriggling little pink creatures at the bottom of the food chain. Godzilla got at them, knocked over their terrarium, and tore them to bits. Church had come home from grocery shopping with Day's Daughter to find the dog in the midst of trying to gobble them up, all at once, even though they were running in twenty different directions. In his frantic attempts to eat them all he didn't bother to finish one before going on to chomp up the next helpless running creature. He seemed overwhelmed. Bits of mice body parts flew from his mouth as he rushed about scooping up first one and then another and then another: he was a messy eater. Soon their half-eaten little carcasses littered the floor in a white, pink and red carnage. A few escaped to live in the walls, breeding and chewing through wires.

Not long after that Godzilla escaped. The mice were left scratching in the walls to tell the tale of his presence. Then Church was allowed to have a cat. The silver lining. His name was

Karl Marx, a mouser with claws set to hunt down the creatures in living in the walls. It was like a miniature ecosystem of kill or be killed, a survival-of-the-fittest contest in their living room. Not long after fait accompli, the cat ran away too. That night, his Nokomis made him soup, to comfort him. The silver lining.

"It's for the best," His grandmother told him. "Wiindigowak aren't meant to have pets." She said it with disdain, red-lip curled back from white teeth. We have indulged his childish desires for long enough, she thought. After Karl Marx, there were no more pets, and Church was less inclined to disagree.

He also knew it was 'for the best.'

July 12th 1872, Drinker's encampment,

We got caught out on the lake in a canoe when a monstrous storm hit. I was with Aabitiba, our Indian guide. Othniel had recommended him to me, as the half-breed was familiar with Ghost Lake and its surrounding areas, and Othniel was willing to spare him, so I quickly engaged his services.

We had set out early in the day to visit those places that Aabitiba, knowing something about the local curiosities and the general layout of the lake, had thought might engage my interest. At first he had directed my attention to great mounds of earth, which were obviously an unnatural feature of the landscape. But he was unwilling to share with me, or was himself uninformed, as to the mechanics of their formation, saying only that it was not his Anishinaabek who had created them. We then set out for certain islands which, floating on their layers of bog and peat moss, were unanchored to the lake bottom, and were said to shift and float about unfettered. Michipocoten-minis, Aabitiba called them.

At my request he'd begun tutoring me in the Indian tongue. If I am to treat the sickness afflicting his people, I will do well to know more about them, and their language, if only for the purposes of communication.

The Michipocoten islands appeared out of the early morning mists like great ghost ships, each one manned by a crew of skeletal spruce. It was this local oddity to which many attributed the death of explorers, lost and unable to gain their bearings amongst the shifting islands adrift on the waters of the lake.

"If you aren't familiar with the lake," Aabitiba told me with a smile, "and the tell tale markers by which to navigate, the islands can easily create an indiscernible maze that has confused even the most experienced men, and led many to starvation and death."

The ground felt as solid underneath my feet as any other piece of dry land, and it was amazing to think that the islands were capable of movement, as I could ascertain none, although my trusty guide assured me that this was the case. He also warned me to watch my step, as there were swallowing places of swampy land that could devour a man whole.

We had only finished exploring one such island, when the weather turned suddenly, as it often does out on the lake. Seeing the black clouds billowing in, we set to paddling, thinking we could return to shore before the storm hit. We were wrong. Even Aabitiba was surprised by the swiftness with which the storm descended.

The ominous clouds amassed themselves in huge columns and blotted out the sun, overtaking us. The rain started to come down like sleet, driven like pins and needles into my exposed flesh by the wind. Soon, actual bits of ice were mixed in with the rain, pelting my hands and face as we rowed heroically.

We decided to head for the nearest point of land which we, at first, thought was another island, but which we later discovered was a small point of land. Loud cracks of thunder boomed across the lake, seeming to tear the very fabric of the sky. More terrifying and filled with raw power than any storm I'd experienced in the south. We were quickly drenched, and paddled as fast as we could for the shore. It was upon this peninsula which the competing team, led by paleontologist, Edward Drinker Cope, had made camp. Any port in a storm.

When we hit land, a few workmen from the encampment were waiting to
help drag our bedraggled canoe onto shore. In the interest of humanity they
were compelled to accept us into their shelters. However, I later came to
believe Drinker's willingness to lend us assistance was less than altruistic.
He was as hungry for information regarding his rival, as Marsh was himself.

On learning of my arrival in his camp, Cope had sent the men to escort me to
his log cabin and requested the pleasure of my company. The cabin was the
most permanent structure in the camp; the rest of the labourers and workmen
slept in canvas tents, or the round wig-wams of the Indians.

Cope was well groomed and neatly dressed for someone in such a remote
outpost. He had a welcoming smile as he offered me the comfort of his
fire, burning cheerfully in a hearth against one wall. Unlike Othniel's
disorganized chaos, Drinker's cabin—though cluttered with all manner
of archeological and paleontological specimens—was clean and neatly
organized. When he smiled, I could see row on row of perfectly even,
perfectly white teeth.

"It is a pleasure to meet you Mr. Lockwood," Cope said genially, offering to
shake my clammy hand, and handing me a dry towel. "Come sit by the fire."

"You are from Haddonfield, are you not?" I asked, in an attempt to exchange
niceties rather than out of any genuine interest in the place. I knew very little
about the man, other than that Marsh hated him with an alarming passion.
"I've passed through the town. Beautiful place."

"Yes. I grew up in Haddonfield, in a stone house called Fairfield. I miss
Fairfield, but it is wonderful here too, don't you think?"

I laughed. I couldn't help being amused by his choice in diction. Wonderful
was not the word I would have used to describe this mosquito-infested
backwater!

"Oh, I know it's a wild place," Cope said. "The storms can be quite
impressive. And the lake is dangerous. There are hostile animals, the weather
is treacherous, and the Indians can also be a . . . concern, but on the whole
there's something invigorating about discovery. The search for something
no one else has stumbled upon. I know you must know how I feel, being
something of a scientist yourself, admittedly in a different field, but I

imagine the landscapes of the mind must be just as intimidating, if not more so, especially considering your chosen topic for research. I'm sure your dissertation on 'Wiindigo Psychosis' will be intriguing."

As Cope spoke, the kettle that was set to boil had begun to whistle, and he placed before me a piping hot cup of tea, steam rising enticingly from the surface. I noticed his fingernails were immaculate, polished to a high luster, and yet there was still grit underneath his nails that he hadn't managed to buff away. Cope was neat—but he wasn't afraid of getting his hands dirty—in fact, I suspect that he loves being out in the field. No amount of personal grooming could hide the calluses and work sores on his weathered hands.

I couldn't help contrasting the marked differences between the figures that the two men struck; Othniel preferred to oversee the field work, and mainly stuck to his studies as fossils were discovered—even of fragmented remains— he spent most of the day alone in his rather opulent field tent. (To Othniel's irritation, he had not been able to negotiate with the Indians for access to one of their cabins, and so he had been forced to make do with a tent.)

"I am surprised you are so familiar with my work!" I replied, "Few people understand what psychiatry is. It is a very new field of study"

"Indeed! I must confess my ignorance, I know very little about your particular branch of science. You will have to enlighten me!"

"It is a different discipline from medicine, in that it focuses specifically on disorders of the mind, and serves a function that was once filled by philosophy, theology and religion, instead of the natural sciences."

"Fascinating," Cope said.

The tea was served in intricately decorated, fine bone china. This bit of elegance seemed out of place in this wilderness. A crack of thunder rumbled as the violence of the storm continued to rage and uselessly expend itself in a powerful display of fervour.

My eyebrows rose even further when I noticed a cabinet set against the far wall displayed an assortment of ornately shaped teacups, carefully arranged. All of the teacups appeared to have the same thin delicacy, and the translucency, characteristic of fine, bone china. I knew that bone china wasn't actually Chinese in origin, and that it was actually an invention of the English. It was an entertaining idea that a man who hunted dinosaurs also collected teacups! And that he had gone so far out of his way as to trouble himself by bringing such a delicate collection with him out into the field, and this most inhospitable of places.

I was absurdly pleased. I felt that I'd found a small bit of civilization, in the wilderness of Marsh's coarse company, which I had been enduring, like the untamed nature of the Indian Territory we inhabited. I found myself wishing that Cope, instead of Marsh, had been William James' acquaintance, and the friend to whom I'd been given introductions. I immediately chided myself. After all, we are all gentlemen here; I was fortunate Marsh had provided me with such a great opportunity to accompany him and pursue my research.

"What kind of tea is this?" I asked after taking another sip. "It tastes . . . unfamiliar."

"It is Moss tea," Cope told me.

"It isn't really moss is it?" I asked. It did taste quite foul.

"It is a tea that seems to be popular with some of the local Indians," Cope said, "so I thought that I would give it try."

"It's been a long time since I've had a decent cup of tea,"" I finally replied. "Even if it is rather peculiar." My hand trembled as I took another sip of tea. At least it was warm. I hadn't realized how cold I was. I was starving.

"I'm sorry," Cope said, handing me a blanket. "Here I am, busy making introductions when you're starving!"

'Starving' is a local turn of phrase that means 'cold', or 'freezing', back in my boyhood home in England. I was surprised at his use of the word, as he spoke what I myself had been thinking. I pulled the quilt tightly around my shoulders, grateful for the warmth of the fire. Even though he was American, we did indeed, seem to have much in common.

I said; "Thank you Cope." And he said; "Please, call me Drinker." Drinker smiled. His teeth were perfectly straight and impeccably white. I also noticed that his eyeteeth, sometimes called canines, were pointed and as sharp as fangs.

We passed the time in some polite conversation, and the violence of the storm quickly past, the black clouds disappearing on the horizon to the east, where flashes of lightning could still be seen stabbing like knitting needles thrust through bundles of purple yarn. The sun reappeared, as warm and yellow as if the storm had never passed by; only the pebbles of ice littering the ground left to mark its passing.

Now that the weather had turned yet again, Drinker insisted on showing me his excavation site. The clothes I had borrowed were baggy and ill fitting on my bones: I felt like a scarecrow. I was less than comfortable. The ice-pebbles from the storm crunched underfoot as we followed a path back through the trees, to a spot a short distance further inland. The site was part of the same ancient riverbed on which Marsh worked, where, Drinker informed me, the river had flowed into an ancient inland ocean called the Niobraran that had once covered most of the continent, millions of years ago.

The excavation site was located in a clearing, where a section of bones was slowly being unearthed. A portion of what had once been a great beast lay half embedded in the ground, part of the ribs, spine, and tail of the monster now exposed. Each successive layer of sediment had encased and impeccably preserved the creature, owing to the nature of the "peculiar geology" of the area.

The bones looked odd emerging out of the forest floor. That one can tread over such beasts, never knowing what is hidden just below one's feet, is disconcerting. Twisted joints and spiky protrusions rose from the earth, like some devil dragged out of the pit of hell, then left to flounder and expire in the soil so far away from its fiery habitation. There was an odd hush to the forest, a silence that gave me a sense of awe as we entered the clearing, like someplace momentous or holy. Overshadowed by the towering branches of foliage; it was also dim, like the interior of a church.

The dinosaurs Drinker is unearthing are scattered about this section of forest in clearings of shale close to the surface, unlike those in the deep excavation pit with cliff-like sides that Marsh is digging. I don't know whether this is owing to their placement in relation to the ancient ocean, and the ancient riverbed, dumb luck, or some difference in excavation techniques. I suspect Drinker received pride of place, having arrived at the scene first, he would have been afforded the opportunity to select the choicest of locations for his dig-sites.

I flinched upon realizing we were not alone, and gave an embarrassing yelp of surprise upon noticing a singular presence, appearing as if out of nowhere, like a ghost. Sitting cross-legged amongst the bones of the nightmarish creature, the ribs of the exposed section rising up above his head, like Jonah inside the whale, was a young Indian boy. I recognized him as Yah-ence, one of Goshko's boys, the Indian from the local tribe who is much respected for his medicine, and who had been attempting with his herbs and song-prayers to cure my patient. The boy sat so still, as if rooted to the spot, I hadn't detected his presence, at first. Yah-ence began to laugh, obviously amused by my reaction.

I looked at Cope, my eyebrow raised in the shape of a question.

"It's one of the best-preserved dinosaurs I've ever unearthed," Drinker told me, by way of explanation. "I've had to station guards to watch day and night to make sure Marsh doesn't deface my discoveries."

"Surely no man of science would stoop to such an act!" I said, appalled. I couldn't believe that Othniel, no matter how gloomy his disposition, would lower himself to carry out such vandalism.

"It has happened in the past," Drinker told me. "I have no proof that it was Marsh, but not long ago we were both working at a site in the badlands. There was no one else around for miles except our two companies, and the Indians. It happened in the dead of night when everyone in my crew was fast asleep. We woke to find that all our hard work had been destroyed, and all the delicate bones we'd been working so carefully to unearth were smashed with sledgehammers. There was nothing left except shards and splinters. It was a difficult day for me, let me tell you. I wouldn't have believed Marsh was capable of it myself, if I hadn't seen it with my own eyes."

Undoubtedly noticing my skepticism, he added, "Who else would have had the motive, interest, and opportunity to do such a thing? Certainly not the Indians. It makes me sad to think of the destruction. The loss to science. There is so much more for us to learn about these creatures. This is why the guards are necessary," he said, gesturing to Yah-ence, "to make sure history doesn't repeat itself."

Whether Cope's assumption is correct or not, I do not know. But it makes me re-evaluate all that I know of Marsh, which at this point remains very little, given that he is taciturn and reclusive in nature. I have no means by which to validate or refute Drinker's suspicions, and so all I can do is keep them in mind, without placing undeserved blame, where blame does not belong. Marsh and Cope both have a personal and emotional stake in their quest, as well as a professional stake, their reputations as men of science, not to mention a considerable monetary investment. They must, of necessity, each regard their work in a very different light.

I have resolved not to place myself between the two men, nor get involved in their dispute. Instead I will try to remain objective. It is not my place to become personally embroiled in their feud. The facts themselves will reveal the truth.

I nodded my head as Drinker continued to outline the main points of his discovery, detailing at length the importance of his findings, and the potential growth in knowledge for paleontology.

"This is a new species," Drinker said, "entirely unknown to science up to this point. It hasn't even been named yet! How would you like me to name it after you?"

"Oh, that isn't necessary," I said demurring, not entirely enthusiastic about the idea of having my name attached to such a repulsive creature.

"It's okay, I've discovered a number of species already. The Elasmosaurus platyurus, the Lystrosaurus . . . Laelaps. It is my privilege as the discoverer to name them whatever I wish."

"It looks like a horned demon from the river Styx!" I protested. I could see the bony protrusions, like horns sticking out of the earth, where they'd begun gouging out the head of the monster.

"Hmm, I see your point," Drinker said, stroking his moustache, "The River Styx you say? I'm sure I'll come up with something. Having a grasp of Greek and Latin comes in handy when you're trying to name new species."

"As it does for medicine as well." I said, and then in Latin: "Monumentum aere Perennius." Some things are more lasting than bronze.

"Indeed!" Drinker said. "You are quite right! Aere Perennius my friend. Some things are more lasting than bronze." And again I was absurdly pleased.

"I do appreciate the thought," I said as we continued to survey the other sites scattered about the forest, none, as of yet, in a state as fully excavated as the 'horned demon' (as I couldn't help but to think of it). There were as many as *twenty sites, marked out with blue flags and roped off to keep large animals like moose from trekking across the fragile bones. "Hopefully I will make a name for myself in a different area of study from paleontology."*

"And what do you think is causing the strange sickness?" Drinker asked. "I know some of the Indians believe that it is our fault, for disturbing the spirits of these creatures," he said, gesturing to the excavation sites.

"That could be part of the cause," I admitted. "Since the Indians themselves believe there is some spiritual element to this malady, I can't help but think that it is that very belief which composes some part of the problem. There is some physical component to the sickness, but to what extent it is biological, I have not yet determined. My Wiindigo Psychosis patient, Ogimaa, does not seem to be displaying the symptoms of a fever one would expect if he were to have become infected. Instead he has an abnormally low body temperature. So far the origin of this illness remains a mystery."

"I myself, am also entirely consumed with the idea of origins." Drinker said, "Evolution explains the proliferation and diversity of modern day species, which have antecedents in the extinct species I study. Our current range and morphology of life seems to have arisen from earlier, more primitive forms."

"What sorts of creatures were these 'primitive forms'?"

"It isn't yet known for sure what class of animals they would have been. Or even whether they were cold, or warm blooded."

"And where do you stand on this point?" I asked.

"Though I lean towards the theory that they were ectotherms, that is, cold blooded, I have not taken a steadfast position on the subject,"

"And Othniel? Need I ask what his judgment is? You seem to be at odds in almost every matter—except your mutual passion for paleontology."

"You are correct. Marsh leans towards the belief in endothermy. That is, that the creatures we study were warm blooded."

"And what is the larger significance to your discipline?" I asked, with genuine interest. This was the sort of academic discussion I had hoped to engage Marsh in on our journey, but this had not been the case due to his withdrawn nature.

"Whether an animal is endothermic or ectothermic can have an impact on their morphology, their life patterns, and can determine every aspect of their survival; how these creatures actually lived. Animals that are endothermic have less capacity to survive variations in their core temperature; it limits their range of habitat to areas where there is a comparative supply of energy, that is to say, food. And while ectotherms can survive a much broader range of temperature fluctuations, they are dependent on their environment to maintain their body temperature. The Niobraran was once a semi-tropical environment, and so I hypothesize that most saurians would have been cold-blooded. It is merely one point, of many, on which Marsh and I disagree."

By this time in our conversation, we'd made our way along the meandering path through the forest and come full circle, ending up back at the site of the 'horned demon' where Yah-ence had now abandoned his post. The workers were making their way to the various excavation sites now that the storm had passed and the earth would be damp and easier to shift. They carried pick-axes and shovels for dislodging the soil and rock sediment built up around the creatures, and which had served to preserve them for an untold number of centuries. More than half their numbers are Indians from the local tribe of Ojibwes, the rest being men Cope had brought with him to Ghost Lake. It is a company of eighteen or nineteen men, and they are digging about the same number of pits.

"Please, come visit me again." Cope said. "And let me know if I can help with your patient. Even my men are worried. With all of these rumours, they are beginning to fear becoming sick themselves. Whatever assistance I can offer, is yours."

"I will keep you updated on my patient's condition," I promised, taking my leave and making my way back to Aabitiba, who was talking with some of the workers who remained in the camp, and waiting by the canoe we'd dragged up onto the shore of the peninsula. My head was full of chaotic thoughts and half-suppositions. I would endeavour to discover Marsh's slant on these matters, to get a more complete picture of their enmity, and so as not to jump to any conclusions.

I am determined to remain a neutral party.

The first death

It was a hot day. It was his first time huffing gas. It was easy to get. Sinunde's uncle kept it stashed away in the garage in a red canister with a yellow spout for the ride-on lawn mower. Rat was the oldest at twelve years old, and therefore cooler than they were, because he knew things they didn't. Like how to get high. Lots of the older kids did it, even some of the kids their age. Bill was Rat's cousin and was a few years younger, at nine years old. Church was sort-of-friends with Sinunde, because Sinunde thought Church was cool because he also knew how to blow smoke-rings. His dad had taught him.

Church had been very different even then, but Sinunde had thought it would be cool to have a sidekick. And Sinunde was nine years old, the same age as his friend Billy, and Billy's cousin Rat knew how to get high from huffing gas. Billy and Rat had both done it before.

Rat stole the gasoline from his uncle's red lawn -mower canister, and they went out to the old shed he'd fixed up with a stereo, Christmas lights, and logs for furniture. They dragged the logs out of the shed and arranged them in a circle.

"It's safer to huff gasoline outside," Rat said, "'less chance the fumes will catch fire or explode." This was said for Sinunde's and Church's benefit. Rat knew neither one had huffed gas before. And he enjoyed playing the role of the wise badass.

Rat held a clear bag with a small amount of brownish looking water around his nose and lips, inhaling the vapors rising from the gasoline, the plastic inflating and deflating like lungs. Church watched with a mixture of fascination and revulsion, unsure yet whether he was more curious or afraid. Rat lifted his head back, eyes unfocused, and extended his arm drunkenly toward Billy. Billy took the bag and poured a miniscule stream of clear gasoline into the bag from a plastic milk jug, carefully unscrewing and then re-screwing the cap.

Church lifted the proffered bag to his face, holding the plastic loosely to his cheeks, the same type of plastic bag people won gold-fish in at the fall fair. There was nothing swimming around the yellowish water except a multicolored tinge floating on the surface, shiny as an oil slick, beautiful as a rainbow. He inhaled and the plastic bag deflated, he exhaled and the bag inflated. Scent of bitumen, coal, and engine oil. His heart beat faster and his head swam. He inhaled and the plastic deflated, he exhaled and the plastic inflated. The ground felt off-kilter, spinning like a tilt-a-whirl, and just as exciting.

He pulled away, breathing heavily from hyperventilating and passed the bag back to Billy. Billy unscrewed the cap on the milk jug, poured out some brownish gasoline from the bag, and added more clear gas from the milk jug, creating a brackish yellow liquid. Sinunde sat watching them, nervously flicking the wheel of metallic teeth-spokes on his brown Bic, occasionally producing a jet of orange flames, but more often than not, only emitting a few restless sparks. He smoked a cigarette as they passed the bag around, waiting impatiently for his turn to huff the contents, and casually blew out smoke rings, trying to be cool. His older sister had taught him. They pretended not to be impressed. Everyone had already seen it before. It was less impressive each time, anyway. No one spoke out about what might have been considered Sinunde's callous disregard for his safety by smoking while they got high (if they even noticed), no one wanted to appear uncool and overly concerned. They all knew getting high was supposed to be bad for you, it wasn't supposed to be safe. Sinunde reached for the goldfish bag with its rainbows. Billy hadn't finished pouring and tried to keep the bag but his fingers were slick, and the bag and its contents ended up sloshed all over the front of Sinunde's jacket.

A few drops splashed across the front of Church's shirt.

Billy dropped the milk jug, and the gasoline glugged into the dirt at their feet. "Fuck" Sinunde whispered.

There was a WHOOSH sound and then Sinunde was screaming. The gases ignited and Sinunde was engulfed in flames, the front of his shirt going up like a papier-mâché effigy, his arms swinging wildly, almost comically and a high pitched keening escaped from his lips like nothing Church had ever heard. A sound that didn't quite sound human. Haunting as the train that passed not far behind their house in the dead of night, filling the valley of their town with its somber howl. This was infinitely worse. Like standing in front of the train as the horn wailed, but it was too late to get off the tracks. Conflagration of black smoke, singed human hair, and the gag-inducing smell of charred flesh. Raw and immediate, painfully close, suffocating in his nose, inescapable.

As the shriek engulfed them, Sinunde reached desperately for Church in a ghastly parody of a hug, imploring him for help, begging, please make it stop, but lighting Church up as well. His shirt caught on fire and he could barely see Sinunde writhing through the curtain of flames and black smoke. Sinunde's eyebrows, his hair, his clothes, and his flesh are burning, and all the oxygen is gone, eaten by the hungry flames, stealing the breath from their lungs. Now he can only scream wordlessly, soundlessly as the flames consume him, the roar and flap of the flames whipped up by the wind as air rushes in to fill the vacuum. Sinunde pitches forward as his hope gives out, thoughtless in the agony, blackened limbs reaching desperately, wrapping about Church's shoulders in a macabre embrace. Don't leave me. Come. Help me. Make it end! Don't. Let. Me. Die. Alone!

Church tried to step back, to pull away, and the terror in Sinunde's eyes doubled. Please! Help me! Don't leave!

Then Billy and Rat were dragging him away from the singed scarecrow of a boy, now a flaming heap on the lawn outside the shed. Rat and Billy had finally been moved from their stunned horror. They dragged Church to safety, away from their friend, slapping at his chest and clothes with their bare hands. Rat threw his coat on Sinunde's body trying to smother the flames with his jean jacket, even though they all feared it was already too late. It had felt like an eternity, but Church knew it had only been seconds. The gasoline burned, and when there was no more gasoline, Sinunde burned.

Church lost consciousness. Burning flesh blackened horror and the sound of ambulance sirens in the distance. He was burning, burning just like Sinunde. Letting himself give up a little to escape from the pain now that help was so close. Rat and Billy rolled his limp, steaming body in the grass, sobbing and crying as they put out the flames, and the sirens came inexorably closer.

Who had called 9-1-1? Church still didn't know. Some concerned neighbour maybe. He was probably in shock.

Pain of burn scars that would never disappear from his chest, no matter how much he healed. Sinunde was the first person he ever saw die. Huffing gasoline out behind Rat's uncle's old shed. Church would have joined him, if he'd been sitting just a bit closer. Rest in peace. Sinunde. Nine years old. Church was only seven. R.I.P. Sinunde.

He still heard the screaming in his dreams. He'd wake up in terror, limbs thrashing, believing he was on fire, and Sinunde was embracing him again, dragging him down into painful oblivion. A slumber that would never end.

Church sometimes wished that he hadn't pulled away from the terror in Sinunde's eyes, reacting with fear, instinct, and self-preservation instead of compassion. Church sometimes wished that he hadn't backed away, pulling from Sinunde's arms. Sometimes Church wished that he had returned Sinunde's hug, just so that he didn't have to see the look of betrayal in his mind's eye. Sometimes, Church wished that he hadn't survived.

He hadn't done enough to save his friend.

Church lay in his bed, slick with sweat from his recurring nightmare, the sheets tangled about his legs. His t-shirt clinging to him uncomfortably, sticky with sweat, but he refused to take it off, even in the privacy of his own room. He could hear distant train -sounds, a horn blasting out across Sterling, a small mining city, the buildings huddled like freezing penguins clustered together for warmth in the valley that had been carved out by glaciers, eight thousand years before.

Long mournful sound of a train's wail. Train pain. Train of coal-fire gasoline death. Noxious smell of burning flesh, then the scent of cherry blossoms drifting in through his window on the summer breeze. Zasaweminaatig. It was something of a small miracle that the cherry tree flourished so well in their backyard, growing as it did, outside its normal habitable range. The smell of burning flesh was only the lingering scent from his dreams.

The train was real enough though.

Its mournful note echoing and re-echoing hauntingly across the valley walls in reverberations that never seemed to end: lasting long after the final note could be heard. It continued on, and on, beyond the range of human hearing, dissipating infinitesimally. Church imagined he could still hear it. Smaller and smaller and further away, but always there, always present, and never really gone.

Down into his bones, down into his cells.

The sound of Sinunde's scream would always be with him. Just like the scars on his chest that would never heal, mottled landscape of melted-frozen Freddy-Krueger flesh. Ugly and scarred. He worried abstractly that no one would ever love him, but didn't worry too much, because the idea felt so distant and hypothetical, barely possible. He was too messed up.

Church had spent hours reliving every moment of that day, trying to piece together what had caused the gasoline to ignite. He'd read that it's next to impossible to ignite gasoline with a lit cigarette. Even sparks won't usually do it. Flick a butt into a pool of petrol and it probably wouldn't explode, only extinguish the smoke.

You need an open flame:

He recalled Sinunde nervously flicking the wheel of metallic teeth on his brown bic. When he pulled the goldfish bag from Billy, it splashed airborne through the distance between them, causing some of the gasoline to evaporate. Gasoline is more flammable as a vapour, than in its liquid state. He'd read that later in his biology textbook, or maybe his teacher had said it. With the shock of getting soaked—doused—Sinunde's thumb pressed down on the wheel of metal teeth when the liquid hit him, it produced a wavering jet of orange flame. He said "fuck," and then the vapors ignited, engulfing him in a fireball, his shirt doused, and the milk jug glugging away at their feet.

Not that it mattered what caused the flames, whether it was his lit cigarette, or a nervous tic, "next to" isn't the same as "impossible," and whatever the source of the explosion, Sinunde was just as dead. Church's torso was just as scarred, and the two cousins . . . never recovered. Though they escaped relatively unscathed, only burning their hands as they slapped ineffectually at the flames.

He never spoke to Rat or Billy again. They both had third degree scarring on their hands, from trying to put out the flames on his chest, and hopelessly rolling Sinunde's blazing corpse in the grass in Rat's jean jacket.

He saw them in town occasionally, at school, on the street. They wouldn't look him in the eye. Walked in the other direction when they saw him. Avoided each other like the plague. Rat kept using, moving on from gasoline, to cocaine, alcohol, heroine, prescription pills, whatever he could get his hands on. He over-dosed four years later when he was sixteen.

Billy killed himself not long after. Someone at school said he had hung himself. Church added Rat and Billy to his list of people that he'd seen die, even though he wasn't actually there when they died. He knew why they killed themselves. He was there when "the accident" happened, and that was the event that set them on their respective paths of self-destruction. He was there when they were dealt their wounds, as fatal as those suffered by Sinunde. None of them had ever really gotten over the horror of Sinunde's death. So both Rat and Billy made it onto his list.

Church slipped in and out of consciousness until the ambulances arrived. He remembered being packed with ice, surrounding him like a blanket, then nothing for a long time. The blackness of non-existence. This was followed by weeks of incarceration in the hospital, and the groggy haze of painkillers. Burn wounds, are one of the most painful injuries a person can suffer, and they kept him pretty doped up. He didn't remember pain, not at first, while he was burning, just a surreal blur. He knew, in the moment, that it did hurt. He remembered that it hurt, but he couldn't recall the pain. Maybe his brain was trying to insulate itself, shying away from the memory of the flames. That was OK. The pain came later. Through the layers of epidermis down to the subcutaneous tissue and muscle, superficial, partial and some full thickness burns to 18% (TBSA) of his total body surface area.

There was steady 'background' pain that was constant, pain as his nerves regenerated themselves—even healing hurt—and procedural pain from the dressing of his wounds. Small contractures formed from the tightening of the surrounding skin, pulling together like craters on the moon, or the leather gathered together around the edges of a moccasin. Church was grateful that he had spent the first few days after the accident, unconscious.

Rat and Billy had remained awake in the immediate aftermath of the tragedy. Giving police statements, describing over and over to family, friends, and authorities, the final tormented moments of Sinunde's life. Reliving it again and again as they were forced to describe, in detail, what they had done and how it had led to their friend's death. Suspicion inevitably fell on the survivors. How had the gasoline ignited? How did Sinunde become drenched in gasoline? Was it an accident? Was there an argument? Why was Church, the only one other than Sinunde, with serious injuries? Church was taken immediately to the hospital, and was in no condition to answer these questions. By the time the police came around to question him, they had already had the full story from the other boys, and were just coming around to crosscheck their facts for corroboration.

Few remembered that Church had been there. He was a victim, another casualty like Sinunde. Sinunde, Rat, and Billy, were the ones people remembered, those poor boys, one burned to death, the other turning to drugs and over-dosing, the third, his cousin, committing suicide. Two deaths in the same family, such a tragedy. People shook their heads, shushing.

"How awful!" they said, while having tea and coffee. "Just awful." It was the sort of thing people said.

Rat, number three. The third person Church had seen die, (Mukade-wiiyas was the second). Rat overdosed on alcohol and prescription drugs when he was sixteen. Billy, number four, death by suicide. Hung himself with a rope when he was thirteen. The fourth person he'd seen die. And, of course, Sinunde had been his first, the first to kick it all off, the first to pop his mortality cherry. People die. He learned this lesson while he was still young. They kept dying. And they did.

Sometimes he thought he was cursed. Maybe it was his fault. Death followed him, and he brought pain to everyone he touched. Death waited behind every corner, in the folds of the drapery, knocking around in the walls like red-eyed mice that had escaped Godzilla, gently tapping, tapping like the scraping branches of the cherry tree boughs on the glass of his windows. Death, he had learned, was never very far. He wouldn't have been surprised if those who knew he had been present at Sinunde's cremation also blamed him for Rat and Billy's deaths too.

After all, he was the only one left alive.

Bloody Knuckles

Thanks to an early growth spurt, Geoff was bigger than most of the other kids in their grade. He was known as a bully. Church had seen him shaking down some of the less popular kids, and no joke, stealing their lunch money.

Church didn't usually have a problem with bullies. He kept to himself, and tried not to bring attention to the fact that he existed. He also had a near supernatural talent for being invisible . . . and . . . some kids seemed to be afraid of him. "People are afraid of anyone who's different," Inri said. The rest Church attributed to his ability to go unnoticed.

There were a few tricks to being invisible. The best trick was: keep your mouth shut. Things that normally remain unseen or escape notice rarely make a sound. The second trick called for blending in to your surroundings. Church always wore camouflage. Not the green and brown of army fatigues, but the same shade of grey as the pavement, the grey of the sidewalk, the grey of a cement wall. Like black, grey contains all colours, and reflects all aspects of light split through a crystal, except grey is less harsh, less dramatic, and less likely to draw attention.

Some of these tricks he had figured out on his own, or had learned from his father, and they were always a good idea, whether or not you were trying to be invisible. Avoid making any sudden movements. Always sit at the back of the bus. Always sit at the back of the classroom. Never volunteer for anything. Never line up first or last. Stick to the middle while in a crowd. Always keep your back to the wall.

Once, for an entire week, Church had actively practiced being invisible at school. He didn't have to speak a single word. No one spoke to him. No one gave the slightest indication that they were aware of his presence. He became like background scenery, a part of the wall, melted into the floor, transparent. People looked right through him, like he wasn't there. If you did it right, you were virtually invisible.

"Hey, wiindigo. What are you doing back here?" Geoff asked loudly so that other kids would hear. "All the people are over there," he said, pointing with his nose towards the other side of the room. —Wiindigo— Geoff had called him wiindigo. The word felt like he'd been hit in the face, or a sudden, cold immersion into a bathtub of ice water, it was shocking to hear spoken out loud. Many people said it; not many said it to his face.

Church stared at him with flat un-impressed eyes as he considered the best way to deal with the other teenager. Church had heard that if you stared into the eyes of a cat for long enough, you could kill it, just by freaking the shit out of it. Church had tried it once on Karl Marx, but ended the experiment early in case it worked. He didn't want to kill his cat. And as his grandmother would say, "you don't kill something unless you plan on eating it." Enough of their neighbour's pets had already gone missing.

He felt nothing as he tried this on Geoff Suture now.

"What are you looking at?" Geoff asked, but Church didn't respond. If he made Geoff think that he was crazy, he might go away. He had seen his father bluff his way out of all sorts of situations by pretending to be unstable. "Nobody wants to mess with the crazy," Peter would say.

Geoff snatched the brown paper lunch bag from his hands and smiled. As if to say, what are you going to do now? Hunh? By the rules of the schoolyard, anyone who squealed would just get beat worse later. So telling wasn't really an option.

"Give it back!" Church said, then gave himself a mental kick. That was pure genius.

"Most cops are just overgrown bullies," Church heard his father's voice echoing in his head. "The same kids who gave you wet-willies as a kid are the ones who are still pushing you around when you grow up. They get a uniform, and they are respected for doing the same shitty things they did on the playground!" His father's hand rested on the stick-shift. He reached over and placed a handicap sticker on the dashboard, then rolled down the window as the cop approached. Peter had 'borrowed' the sign from Day's Daughter, and found it useful on all sorts of occasions. Peter detested the police. He called them pigs.

"Why should I?" Geoff sneered.

A sneer is a cross between a smile and a leer, and it always made people look ugly. The lips peeled back from one side of Geoff's mouth displaying his teeth. It was a smile in its truest form—a distillation of contempt. It reminded him of the way Godzilla showed off his teeth when he growled, their sharpness complemented by the metal spikes around his collar. Church wished Godzilla was there now so he could let go of the leash and watch the dog rip out Geoff's throat, then stand transfixed as the bully gurgled and choked.

Involuntarily, a sound escaped from him—a rumbling in the back of his throat, not unlike the sound Godzilla made when he growled. Instinctively, Geoff took a step back, and lowered the stolen lunch. For a moment, the sneer flagged, held half-heartedly at half-mast.

"Give. It. Back." Church snarled. Trying to keep the surprise out of his voice. Like he had meant to do that all along. Yeah, that's right, I meant to growl.

"Why should I?" Geoff asked.

And Church shouted "BLOODY KNUCKLES!"

'Bloody knuckles' was a brutal method of conflict resolution that was currently popular at their school for settling any dispute, and sometimes it was played just for fun. It was called bloody knuckles because it sometimes ended in blood, though it was more likely to result in bruises when someone forfeited. The game was basically an endurance contest, and Church knew this was something that he could win. He had a high pain threshold, and the scars to prove it. A small crowd of kids began to form around them as word spread.

The rules were simple. The players placed their fists next to their opponents, and took turns smashing the other person on the back of the hands with their knuckles. When someone pulled their hands away in time, and the other person missed, that meant it was now their turn. The object of the game was to smash the other person's hands as hard as possible before they had a chance to move, and the game continued until someone forfeited—or until someone drew blood.

The game drew crowds the same way a fight did.

Geoff and Church headed outside, with a small troop of hangers-on trailing after them. Nothing like a bit of blood to brighten up their otherwise colourless day. There was a grove of trees called the Devils Glen just off school property where kids went to play hooky, smoke pot, and drink beer. The Glen was littered with cigarette butts, garbage and the rusted remains of a spring mattress.

Bloody knuckles was sort of like a duel. Duels were once considered a legitimate solution for settling any dispute, except they usually ended in death. There was an elaborate system of rules for engagement whereby it was made acceptable to kill. Seconds had to be chosen to hand you your pistol, foil, saber, broadsword, small-sword, or rapier. An appointed time had to be agreed upon (and dawn was usually chosen to give the participants time to sober up). Then locations had to be put forward and agreed upon. Preferably somewhere isolated, and outside the jurisdiction of the law.

Bloody knuckles was not as lethal as a duel, but it wasn't quite as wholesome as slap-jacks either, which was basically the same game as bloody knuckles minus the fists. No one played slap-jacks because what was the point? A game that didn't involve pain and fists wasn't going to win very many hearts.

Geoff placed his fists next to Church's and said, "I go first." Geoff's knuckles seemed huge. His jaw stiffened as he imagined what it was going to feel like to have those knuckles slam down against the back of his hands.

Geoff made a few fake nudges trying to make him flinch, then slammed his knuckles down on the back of Church's hands three times in quick succession. Each time he placed his fists back in place next to Church's before making his next strike. Fuck. For a moment, Church turned away and held his fists to his lips blowing on them, and Geoff laughed. The crowd of milling student hissed and jeered.

His knuckles were already red, and they would soon be swollen.

Church put his hands back in place and stared Geoff down, trying to psych him out. Church's brown eyes, so dark they almost blended into the black of his pupils, stared into Geoff's indeterminate shade of grey-green. They seemed to change colour, from one moment to the next. Trying to catch some flicker of warning in his eyes. Church's pulled his fists away, and Geoff missed, coming down on nothing except empty air.

It was now Church's turn.

He stood still for a long time, looking Geoff in the eye again and drawing out the moment. He wanted to make Geoff wonder when the first attack was going to come. When Geoff's eyes shifted away for an instant, Church slammed his fists down hard on the back of Geoff's hands, catching him off-guard before he had a chance to pull away. There was another long, drawn-out moment, and then a series of blows, with a series of alternating spaces of time in between. Then combination blows, two quick double taps in the same sequence, coming in at random moments interspersed with one-hits and two's. Double taps were risky because the other person could already be pulling their hands away on the first strike, but they also did the most damage.

Geoff pulled away and Church missed. It was now Geoff's turn to go again. Oh Fuck, he thought. But then Geoff only landed two hits before he missed, and then it was Church's turn again. Geoff was stronger, but Church was quicker.

Even though Geoff could do more damage with his fists, Church was still landing more blows. Geoff's knuckles were red, and he could tell that Geoff was in more pain with every strike that landed. He caught Geoff's fists on the edge of his knuckles as he was pulling them away and it broke open the skin like a gash in an orange peel and blood oozed slowly out.

Church had won. Geoff's knuckles were bleeding. Tiffany and
Jason who'd been standing by watching, proclaimed Church the
winner, and the crowd of milling teenagers cheered and booed,
some patting Church on the shoulder

Geoff picked up the brown lunch bag and pushed it
unceremoniously into Church's chest with a disgusted sneer
and then walked away. He was a sore loser because losing this
game hurt. A few kids even hurled insults at Geoff's retreating
back, feeling suddenly brave at his defeat. They would have
been pleased no matter who had won—bloody knuckles
was entertainment. For a moment he felt sorry for the other
boy—but that didn't last long. When Church looked into the
bag he discovered that his sandwich was missing. His stomach
grumbled loudly in complaint.

Geoff consoled himself with the sandwich he had stolen from
Church—the Indian kid who didn't look very Indian. He took
a bite out of the sandwich and stared at it in disapproval. What
was this? Geoff peeled open the slices of bread and peered
inside but all there was, was some relish, mustard, and onions.
There wasn't even any baloney! Geoff threw the slices of bread
away in disgust. Geoff's own parents hadn't thought to make
him anything at all for lunch.

MEDICAL CHART   DATE: *July 13th 1872,*

NAME: *Ogimaa, (waabzheshi dodem)*

ADDRESS: *Ghost Lake*

AGE: *30*

GENDER: *male*

OCCUPATION: *trapper/labourer,*

HEIGHT: *5'8"-5'9"*

WEIGHT: *approx. 13 stone*

NOTES: *I have conducted a fuller, more detailed examination of the patient.*

SYMPTOMS: Drowsiness. Fatigue. Inability to sleep at night—and when he does sleep he complains of constant nightmares. He complains of an overpowering hunger (though he refuses to eat—possible dysphagia—difficulty swallowing. Anomalous pupillae—wide black pupils dilated to over-shadow the natural colour of his retina (even when there is light to stimulate his pupils, there is very little contraction). He has a pale sickly complexion, a slight blue-ish tinge, which could be caused by hypoxia—an inadequate oxygenation of his blood. He has an abnormal respiration and decreased metabolism. He has an erratic pulse, tachycardia (above 200bpm!) and bradycardia (initially his heartbeat was so slow I had trouble finding his pulse!) This irregularity could be a result of the low oxygenation of his blood cells, high blood pressure, or cor pulmonale, a partial failure of the right side of the heart. He has a low body temperature—not quite ambient room temperature, but still quite low (his feeling that he is too warm could be due to this low temperature, which would make the surrounding air seem unnaturally warm, and could also explain his paradoxical undressing. I wonder if he could be experiencing some form of congenital disorder, or if it could be an acquired condition, caused by some trauma to his head, or injury to the spine—although Ogimaa insists that there has been no such injury. The symptoms did not appear until some time after he began digging for Othniel, and they grew progressively worse, until they became debilitating.

PSYCHOLOGICAL STATE: *Melancholy, depression and sadness regarding his supposed transformation into a "wiindigo," with short periods of mania, thrashing, shouting and raving—so much so, that he has had to be restrained. He truly believes he is becoming a wiindigo, and that these symptoms are the result of his transformation.*

DIFFERENTIAL DIAGNOSIS: *Insomnia, paranoia, and neurasthenia. His nightmares have led to an inability to sleep, which in turn has brought about paranoia and much mental agitation in his sleep-deprived state. My first instinct is that simple rest should afford some reprieve in his symptoms, and that once he is rested, we can then tackle the disturbance to his unconscious mind in the form of these dreams.*

DIFFERENTIAL DIAGNOSIS: *Hypothermia, torpor, and inanition. Ogimaa's vital signs are abnormal. His respiration rate is as erratic as his pulse. His sensitivity to pain is low, or else he has an otherwise high threshold for pain. According to the mercury, his body temperature appears to be below the normal range of 96 degrees Fahrenheit. His temperature hovers and fluctuates at, or around 87 degrees, and so he appears to be suffering from a mild hypothermia. This in of and itself, could explain the slow down in his metabolism, and his various symptoms. Though I am at a loss to explain his mydriasis, the size of his pupils, and their lack of reactivity to light, this is not always considered a "vital sign" for the obvious reason that there are occasionally other causes for this other than death. Dilation of the pupil is normal under low-light conditions to draw in more light and improve night-time vision, though Ogimaa's remain fixed in all light situations, like certain nocturnal species that only emerge at night. The tachycardia and increase in his heart rate is consistent with hypothermia, although the initial slow down in his respiration and pulse, and the erratic changes in his pulse and respiration, are not. He shows no signs of shivering, which is what one would expect given his temperature reading, even though he complains that he feels he is too hot, and that his heart is cold. The change in skin colour—he appears pale and drawn—could be the result of vasoconstriction, narrowing of the blood vessels, which is also what one would expect from the body's response to cold, by reducing heat loss from the blood to the surrounding air. He is physically cool to the touch.*

Again I am reminded of certain animals that hibernate in the winter, and intentionally slow down their metabolism during periods of scarcity in order to ward off starvation. His symptoms, low body temperature, slower breathing, his torpor-like condition for most of the day, and his slowed-down metabolism can all be consistent with hibernation—if hibernation could be considered to be a disease among humans.

Now that I reflect back on Ogimaa's symptoms, I see in retrospect that the change in his pulse and respiration, from depressed to active, was sudden and dramatic. This change did not occur until I made some comment upon its strangeness, at which point his pulse jumped and changed to something resembling a more normal speed. I almost believe my own observation of the symptom caused Ogimaa to subconsciously change the speed of his pulse to something that was more in accordance with my expectations. The French physiologist and scientist Claude Bernard* has demonstrated the importance of blind experiments to ensure the objectivity of his scientific endeavors, and I suspect my reaction to Ogimaa's symptoms, may have altered and invalidated those observations.

If my observation of Ogimaa's symptoms caused them to change, and I believe that it did, then his symptoms would then be in accordance with a diagnosis of hypothermia, and possibly a state of torpor-like hibernation. In that case his slowed metabolic rate would be caused by of his cool temperature, and not the other way around, as the bedside-fire in his chamber has had little effect in keeping him warm—which would also be consistent with this diagnosis—a slowed metabolic rate resulting in a lowered core body temperature. This would also explain his feelings of hunger as his body uses up its reserves of fat as an energy source. His symptoms are consistent with inanition, or the effects of starvation. If he continues refusing to eat his meals, he will be in a dire situation when his body consumes all of its energy in the form of stored fat, and begins breaking down muscles and other tissues to keep his vital systems functioning. His body will in effect, begin to consume itself, and he will truly be the cannibal he fears becoming. Except that he will be the only victim.

Ogimaa's 'paradoxical undressing', usually a cold response in the most extreme cases of hypothermia, where the victim becomes delirious, usually in a state of extremity, lost and wandering in the snow-swept wastes, is also strong evidence for the diagnosis of hypothermia. The body temperature drops, the surrounding air begins to feel warm in comparison, and the confused victim removes their clothes, further lowering their body temperature, and hastening their own death. We must remain vigilant to keep Ogimaa well bundled, and the fire in his room well stoked.

*I am in agreement with Bernard's use of the scientific method as it applies to medicine—though I am in equal disagreement with his practice of vivisection on animals, which I regard as unnecessarily cruel.

DIFFERENTIAL DIAGNOSIS: Anorexia Nervosa, in some form or variation. Ogimaa refuses to eat—not due to any fear of gaining weight, or distorted perception of his own body—but because of the irrational fear of turning into a Wiindigo Monster. It is only by happenstance that I am familiar with the condition of Anorexia Nervosa, as it was first described by my friend Jack—Sir William Gull. And I say Sir because he has recently been raised to Baronet—I only heard the news a short time ago—for successfully treating the Prince of Wales, Edward VII, during an attack of typhoid fever. I received a letter from Jack, when I went last week to the trading post at Koo-koo-ziibii, Owl River, to collect and deliver my correspondences, and he is now physician-in-ordinary to Queen Victoria herself!

It is a coincidence that I have come to study, what may well be some derivation of this disorder, in the form of Wiindigo Psychosis. Ogimaa feels hunger, but denies himself all but the smallest quantities of food we can encourage him to ingest, through our constant cajoling. Starvation, for whatever the reason, including self-imposed starvation as a result of Anorexia Nervosa or Wiindigo Psychosis, can cause abnormal heart rhythms of the sort I've noticed in my patient. The obsession with food and body image, in this case, is instead an obsession and anxiety surrounding eating human flesh, and becoming a monster. Poor blood circulation, hypothermia and a lowered body temperature could be a physiological attempt to conserve energy. His lethargy and torpor, fatigue—even his apparent growth spurt or the swelling of his limbs—reminiscent of certain species of birds that fluff up their feathers to capture their own body heat—all are consistent with this diagnosis: self-induced starvation, Anorexia Nervosa and Wiindigo Psychosis. Even his perception of himself and his symptoms, feed into his conviction that he is turning into a wiindigo, and he points to those symptoms as proof of his transformation.

DIAGNOSIS: Wiindigo Psychosis. This case is consistent with the extant literature on the subject, which is scant, though all his symptoms do seem to be consistent to the other instances I have read, right down to his craving for human flesh. My examination and analysis of this patient brings to mind my earlier conversation with Drinker regarding endotherms and ectotherms— warm-blooded and cold-blooded animals, and it strikes me that it is possible for all of these symptoms to be attributed to metabolism and metabolic processes, which are themselves subject to and regulated by the mind, and psychical processes. Like certain animals that are warm-blooded during the summer, but cold-blooded during the winter months when they hibernate, his metabolism and physical state seem to be in a state of hibernation, and his mind is fixated on the dream of wiindigo transformation.

July 13th 1872, Ghost Lake,

I awoke suddenly. My eyes snapped open to zero-in on the slight tickling sensation that had, oddly, been enough to rouse me from my sleep. A mosquito had landed on my arm, and was now testing the porosity of my skin with its proboscis, searching for blood passing through the conduit of a vein, and a weak point at which to make an incision.

I studied the insect with a clinical, dispassionate curiosity.

I felt a slight pinch as it found a suitable extraction site, and inserted its mouth, hollow and pointed like a syringe, and began to inject me with its saliva, which contains an anti-coagulant that would prevent my blood from clotting. I couldn't help wondering if Alexander Wood had drawn inspiration from these insects in his development of the hypodermic needle. The mosquito began to drink, drawing the blood up through her mouth like a straw, and I could see my blood filling her belly through the clear translucency of her body, tingeing her abdomen first pink, and then a darker shade of ruby.

Reaching forward with my free hand, I carefully pinched the flesh surrounding her tubular mouth, and squeezed, trapping the tube in my arm so that the insect could not withdraw after it had finished gorging. The insect pulled, attempting to withdraw from the extraction site, but found that it was trapped and forced to continue ingesting my blood, long past the point that it would have normally had its fill. I felt the tiny creature tugging, trying to withdraw its appendage with increasing urgency, but to no avail, her body swelling, growing fat on my blood, she trembled slightly, and then burst, exploding blood and bits of mosquito wings, her limbs spattering across my forearm in a satisfying display of crimson carnage. The little bastards are eating me alive in this godforsaken country, and it was time they had a little taste of their own medicine.

I must speak with the healer, Goshko, regarding the matter. There is bound to be some local method of warding off the vile creatures, or the Indians would all have been sucked dry, long before it would have been possible to make this place fit for human habitation.

Baakaakwenh

A few illegal chickens ambled about their backyard, pecking furtively at the ground in an aimless search for a meal. A meal they would one day become. They provided a regular source of eggs, and when they were ready, a source of fresh meat. Free-range chicken tasted much better than store-bought meat, although slaughtering and plucking the birds was a chore.

One day, Church was watching Inri slit a chicken's throat, but before he could upend it neck-first into an empty bottle of javex to bleed out, the poor bird somehow managed to wriggle free, convulsing. The head was almost completely severed, and attached only by a few ligaments—it dangled as the bird ran about their backyard in a panic, blood spurting out the stump of its neck as the legs continued to pump, making a bloody mess of their garden, before finally flopping on its side and twitching spastically.

Death isn't pretty, just necessary. If you don't eat, you don't live. And everyone needs to eat. Especially wiindigo. There wasn't much choice, in life, or in death.

Inri picked up the limp body, upended it neck-first into the cut-off top of the javex bottle, and then went back to the coop for tomorrow's meal, a smear of blood decorating his cheek from where his hand had brushed against his face, brushing away a stray strand of hair, or from taking a haul on the menthol cigarette perched free-standing from his red lips.

Moss tea

Sometimes, he had a drooling problem.

Church was in class. He heard the teacher's voice, but he was not listening. He was busy fantasizing about the salty taste of bone marrow quivering in his mouth like warm meat-jello. A little known fact: gelatin is made with ground up bone. Fe-fi-fo-fum, he thought. If kids knew what was in Jello they might be less willing to eat it. People are monsters too. Fe-fi-fo-fum, Church thought, I'll grind your bones to make my Jello!

His stomach grumbled like a bear awakening from its winter slumber. Some of the other students glanced his way, but Church didn't notice. He was too busy daydreaming.

And his dreams were bleeding. The iron taste of blood, the melt-in-your-mouth savory-sweetness of cotton-candy flesh, so tender it dissolves on contact with your tongue. A gob of saliva dripped from his mouth to touch the paper on his desk six inches below his chin, still connected to the spittle in his mouth by a long translucent strand.

Geoff stared forward. There was a sound coming from the desk next to his. He looked over at Church. The kid was drooling. Church jerked awake and the drool bounced back into his mouth with the elasticity of a spring, leaving only a small glistening pool of goo on the table.

What a freak, he was like a frigging St. Bernard!

Church wiped his mouth with the back of his sleeve, and realized the paper on his desk was now wet. Students were looking at him. Maybe it was things like this that made the other students avoid him?

Sometimes his salivary glands kicked in at the worst time, and he'd have to struggle not to drool. It could be embarrassing, as it was now. The teacher squinted her eyes at him as if he were on drugs.

Church spent the remainder of the school day practising invisibility, and trying not to draw more attention. It was math class, so Church was sitting beside Geoff. He stole glances at Geoff's neck, and the meaty calves sticking out of his shorts, while the hunger in his stomach gnawed at him. He had the calves, Church imagined, of a well-fed German boy in lederhosen.

Geoff was Swedish, German and Ghost Lake Anishinaabe—as much of a mutt as Church was. He imagined Geoff was one of those hapless children in fairy tales, like Hansel and Gretel, who get eaten by a witch. He pictured Geoff as Hansel. The witch knocks Hansel over the head with a frying pan. Hansel falls to the ground like so much dead weight. Hansel regains consciousness half submerged inside a pot of cold water. The lid is chained on and the pot is placed over a fire. The water temperature slowly rises. Hansel whimpers and begs for his life.

"What's going on? Where am I?" the muffled voice of Hansel can be heard coming from inside the pot. "Let me out. Let me out. Let me of here!" Hansel cries, "I want to go home!"

Church wonders what he'll taste like? Swedish boy filled with porridge, and other peoples' lunch. Swedish sausage, Sweetish schnitzels, Sweetish meatballs!

"Please!" Hansel says beginning to panic, "it's getting hot in here. OWWW! OWWW! LET ME OUT. LET ME OUT!" Hansel howls inside the pot.

Church laughs and the whole class turns to look at him. The teacher turns from the math problem written on the board. Church notices that he is drooling again and wipes his mouth on his sleeve. Geoff squints at him as if he knows that Church was imagining what he would taste like if he were roasted alive.

After school, Church pours himself a cup of moss tea.

Mukade-wiiyas raises an eyebrow but says nothing.

"I guess it's about time you started drinking moss tea," his grandmother says. "I was hoping you weren't wiindigo enough to need it." No one asks why he decides to start drinking moss tea. Day's Daughter figured she had a pretty good idea what might have happened. It was bound to happen eventually.

"It is good for you, and delicious!" Inri said.

Church still thought that it tasted like sticks.

Aluminum

It takes 8.2 minutes for each ray of light from the sun to travel through the vacuum of space and reach the surface of the earth. The sun is a yellow dwarf star, and its starlight shines down on everything equally; the red bricks of the school, the see-saw, and the blood dripping from the boy's busted lip onto the chalk outline of the hopscotch scrawled on the ground.

The light falls on everyone and everything regardless of worth. The light falls on the plants and the mice, the insects and the birds, the sand and the slime, burning the desserts and depriving the arctic of its presence for six months out of the year; it falls on saints and sinners, children and drunks, bums and beauticians. The school receptionist is wearing a cardigan and has fake pink fingernails. Somehow she is clacking away on her keyboard despite her grotesquely long nails, and she tilts her head to the side as she listens to the radio. The radio didn't care who was listening. The light didn't care who it touched.

The receptionist frowned, looking over the top of her glasses as she watched Geoff troop by into the boy's bathroom, a clod of white napkins held to his lips slowly turning red as it absorbed his blood, tears slowly drying on his cheeks.

Geoff Suture had been beaten up again. The receptionist said nothing, and went back to her work.

Geoff was a strange child. He was small, and overly fond of the sun. He'd sit for hours in the light, eyes closed, head tilted back to absorb the rays. Skin tanned a deep copper-brown thanks to his Native heritage. He never seemed to burn. But neither did the grass or the trees. If they liked the sun, why shouldn't he? And he did like the sun. He stretched out like a cat on the asphalt on the east side of the playground to catch the morning rays.

A shadow fell across his face, and he opened his eyes to find himself surrounded by several kids looking down on him. They called him names, punched, kicked, and spit on him.

He had quickly learned to change those aspects of himself that other kids found objectionable. After the fifth or sixth time he was beaten up, he thought it was better to hide, and before long he didn't get picked on anymore. Of course, he soon discovered that he had actually grown larger than most of the other boys. More often than not, he was the one doling out the beatings now.

Church carried a burlap sack with their dinner inside. He was on his way home from checking the snares he and Day's Daughter had placed around the green spaces in Sterling. Church passed Geoff's house on his route. There was loud music, and figures clutching beer bottles as they paraded before the windows. It sounded like a good party.

"Hey," Geoff said, stepping in front of Church.

"Hey," Church said back. Geoff took another step forward and pushed Church in the chest, shoving him so that he had to take another step back.

"What?" Church asked. What had he done? Was Geoff still angry about losing the game of bloody knuckles?

"What's that?" Geoff asked pointing at the burlap sack tied at Church's waist. One of their snares had been successful. The burlap was stained, and something red was dripping from the bag. Geoff snatched the bag from him and looked inside, his lip curled. The carcass had become tangled in the snare and Church had accidentally ripped the head off.

"You're such a freak," Geoff said, thrusting the dead rabbit into Church's chest. "My grandpa says you're Ghost Lake."

"Eennhyaanh," Church said. The nasal-sounding Ojibwe word for 'yes'.

"You don't look very native," Geoff said, looking him up and down.

Church shrugged noncommittally. He'd given up trying to explain the disparate parts of himself. It was too difficult to add up. Human. Non-human. Anishinaabe. Whatever his father was supposed to be— with those numbers written on his arm.

Tattooed onto his flesh as if by a red-hot cattle brand. But Peter did not like to talk about the past. Church knew what he was though. He was wiindigo.

"I know who I am," Church said. "Do you?" Geoff was one of Gzhaate's brood. They were adopted cousins or something, though they weren't blood related. And they were cross-cousins at that. Church didn't think that even qualified. According to traditional kinship relations, cross-cousins weren't technically considered to be a relation.

"What do you want?" Church asked. He figured Geoff was trying to pick a fight. He'd seen him do that on multiple occasions. Sometimes Church wished he really was wiindigo—that way he could eat all of his enemies, and satisfy his hunger while disposing of their bodies. Three birds. One stone.

Church wondered if he should play dead—why stab a dead corpse? —Or fight back. If he inflicted as much damage as he could, it might convince Geoff that he was more trouble than he was worth. Like a dog hassling a porcupine. There were other kids Geoff could pick on who would take twice as much shit without giving half as much resistance. Why did he pick fights with everyone anyway?

A man grabbed Geoff by the shoulders and began shaking him. "I thought I told you to stay in your room!" the man screamed in Geoff's face, spittle flying from his lips, "And now I find you out here hanging out with your friends!" The man gestured towards Church, and he took a step back, surprised by the sudden interruption, and the intensity of the man's rage.

Friends? Church thought. He almost laughed, but couldn't quite manage it. Geoff's tough expression was gone, replaced by the same fear he no doubt inspired in the kids he bullied at school. For a moment, it gave Church a small thrill of satisfaction, but then the delight in his stomach died, like a cold, hard pit of aluminum. He felt sorry for Geoff. They were, after all, supposed to be distantly related. The man shoved Geoff in the direction of the house, his shoulders slumped as he made his way up the stone steps. Church picked up the sack, from where it had slipped from his hands, a dark red stain growing larger as the coarse material slowly absorbed the carnage.

Could violence be inherited, from one generation to the next? Church wondered. Recycled, like pop-cans melted down to make new ones. Maybe Geoff was caught up in a cycle of violence, the frustration and pain, spilling out over onto the other students at school? Hefting his dinner, Church made his way along the cracked sidewalks of Sterling, taking all the short cuts down side streets to get home faster with their meal. Like always, Church was hungry.

July 15th 1872, Ghost Lake,

Dear James,

Each day brings with it another lesson in the Indian tongue, in which the medicine man, Goshko, has been kind enough to instruct me—and to some extent Aabitiba—by virtue of simply being continually in his presence. Aabitiba still remains in my service, in the position of my occasional translator and guide. As a result, I am becoming increasingly confident in basic conversation, and feel that I am almost fluent already!

The air is filled with the high pitched whine of the mosquito, a ringing sound almost outside the range of human hearing, but magnified so many times over, it becomes a palpable force. Wings beating the air like a thousand, miniscule, pulsing hearts.

They are a plague in this God-forsaken country, which the Ojibwe call zaagimay, or machi-minadoosh—small evil spirits. I have no doubt why they are so named. Their thirst is so great, there is scarcely a place on my body from which they haven't yet drawn blood. The itching is unrelenting. They seem able to get at my flesh, right through my clothes! In the evenings, at that twilight hour between day and night, or night and day, the air is so thick with the little creatures one can barely breathe without choking on their bodies. Disgustingly enough, some are already fat with their victim's blood. When I swat at them, I can tell which ones have feasted, by the red smear left to decorate the walls of my tent, which are already cluttered with crushed bodies like gruesome wallpaper.

There is a myth that the Indians joke about, of a mosquito the size of a bear that can swoop down from the trees and carry off a man whole. It takes its prey to its nest, where it can nourish its brood of children on the victim's blood. Thousands upon thousands of children. I gave a shudder at the thought, but I refuse to give in to such childish flights of imagination.

I have not yet determined the triggering factor for these incidents of Wiindigo Psychosis, but I can say this—it does not appear to be entirely a problem of the mind, as I had at first assumed. There is some cultural understanding of the sickness that is obscuring my diagnosis. But it is still early in my observations and treatment of my patient. I am coming to believe that some combination of western scientific medicine, and the continued application of Goshko's magical treatments, may be required to take care of those aspects of the patient's symptoms that are being brought about by belief. Without that spiritual element, whether or not it has any actual medical merit, I would fear for the patient's ability to recover.

I miss our discussions, James. If only I had your steady companionship and insight to guide me on this expedition, I would feel much more confident. Tell me, how is your metaphysical club progressing?

This is truly a wild country! Civilization feels so remote here, though I know it is only a day's journey to the nearest trading post at Kookoo-Ziibii—Owl-River, where I periodically go to pick up supplies, and send postage.

I hope this letter finds you well. Your friend,

Harker Lockwood,

July 17th 1872, Ghost Lake,

I went to visit Goshko in his cabin this morning, for what has become my regular instruction in the Ojibwe tongue. He gave me a baashkinejiisijige, a smudge—filled with acrid herbs and plants—that are burned to keep the mosquitoes away.

I am constantly scratching the mosquito bite on my arm, where I foolishly allowed the creature to sink its teeth into me. It is uncommonly irritated, forming a large, itchy red bump, probably owing to the length of time I allowed the insect to withdraw my blood, and inject its saliva into my veins.

"Zaagime mchi-minadoosh!" the old healer calls them, or blood-sucking little-devils. It is an apt description.

Shrinking Violence

"We're not the only ones." Day's Daughter told him. "Immigrants brought their own monsters with them. Their own hungers, their own forms of wiindigo." The word vampire echoed in Church's head, but he dismissed the idea, chalking it up to another one of his Grandmother's stories, reminding himself that she was crazy. It wasn't her fault. This wasn't about blame. Day's Daughter wasn't lying, because you couldn't be lying if you thought you were telling the truth.

"Don't believe everything Day says," Inri told him. "Those stories of hers just help her deal with the business of living," And then, hitting upon a metaphor he thought Church would understand, he added, "like dinosaurs that evolved to have sharp teeth. We have stories, and they have teeth." And then Inri smiled. "But then, so do we."

Despite Inri's cautions, Church couldn't help but to sort-of believe most of the stories Day told him, even if they weren't all completely true. "—'Bought that story hook, line and sinker," Peter would say. Although as he grew older, Church began to notice certain . . . inconsistencies.

One day, they were walking along the paved path that meandered about the edges of town, circumnavigating the heavily forested areas where they often foraged for morel mushrooms, baby ferns, Saskatoon berries—whatever was in season—and checking the snares and traps they'd set up here in there along the way. So far they'd been coming up empty. They wouldn't be having any meat for dinner.

The paved path gave way to gravel, and Day's wheelchair bumped and hobbled over the rougher terrain, though it was no difficulty for Church. They'd traversed this path many times, and the weight had long since become something he was accustomed to—even after it rained and the rubber treads of bikes left gouges in the softer soil of the path—and Day's wheels would get caught in the ruts. The older he got, the more his upper body strength increased, and the easier it was for him to manage this trek. A man came walking towards them on the path. He wasn't dressed for going out for a jog; sweats and a t-shirt, headphones—the gear that people usually wore, especially this far out along the path.

The man wore a fancy suit, though it looked slightly out-of-fashion, which wasn't saying a lot, since according to Mukade-wiiyas, the style of men's clothing seemed to have changed very little in over a century. Their uniforms remained mostly the same. Black tie, dress pants, coat, vest, pocket watch, cuff-links, shoes that had been shined to a high lustre. Lank, ash coloured hair tucked behind his ears, hands behind his back as he strolled towards them like a junky-version of Benicio del Toro. Day's hands squeezed the armrests of her chair, her knuckles white.

"Good evening," the man said, nodding to them as he passed. Day shriveled back in her chair as if afraid he would attack her, but said nothing in return. And he was right; their shadows had lengthened. The sun had gone down. The golden light of the late afternoon sun had now given way to crepuscular rays punching through the clouds on the horizon.

Other than a casual greeting, the man had made no threatening movements towards them, and he continued along the path in the direction he had been walking; but Church noticed Day's unusual reaction. Her back went stiff, and every muscle in her body tensed from some unknown disturbance to her state of mind. Church kept pushing the wheelchair, and Day swiveled in her seat, unwilling to take her eyes off the well-dressed man for an instant. She let out a breath in a rush as he disappeared around the corner in the distance.

"Nokomis. Wegonesh na maazhise?" What's wrong grandmother? Church asked Day in a whisper. What had made Day so frightened?

"Gii-gi-waabaminaan na nini bijiinag giiwitaashkaw giinawind?" She asked. Did you see that man that just walked by?

"Enyaanh." Church said, drawing out the nasal sounding vowels slowly; Ennh-yanh. Yes.

"He wasn't human." Day told him, "I don't know what he was, but he wasn't a man. You stay away from him. If you ever see him again, and I'm not with you, I want you to run. Okay?"

"What was he then?" Church asked, confused. The man had looked normal to him. Other than the nice clothes, he hadn't seemed at all unusual, and Church couldn't see how Day figured he wasn't human.

"We aren't the only monsters in this world." Day said, twisted around as much as possible in her chair so she could look back up at him, her face twisted with worry. "Europeans brought their own kinds of madness with them. Just promise me okay?"

They followed the curving path that led back onto the paved streets of Sterling, the streetlights coming on as they emerged from the park. His grandmother set a brisk pace now, wheeling herself along the cracked sidewalks, as Church trotted along beside her. Day was not a frail woman, and she could get around on her own if she needed to, although it was always good to have help getting up a step or two, or traversing the cratered paths and bike-trails. Day was fat for a wiindigo, and Mukade-wiiyas liked to say that Day was no "Shrinking violent"— whatever that meant.

To be clear, Day was not "fat" by anyone's measure of the term, though she did manage to keep a bit more meat on her bones, probably owing to her limited mobility. She was only fat for a wiindigo, the rest of her family being almost starvation thin. "Runway sheeek," Day called it, claiming that Marie could have been a "supermodel," walking "the runways of London, Paris, and New York. Her beauty could have taken her all over the world, anywhere she wanted to go." Day said this as she fussed over Marie's make-up, blush, eyeliner, lipstick, brushing her hair to a high black lustre, and then braiding it—all while Marie remained motionless and unresponsive, more like doll or a mannequin in a storefront window, than a living being capable of agency and movement.

"You know Marie never liked to travel," Inri said, "She's always been the one who wanted to stay put. When we were young, she never liked leaving the school. She was always scared to go anywhere."

"I can dream for her," Day said, carefully layering the strands of Marie's hair into a tight braid. "Someone has too."

"Dreams are all she has," Inri said, "And I travel enough for the both of us. I've been to Paris, London, and New York—and I'm no supermodel."

"You could've been too—if you were born a girl," Day said, still daydreaming on could-have-beens, should've-beens, and never-were's.

"She's happiest where she is, here at home," Inri assured his mother, though the glazed look never left Day's eyes.

Phys. Ed.

Church's least favourite class was Phys Ed. because of the change rooms. He would come early to change, wear his uniform underneath his clothes, or wait until all the others had left the room to change. He didn't want anyone to see his scars.

One day after class, he was still getting changed when the other boys began streaming into the change room. They were loud and keyed up from their activity, smiling and joking with one another, twirling up their T-shirts and whipping each other. No one had ever taken notice of Church's presence or absence, but for some reason they took notice this time. Church preferred it when he was invisible.

"Hey Church, I've never seen you in here before," one boy commented.

Church quickly pulled his gym t-shirt off with the school logo of a Martin on it from underneath the large sweater he was wearing, and began to put on another T-shirt without taking off the big sweater. He dressed quickly but not quickly enough; he wanted to get out of there, fast.

"I bet he's got titties under there," one of the boys said, noticing the way he changed his shirt like a girl, without taking off his sweater so that no one could see his chest. Church took off the big sweater once he had his t-shirt on and began collecting his things and silently stuffing them into his army-surplus bag.

"Maybe he gets changed with the girls?" another boy said.

Church quickly tied his shoes and stood up to leave.

"Yeah, I bet that's why we haven't seen him in here before," the first boy said.

"Aaaw. Maybe he's just shy!" Another boy said with false sympathy. "Poor baby."

"Let's see what kind of titties he has," one of the boys said, coming to him with his arms outspread to cage him in and laughing as he struggled to lift up the t-shirt over Church's head.

Church fought back, slapping the hands away.

"Ahhh. Poor baby, he is shy!" the boy said, inciting more laughter from the other boys in the room.

Church tried to dodge around the boy, but he had him backed up into a corner, and when Church tried to get around him, the boy managed to grab a corner of his t-shirt and pull it over his head, jerseying him like a hockey player on the ice. The t-shirt ripped but, suddenly, none of the guys were laughing. They were staring at Church's scars, the burn marks that mottled his chest like Freddy Krueger's flesh.

The sudden silence registered their shock. Church pulled out his gym t-shirt with the school logo of two fighting weasels, putting back on the un-torn but sweaty shirt. Church discarded the torn t-shirt in a trashcan on his way out, leaving the change rooms without saying a word.

For a long time after that incident, he could feel eyes on him, and hear whispers whenever he walked by. No one teased him anymore about getting changed after Phys Ed, and he used the teachers' bathroom in the hall instead. Church thought that, in some ways, it had been better when they were teasing him. At least then they weren't talking about him, or feeling sorry for him.

His secret was out. They all knew about his scars, and they all thought he was even more of a freak than they had before. Word had spread that he'd been horribly abused as a child, or that he had some terrible skin condition. But at least no one knew the truth.

No one knew he was there the day Sinunde died.

July 18th 1872, Ghost Lake,

Dear James,

There was a terrible accident in Marsh's camp today. The scaffolding that supported the excavation of bones being dug out of the side of a cliff, collapsed. Several of the workers have been severely injured, and Marsh is furious over losing more men, and falling behind in his task. Now that he is short-staffed, Cope has an advantage and will be unearthing more of the giant creatures, and at a faster pace, than Othniel could hope to accomplish now. His efforts at enlisting more members of the local tribe have failed, since many of them fear some sort of superstitious retribution from the spirits, who they say have cursed both the bones being unearthed, and any men foolish enough to dislodge them from their century upon centuries of rest.

Aabitiba tells me that the Ojibwe believe it is this disturbance that has caused the outbreak of Wiindigo Psychosis, which they truthfully believe to be, not a sickness of the mind, but an actual transformation into one of these cannibalistic monsters from out of their legends.

The news of Ogimaa's sickness has somehow circulated, and neither can the nature of his sickness be concealed. Everyone now knows that there is another case of this illness, or wiindigoowi, as the Ojibwes call it, meaning to turn into a wiindigo. They are frightened.

There is also a young woman in the area, Goshkǫ's niece, who is said to be a wiindigo. Everyone is afraid of her, and avoids her, though I am told that she causes no harm to others and stays to herself. She is virtually a hermit, isolated and set apart from the rest of her tribe. She lives alone at some distance from our encampment, on the other side of Drinker's peninsula. In some way I do not understand, these cases of wiindigo sickness are somehow different. The woman is said to have always been wiindigo. These new wiindigo are human beings who are believed to be transforming into wiindigo. I would like to compare her condition to that of my patient. All manner of numerous, irrational rumours abound. Whether caused by witch or wizardry or the unearthing of desiccated bones, there is no consensus with regards to the cause.

Strangely, no blame has fallen on the hermit-woman known variously as Mukade-wiiyas, which translates as black meat, or Weetikowim-O'daanisi-kwem, the Wiindigo's daughter. She's always been wiindigo, they say.

 She is a mystery I intend to solve.

I have prevailed upon Aabitiba, despite his own grave misgiving and superstitious trepidation, to lead to me to her remote cabin, at a distance from the sites where most of the rest of the tribe have chosen to congregate on the edges of the lake. On the other side of the Jiibay River, which feeds into the lake. Much like the witch woman Marsh insisted we visit, I believe this woman has been ostracized. Not even her own uncle, Goshkǫ, will visit her.

But that is an expedition for another day.

When Aabitiba rushed in, breathless from running to inform him of the accident, Marsh's anger was unseemly. If you could have seen his reaction James, it would have shocked you. I'm certain that, had you known the nature of this man's character, you would not have recommended me to his company. As luck would have it, I happened to be in Marsh's tent when the news of the accident reached him. Upon learning of the disaster, his face turned red with rage, his brows furrowed, and his face contorted into such an expression, he scarcely looked human. I have rarely seen such a fervour of emotions. The glass out of which he'd been drinking a Rusty Bourbon shattered in his hand from the pressure of his grip, the shards imbedding themselves into his flesh. Blood dripped down his forearm. He scarcely seemed to notice his injuries as he wiped up the blood with a crisp white towel, staining it a bright crimson as he gave instructions for the men with the worst injuries to be sent to Sterling, and those who could be patched up, given enough time to recuperate so they could continue to work after they healed.

His emotion was not on account of the safety of his people, but on account of "falling behind," and his near-obsessive fear of letting "that damned Drinker Cope get the best of him!"

He asked Aabitiba to recruit more local tribesmen to replace the ones who have fallen lame, and when he learned that this was not likely because the Indians feared falling ill to this wiindigo condition, and that two in his company had already quit out of fear, his fists clenched and the wounds that had in the interim, clotted and begun to close, reopened and bled out onto the carpeted interior of his tent; it was most disturbing to behold. I thought he would throw himself down on the floor, like a child throwing a tantrum, but instead, his face slowly returned to its normal shade, from purple, to red, to beige. He unclenched his fists, and the flow of blood slowed, but continued to drip, soaked up greedily by the Persian rug at his feet.

"Fine, I'll bring in men from Sterling. It will be a delay of some weeks at least, if not more. With so many men injured or deserted, all that will be left is a skeleton crew while I go to retrieve more men. Brennen," he said to one of his more favoured students from Yale who'd also agreed to undertake the expedition, "I will leave you in charge in my absence."

Then, knowing that I had at first trained as a physician, and earned my Bachelor of Medicine and Surgery before turning to the field of Psychology, Marsh also gave me instruction: "Harker, tend to the injured men. I implore you to do your best to cure this sickness. We must dispel these superstitious delusions."

It is lucky that I happened to be on hand. I have gone from one patient, to four. I spent the rest of the day and night tending to the injured, setting broken bones, creating casts, slings, bandages, and administering drugs to relieve suffering. Five men in all were severely injured, and will need months to recuperate. One man was sent home, another sent to Sterling for surgeons more capable than I, and three remain to recuperate. Marsh is out seven men in total—together with those who have deserted.

I begin to suspect both Marsh and Cope, and their motivation for their archeological research. I think their spirit of discovery has less to do with the science, and more to do with a competitive relation to each other. They are driven to out-do each other at all costs; a sort of brother-in-arms rivalry, and each, it seems, would rather see himself destroyed, than the other succeed. I do not know where this enmity between the two men began, but I have little hope that this endeavour of theirs will end well, even if I do owe my own presence here, to their battle, raising as they have, the spectre of the wiindigo.

Always yours, and in good faith,

Harker Lockwood

Blood Money

"Stand here." Peter said.

Church yawned and cooperated. It was late, and he was too tired to object. Besides, he'd been bribed with a few mouthfuls of C-Six, and the promise of an all-you-can-eat buffet, so he stood where he had been instructed. Peter slinked away and hid in his Cutlass, waiting up the street a block away. Church didn't know what kind of scam this was, but he had learned that sometimes it was better not to ask.

"Shut up, and do as you're told." Peter said. "Now a man is going to pull up and roll down his window."

"What man?" Church asked.

"You don't need to know that," Peter told him.

"Okay." Church shrugged.

"Good. Now what do you say when he rolls down his window?"

"I ask him for money?"

"Right. Good. He'll ask you to get into his car, and then I want you to get in."

"Then what-do-I-do?" Church asked, the syllables rolling out of his mouth like a single word.

"Then you don't do anything. You sit there and wait until I come and get you," Peter said.

"All-right," Church said, shuffling his feet and squinting one eye as his father retreated to his Cutlass, leaving him alone on the street.

The street lamps are spaced widely apart in this neighbourhood and most of them flicker or don't work. The ones that do leave scattered pools of light collecting on the pavement beneath them.

He counts the streetlights and watches bugs swirl around under each of the lamps, mashing their bodies into the light, trying to commit suicide. Immolation by fire. But the protective layer of glass around the bulbs protects them from their own death.

Church slump his shoulders, but straightens again when a car pulls up. A man rolls down the window but leaves the engine running, and the bugs swoop around in front of the headlights. Church knows he isn't supposed to get into the car unless the engine is turned off.

"Do you want to go for a ride?" The man in the car asks him and smiles.

"Do you have any money?" Church asks, sticking to the script. The man's smile gets wider and he slides over from the driver's seat and pushes the passenger side door open. "Get in."

"Turn off your engine," Church tells him. He waits until the man turns the key back in the ignition before climbing into the passenger's seat, his butt sliding over the leather seats of the interior. Church slams the car door closed behind him with too much force and winces at the sound it makes. He isn't used to a car door that you don't have to slam hard in order for it to close.

"We'll do this here then?" the man asks.

"What about the money?" Church asks, unsure what is supposed to happen next. His stomach feels weird, and for once he isn't hungry. No that isn't true. He is still hungry, but the hunger was being overtaken by a fluttering in his stomach, like the fluttering of the moth's wings, beating themselves against the glass in their haste to get to the light. A creeping suspicion begins to grow, but he quickly squashes it. Peter might be a deadbeat, but he couldn't be that awful.

"We'll get to that later," the man says, picking up Church's hand and placing it on the brown thigh of his pant leg. Church's suspicions are confirmed. The frenzy in his stomach drops, like all the moths have died mid-flight. He knows what kind of scam Peter is running, and it makes him feel suddenly numb. He hadn't thought his father was capable of this. There must be some other angle to this. Peter wouldn't do this—would he?

Church leaves his hand where the man has placed it but finds that he is unable to move—all the muscles have seized up. The man makes a small groaning sound in the back of his throat. "Rub it a little bit," he moans as he lifts his hips slightly off of the seat. Church moves his hand in incremental circular movements on the brown surface of the cloth, feeling trapped. A moth has somehow managed to slip past the glass, and the beautiful light that had irresistibly drawn it in, has now lit its gossamer wings on fire, as they continue to beat the air, struggling uselessly to get closer to the burning light as its wings slowly blacken to ash.

The man rests his arm on the back of the seat, hand resting on the back of the head rest as he unzips the metal fly of his trousers and sticks Church's hand into the opening so that it rests on his underwear. Then he leans back and closes his eyes. Peter said that he would, "come and get him," but when would that be? Is this really the sort of scam his father had intended?

Church's hand continued its incremental movements. His eyes darted back and forth, looking for some escape. He couldn't go through with this, he decided. He was going to have to start running. This is when Peter snatched the driver's side door wide open and the man jolted upright, his eyes snapping open in terror.

"Fucking pervert!" Peter screams, lifts the man out of the car by his collar and begins slamming him against the hood of the car, yelling. "I'm going to kill you. I'm going to fucking kill you!" The man is sobbing, covering his face with his hands, and Church watches as the blood drips down the windshield from where part of his face had connected with the vehicle. The man reaches into his back pocket, takes out his wallet and flaps it in Peter's face. "I don't want your money!" his father says disgusted, his face turning red and spittle flying from his mouth.

"Take it!" the man says, offering Peter the wad of bills and trying to get back into his car. Peter knocks the money out of his hand, grabs him again, and brings his knee up into the man's groin, punching him in the face while he is doubled over, then kicking him in the ribs when he's on the ground. The thing about his father is that even though he is old, he is far from weak. A lifetime of training had left his withered muscles wiry and strong. Throughout the beating, he hadn't even dropped the hand-rolled Heller decorating one corner of his lips, though his face was now splattered with droplets of blood.

Church's paralysis finally seems to lift, and he snatches the car door open and runs, the splotches of light from the street lamps disappearing under his feet like the dotted lines on the pavement. He is crying without making a sound, the tears welling up in his eyes and silently sliding down his face.

Church climbs into his father's Cutlass and waits, wiping the moisture from his face so Peter won't see that he was crying. He watches in the driver's side mirror as his father steadily marches towards the car, his face set like a stone. Peter opens the car door. He is holding a wad of cash that he has picked up from off of the ground. He doesn't say anything to his son as he starts the car and they drive off. The money also has a few spatters of blood.

They don't speak to each other on the way home. The next day, Peter takes him to an all-you-can-eat buffet—as promised. Peter pays the bill with the blood-splattered money that has now dried to a brown crustiness. It would soon flake off. Good as new.

The Poker Game

As they ate dinner, Church studied the gouged and marred
surface of the table. Spirals and circular growth rings marked
the life of the tree that was now a slab of wood six inches thick,
and six feet long. He had forgotten which ancestor populating
the landscape of his grandmother's stories, had hewn the log
where they now ate their evening meals.

He searched the knot-work for bloodstains, as the surface often
doubled as both a dining room table and a food preparation
station. But even though he could find no trace, as the surface
had been thoroughly scoured, the wood still remembered. It
soaked up a bit of everything it touched, and every moment of
its life was recorded in the fibre of its flesh. All you needed to
read this history was the knowledge that would let you decipher
it. Like the 1's and 0's that made up the genetic code, it was a
map, not only of how its body was made, but also of what had
happened to it during its long existence.

One night, Peter had been celebrating.

Peter was always more unpredictable when he was in a good
mood, expecting everyone else to be happy too, and angry when
they didn't share his humour. Day's Daughter, Mukade-wiiyas
and Marie had gone out to Ghost Lake, and left Church to
spend time "bonding" with his father, and as Day said, "learning
how to be human."

"I don't know how you can stand that bastard," Inri told Day, lip
curled.

"Never-mind," his grandmother said, "Church is lucky to have
any kind of father, even a miserable old deadbeat like him. None
of us were given the same chance. He needs to learn how to be
human, and we certainly can't be any kind of example for him."

Inri chortled, an exhalation of breath somewhere between a laugh and a snort, and rolled his eyes. They'd already been through this argument many times. Church deserved to spend time with his father.

Church and Peter's time together often entailed a deck of cards, and a bottle of whiskey. Other times it entailed some kind of scam where the skinny arms and small wrists of an adolescent were useful, or as a cover story in case things turned sour. Church had come to enjoy the burning sensation of whiskey as it slid down his throat—and he had become quite good dealing cards.

Peter invited some of his buddies over to play poker. Church played a few rounds, hoarding all the cigarettes they used in place of poker chips. Squirreling away smokes for later like a chipmunk collecting for the winter. When they switched to using money, Church wasn't allowed to play and he'd have to be the dealer. He paid close attention to the elaborate system of scratches and coughs that made up Peter's early warning system, their own complex language of signs telling Peter when to raise, bluff, fold, or ante higher.

After a night of drinking more bottles of C-Six than was healthy, one of Peter's buddies became irritated over losing, and shoved Church, pushed him hard, and he landed awkwardly on a fallen-over chair leg. He felt something *snap*.

"Deal the cards," Peter said. "Stop being such a whimp."

Through the haze of cigar smoke, Church drank more C-Six hoping to dull the pain. He dispensed the cards gingerly, trying to use his fingers to fling out the cards, and winced every time he jostled his sore arm.

"What a crybaby," Peter said, and his friends laughed.

After Peter had passed out, and his drinking buddies had all gone home, Church used his good arm like a sling and considered walking to the hospital, but decided against it. Wiindigo did not go to the doctor. He could just imagine how that conversation would go.

"How'd you break your arm son?" the doctor would ask.

"I fell," he'd say.

"Oh yeah? And where'd you get the black eye?"

What was this anyway—an interrogation—Church would wonder. Was he a patient, or a criminal?

His eye had already swollen shut so he could barely see anything out of his right eye. He wouldn't be joining the rest of his family at their cabin on-reserve until the bruises faded. Peter would have to make up some excuse for the broken arm.

To be fair, Peter didn't usually hit him in the face—black eyes were too hard to conceal—and his friend hadn't meant to break his arm; that had just been an accident. But he would be in trouble if he went to a hospital. Social services could begin asking questions, and that was something Church didn't want to happen. His mother was insane and incapable of looking after him, his grandmother was disabled, and Mukade-wiiyas was ancient.

So Church sat and waited for Peter to wake up so he could re-set the bone. They cleared a spot for him to lie down on the kitchen table and prepared for the procedure. Peter tied him down so he couldn't struggle, and they took turns hauling on a bottle of C-Six and smoking Heller's. Peter was being uncharacteristically nice, talking to him gently, and offering him all the cigarettes he could smoke.

Peter glanced back and forth between Church's arm and a medical textbook he'd managed to find somewhere amongst all the cookbooks on their shelves. Peter stuck a cherry branch into his mouth so he'd have something to bite down on. Church had a high threshold for pain, but it hurt so much, he didn't remember when he passed out, only the sound of the branch, *snapping*.

Darkness.

Empty darkness, free of stars. Darkness like the space deep inside him where all his hunger stayed. A darkness free of pain, but a darkness also free of hunger.

Darkness.

Then hunger.

Darkness.

Hunger.

Then pain. Light. He was hungry. His eyelids cracked open. His arm was held in a sling resting on top of his chest. The bone had been set. The throbbing ache in his arm was matched by the familiar hunger in his solar plexus. Like two friends, one old and one new. The pain and hunger welcoming him back to consciousness. Yep, he was still alive.

He didn't think that it hurt this much to be dead.

Peter had dozed off on the sofa near the bookshelves.

Church was still lying on the slab of wood that doubled as a food preparation surface. A drop of water fell from the ceiling and splattered against his forehead. His good hand found the bottle of C-Six at his side, and a package of his mother's menthol cigarettes. He took first a careful swig of the whiskey, and then fumbled to light one of the menthols, drawing in the minty flavour. They had eaten countless meals at this table. This was the place where their wiindigo family ate almost every meal. Breakfast, lunch, and dinner. It was stained with the effluent of countless meals; blood, bone, grease and gristle, white wine & vinegar, and now also infinitesimal traces of his own blood which had soaked into the grain of the wood, new 1's and 0's to add to the make-up of the table. Heavier and weightier with the years, it seemed to grow more and more tangible, even as they ate far more than they should have been able, and yet their appetites remained insatiable.

His eyelids closed and he dozed off again—despite the pain— thanks to a few more swigs of C-Six. This time, his sleep was not dreamless. Images flickered across the black screen of his unconscious:

"What's so great about these bones?" the man with the blotchy pigmentation of a half-breed asked, acting as interpreter and relaying the question in English, translating the words of the old chief Mookman.

Rather than respond directly, Drinker reached into his mouth and slowly removed his false teeth, holding the rows of perfectly glistening bicuspids up to light like Hamlet holding up the skull of Yorick, so that the teeth glistened in the light from Mookman's fire, grinning like a court-jester's smile, grinning like a skull, because underneath the soft tissues, even humans are just a pile of bones and teeth, because they were the last to rot and decay, and therefore also the most likely to become preserved, encased in mud, and slowly replaced by minerals as fossilized rock, unlike the softer tissues, which are so quick to decay.

Unfortunately, Drinker had a sweet-tooth, and liked to drink his Congou—his English Breakfast tea—with four, count them, four lumps of sugar, which he knew, had prematurely rotted the teeth from his head, and had caused him such pain, that he had gotten roaring drunk one night and had them all removed, ripped out of his jaw, one by one, with plyers so that they could never trouble him again—his skull would now be a toothless skull, unless he was buried with the false teeth left intact inside his head.

He had never been willing to give up his vices, his beautiful bone china, and his sweet Lady Grey—just the thought made his eyelids flutter—evaporating swirls of citrus bergamot mist wafting on an updraft in the play of light angling through his window. Drinker had even taken to growing, cultivating and pruning his very own Camellia Sinensis Assamica in one corner of his cabin so he could prepare his own tea, keeping the small plant well pruned like an ornately trimmed bonsai. He'd also been trying some of the indigenous varieties of tea—the moss tea that seemed to be so popular amongst some of the Ojibwe tribesmen. It tasted like nothing to him, like dust, but with an earthiness that he found too raw, but which he still insisted on drinking, in order to get a better sense of the land. The place where he sought to recover his greatest finds, retrieving from the dark earth his treasures; undiscovered, undocumented, and previously thought to be fantastical creatures, never before been imagined to actually have walked the earth.

Drinker removed his teeth and briefly resisted the urge, before saying; "Alas, poor Yorick! I knew him." Drinker knew it was a melodramatic gesture, and under normal circumstances, in poor taste, but he knew, that these Ojibwe were unlikely to have come across many white men, let alone white men with false teeth. They were suitably impressed, one of Mookman's advisors even let out a sharp gasp in shock—possibly believing his act one of magic, a show of power, rather than the mundane action that it was.

"There is power in bones," Drinker began, allowing time for his half-breed translator to relate his words to the old Chief named Mookman, who true to his name, seemed sharp as a knife. Mookman's eyes were bright, taking in the appearance of Drinker's companions calmly, and noting every detail of their exchange. "There is power in bones," Drinker said again, "history, spectacle, knowledge, science! These are things that will, I believe, catch the imagination of the Dominion, and you, and your people are sitting on a gold mine of powerful knowledge. The bones may not be of interest to you, but it might be of interest to those White men in the cities and universities, and those with enough influence to sway the hearts and minds of those in political positions, to safe-guard access to the bones, if not your gold, or your timber, or your other resources, which you fear are threatened—the extraction of which has been causing you some heart-ache already, you've told me this yourself—the intelligent men in the white man's schools and universities—they won't allow their access to this historical knowledge, these paleontological discoveries, to be damaged or put at risk—where these bones are discovered, your lands should be safe—for fear of damaging these bones— if not for the well-being of you or your people. Gold, timber— this is a vast new country and these can be found in other places, but the bones of these monsters? They have been found in few and far-between places, and they are more valuable, because they are rare."

Mookman nods his head in understanding, as his translator recites Drinker's words. Mookman had not been one of those to gasp when Drinker had removed his teeth, but he had listened carefully to his advisors, and to the translation of Drinker's words.

"I believe you speak wisely, in your own interests, and from your own heart. I will allow you to dig up our bones—on the condition that you do not disturb certain sites, or burial grounds for our dead. The Burnt Grounds are off-limits to your people, as are the spawning grounds, the moose and elk habitat, everywhere Ghost Lake Anishinaabe have taken up residence as their homes and sites for camp, their gardens and their traplines must remain undisturbed. All other lands are open to your men's exploration and digging crews, although I suggest you look here," and Mookman pointed, dropping a wrinkled finger onto Drinker's yellowed map, landing on the base of the peninsula that stuck out into the lake. "Here is where you will find most of the numsookan-okaanag that you seek."

Church woke from his strange dream.

It had felt like he had been watching the flickering from an ancient, 16mm movie projector. It had felt like the dream had, had him, rather than him being the one to have the dream. He was merely carried along for the ride as a passenger, a passive witness to the unfolding of past events. At least, it seemed to be more than a dream; it flowed, not with the logic of a dream, but with the order of an actual event, one that had taken place, over a hundred years before he had even been born. Maybe Inri was right? The X-ray vision his uncle thought that he possessed was his gift, drawn down through the blood from that magician-warrior ancestor Kakiigan—or maybe he'd just been reading too many books about dinosaurs? Church shook his head, shaking off the ghosts, and the memory of voices of men who had been dead for close to a century.

July 21st 1872, Ghost Lake

Tragedy seems to befall this expedition at every turn. One of the injured men has fallen ill with fever, and I have stayed up all night with the sick man, tending to his needs. He continued to worsen, and I feared for his life. It got so bad, I sent for Goshko late in the night, willing to accept any help he could provide, even the folk cures and talismans of the medicine man. He prayed and sang his songs, wafting his acrid herbs over the sick man, while I administered 1mg of quinine on the hour, every hour, changed and sanitized the bandages from his scaffold injuries, and ensured that his room was properly ventilated to let in fresh air.

Around dawn his symptoms grew worse, and I gave him up for a dead-man, but as I was administering a dose of quinine, the first rays of dawn came through the window, causing the Cinchona extract to fluoresce and glow due to the peculiar nature of its chemical resonance, and the moment the light, and the dosage of quinine reached his lips, he seemed to deflate, his fever seemed to break, and he fell into a deeper, more restful sleep.

Both Goshko and I were exhausted and retired to our respective places of rest to sleep for a few hours, checking upon our patient periodically throughout the day. He seemed to be recovering, and we let ourselves relax, feeling that the man would now recover. But as the sun sank to the west, his symptoms rallied and grew worse. Goshko and I were again at his side, applying every medical trick we could think of, every prayer-song, talisman, and tincture. But it was all for naught. In the early hours past midnight, the man succumbed to his illness.

Despite doing everything we could, it was not enough.

There was a general sense of unease in the air, as the other workers soon learned of the man's death. Sadness, shock, subdued speech—and when it occurred—laughter was hushed. It was clear everyone was upset by the death. There were rumours that he, too, had come down with wiindigo sickness, that in his cannibalistic hunger, he had bit off and swallowed his own tongue, and then drowned, gurgling in his own blood. No matter how much Goshko and I protested, insisting that we had remained with the man throughout his sickness and that his death had been perfectly natural, the rumours persist, whipping up already heightened fears amongst the Ghost Lake Indians, and the workers in both encampments.

Marsh, surprisingly—in an act of revealing humanity—gave all of his workers the day off, allowing the dig site to remain fallow in honour of the man's passing. Cope's men worked throughout the day. Digging in the soil to unearth bones, just as we dug up the earth to inter those of the fallen worker.

August 3rd 1872, Ghost Lake,

Another man has fallen ill.

This time it is another case of wiindigo sickness, and this time, it has stricken a worker in Drinker's encampment. Upon making our landing on the peninsula, Drinker led us stone-faced to the appropriate lodge, where the man named Eniwek lay afflicted with this extraordinary malady. Drinker's manner was stiff, yet cordial, his mustache and goatee impeccably groomed, as if he were going to have his portrait captured in tintype.

I entered the wigwam alone to examine the patient. His symptoms are similar to that of Ogimaa's, who still remains chained to his bed, with no improvement or deterioration in his condition. Eniwek raves about his craving for human flesh, an unrelenting hunger that refuses to let him sleep. This despite the fact that when wholesome food is offered to him, he will not eat. "Bakaade, bakaade, bakaade. Nbakaade." He chants, over and over again, in an unrelenting loop. "Hungry, hungry, hungry. I'm so hungry." In both English, and in his own tongue: "Hungry, hungry, hungry. I'm so hungry." "Ngawaji. Ngawaji, apiji-nbakade."

It's enough to drive anyone to madness. After only a few minutes in his presence, I felt myself deranged. Some of the details of this new case are eerily similar— precisely the same in fact—and I would have believed that the details of Ogimaa's illness had somehow become known, were it not for the fact that I am certain that I am the only one aware of these details. And I have told no one.

The man claims the witch woman cursed him. He claims that the spirit of a Wiindigo came to him in a dream, and offered him human flesh to eat from a bowl made of ice. The details of the case are so alike, that I would have doubted Aabitiba's translation, if I hadn't picked up enough of the language, to get the general sense of Eniwek's words. I have had the man moved to

Drinker's own cabin; when I recommended that he be brought indoors, and isolated from the other workers, so they should not be subject to the influence of Eniwek's deranged mind, Drinker bravely volunteered his own lodgings.

I am exhausted from all my new patients—that damnable scaffolding disaster—I've been busy treating the ailments of the body; I am unable to make sense of this puzzle, this ailment of the mind. How can two men have the same dream? Even down to minute details! Is there some sort of physical or biological origin for this strange infirmity? There are too many unknown variables. And, as the saying goes, God—or in this case—the Devil, is in the detail.

"Consciousness is just a means of collecting the sorts of things we need to keep up with the business of dreaming. Our waking experiences are merely the sorts of material that can be stitched into the fabric of our dreams."

~Inri

Numsookan

Church stood on a deserted street, the light pooling in widely spaced puddles beneath the streetlights. He watched the bugs beating themselves against the glass, attracted by the light, trying to get closer to the electric flame, and their own death. Death by immolation. This time, Peter had brought a baseball bat with him in case anything went wrong. Church could see his father's brown Oldsmobile Cutlass parked in the shadows a block away.

A Crown Vic cruised down the street, slowing as it caught sight of Church. He stepped forward as the sedan eased to a stop at the curb in front of him. Church squinted nervously into the shadowy interior of the car, seeing three men, two in the front and one in the back. Church couldn't stop his gaze from straying to the brown Cutlass parked up the street, as if the sight of it could give him some idea what he was supposed to do.

The man in the passenger-side front seat rolled down his window and smiled, scrutinizing Church over the top of sunglasses, even though it was night. The man's skin was pale, his hair was long and lank, and the colour of burnt straw. Church noticed that his eyeteeth were pointed, as if they'd been filed down to an exquisite sharpness resembling fangs. Church gave his head a little shake. Maybe he was hallucinating? Madness ran in their family, maybe he was having trouble differentiating between what was real, and what was fantasy. Just like his Grandmother.

A feeling of stillness rolled off the man, a patience that drifted out of the car with the smoke from a flavoured cigarillo. And for some reason Church was reminded of the story Day's Daughter told, of monsters that came alongside the European settlers disguised as men. Church looked down at his fingernails and anxiously chipped at the faded black nail polish on his middle finger with his thumb. Maybe these men were some kind of Wiindigo?

Church felt like Little-Red-Riding-Hood confronted by three large wolves with three sets of teeth. Why, Grandmother, what big teeth you have! Except Church already knew that all the men who pulled over on this street were predators. What should he do? Peter was outnumbered. Again he looked towards the darkened Cutlass for guidance, but there was no advice forthcoming.

Burnt-straw caught his eye and the man's smile grew wider. Church felt as if he were falling into dark-blue pits, drowning in the endless depths of two deep wells. He recognized that look; the man looked hungry.

"My name is Hundsfordt," Burnt-straw said, as he stepped out, and held the car door open with a flourish, his coat falling open like a cape as he gestured for Church to get in. The tall compact driver is wearing a dark suit that looks too small, and a thin tie, he barely seems to fit into the car, there is a cigarillo perched between his lips. He has the same pale skin, but his hair is a pale cornflower cropped close to the skull. Church hesitated for a moment before sliding his butt across the leather seats. Hundsfordt climbed in behind him slamming the door. Church was now sandwiched between the two large men, the black-suited man in the driver's seat, Hundsfordt in the front-passenger seat, and a shadowy man in the back.

"I'd like to introduce you to Ox," Hundsfordt said, gesturing to the tough-looking chauffeur, "and Grundel," he said, gesturing to the man in the backseat. The three men smiled, light glinting off of their white teeth.

Involuntarily, Church heard the words from one of his grandmother's stories: ". . . to distract the creature—and pay attention now, this works for both men and women—Gaawiin had to satisfy the Wiindigo's hunger in other ways, instead of letting it eat her . . ."

Ox turned the key in the ignition, starting the car. He pulled away from the curb and they passed the darkened Cutlass, beams from the streetlights shifting across the interior of the car, shadows slanting as they cruised smoothly down the street. In the rearview mirror, Church could just see the flare of headlights roaring to life as they turned the corner at the end of the street.

Church wasn't alone. Peter would be following at a safe distance. He had to keep reminding himself of this fact to remain calm as the Crown Vic haunted empty streets, prowling the ugly industrial park. Where were they going? Church wondered. This was a bad idea. Bad, bad, bad, bad idea. This was Peter's worste scam ever. Church hadn't believed, after the last time, he would have been willing to try pulling it off again. Bad, bad, bad, bad idea. There were so many ways for this scheme to go wrong.

Hundsfordt handed him a stainless steel thermos and indicated that he was to drink. The way the Hound looked at him, Church knew he wasn't really being given a choice. He could drink from the thermos, or they would hold his jaw open while they poured the liquid down his throat. The threat was real, and Church had no doubt Hundsfordt would follow through with it. Church drank.

He didn't know what he had been expecting, alcohol possibly, certainly something potent, or something that would taste unpleasant, but whatever the contents of the thermos, it tasted like water. Water, with the slight hint of something else. Certainly it wasn't water. Earthy and rich tasting, like water straight from the spring, tasting of rocks and the irony taste of minerals, the "water" had reddish tinge, like punch, but only a slight sweetness. It was refreshing and ice, ice cold. It actually tasted quite pleasant. After swallowing only a few small mouthfuls Church handed the thermos back to the Hound—as he continued to think of the man—and he seemed satisfied.

"Now then." Hundsfordt said, "Now that the formalities have been observed, we can get on with our business. We were hoping to get the chance to speak with you—and now here you are. Isn't that a coincidence?"

"What do mean?" Church asked. "Why would you want to talk to me?"

"Nous atteindrons en fait le contraire," Hundsfordt said, speaking in French. Church had never paid much attention in French class, but he understood the phrase to mean something along the lines of, 'on the contrary.' He hadn't yet been able to place the man's accent; he at times sounded Eastern European, but now he spoke French. He was certainly European.

"Our employers at Magnon Incorporated have requested that we speak to your family regarding your ownership of several hectares of land lying adjacent to a certain lake. Unfortunately, neither of your grandmothers have been willing to discuss the matter, and so then we hit upon the idea that you might be more amenable to hearing us out."

"Property?" Church asked. They didn't own any land, only the cabin on- reserve and their house in Sterling. How would they have come to own land, let alone several hectares of land? "My family doesn't own any property."

The three men exchanged glances with each other, Ox looking first towards 'Hundsfordt' and then raising his eyes to the rear-view mirror to make eye contact with 'Grundel.' Church hadn't yet had a good look at Grundel, who was sitting in the back seat. He turned and caught a glimpse of the hulking shape, cornflower hair cropped short in a military style buzz-cut, like an exact replica of the man who sat in the driver's seat. They must have been brothers, if not twins. In fact, all three of the men had an unsettling resemblance.

"I see, well, let me be the first to assure you that your great-grandmother, Bah-goan-nah-gee-zhig," Hundsfordt read, slowly pronouncing his great-grandmother's name from a sheet of paper he had produced from somewhere about his person, "was the proud owner of thirteen hectares of rocky, swampy, and desolate land that lies just north-west of the Ghost Lake reserve."

"Thirteen hectares?" Church said. He couldn't believe it. "I don't believe it." Why would Mukade-wiiyas own so much property? Where would she have come up with enough money to buy that much land? For as long as Church could remember, they'd been scraping by, struggling to put food on the table, to pay their bills, and unable to afford basic repairs, like the front steps or their leaky kitchen roof.

"A certain Mr. Harker Lockwood began buying up the land near your reserve around the turn of the century, and for some inexplicable reason, when he died he deeded all that land to Bah-goan-nah-gee-zhig, and to your family."

Could this be true? Church wondered. Who was this Mr. Lockwood? Why would he have deeded so much land to Mukade-wiiyas? Why would these Magnon goons lie? What did they have to gain? And why did Magnon want the land so badly?

"Doesn't it strike you as odd, that this Bah-goan-nah-gee-zhig has the same name as one of your grandmothers, Church? We managed to dig up her birth certificate, and the date seems to indicate that she would have lived to quite a ripe old age, but it could not conceivably have been this same Bah-goan-nah-gee-zhig to whom Lockwood deeded the land. As with many families, I'm sure the name has been passed down, from mother to daughter for generations—maybe even centuries! But nevertheless the land has now fallen to you. Since Day is mentally . . . indisposed, you are now, or soon will be, the legal executor of her estate."

"You are the most-likely future owner of this property. Should anything happen to your elders you would stand to inherit this sizable estate. Which is why my associates and I have whisked you off the streets to broker a deal."

Church scrunched his eyebrows together. He didn't like the way Hundsfordt had said, "Should anything happen to your elders." It sounded like a threat. Real or imagined, he didn't like it at all.

"What kind of a deal?" Church asked. "If my grandmothers didn't want to speak to you, it was probably because they don't want to sell. Why do you want to talk to me?"

"Sometimes our clients can be irascible, which is why we have been hired to try to convince your family to change their minds. Your grandmothers wouldn't even listen to our offer. So we thought we would make our offer to you, and then you could be our emissary to your stubborn guardians." Hundsfordt smiled again, showing off his pearlescent fangs. "We are willing to pay half-and-again the current market value for the purchase of your land."

"Why does 'your employer' want to buy the land so badly? What's so great about this thirteen hectares? 'Rocky,' 'swampy,' and 'desolate' as you've described it. It's not exactly prime real estate. So why do they want it?" Church's thoughts had gone to the dinosaur bones littering their reserve—an archeologist's gold mine. Day's Daughter had told him the story of two paleontologists who had once taken an interest in the bones, and it had only brought misfortune. These men didn't seem like paleontologists.

Hundfordt stared at him, the twin pools of his eyes turning a dead steely grey in the darkness, evenly assessing him. "You know, you're very bright for a boy of your age. What are you, thirteen? Fourteen?"

Church stared back into Hundfordt's eyes, unwilling to answer the question. Something Inri had once told him came back to him: "When you look into the darkness, the darkness looks back into you." One of his endless snippets of wisdom. And also something from his father: "Never give out more information than you have to." Peter had once said, "Always keep your lies as simple as possible, the less information you give out, the better. Let them draw their own conclusions." He'd been talking about how to pull a scam on an insurance company at the time, but the advice still seemed to apply.

When Church didn't flinch from Hundsfordt's gaze, or even appear to be intimidated, Hundsfordt frowned. "There's something very different about you," he said, tapping the lower incisors on his jaw with a fingernail. "But I haven't quite been able to figure out what that is. I feel like I'm missing something—and I don't like it. I don't often overlook details. That is, after all, what we've been hired to do: take care of the details." The darker-haired man looked over at his companions, and then peered pensively out the windows. "Ah, never mind. We've almost arrived, and then we can deliver our message."

The Crown Vic came to halt and Church sat up straighter, stretching out his neck to see where they'd brought him. In the strange hallways of the conversation they'd explored, Church had forgotten all about his father. He couldn't see the headlights of the Peter's Cutlass anywhere. Maybe he'd lost sight of them? Apparently they had only been driving aimlessly, and had now come around to the same deserted stretch of road where they'd first found him.

"What message?" Church asked feeling suddenly less hungry. Less hungry was not a feeling that he was used to feeling. All three men turned, and were looking at him. These men might not be wiindigo, but Church also knew hunger when he saw it, and these three men were hungry. Hundsfordt picked up Church's right hand and began stroking his palm with his fingers, Grundel sitting in the backseat began nuzzling at the side of his neck, he could feel the un-shaved stubble tickling him like the blades on an electric razor, Ox had picked up his arm and was rubbing his cheek rhythmically against his forearm. Like a cat rubbing itself against his leg and purring.

They smelled funny. Underneath the smell of anise and cloves, tobacco and labdanum; there the scent of something unfamiliar, something slightly sickly-sweet, like fallen leaves left to mouldering. Church wasn't sure what it was, but they didn't smell like other people, they smelled like their own sort of creature, with their own sort of musk. The heady smell of his mice's cage. The scent became overwhelming, crowding his senses.

Church gasped, a sharp intake of breath as he felt the puncture of filed-down teeth break the skin at his wrist. The pain was similar to that of an injection, when the hypodermic needle slides in, but then his whole arm went numb, and he couldn't feel the pain, only a pressure on his veins, and a drawing and spreading out from the numbness. Almost simultaneously he felt the same pain, pressure and numbness at his elbow and then at his neck, twin hypodermic pin-picks puncturing the soft tender flesh on the under-belly of his elbow, twin hypodermic pinpricks puncturing the vein just above his collar bone in the alcove between his shoulder and neck. There was a reeling, falling, pleasantly drunken spinning sensation as wounds erupted on his body like the stigmata of Christ nailed to the cross. Church could feel his blood slowly being drained away, and the numbness faded as the mouths became more insistent and the drawing became painful; he felt like an anatomical drawing done in hues of blue and red, an ache running through all his veins, from his arms and legs, down through his thighs, to the veins in his finger tips and at his temples, he could feel every tendril, curly-cue and interstice of ventricle, a blooming dendric proliferation of pain, in and out from his heart, pulmonary blue as he inhaled, pumping red as he exhaled. Their Adam's apples rose and fell as they drank—drinking from him like fat, pale leeches letting the bad blood from his veins.

Church cried out and tried to sit up, but three sets of arms held him down like iron bands. They made wet sucking-suction sounds as they drank. Church felt increasingly light-headed, and he wondered how much blood there was in a human body? How many pints of blood could he afford to lose? How long before lost consciousness?

His father ripped the passengers' side door open, almost
breaking the door off of its hinges, baseball bat held firmly in
his grip, the veins on his forearms thrown out into relief by
the rolled up cuffs of his shirt, and showing off the numbers
tattooed on his left arm. AW7906. Peter's face was red, his jaw
was clenched tight, and his eyes had bugged out slightly. The
brown spots at the edges of his vision finally coalesced, and for a
moment Church lost consciousness with the image of his father,
standing frozen in fury by the tableau of his teenaged son being
mauled by three strangers. Sensation returned to him with slow
slurping sounds as Ox, Hundsfordt and Grundel continued to
drink; the sound of rubber boots suctioning through mud.

"What are you doing to my son?" Peter shouted angrily.

"You owe us some money," Ox said. Church could hear what
was happening around him, but he couldn't see anything. His
vision had shrunk to a thin horizon line as his eyelids slid shut.
Why wasn't Peter attacking the men with his baseball bat?

"But I still have time!" Peter said.

"Your time just ran out." Grundel said.

"Give me more time," Peter demanded.

"We already gave you time," Hundsfordt said. Church struggled
through his dim, garbled consciousness, trying to make sense
of this conversation, but it wouldn't seem to fit together, like
a jumbled crossword puzzle, the words didn't make sense. Did
Peter owe them money? What was going on? Was he dreaming?

When he opened his eyes again, he didn't seem to have the
strength to move, all he could do was watch the world through
heavy-lidded eyes. Drool leaked from his mouth to pool under
his face resting on the leather seat.

The door had been left ajar, and from his sideways position, Church had a front seat view of the events as they unfolded. Peter was surrounded by the three vampires, and swinging his baseball bat wildly. Every time one of the men got too close, Peter would take a swipe at them, and the other two would leap forward to take advantage of his exposed flank and he'd have to swing around to face his other two attackers. Hundsfordt moved in and grabbed Peter from behind, one hand holding him across the chest, the other hand pulling his forehead back to expose his neck. The ash-haired man moved quickly. There was a flash of white, Church barely saw what had done the damage but he was pretty sure that it had been one thumb-nail grown unusually long and impossibly razor-sharp.

A ragged, red line appeared written across Peter's pale throat. He tried to swallow, but instead, blood spurted out like when you press your thumb over top of the nozzle on a garden hose. The blood spurts out in exactly the same way that it does in horror movies, and Church thinks oh that's soo fake, except this time, it is real. He can't help replaying the scene from the Addams Family Values inside his head; the scene where Wednesday and Pugsley are performing an abridged sword-fighting scene from Hamlet in a school play:

Wednesday: How all occasions do inform me and spur my dull revenge. O, from this time forth, my thoughts be bloody or nothing worth. If I must strike you dead I will.

Pugsley: [slashes Wednesday's left wrist; blood sprays out] A hit! A very palpable hit!

[Wednesday cuts off Pugsley's arm, Pugsley slashes her throat; there is lots of blood spraying everywhere, getting the front rows]

Wednesday: O, Proud Death. What feast is toward in thine eternal cell?

[drops both swords and falls to her knees]

Wednesday: Sweet oblivion, open your arms!

[choking and gasping for breath, collapses, and dies]

[the audience sits aghast in stunned silence, covered with blood while the Addams give a standing ovation]

Gomez: Bravo!

Morticia: Bravo!

Gomez: Bravo! Bravo!

The front of Peter's white dress-shirt, the cuffs rolled up, is drenched in blood. Hundsfordt must have hit an artery, because in seconds his face is a deathly shade of white. Peter falls to his knees, his hands reaching up to clutch at his throat. Number Five Church thought. The fifth person he'd seen die.

There is nothing but darkness for a few moments.

When he opens his eyes again, he finds himself looking at the lifeless body of his father, a heap of cloth and bones lying on the concrete. Ox and Grundel are lapping up the blood that has puddled in the street, and Hundsfordt is feeding from Peter's still-warm corpse.

Church climbs out of the Crown Vic, struggling not to pass out again. Shambling on wobbly legs, Church circles back around to hide behind the vehicle before taking off at a loping pace, running as fast as he can, which isn't very fast—more like a loping Zombie shuffle—than a run. He picks up speed as he hobbles along, the spots of pooled light from the streetlights disappearing under his feet as they had once before. Adrenaline and momentum lending themselves to his feet like a second wind.

When he was younger, Church used to be scared of the night, imagining some shadowy monster, racing closely behind him, so close that he could feel the brush of its fingers grazing the back of his neck. It always made him feel slightly embarrassed; he was supposed to be a wiindigo. Monsters weren't supposed to get scared. Except this time, he knew for certain that the monsters were real, which is an entirely different kind of worse, from that formless fear.

Church looked back before dashing around a corner, but the monsters were still busy with his father. As soon as he was out of sight, he felt his burst of energy fade. He stumbled and almost fell. He was tired, so tired. He wanted to lie down on the pavement and go to asleep, but that was a bad idea. Like falling asleep in the snow. It might look soft and inviting, but the snow was cold. So he kept running, and running. Cutting down side streets, through backyards, and the narrow space between buildings, until the brown clouds started coalescing again, the dark motes circling in his vision like hungry vultures, and he knew that if he didn't slow down, sleep would come to him again, whether he liked it or not. He slowed his pace to a walk, but kept moving.

When he got home, Mukade-wiiyas, Day's Daughter and Marie were still away. They were out at Osedjig's cabin on Ghost Lake. Leaving him time to 'bond' with his father, and learn how to be human. He kept thinking: Peter's dead, Peter's dead. He had seen the blood spurting out of Peter's neck as if it were a scene in a Tarantino film, but he still couldn't get it to sink in. Peter was dead. It didn't make sense. Peter was too slippery to die.

"I was named after my Grandfather," Peter had once told him, "so that the Angel of Death might be fooled into believing that I'm already dead, that I've already been taken." Even Peter's name was a scam, meant to fool death.

Then, he thought, "Ding-dong, the Witch is dead. Which old Witch? The Wicked Witch! Ding Dong the Wicked Witch is Dead," replete with munchkins dancing in his head like smirking sugarplums. Church suspected that maybe he'd lost a lot of blood. He could be in shock. His thoughts had gone loopy. His brain was a contorting collision of strange thoughts. "Bugs-Bunny ran across the Star-Ship Enterprise," which was a line from a Bruce Coville novel. His reality mediated by fictional versions of reality. Allusions. Illusions. Maybe he watched too much T.V.? His mother's television set was always on, even when no one was home. Maybe his brain was fried like Sarah Connor in the Playground Scene of Terminator 2? Sarah Connor screams as she bursts into flames, in a process of almost instantaneous skeletalization she is burnt to ash, clutching to a chain-link fence, a truly Apocalyptic vision like the grainy black-and-white footage of an Atomic bomb test-detonation in Dreamland.

Church didn't fall asleep so much as lose consciousness. Jumbled images clogged his dreams in a chaotic flood of Cubism. The next morning Church's first thoughts were; I'm hung-over. Peter is dead. And then: maybe it was just a dream? Church came down the stairs, expecting to find the house empty.

The house was empty.

But this proved nothing. Peter often came and went as he pleased, even when he was supposed to be 'bonding' with his son. Still. If Peter was alive, he should have returned by now.

On the morning of the third day, he was woken up by an odd silence. Something was different. He had already given Peter up for dead, when he came downstairs to find the old man sitting at the kitchen table, reading a newspaper and drinking a beer. Marie's television set had been switched to off.

Maybe it had all just been a bad dream? Maybe Magnon's goons had drugged him? What had been in that thermos? Rohypnol—the rape drug—or maybe something more hallucinogenic? Certainly it hadn't been mineral water. They had been adamant that he drink.

After a certain point everything had grown so confused. And he had jumbled-up dreams of blood and violence, his wiindigo physiology reacting to the strange concoction of drugs that had been introduced to his system? But this explanation didn't seem adequate to explain what he had experienced. He'd never had dreams like that when he was high. Maybe he was just going crazy, and the madness gene was finally kicking in? Maybe he was losing touch with reality?

Whether madness or hallucination, Church was certain that he'd seen something happen that night. His mind must have formulated some sort of fantasy where the predators who cruised the streets in old Crown Vic's were actual predators, feasting on human blood.

As Church sat down to breakfast, Peter smiled and he could have sworn he saw a pair of sharp, gleaming teeth, glittering like the fangs of a vampire from any B-rated horror movie. But a moment later the hallucination cleared, and Peter was crunching away on a bowl of cereal. It was the fading echoes of the drug still leftover in his system, or maybe his overactive imagination. Peter was alive and whole and eating cereal. Sunlight was streaming in through the window, and the undead weren't supposed to be able to tolerate sunlight. So Peter couldn't be one of the undead either. Another nail in the coffin to the theory, which couldn't help springing unbidden to his mind, that Peter had died, and then been brought back to life amongst the ranks of the undead. The absolute normalcy of the moment squashed any such wild imaginings. Vampires weren't any more real than wiindigo. There was soil on Peter's shoulder.

Church made sure to take his anti-psychotics that morning. He'd been on thorazine since he'd made the mistake of confessing his belief, to the school nurse, that he was a cannibal. As it turned out he wasn't inhuman, the nurse had assured him. He was just crazy.

"You're not a cannibal Church, you just have a psychological disorder. These things happen to a lot of young people. It's a very normal medical condition that can be treated with anti-psychotic drugs to dissipate your delusions. It's also important to recognize when you're having a delusion, so you can differentiate between what is real and what isn't real."

He was sent to a psychiatrist. Day's Daughter had been terrified that they'd lock him up like Marie so they could study him, another case of Wiindigo Psychosis for them to write about in Medical Journals. But Day's hands were tied. Church had screwed up royally, and social services would get involved if he didn't see the psychiatrist. So he promised his grandmother to clean up his narrative, leaving out any mention of wiindigo. The psychiatrist listened to his edited confession and diagnosed him with schizophrenia. He was prescribed respiridone, an anti-psychotic drug that was supposed to control his "delusions." Most days he didn't bother taking his meds, but after what he had witnessed the other night, he thought that he had better start.

Jenna, the girl who always wore black, came up to Church during lunch.

He was sitting in his usual place on top of the stack of piled up folding tables, watching everyone as they ate. Jenna was one of the Goth kids at school who was willing to talk to him.

"Are you all right?" she asked, peering up at him through the sweep of raven coloured hair concealing her face.

"Yeah," Church said, not taking his eyes from the room-full of people eating their lunches like one beast with multiple mouths, chewing and swallowing, chewing and swallowing.

"My little brother is missing. No one has seen him since yesterday. The police think he ran away, but I don't think he did." Church's first thought was that Jenna's brother was dead, that the vampires had gotten to him, just like Peter. There were always predators out there ready to thin the herd. But then he remembered that his father wasn't dead, it had just been a delusion.

"You haven't seen him have you?" Jenna asked.

"No, I haven't seen him," Church said. His stomach grumbled and seemed to gnaw on itself, almost as if his body had started cannibalizing its own reserves of muscles and fat. "Maybe he'll turn up," Church said. "It'll be okay." But he didn't really believe it.

"I hope so," Jenna said, but she knew that it wasn't.

After school, Church and Jenna went over to Jason's Fort, a pimped out treehouse strung with Christmas lights, Sally-Anne furniture, and a banner of Sterling Martin, their school mascot. They smoked a joint, even though he wasn't supposed to because it could interact with his anti-psychotics. They watched, silent, and lost in their own worlds, as the light slowly drained from the sky and shadows infiltrated the fort. The blinking lights decorating the treehouse reminding him of another time, another place, and another ramshackle hangout, when everything in his life had changed.

Reclining in an old armchair, Church closed his eyes and began to dream. In his dream he saw three vampires sitting in a motel room having a discussion about him, discussing the nature of his blood. Its taste. Its consistency, its bouquet and bite.

". . . his blood tasted like... like . . . perfume," Hundsfordt was saying to Ox and Grundel who weren't really listening anymore as they lounged about their motel room. This was about the millionth time Hundsfordt had attempted to describe the taste of the young man's blood, which they had only too briefly tasted. They had decided to stay in town while they were still on retainer.

"His blood was like . . . like wine, with a cloying sweetness and cassis, like a baby's tears, crisp and pure... and with only a slight salinity . . . It was like nothing I've ever tasted."

"Then why did we let him get away?" Ox asked annoyed, looking up from a sculpture of Apoxyomenos in a Volume on Art history. The caption read:

A Roman marble copy after a bronze original by Lysippus in 330 B.C.

"Because," Hundsfordt said, "his blood is intoxicating. I don't think we could have handled it all at once, and besides . . . " Hhe pointed to the body propped up against one wall, "his father was distracting us." Peter's corpse lay on the floor like a sack of potatoes.

"He's not going to wake up for another three days." Grundel pointed out. "We're not going to get any answers from him any time soon. We'll have to wait."

"Who's going to go and bury him?" Hundsfordt asked. "He should be properly planted in the ground before his resurrection."

"There was something strange about his blood," Grundel commented. Grundel and Ox were identical twin brothers, like living mirrors of each other, differentiated only by Ox's preference for suits, and clove cigarettes. They were triplets actually, and Hundsfordt was their eldest brother, who often took the lead in any given scenario, by right of constant habit. Different in height, shape and colouring from his younger twins, Hundsfordt was their fraternal twin, though they had all shared the same birthing sack. They were blonde, where Hundsfordt was a darker ash.

"Yeah, he was . . . hungry," Ox said, at a loss for words to describe it.

"I'm hungry!" Grundel volunteered, perking up at the possibility of food.

"No, No. You don't understand," Hundsfordt said. "Ox is right. For a moment, I was afraid that the boy was going to eat me. Even though I was the one drinking his blood, it was like I was the one who was being consumed."

Grundel and Ox were now listening attentively to their older brother's words. They had felt the same thing, and were not sure what to make of it. Human blood had never tasted this good. This strange boy's blood was ten times better than the finest human blood they'd ever tasted. And they had tasted a lot. Simultaneously fat and delicate with subtley layered complexity and depth. A depth that drew them into it's richness, to the exclusion of all else, even as they drew the blood into their bodies. It was all consuming, intoxicating, enthralling. They grew drunk on his blood, and could easily forget themselves, following the slowing beat of his heart into death.

"Why don't we find him then?" Ox asked.

"Yes, let's find him," Grundel said. "I'm thirsty!"

"We will find him," Hundsfordt agreed. "But not yet. After all, we still have a job to do, now don't we?" He pointed at the shovels and said, "You two go start digging."

Church jerked awake, to find himself alone in the treehouse. Jenna had gone. The Christmas lights were blinking rhythmically in time with his heart. That had been an odd dream. It had felt so real. More like a vision of things that were actually happening, than the amorphous shapes and images that usually occupied his dreams. The lumped- together narratives, and cannibalized parts of his day.

Jenna's little brother was missing. Church hoped that nothing bad had happened to him. He debated sleeping in the treehouse, but it was already getting cold, and Church wanted to be there when Marie and Day's Daughter returned from Ghost Lake. They were supposed to arrive in the morning.

It wasn't the same without Mukade-wiiyas. Church had thought that she would always be around. Inri was rarely home these days, so Marie and Day's Daughter were all he had. Peter didn't really count.

When he got home, Peter was out, so Church had the house to himself. It seemed too quiet with Marie's television shut off. He flicked it on to have the company of light and sound. Then he fell asleep on Marie's ratty but comfortable sofa-chair, flashes from the shifting images on screen splaying themselves against the walls in the darkened room; blue-white, orange-red, blue-green. While he slept, he had violent dreams.

But they didn't feel like dreams. Again they felt too real to be mere dreams. They felt more like visions of something that would happen, or could happen, in the near future; or the way things had already happened in an alternate universe. Was it a warning of what could happen, or what already had? He had difficulty disentangling from this potential future, the paradox of seeing things that have not yet occurred, but might yet still come to pass:

Hundsfordt and his two triplet brothers, Ox and Grundel, stepped cautiously up the ramp at the back of the house. The boy was close. They could smell him. His scent was much stronger here. They could almost taste his blood on the air like a fine misting of the most exquisite par fume. A fume that that smelled as divine as it tasted. A subtle, almost molecular excitement of the air particles—the closer they came to the source of the disturbance, the more frenzied the agitation. It was so subtle, that had they not been actively searching for it, it might easily have gone undetected. But having tasted the blood, and catching a whiff, there was now no mistaking the strange quality it had.

The occasional figure could be seen in the windows, dark shadows against the squares of yellow light. Hundsfordt raised a hand, and all three of them advanced. They had ordered their thrall to leave the door unlocked.

They followed the flickering light and sound from a television, like a beacon of human habitation. They entered a large kitchen space where a woman sat in one corner staring at a TV screen and smoking a menthol cigarette. The unusual scent of her blood filled the room like rotting flowers over-riding the odours of tobacco and mint. Her blood was as miraculous as the boy's, if not more so. More heady with age and edelfaule, the noble rot, her blood had only deepened in flavour and complexity, with only a hint of acescence and a smoky caudalie that tasted of volcanic ash.

They moved quietly through the dark house like shadows themselves, decanting first from the immobile woman in the kitchen, who made no move, and said not a word of exclamation or protest as each of the brothers sank in their fangs, and began to drink. What had begun as one kind of mission, quickly became another.

As they drank, they became drunk. Their self-control dropped like a gauzy shroud, an insubstantial mask that merely hid but did not negate the truth that lay underneath. Like sharks driven into a feeding frenzy by a drop of blood in the water, once they had had a taste, they couldn't seem to hold back or stop themselves. They drank the woman dry, down to the slow beating of her heart, until it had stopped, and still they drank, and then like drunkards, they moved on from one room to the next, searching for more of the deciduous blood.

They found her in an antechamber as she came out of a front room which had once been a drawing room, but that had now been converted into a bedroom. Having somehow become alarmed, she came rolling out of the bedroom calling out to her daughter, "Marie! Marie!" A shotgun rested across the arms of her wheel chair as she turned the metal grips on the side of the wheels.

She stopped calling out, her voice dying mid-word as she saw the three hulking shapes coming towards her. Inexplicably—the glass globe on the ceiling exploded in a shower of sparks— plunging the hall into darkness, the shards of frosted glass raining down and crunching under their feet as she struggled to bring the muzzle of the shot-gun up to bear. She wasn't fast enough, and in the enclosed place, they were upon her before she could level the gun at head or heart, the barrel was forced down, and then ripped from her grasp—at least they tried to—but she wouldn't let go. She was abnormally strong. And so they let her have the gun, the barrel was too long and could do no damage in such close quarters if she could take no aim, held down so that it pointed at the ground. She gasped as they sank in their fangs, each to their own, choosing their preferred arteries, which they often did when they hunted together; Hundsfordt taking the right common carotid, Ox taking the left subclavian, and Grundel taking the right radial, or alternatively the left common carotid, right basilic, and left ulnar.

The older woman's blood tasted even more vital, and even more intoxicating, overwhelming them with its power, its tidal force. More like ice-wine than noble grapes, her blood was beyond late harvest, it had been left to freeze on the vine, thick with clots of lie, the sediments of a longer life in the cask. An oakiness of garrafeira. Invecchiato. The cruor was thick, with a mead-like consistency like molasses, drawn sluggishly from her ropey veins, more rendered syrup than sap. They glutted themselves on her blood, unable to stop themselves. Though in reality they did not even try. They were monsters after all, and this is what they did best. And they enjoyed it.

As in the nature of some dreams, Church 'watched' as a disembodied spirit, unable to halt or alter any of the events as they unfolded, and able only to witness. His dream self only became an actor in the drama, when the scene shifted to the moment when he found himself coming home, long after the triplets had left.

He suspected something was wrong when he walked up the ramp to the back door. The house was silent. He couldn't hear Marie's television, that constant low-level symphony droning on the air. When he turned the knob to the mudroom door (which was unlocked, setting off more alarm bells) he knew something was wrong.

He entered the kitchen and everything was in a disarray; recipes had been torn from the walls and scattered like multi-coloured confetti, a bookshelf had been knocked over spilling cookbooks onto the floor in gourmet slaughter. The table and chairs had been overturned, and Marie's TV had been smashed in, but it was still plugged in to the wall so it exuded a poisonous glow, and lit up a cloud of phosphorous dust like green fog.

Marie's twisted corpse lay amongst the rubble, pale now that she'd been robbed of her vital fluids; she was dry and desiccated like a mummy. He found Day in the hall, her wheelchair over-turned, one wheel spinning ever so slightly with the creak of the floorboards as his weight shifted. Day was as dry and desiccated as Marie. She was clutching fast to her shotgun, though not a single round had been ejected from the chamber. Not a single shot had been fired.

Church returned to the kitchen and sat in the only remaining chair still standing. It had somehow managed to escape being upended during the scuffle. The chair appeared miraculous. It was the only thing that seemed to have escaped unscathed, because everything else seemed different. Everything else seemed out of place. Nothing was where it belonged.

It felt like a war-zone; a bomb had been dropped and the soil would be radioactive for fifty years. No one would live here, because they would know people had been killed here, and maybe the walls still held an after-image of the violence that had once taken place. Burnt onto the walls like Hiroshima shadows. The real estate value would plummet in the murder-house. And he supposed that the house was now his. And so was 13 hectares of land.

Church sat amidst the carnage and prayed—who knows—maybe the tobacco would take his prayers with them? The smoke curled up around the ceiling, staining the drapes yellow, and curdling the paint on the walls.

It turned out monsters were real after all. But wasn't he a monster too? Wasn't he descended from a Wiindigo? If he wasn't so sure before, didn't the existence of vampires prove it now? He was going to find the monsters that had done this, and he was going to have his revenge, because he was a monster too. They didn't know what they were dealing with.

Church woke up from the dream—confusion of the dream-world reality blurring into the waking world. It had felt so real, but he found himself in the kitchen where he had fallen asleep in front of Marie's TV. There was no damage, no destruction—no bodies on the floor. Just the comforting glow of Marie's TV and the distant sound of Peter snoring in the upstairs guest bedroom. Everything was as it should be. Peter had come in while he slept, and Day and Marie would be home from the lake soon. There was no reason for him to be upset. There was nothing for him to be afraid of. Vampires were not real. Were they?

Cryptozoic, adj. **1.** In geology it refers to that part of the Precambrian time whose stratigraphic record reveals only sparse or primitive fossils. **2.** In zoology it means to live in a concealed or secluded place.

August 13th 1872, Ghost Lake,

"Harker, you must see this!" Marsh said, sticking his head through the flap of my tent, with a rare glint of enthusiasm in his eye. For as I'd come to know him over the course of the past four months, I could tell—Othniel was positively elated. "Join me at the excavation site!"

I quickly dressed, and met Marsh at the pit he'd been digging. The steep slopes like cliffs required scaffolding to descend, and for the workers to exhume their finds.

"Come see!" Marsh said upon seeing me. We descended the scaffolding to where most of the workers had abandoned their stations and were congregated around the newest discovery. Marsh swiped his hand across the stone, blowing and wiping away the dirt. Imbedded in the rock was the skeletal structure of what looked like an enormous prehistoric fish, its mouth evidently filled with razor sharp teeth, two inches long. They'd been diligently freeing the fish from its encasing of stone, chipping away at the rock with chisels to reveal the preserved bones, at least nine feet long, from head to tail, and they hadn't even yet finished revealing the whole length! It is a matter of some amazement, to both Marsh and his workers who have experience on many of these digs, as well as to those newly hired workers.

But what had Marsh most excited, was not just the size of the fish, but also the outline of a smaller skeletal structure, at least six feet long, the length of a man, imbedded backwards within the belly of the beast, which the larger monster had apparently swallowed whole, and which had undoubtedly led to its untimely death. Most likely it had then been washed up on the shore and buried under the layers of sediment, which had preserved it.

Marsh gave a cry of success, raising his arm in the air and laughing in excitement. He whooped, and threw his hat on the ground. I'd never seen him this joyous, and marveled at the change in demeanor, which I would not have thought possible given his gloomy character. His face was red and aglow with passion. This was what he lived for: the discovery, the honour of naming newly found creatures, and gaining credit for his efforts in his scientific and social circles.

And indeed, it is a marvelous find!

"The bastard was so greedy he bit off more than he could chew!" Marsh explained. "Look at the bugger! The animal was so voracious he swallowed his prey whole even though it killed him. It probably ruptured every organ in its body—the mindless glutton!"

It is, I have to admit, something spectacular to behold. I couldn't help but get swept up in the moment, running my hands over the fossilized bones, feeling the texture of something so ancient that it had lived millennia before the birth of Jesus Christ. A dark and disturbing chapter in the history of the earth, well before the light of humanity or civilization—as if God had abandoned this world for a time, to wallow in its own vicious darkness.

Though he has spent a tidy sum mounting this expedition, and he seems hell-bent on spending every last cent on this obsession, I begin to understand why Othniel is so determined in his quest for fossils, after witnessing and partaking in a discovery first hand. It is this knowledge that has shed light on his perpetually gloomy disposition.

"His uncle," Drinker told me, "George Peabody, was quite rich, and financed his expeditions in the past. Now that Peabody has died, and left Marsh a sizable chunk of his fortune, he is left to his own devices. But I'll have you know he didn't gain his professorship until Peabody donated $150,000 for the establishment of a Museum of Natural History at Yale. That is not the sort of credibility I seek."

It now looks as if Othniel's gamble in making the trek to this far-flung outpost, has paid off. Though I try to remain impartial, I do hope Marsh finds satisfaction in his discoveries, and that he might be able to restrain his passion, and stave off bankruptcy.

August 14th 1872, Ghost Lake,

I was shaken awake in the early hours of the morning. "Shkozin! Shkozin! Goshkozin!" Aabitiba said. Roughly shaking my arm.

"I'm awake! I'm awake! Naabiziingwashi!" I insisted. "No need to rattle my skull! What is it? What has happened now?" I must admit, I had no sunny outlook at being woken so early, and given all that has happened since my arrival, had little hope that the news would be agreeable. My suspicions were soon to be confirmed.

"Marsh has sent me to bring you to the excavation site," Aabitiba said.

"Why? What is it?" I asked. "Aaaniish na? Wegonesh?" But Aabitiba only shook his head, refusing to explain further, insisting only that I must see with my own eyes. So rousing myself, I dressed quickly and followed the half-breed out into the early morning light, grey-blue, with a scattering of stars in the darkness to the west. The sun had not yet risen, and the sky was only beginning to lighten in the east. It was even earlier than I thought, and my presentiment of doom increased as we made our way to the bone-bed.

Whatever the source of alarm, even Aabitiba seemed concerned. He was frowning, which was one of the first expressions of anxiety that I'd seen troubling the mottled complexion of his face. His normal bearing is one of stoic reserve.

By the time we made our way down the scaffolding of the quarry, the sky had already lightened significantly, even in that brief space of time, and a few men were already standing around, milling about the large matroyshka fossil Othniel had only partially exhumed the day before, like a set of Russian nesting dolls, one fish resting inside the body of the other.

When the workers parted to allow us near, I was almost certain that I would see the body of one of the workers, some tragic twilight fall from the scaffolding, a broken neck, and a body left cooling until it was discovered in the early hours of dawn, all the warmth of life having already seeped out of the body during the night to rise up and out to the stars. To my relief this was not the case; it was not a body. But to my dismay, it was something almost as equally disheartening.

Othniel crouched on the ground, kneeling at the centre of his milling diggers, hands gripping the corners of his scalp in a posture of abject loss, like a father kneeling over the body of his murdered son. Kneeling amidst the dust and gravel of the crushed and broken remains. For that was all that was left of the gluttonous matroyshka fossil, one of the crown jewels in his career of discoveries as a paleontologist—crushed and broken remains.

It appeared as if someone, for there could be no other explanation for this sort of, of vandalism, had whaled upon the ancient, mineralized bones with a sledgehammer, with the intent to destroy, possibly one of the only extant examples of the horrendous creature.

"Oowwww." Marsh moaned, rocking back and forth on his knees, insensible to the grit and stone-shards crunching against the weight of his flesh, in a way, that had he been in any other state, must have been quite painful. The pain was nothing to the anguish on his face. It barely registered.

"My poor boooones!" Othniel moaned, like a ghost or pale, haunting specter. "My bones! My bones! What has he done to you? Oh, no. Oh, no. My poor boooones!" He held a shard of the bone in his fist, six inches long like the blade of a knife. The largest piece he could find that had survived the bombardment, cupping it to his face, and caressing his cheek against the petrified fragment.

I felt ashamed to be witness to such a profusion of emotion, but I can only imagine what he must have felt in that moment, and couldn't help but feel pity for the disagreeable man. In an instant, Othniel leaped to his feet, his sorrow abandoned in the dust and pulverized stone. He was still clutching the shard of bone in his shaking fist.

"Cope did this!" He shouted. "That underhanded rat! I will have his hide for this! That bloody misfit! That Damned bloody devil!" And all manner of oaths only fit to be heard in a hole dug in the earth, hundreds of miles from the edge of civilization.

"I really can't believe that Drinker would be capable of this!" I said, gesturing to the destruction littering the stratified layers of the bone-bed.

"Drinker! Drinker is it? Well, you tell your friend Drinker that I know what he's done and that he's not going to get away with it! He will pay for what he's done to me!"

"You don't know for sure that Cope has done this. You can't condemn the man without evidence!" But even as I said this, I couldn't help remembering what Drinker had said regarding the necessity of enlisting the aide of Yah-

ence to guard his fossils, for fear that Othniel would sabotage his bones. It was almost too much of a coincidence to believe that he had no part in this destruction, and I was at a loss to conceive who else would have a stake in Marsh's discovery, and a strong enough motive to perpetrate this act of sabotage.

The more I protested, the deeper my own suspicions grew, but in the interests of de-escalating the situation, and potentially deflecting a possible retaliation, and a cycle of attack and retribution, I sought to de-legitimize Drinker's guilt in this instance. Though I have my own strong reservations in the matter.

"No proof! No proof! The proof lies at your feet!" Othniel insisted.

"It does look bad," I agreed, "but the appearance of guilt, is not the same thing as guilt. You still have no proof, and someone else who has an interest in your activities here, might have had reasons to damage your discoveries."

"Like who?" Othniel asked.

"Well," I said, though I didn't truly believe it, "I've noticed that ever since the newest case of Wiindigo Psychosis has developed, the Indians are less and less pleased with your presence here. Might not one of the tribesmen have destroyed your finding, believing that this would dissuade you from your enterprise, or cause discord amongst your two competing teams? Say that this is not a possibility before casting aspersions onto the character of others."

My speech seemed to have had some effect, as Marsh looked thoughtful, and gave off his raging against Edward Drinker Cope. I know not how this fiasco will end, but I fear it is an omen that forebodes ill, for anything good ever coming from this expedition, the same as the presentiment of doom with which I was roused.

"Movement is life, and stillness is death."

~Inri

How Peter Died

Church sat in the front seat of Peter's Cutlass. He'd snuck out to steal sips of C-Six from Peter's flask hidden under the visor, and smoke the Hellers stashed in the glove box. He heard the back-door slam and the windows of the house rattle. Peter was on his way out. Church flicked the cigarette away and hopped in the back, crouching down in between the seats and hiding under filthy blankets. When he saw that his cigarette had bounced off the half-closed window and landed on the dash, he thought for sure that he was busted. But when Peter got into the car muttering something about "crazy wiindigos" under his breath, he picked up the smoke from the dash and started smoking it, without realizing that he hadn't been the one to light it.

As Peter drove he adjusted the rear-view mirror and kept looking behind him as if he sensed Church's presence. Church held his breath, trying to keep the beating of his heart silent. They drove along Tarpaulin Road, and for a while Church assumed they were heading towards Nally's Pool-Hall, but then Peter turned, heading north-west on a route out of town.

Peter kept wiping sweat off his forehead. It was Peter's only flaw in an otherwise perfect poker face. When Peter was anxious, he perspired. Church could see the sheen of sweat on his forehead. Maybe he was scanning the forest, looking for a suitable place to kill him, and then hide the body.

They turned down a deserted logging road. This would be the perfect place to kill someone, Church thought. There were so many predators around you wouldn't even have to worry about burying the body. In less than a week there would be nothing left but the bones. Church knew he was letting his paranoia get carried away. Peter was a bad father, but he wasn't that horrible.

Branches scraped themselves on the windows, pine needles screeching on glass and painted metal-like fingernails on a chalkboard. The rough path through the trees was pitted and the car bumped wildly over the rutted tire marks.

Where were they going?

Church had a road map of Sterling on his bedroom wall. A snarl of scribbled lines half-grid, half organic evolution. Some roads didn't appear on any map because they were too small, or because they were little-known shortcuts. And some roads were just dead-ends that led nowhere, but which a certain number of people would inevitably follow, only to turn back, each time drawing the lines of the path deeper. Church had penciled in the roads and footpaths that had gone un-marked. The logging road was one that he had never seen before.

The route became increasingly steep, and Peter had to gun the engine to get enough traction to get up the hill. The wheels caught and then they were up and over the lip. Peter drove down the path a short distance and then stopped at a point overlooking a forest terrain far below them.

Peter got out of the car and slammed the door. Then Church heard the sound of other car-doors slamming, and he knew they weren't alone. Peter hadn't driven all the way out here to kill him. Peter was scared.

That's why he'd been sweating. He'd been looking in the rear-view mirror because they'd been sandwiched between two cars. He'd been following someone, and someone had been following him. Church raised his eyes above the level of the window and peaked out to see his father making frantic gestures. His arms out-stretched, his hands facing palm-outward in a non-threatening and co-operative gesture, but empty-handed, as if to say he was broke. Not offering what they wanted.

There are many moments in life that are fleeting. They are here, and then they are gone, without anything to mark their presence. And then there are others that, though short, are indelibly burned onto your consciousness forever. You can't get rid of them, no matter how much you wish you could forget. This was one of those moments. It happened quickly.

The two larger twins, Ox and Grundel, stepped out of one car, and Hundsfordt stepped out of the other. Both black Crown Vics. The triplets wore matching suits, accentuating their similarities. Hundsfordt less massive than his brothers, his darker burnt-straw hair hanging lankly to his chin, Ox and Grundel almost interchangeable, one from the other, differentiated only by a cigarillo hanging from one corner of Ox's lips. They both carried baseball bats. The batons looked small in their meaty palms, and Church could see the muscles in their arms bulging even through their suits.

"This location was chosen for a particular purpose," Hundsfordt said, like the monologue of an evil villain revealing his plot. "I chose this location because my brothers rarely receive carte-blanche to do whatever they want. We always have to worry about evidence. Blaach! Things used to be so much easier before DNA. But that's the beauty of this location, it provides a convenient alibi: the Genosee Falls is known for its jumpers." The lovers leap.

Now Church knew where they were, and he could put a red dot on his mental map of their location. He could also hear the trickling sounds of the subterranean stream as it emerged from the cliff face, and cascaded down the steep drop. There were many stories about the place, though he'd never seen it before.

Hundsfordt's calmly delivered speech was punctuated by the sounds of groans, and the scuffling of feet on gravel, the sound of wood pounding into bones and meat as the brothers beat the living shit out of Peter.

"I did what you asked. I complained to the Department of Social Services. I've tried to convince Day to sell her land, but she's stubborn. She won't budge. But if you kill me, you'll never get your money back." Peter said, through purple-black lips, the desperation starting to enter his voice as he realized that this wasn't just another death-threat tactic to make him pay up, but a tactic to make him dead. This was how he could pay his debts.

"Oh you've done well. When Day's Daughter is out of the way, we'll only have Church to deal with. Young people are so impressionable. He'll inherit the land, and then we will purchase it from him."

"Wait! Wait! I can still be useful to you! I can help you with Church. He'll listen to me! He'll do what I say. I promise."

"I'm sorry," Hundsfordt said with mock sincerity, "but I'm afraid you've outlived your usefulness."

Peter groaned as he received another fist to the gut.

"That's enough!" Hundsfordt said, "You don't want him to bleed too much, that'll leave physical evidence up here when we want to make it look like the rocks down there did this to him."

Peter struggled weakly as the twins dragged him bloodied and beaten to the cliff and then tossed him unceremoniously over the edge like a sack of potatoes. He disappeared over the edge and then he was gone. Gone like magic. Church didn't even hear the sound of his body hitting the ground. Church had half-expected something to save Peter at the last possible moment, like in a movie, but nothing did. Number six, Church thought as he watched Peter's body disappear over the cliff. Number six. Peter had also been Number Five, since this was the second time he'd seen his father die.

Church wanted to crawl to the edge and peer over to see what had happened to Peter's body. Was it twisted and mangled? Was the cliff a sheer drop of forty-feet or was it punctuated by protrusions of sharp, jagged rocks? Was there a chance at all that he could have survived the fall? Was he really dead? Maybe he was clinging to a branch? He couldn't believe that Peter was actually dead.

It had all happened so fast. One moment Peter had been bargaining and cajoling, and the next he was gone. Hundsfordt tossed Peter's keys to Ox and told him to "get rid of the car." Ox got into the Cutlass, and adjusted the driver's seat for his significant bulk. Crushing Church in the small space where he lay hidden under the dirty blankets reeking of diesel and motor oil.

Church squeezed his eyes shut tight. He wasn't just physical evidence - he was an eyewitness. The car made grinding sounds as Ox changed gears. He raised one arm over the seat as leverage, looking backwards over one shoulder to negotiate the rough path through the woods in reverse. Ox was focused on his task, and didn't notice his presence. The smell of diesel, oil, whiskey, and cigarettes must have masked his scent. As they drove Church tried to keep track of where they were going by the few landmarks he could see, but it was useless. Night had fallen, all he could see was the sky, and he'd never learned how to tell directions by the stars.

Eventually they came to a stop and Ox got out, slamming the door behind him. Church stayed in his hiding place, waiting until he was sure the vampire was gone. He peeked out the window to see where they were. Aesop's junkyard. Church recognized the corrugated metal walls of the fence. There were stop signs and scrap pieces of metal. Mounds of twisted iron and hollowed-out cars piled up in shadowy heaps like the skeletal remains of dinosaurs.

Church quietly slipped out, leaving the car door ajar as he made his escape. For a moment he felt a sense of elation as he sprinted towards the fence, but then he remembered Ox and Grundel, swinging the limp form of his father over the cliff edge, and his elation died. His father hadn't escaped. Church threw himself at the fence and began to climb, plotting his home and Aesop's scrapyard on a map of the city, and then in red, penciling in the quickest, and most direct route.

He could try to forget Peter, black out every memory of his father so that it was as if his death had never happened, but Church's body would remember, that elephant. His arm would always be a little bit crooked, and he would always have the half-moon scar from a botched scam gone wrong. The body would always have those telltale scars, even if he forgot.

Church ran. Movement was life, and inertia was death. If he slowed down, it felt like he'd die, so he kept moving. Tears threatened to fall but he forced them away. He was like a rolling tire, momentum kept him going, gravity kept pulling at him, if he slowed down, he'd fall. So he kept running, following the map in his head. Movement was life, and inertia was death.

`Homeostasis:` or Milieu interieur, is the process by which a body or system regulates itself to keep internal conditions, like temperature, at a constant.

August 19th 1872, Ghost Lake

Attempting to understand the source of the antagonism between Drinker and Othniel, I questioned Brennen, one of Marsh's faithful Yale students that he'd dragged with him from New Haven, in order to act as a source of free labor I suspect, as much as to be a hands-on learning experience for his pupils. I intercepted him on his way to the excavation site, bucket and shovel in hand.

"I think Jones— err Ah, Drinker that is—I think he's just jealous of the professor's success, and what he sees as an unfair advantage. Professor Marsh's Uncle was George Peabody, you know?"

"Yes I had heard. I guess I can see how that could make one's path through life somewhat easier. Peabody died the year before last, did he not?"

"Yes, they even buried him in Westminster Abbey. Although I think his remains have since been moved to a cemetery in Salem."

"So you think they are just playing out some sort of class struggle?"

"Those with the capital own the means of production." Brennen said, picking up his pick and shovel, continuing on his way and whistling a jaunty tune as he walked down the path towards the deep pit dug into the earth below.

"Cheer o!" he called back over his shoulder.

And when I asked Othniel the same question, I got a different answer:

"That damned Elasmosaurus! —I haven't gone out of my way to advertise his failures, whatever he chooses to believe. I am much too busy with my own endeavors to waste energy sabotaging his—after all, why would I bother? It is clear I need do no such thing, as he is perfectly capable of undermining himself—with his own shoddy work!"

Othniel's large, palatial-sized tent, was a disorganized mess. Books, crates, maps, and various camping and excavation supplies littered the dim interior, lit only by a small oil-lamp, and the buttery-orange light of the sun filtering in through the canvas.

"What do you mean?" I asked.

"He is a hack! There is no one he can rightfully blame for his own short-comings and his own short-sightedness. It was his own professor, Joseph Leidy, who was the one to pronounce his error in an address to the Academy of Natural Sciences. I had no part in publishing his errors. I was merely the one to first point out the mistake on a visit to Haddonfield, and we brought in Joseph as a neutral party to adjudicate the dispute. This is the grudge he holds against me!"

I listened to Othniel's point of view, but couldn't help thinking that his assessment of Drinker's character was misguided. It sounded like it was all just one big misunderstanding.

"As for that thing with Vorhees: it was Edward himself who introduced me to the man, and showed me around the marl-pit. He must have known I would jump at the chance to examine some of the fossils myself. It was an opportunity I couldn't pass up! And it's not as if my descriptions of any species can detract from his work. If he didn't intend on sharing, he never should have shown me the marl-pits. I don't know what he was thinking when he flaunted his discovery in my face like that? He wants all the bones for himself, and would keep me from this site too, if that were within his power."

No matter the source of their animosity, I can see it is no use trying to reintroduce them to each other on friendlier terms, they are too set in their injuries, pitted against each other like rabid dogs.

"What do you think the Indians make of these bones?" I asked Othniel, changing the subject. "These creatures that you are digging up from the earth, on their Anishinaabe-aki?" I had decided that if I am to understand more about the Indian psyche, it might give me a greater insight into the affliction of this wiindigo malady. "On the whole they are a superstitious lot are they not?"

"Superstitious?" Othniel looked up from his scribbling, one cheek smeared with a spot of dark ink where he'd rubbed at his face, the ink from an Esterbrooke pen nib staining his fingers. "The Indians might be a superstitious lot, but they are no more foolhardy than a lot of the falsehoods others tell themselves."

"They aren't shocked by the monsters you are unearthing?" I asked Othniel. The plumage on his dip-pen danced back and forth as he wrote, most of the barbs had been removed from the vaned pinion feather, leaving only a decorative on the tip of the rachis. Othniel was using the hollow calamus as a pen-nib holder, rather than as a reservoir for ink. The metal pen nib scritching against the paper like a cricket's stridulation.

"Red Cloud once told me that the Sioux had a name for these bones, a legend of a giant called Uncegila, who was slain, and whose bones still litter the earth. But this is Anishinaabek territory," Othniel said, gesturing with his quill, "and I'm not familiar with the local legends. Ask Aabitiba, or one of the other salvages."

Sitting on Marsh's desk was a strange amber orb, like a large paper-weight holding down a stack of papers—I knew that he wrote almost non-stop in his attempts to keep up with Drinker's output of publishing, to make reports on his findings, and describe the various species first, before his competitor could describe the species, and take the credit. Alas! Such was the nature of academia, if one happened to stumble across the same discovery as another, whether better researched or not, the man who published first, often got all the glory. Othniel frequently grumbled about this when I came to visit him in his tent, scribbling furiously away in his books.

I could only sympathize with his pain—apparently Drinker was very prolific despite his preference for fieldwork. "Let others dig in the dirt like salvages," Marsh said, "I have more important work to be doing. All I need is access to the finds. I have no inclination to waste my time on such labours myself, when I could be studying, and describing those same finds as they are harvested from the earth." My own field of study was so new and so little explored, I had no such fear that a similar competitor would stumble upon, or steal my work.

Picking up the amber, I held the rock up to catch and diffuse the light and show off its jewel-like lustre. Inside the yellow stone, to my amazement, was a rather large insect, and not just any insect, but a perfectly preserved mosquito. Somehow it had been swallowed inside a gelatinous lump of ochre-coloured bone marrow, and frozen inside like an embryo.

"That is fossilized tree resin, often called ambergris—or amber. It also has some interesting electrical properties." Othniel took the stone from my hands and rubbed it vigorously against his vest, showing me the lint now clinging to the stone. A few hairs on his head stood up perfectly straight, acted upon by the invisible force of static electricity. "This specimen is from the late

Cretaceous, and it is unique for one reason—you might have noticed the Culicidae inclusion? Mosquitos are a species as old as the dinosaurs, and they have been feeding on generation after generation of vertebrates since before the dawn of Adam."

I hadn't realized that the little beasts were so ancient, that they were themselves virtually dinosaurs. Maybe there was something to the vampire myths after all; as long as there was a source of fresh blood, they would sustain themselves through all eternity. I shook my head, trying to dispel these foolish thoughts.

"I find it hard to believe that one man could publish so many academic articles worthy of study." Marsh complained, not for the first time. "They are either poorly written, or not all of them are written by his own hand! He must surely employ a team of ghost-writers!"

I didn't have to ask whom Othniel was referring to. I left Othniel to his grumbling and scribbling and went to visit the object of his derision out in the field. A few hours later I came upon Drinker, sleeves rolled up to his forearms, working hard at shoveling a pile of dirt into a wheelbarrow.

"There you are Drinker! I've been meaning to speak to you about—are those ants?" I asked curiously, watching the frantic movement of tiny fretting insects as their warren of tunnels was destroyed, shovelful by shovelful.

"Let me show you something," Drinker said, leading me to a pile of dirt that had already been transplanted—a large anthill in fact, had been dug up and relocated to sit on top of one of his fossils. "You see? We let the ants do the hard work of removing the heavy soil, one grain of sand at a time." The industrious creatures were working tirelessly, like indomitable little soldiers, or an interminable force of nature.

"Each insect is able to carry ten times its own weight! That's better productivity than a mere man I'll lay you odds—at least when there isn't enough manpower to go around. They're slow workers, but slow work is better than no work. And they work for free!"

"That's very ingenious." I watched the mass of wriggling, panicking ants swarm around the wheelbarrow. Given the number of men who have deserted, it was quite clever. "It is a shame you and Marsh couldn't put aside your differences and work together. Imagine the work you two could accomplish, with two minds working towards the same goal, instead of this antagonism and division."

"I know. But that is not going to happen. Our differences are irreconcilable I'm afraid." And after a pause, Drinker added: "We were colleagues once. Friends even."

"What happened?" I asked, my curiosity piqued. "From where does this dispute stem? Help me to understand this strife between the two of you."

"I guess you could say it is a philosophical disagreement. About the manner in which we conduct ourselves, both on the field, and in our personal business." Drinker took a deep breath, exhaled, and then continued. "As a professional courtesy, and to share in our mutual interests, I introduced Marsh to Albert Vorhees, the owner of a marl pit in New Jersey where I had been finding many interesting specimens. And then, like a scoundrel, Marsh went behind my back and made a deal with Vorhees to have all the fossils delivered to him instead of to me."

—Now, we were getting to the heart of the matter—

"This was more than a professional malfeasance, it was a betrayal of the friendship I had extended. Even then I could have let it go. There are other bone-bed sites—like this one here. But he also went out of his way to publicly humiliate me. He discovered an error I had made in the arrangement of an Elasmosaurus skeleton, and he made damn sure anyone who would listen, heard about it."

"You see, the truth is, Marsh is jealous. He sees me as a threat, instead of as a colleague. He would rather see me ruined than to allow any measure of success to settle on my shoulders."

I could tell there was no point in trying to sway Drinker's opinion on the matter. They were both such stubborn, ambitious men, too similar for their own good.

"We are not colleagues," Drinker finished, "we are enemies."

And with that, I thought it best to stay out of their conflict, lest their hostility for each other, come to be transferred to me. I came to Ghost Lake with the intention of studying Wiindigo Psychosis, and that is exactly what I plan to do. They will have to sort out their enmity towards each other on their own, because I am not able to untangle the knot of their aggression. I fear it can only be solved in one way, like a Gordian Knot. I only hope the rope will not become their noose.

Deflection Strategies

In Grade Five, Church's class went on a field trip to the Sterling Museum.

Church spent the entire day reading the plaques beside each display in the dinosaur exhibit. He wrote down the names of the dinosaurs in tiny letters on both sides of a cue-card until there wasn't any space to hold more words. In red ink he drew a field of dripping blood, to symbolize the fact that they were extinct, and blotting out the names.

One display held rocks of varying shades and sizes—shiny like stones that had been through a rock-tumbler. On a plaque Church read: "Like certain modern species alive today, some dinosaurs ate rocks to aid in their digestion." Amber-pink rose quartz, red-violet amethyst, and green marble opal. Church examined these stones with fascination. The stones had once been inside the living body of a dinosaur. Church had eaten stones himself, to help stave off his hunger.

The plaque standing before a Sauropod exhibit read:

It is estimated that the largest plant-eating dinosaurs would have had to eat 300 pounds of food per day if they were cold-blooded, and up to a ton, if they were warm-blooded. These numbers are calculated by comparing dinosaur size to modernday animals like cheetahs that are warm-blooded, and can eat their own weight in food every ten days. It takes more calories, which is a unit of food-energy, to keep the blood circulating and the heart beating in a warm-blooded animal, than it does in a cold-blooded animal, which uses the temperature of their surroundings, and various deflecting strategies, to maintain their body heat.

Apparently, Church thought, there were some advantages to being cold-blooded. And he wondered what deflection strategies a cold-blooded animal would use, and whether he should take notes.

August 21st 1872, Ghost Lake, Drinker's encampment

When I go to the other encampment of dinosaur hunters on the peninsula, ostensibly to visit my other Wiindigo Psychosis patient, Eniwek, I often visit with Drinker too, and I must admit, more often than is strictly necessary.

Deprived of civilized conversation for these many months, Drinker has taken to imparting to me his thoughts on myriad of topics, and, occasionally, requesting my expertise. He has shared with me the descriptions of monstrous dreams that plague his sleep, where the extinct creatures he digs from the ground are given terrible life and form. I have prescribed a small dose of belladonna to help him sleep, and when this failed, a tincture of laudanum.

Eniwek's illness seems to be progressing, much the same as Ogimaa's, with little response to my treatments and ministration. If I was not aware of the deep divide the bone-men have created—fraternization between the two camps is strongly discouraged—I would not feel as if I were crossing enemy lines under the flag of neutrality. They both fear that the knowledge of their respective discoveries might reach the ears of their adversary. It is possible one could preemptively publish a quick article in an academic journal claiming a discovery as their own. Marsh has told me that all he needs to identify a new species, is but a fragment of bone, the whole corresponding to the arrangement of the parts, even a shard could be enough to claim the right of "discovery" to any particular species. "Symmetry" is the word he used to describe it. And Drinker has told me that Othniel seems to delight in swiping his discoveries in just this manner—and he has done so on more than one occasion—naming, and gaining credit for discoveries he himself had made mere days before his publication was to come out. Under the guise of 'neutrality' I must take no sides, or risk losing my immunity—the ability to cross no-man's-land on this peculiar field of battle.

On Drinker's desk, I noticed an exceptionally beautiful stone being used as a paperweight. "That's a crab's-eye." Drinker said as he prepared a batch of pungent moss tea, "Also called a gastrolith or a gizzard stone. I have many of these stones in my personal collection." I couldn't help but think of the corresponding stone on Othniel's desk, a mosquito trapped forever within a fossilized chunk of amber. Again it struck me how similar the two men were, and that what each hated in the other, was also found in themselves.

I hefted the weight of the stone. "It's much too large."

"That's because this one was not formed inside a crab or a chicken. Some species of dinosaurs also ate rocks to help with their digestion. The stones would rub against each other like a pestle inside their bodies." He rubbed his fists together in a circular motion to illustrate the friction. Like a pebble worn smooth by the action of tidal forces, except the crystalline structure of the purple-pink quartz had been slowly revealed by a monster's grinding digestion.

"How do you know this isn't just a river stone?" The surface was completely smooth to the touch.

"It is entirely unlike the surrounding geological strata surrounding the bones where it was found. And the highly polished surface is consistent with gastroliths that are common among living vertebrates like crocodiles and domestic fowl."

"Are they always this beautiful?" I held the gastrolith up so the crystals sparkled, seeming to glow with an inner light.

"No. That is an unusual specimen. More often than not, they are dull, rather than beautiful."

I passed a few moments in pleasant conversation with Drinker, and after seeing to the treatment of Eniwek, I concluded my visit, collected Aabitiba from his fraternization with the Ghost Lake diggers amongst the camp, and returned to Marsh's situation across the bay.

The Farm

Church was in the Farm—or the Home—the Home for the-most-fucked-up-boys-and-girls. His mom had been declared "unfit", his grandmother was disabled and insane, and his father—Peter—Peter was de-ceased. At least, he was pretty sure that his father was dead. Church had watched him die. But the first time had been a hallucination. He was pretty sure the second time had been real. Is that what triggered Social Services to get involved? Sometimes he thought Day and Marie were dead too. Other times he knew they were still alive. Locked away in the Sterling Shores Mental Institution. Inri could be almost anywhere. And Church was in the Farm, plotting his escape.

On Church's fifteenth birthday the foster parents he had been living with for the past nine months were blessed with the unexpected news that Marianne was with child, after years of trying, and the doctor's frequent assertions that their chances for impregnation were next to zero.

The sounds of their excitement filtered upstairs to the room painted in nursery colours. The room contained a bed, dresser and bookshelf, as clean as an institution. Church knew that it was time for him to leave.

Robert and Marianne had been decent foster parents, they never yelled at him or beat him up, they fed and clothed him, and they were scrupulously polite, though they remained strangers. They ran their house like a ship. Every few years another kid was successfully raised to the age of majority and transplanted into the "real world," a useful citizen, and then it was time to start again. They tolerated no "bullshit" and since you were going to be out of there in a few years anyway you might as well "shape up or ship out."

Church fit right in because he had no intention of getting comfortable living there. He had only unpacked his clothes into the dresser because they had insisted. He followed every one of their rules. He never made any demands on their affection, and he was quiet.

They never adopted a baby because it would require an emotional commitment they weren't willing to make to someone else's child. They only fostered teenagers. All they had to do was be strict and provide food and shelter. Church accepted what they gave and was thankful for it, but he had a feeling that he wouldn't be able to compete with the miracle baby for whom they had been saving all their love. Pigs with pink wings flew across a band of wallpaper along the ceiling as a testament to their unfulfilled dreams.

Church packed up all the essentials; a few changes of clothes, a few dog-eared paperback novels, a walk-man with a few Rrivven cassettes, and then he was ready to go. The books had gotten him through hard times, taking him to far off places when he wanted more than anything just to be somewhere else.

Church waited until the Foster Parents had gone to bed, then snuck downstairs, stole the three hundred dollars hidden in the den and the fifteen dollars in a basket on the kitchen counter, and left. Slipping out quietly, Church locked the door behind him, hid the key under a potted fern, and then walked away. He didn't look back at the house behind him.

Part III

(Three years later)

*"You taught me language; and my profit on't Is,
I know how to curse. The red plague rid you . . ."*

~Caliban's speech in The Tempest, Shakespeare

*Row, row, row your boat,
Gently down the stream.
Merrily, merrily, merrily, merrily,
Life is but a dream.*

~Eliphalet Oram Lyte (1842 - 1913)

"Isn't that just like a wop? Brings a knife to a gun fight."

~Sean Connery, The Untouchables, 1987.

writhe, v.i. & t., & n. **1.** To twist or roll oneself about as in acute pain; to squirm; to shrink mentally, to be stung or bitterly annoyed (under, or at, an insult etc.; ~with shame, for example). **2.** n. The act of writhing. [From the Old English word 'wreathe(n)', to 'interweave' or 'entwine,' and related to the word 'rive(n)', to be 'torn,' 'rent,' or 'divided']

Church

A large orange goldfish drifted lazily down the centre of the highway like the surreal wedge of an orange, floating ghostly two feet above the wet black top, its left fin waving leisurely.

Church woke up. Wetness had soaked through his clothes and into his bones making his teeth chatter. It was drizzling slightly, though it was too cold for rain. Droplets absorbed into the fabric of his hooded sweatshirt. Hail made a clicking sound as it bounced off the synthetic material of his jacket. Church recalled with startling clarity the images that had appeared to him in his dreams. The giant fish that had hovered in space, determining a course of action with one swish of its tail, or changing direction with one flick of the wrist. Fluidity, and freedom. The dream-power-magic had punched him in the face, and some of it was still clinging to him like bits of fluff caught in his hair, like the drowsiness following sleep.

All cold-blooded creatures are dependant upon the weather to moderate their body temperature. Transportation is key. Movement is life and stillness is death. If they stayed still for too long, they would die. If they just went wherever the current took them, they'd freeze to death, starve, or fry.

Church hefted his backpack, hiked out to the road, and stuck out his thumb. He'd spent the last few hours sleeping on a bench in the small roadside park that overlooked a sweeping panoramic view of a silver lake, and green, boreal forest. He watched the cars go by like a batter stepping up to the plate, then watching the baseballs whiz by. It was all in your stance. The cars zoomed by like speeding metal coffins hurrying towards their deaths. Ahead there were red brake lights, and behind, there was a string of white headlights, like red and white blood cells careening in opposite directions. Church had his thumb pressed up against the artery; he could feel its pulse.

Transport trucks roared by, rumbling like thunder, pistons pumping black bile through mechanical veins, the preserved remnants of prehistoric life. That's why they were called fossil fuels. He imagined the ghosts of dinosaurs filling the sky like smog, taking out their revenge at a sub-atomic level, hacking apart the atoms between particles of ozone. No one knew what dinosaurs had really sounded like, but Church thought that they would have sounded something like transport trucks. Growling up and down the black top at 120 klicks. Their souls encased in snarls of living metal.

Stratified layers of living rock rose up on the other side of the road. Dynamite had been used to blast through the archean rock of the Canadian Shield to create these roads, dinomite for the tyrannosaurus trucks. In his mind he saw explosions ripping the earth, and for a moment he smelled brimstone, but he knew it was probably just his imagination.

Church watched the traffic whiz by. All he had was a direction.

That was enough. Inri had told him that you could get anything you wanted, by going in the right direction. "If you want to be smarter, go East. If you want to be stronger, go West. If you want power, go North. If you want beauty, go South. You can have anything you want, as long as you know how to get there." At the time, Church hadn't been sure what Inri meant—and he still wasn't sure—but he thought he understood a little bit better now. It was all about choices, and paths, and there were a million ways to get where you wanted to be. But mostly Church wasn't going anywhere, he didn't have any destination in mind. He was just moving. He had been captured by the same mania that afflicted Inri. Movement was life, and stillness was death. So he kept moving. It was a law of physics: an object in motion tends to stay in motion.

There was a certain art to hitch-hiking. No one wanted to pick up a bedraggled stranger, so Church pretended wetness wasn't slowly seeping into his bones. Without exactly smiling, he pretended to be cheerful, and a car pulled over. Church hoisted the army knapsack and jogged over, his shoes leaving imprints in the soft gravel.

"Where you headed?" the man asked.

"Sterling." Church said. Those two syllables tumbling from his mouth, before he knew that he would say them, ringing out as clear as the metal alloy after which the city was named.

He had been away from Sterling for three years. He couldn't go back home. They would be waiting for him there. The triplets were still searching for him—he could feel them like throbbing presences in the back of his skull—ever since he drank out of that thermos, he had slowly become more and more aware of their triumvirate life forces, like the blips on a radar-screen. He always felt the need to be on the move. He couldn't stay in one place for long. He had to keep moving. But if you went far enough, you'd end up in the place where you started. So Church formulated a plan. It was time to return to Sterling. He'd been running for too long.

His plan was simple. He was going to let the hunger grow. He was going to let the hunger grow to unreasonable proportions, making himself more wiindigo, and letting his inhumanity begin to show. If he was going to combat monsters, he needed to be more monstrous himself. Wiindigo versus vampire; it sounded like it would make a good comic book. There was only one question: could Superman outrun the Flash?

The roads unfolded like a flower, eternally blooming beneath the wheels of the truck. The scenes changed but the yellow lines always remained the same. He thought that he now understood Inri's need to be constantly on the move. Movement was life, and stillness was death.

Church closed his eyes and the dreams came like driftwood, the flotsam and jetsam of his day cast onto the shore, and thrust for a moment into the spotlight, to play themselves out against the black screen of his unconsciousness.

In his dream Church saw three dinosaurs running across a field. Coelurids. Their long hind-legs designed for speed. The coelurids ran across the area of land that had once been used as the pow-wow grounds on the Ghost Lake reserve, their powerful legs propelling them forward across the lawn. What happened to the spirits of extinct species? Church wondered. Did their spirits still run across fields as they once had when they were alive? With these images in his mind, Church fell asleep as the truck carried him further down the road, and on to the next town—and closer to the city of Sterling.

August 24th, 1872, Ghost Lake,

Laudunum. Strychnine. Arsenic. Quinine. Ether. I've tried them all in the vain hope that one of my medicines might have some restorative effect upon my patients. Fowler's medicine. Pemberton's French Wine. Globe flower. I've tried them all, with little to no, effect. Easing the symptoms, allowing the patients to rest, calming agitation, but curing the sickness? No.

Despite my natural reticence—blood-letting is not one of my preferred methods of treatment—I've been reduced to bleeding my patients on the off chance their symptoms are being caused by bad blood. This is not a theory to which I myself ascribe, but feel that it is at least as important to be seen to be doing something as it is to observe the patient's symptoms in the search of a cause, and so as to provide the patient some measure of hope. It is never good idea to underestimate the role of a positive outlook in a patient's prospects for recovery.

Othniel took an interest in my employment today, and chose to sit in on my examination, and treatment of the patient, having a vested interest in the returned health of his employee.

Marsh watched, as I slowly stoked and fed the fire, and then patiently waited for the water in the pot to boil and then cool enough so I could wash my hands before examining the patient. Othniel said nothing, though he watched all my movements with a hawk-like gaze, trying to decipher my every action. Rather than keep him in the dark, I spoke, answering his silent questions.

"Dr. Semmelweis showed conclusively that medical students coming from dissecting classes, carried infections from their exams to birthing mothers in the maternity clinic. A simple chlorinated solution was enough to halt the spread of disease. Though Semmelweis has been derided, I am a strong adherent to the idea of germ theory, and I believe that hygiene is a simple way of preventing sickness."

I must admit I felt a bit self-conscious under the strength of his unwavering gaze, and found myself rambling, though Othniel made no complaint. "Joseph Lister has also demonstrated that the sterilization of medical instruments with phenol proves the existence of germs."

"These germs?" Othniel asked. "They are alive?"

"Yes, microscopic organisms which cause disease. I don't place much merit in the concept of miasma. Dr. John Snow has shown that a contaminated well on Broad Street was the source of a cholera epidemic—not bad air. Illnesses have causes, and a large part of curing or preventing sickness, is finding their origins."

Othniel listened to my explanation but made no comment until I finished lathering and washing my hands in the warmed water. Ogimaa lay, as usual, in a lethargic state. "I thought Ogimaa's sickness was of the mind."

"It may be. But I try to refrain from making too many assumptions. It is possible that there may be some other cause for these symptoms."

With Ogimaa, I used the small ivory-handled lancet James had given me on the commencement of my journey, spring loaded, and engraved with a dedication from my mentor. The lancet came with a matching ivory case. Upon seeing the ivory, Othniel raised an eyebrow, but made no comment.

I can appreciate why the lancet might engage his interest, as it is almost the same colour and texture as bone. A fancier lancet than any I have previously owned. "A gift from James," I answered again, to his unspoken question. Marsh made no comment, allowing me to continue with my work.

I explained to Ogimaa, in broken Indian, what the process entailed. He agreed to the procedure, seemingly willing to try anything to halt his transformation. "Gaawiin andawenimsii aansinaago wiindiigoowi!" he said. I do not want to turn into a wiindigo!

I wrapped a linen cloth around his bicep, just above his elbow where I intended to make the incision, and placed a bowl below the forthcoming wound. Placing the clover shaped blade against his skin, I drew the lancet across his arm with a sufficient depth to breathe a vein. The blood came out slow, trickling down his forearm and into the pewter bowl. I watched intently as the blood flowed, and the puddle grew, spreading outward along the inner concentric rings of the bowl, measuring out in increments each ounce of blood.

Ogimaa's remained quiet, his fist gripped loosely around a small leather satchel hung around his neck—such misguided trade in charms and amulets being the mainstay of Goshko's so-called "medicine."

The minutes passed, and Othniel observed from one side of the room, leaning against the wall as he watched the treatment unfold. For his part, Ogimaa seemed quite relaxed and restrained, though he refused to look, as the blood flowed. He stared at the ceiling and showed no reaction to the pain. If he felt any, he kept it to himself.

When the wound clotted, I breathed another vein, drawing the lancet across Ogimaa's arm, an inch-and-a-half above the first wound. The blood flowed more quickly, and when the concentric rings measured out 12 ounces, I dressed and bound the shallow incisions, taking great care in cleaning the wounds, so that they would not become infected.

After sterilizing the lancet, I placed the ivory-handled blade back into its matching case. Othniel watched all my actions with the same absorption with which he had observed the entire operation, arms folded across his chest.

Ogimaa insisted he felt better, much to his own surprise. Smiling, and shaking my hand, thanking me profusely. "Gchi-Miigwetch! Gchi-nmino-ayaa! Miigwetch-miigwetch!" Thank you, I feel better! Thank you-thank you!

At some point, Marsh slipped out of the room while I tended to Ogimaa, and took notes on the alleviation of symptoms. Seeing the general improvement in Ogimaa's condition, and it being too late in the afternoon to make the passage today, I have resolved on the morrow to visit my patient in Drinker's encampment, and apply the same therapy.

Upon quitting the chamber for but a moment to speak with Othniel about the man's condition, I stepped back into the room where 'the wiindigo' was convalescing. Othniel had already gone, and I would have to wait to speak with him. It was with great shock that I witnessed the activity that was taking place in my brief absence. Ogimaa had taken up the letting bowl with which I had just measured out more than eight ounces of his own blood. . . and from which he was now drinking.

Ogimaa's Adam's Apple rose and fell as he swallowed, taking great gulps of the precious liquid. He drank with such greed and enthusiasm that the blood trickled out the corner of his mouth and dribbled down his neck and chin like milk. He couldn't drink the blood fast enough. For a moment I was transfixed, rooted to the spot, as I watched the spectacle before me. I felt a sense of nausea and vertigo, as if my surroundings had suddenly become distorted in relation to my body; I remained the same, but everything else shifted around me, growing in size and detail. Finally, Ogimaa lowered the pewter bowl, wiped his mouth with the back of his hand, and belched loudly.

"BRAAAAEEeeGCHH!"

I could only stare at him, speechless. A slight smile turned up the corner of his lips as he lay back against the headboard of his bed. I fear that whatever benefit Ogimaa might have gained from the letting of bad blood has been reversed, or made even worse, by its regurgitation.

After seeing to Ogimaa's comfort, I promptly took my leave, again warning him of the risks of overtaxing himself, and prescribing as much rest as he could stand. I felt a restless need to be away from the man's sickbed, leaving him to his convalescence. The next time I breathe the vein of a Wiindigo Psychosis patient, I will make sure to take the letting bowl with me when I leave the room.

Sterling

Sitting in a booth in the empty restaurant of the bus terminal, Church worked on one of the sketches that he would sometimes draw, letting his hand travel freely across the paper, working out the contradictions worrying themselves at the edges of his awareness. Sometimes he could sell these pictures on the street for spare change.

Church looked down at what he had drawn. A gaunt-looking face stared out at him from the page: flat planes, narrow angles, hollow cheeks, and bottomless black eyes. Two dark wells into which he was drawn like a tunnel, until the world became a distant pinprick of light, a single shimmering star in the all-consuming darkness. Church shook his head, the pinprick of light expanding as he withdrew backwards through the tunnel, hungry eyes diminishing to the glimmering black holes in the hollow face. It was the face of hunger: starvation, famine, and greed. He'd drawn his great-great-grandfather.

Church caught his reflection in storefront windows, and in the eyes of people who walked by, and unsolicited, offered him their spare change. He was beginning to resemble the image of the face of hunger he had drawn. Church scratched out his grandfather's eyes so he wouldn't be drawn back in every time he flipped through the pages of his sketchbook, and then headed to the offices of Magnon Inc.

Ox, Hundsfordt and Grundel had been hired by Magnon Inc., they hadn't kept that a secret—maybe they didn't believe he could do anything against Magnon directly, and they were probably right. What could he do to Magnon Inc? Church had decided to stake the place out. The industrial area of town harboured one of the main offices of the company and Church wanted to get a better idea of who, or what, he was up against.

The sunlight felt warm on his back, attracted to his t-shirt, it was absorbed into the dark material, and radiated back outward as heat. Of course, if the shirt had been completely black, it would have absorbed all light, and he would be invisible. If his shirt had been completely white, the combination of all possible visible light, he would be a mirror. Shades of grey, Church thought as he sat observing all that occurred around him.

The birds chirped. People walked back and forth across the interlocking cobblestones of the courtyard. If he had been more like a lizard, he would have luxuriated in the heat. Instead, he had to squint against the glare as he watched the the complex of corporate offices, the glass in the revolving doors shining brightly for a brief moment as it caught the correct angle from the sun to pierce the back of his retinas. Church liked moonlight better. The courtyard was busy with people coming and going on their lunch hour, but if it had been 12 midnight the courtyard would have been deserted.

There was an ugly corporate sculpture dominating the courtyard, something horridly geometric and utilitarian in design: solid, blocky and heartless. The complex was located on the outskirts of Sterling, and was basically industrial wasteland, but with immaculately manicured lawns, like a golf course. It was overrun with Canadian geese and their feces. The land that had been zoned for industrial development had been chosen directly along a flight path, the artificial ponds with their fountains and neatly tailored shrubbery creating the perfect simulated habitat. The geese where everywhere! Shouldn't they be flying south for the winter soon? Church wondered, Stupid birds, maybe the magnets in their brain were out of whack or something?

Church already knew the vampires—as he continued to think of Ox, Hundsfordt and Grundel—could tolerate sunlight at least as well as a wiindigo. Contrary to popular belief, the sun did not make vampires disappear in a puff of smoke—at least not these ones. He also knew who the vampires were working for, so if he had to start looking anywhere, this would be the place to start, and it also gave him a chance to gather a little information, before springing the trap, baited with his own flesh. He was the lure.

Of course, if he stayed in one place for long enough, they would come to him, but Church couldn't afford to be patient—he was hungry now. He had carefully cultivated his hunger, alternatively stoking and starving the flames until they were banked almost to the point of supernova, licking up his face and arms like invisible pins-and-needle spiders crawling outside his flesh.

He felt as prepared as he could get. So he watched the people come and go, entering and exiting the glass doors of the building, reflecting the light of the sun for a brief moment each time the doors were opened, and then closed. Each individual flare of light was like the squeak of a swing set sliding into his brain. The squeak of a see-saw, see-saw, see-saw.

The building had a high level of security. Everyone entering the building had to pass through a turn-style gate, sliding a keycard through a magnetic strip detector, or else they stopped at the security desk adjacent to the turn-style and, after showing what Church assumed were two pieces of ID and signing in, entered the building through a separate gate with visitor passes hanging from lanyards around their necks.

His enemies were like Doctor Claw, the bad guy in the Inspector Gadget cartoon that he used to watch on Marie's television—you never got to see his face. All you ever saw was his arm petting the pampered Angoran cat. Church's enemy was a faceless corporate office, and it was hard to fight an enemy you couldn't see. The people hiding in that building were making decisions that would affect the lives of other people and the land, yet they would have to deal with none of the repercussions directly. At least Ox, Hundsfordt and Grundel, were something he could confront directly.

ozagask-waajime, n. (animate) A leech, a bloodsucker.

August 25th 1872, Ghost Lake,

Dear James,

I have another debacle to relate.

I made preparations with Aabitiba for the trek across the lake by canoe, which is the surest and easiest method of conveyance in this wilderness, but I have been unable to locate my ivory-handled lancet! It has been mislaid or misplaced, and I am unable to find it. So, having no other recourse, I have gone down to the water's edge to collect some leeches for Eniwek.

Unfortunately, I have no access to the European species of leeches, which can ingest several times the amount of blood as those that can be found in America. To make up for this deficiency I collected several leeches, choosing thirteen unusually large, fat, black leeches—hopefully sufficient to purify and cleanse the body. I had only to turn over a few rocks to find them. They attached themselves to the algae covered stones to keep themselves from the tug and ebb of the current, lapping in and drawing out against the shore. When freed, they wriggled and swirled in the water, as the waves buffeted their twisting bodies. I lifted their writhing forms from the water with a stick, and attempted to gather the little creatures into my pewter case without allowing their serrated mouths to touch my flesh.

I was not entirely successful.

One of the little beasts managed to affix itself to my wrist, and from there immediately began draining my blood, its little jaws securely latched. I tugged on the slimy creature, but it wouldn't let go, so intent was it on the meal. I pulled until finally the jaws ripped free. The leech hadn't let go willingly, and left behind a ragged, gaping wound, which, owing to a natural anti-coagulant they secrete, did not immediately clot. It bled profusely.

I reminded myself to keep an eye out, the next time I went for a swim to bathe in these waters. I had not realized that the vampires were so plentiful. The waters must be teeming! Every other rock I turned over seemed to have another leech. The little devils are also known to secrete an anesthetic, which prevents their victims from feeling the graze of their fangs.

Once the bloodsuckers were secured inside my pewter case, where they could do no more damage, I went back to transfer the leeches into a masonware jar, and to collect Aabitiba for the journey across the lake to Drinker's peninsula.

Upon arriving at Drinker's cabin, where Eniwek lay chained to his bed convalescing, my patient appeared to be in a sedate, and even cheerful mood. I explained, as best I could, the process of leeching, and the potential health benefits he could expect from the letting of bad blood.

I had him remove his shirt, and then I blindfolded him. I had experiences in the past with those who were squeamish of leeches, so I thought it best, especially after the incident with Ogimaa, that Eniwek not be able to witness the procedure, lest he become tempted to replicate similar grotesque compulsions.

I dipped a cotton ball into a jar of phenol, and sterilized first a portion of Eniwek's flesh, and then the metal tongs I would use to pick up the leeches. Eniwek was compliant, and sober throughout the entire period of questions and answers, blindfolding, and sterilization. I could only marvel at the changeability of the Wiindigo Psychosis psyche. I did not believe for one second he had made a full recovery, though at the moment, he appeared entirely sane.

Removing the lid on the glass jar, I selected one of the largest leeches, as if removing pickles from their briny fluid. Placing the writhing, wicked creature to the portion of Eniwek's sterilized skin. It thrashed about, twisting and flopping its body around in strenuous exertion, as if attempting to return to, and uncomfortable away from its watery abode—but upon finding itself atop a warm-blooded mammal, quickly affixed itself by its hungry jaws and began feeding. Eniwek groaned, though I knew from personal experience, it did not hurt, owing to the anesthetic effect of the saliva the small creatures could excrete; the pain came later, when you tried to remove their jaws from your flesh.

Luckily for Eniwek, I had come prepared with a shaker of salt. Though the water in the jar appeared to be briny, it was not; the colour was owing to the natural silt in the lake water. Leeches cannot withstand salt-water, as they are a fresh-water fauna. When they had had their fill, they should release their grip instinctually, though I had brought salt just in case. And owing to the fact that the North American variety could not hold as much blood in their bellies, I had collected more than I would strictly need.

Picking up another of the little beasts with my tongs, I placed the wriggling mass next to its brother, and another, and another, until I had seven of the slimy worms placed next to each other. With each leech I applied, Eniwek groaned, as if in pleasure, raising himself as far off the bed as the restraints would allow. Maybe it was merely the thought of the slugs that bothered him? I knew he could not see. I also noticed the distinctive vocal peculiarities that I have also noted in Ogimaa. This, too, could be a symptom of the psychosis if it represents a change in the regular cadence of speech. Not knowing either of the gentlemen before their sickness developed, I cannot know with any certainty.

I looked at my pocket watch, timing the process. Much like the mosquito that I had foolishly allowed to gorge upon me, the black leeches grew engorged as they ingested Eniwek's blood, growing slowly larger and larger. But though they grew swollen and fat, the slimy things were not translucent, and so did not change colour as they fed. Eight. Nine. Ten. With each leech that I applied, Eniwek moaned louder, and louder, becoming more distressed with every bloodsucker I applied. I could see sheen of sweat beginning to bead on his forehead. He must have been more alarmed by the leeches, than he had let on. He had displayed no fear of them prior to the letting, and so I had believed he would do fine. Eleven. Twelve. I used more than I would have used under normal circumstances—again, owing to the fact that the leeches were of the North American type.

Eniwek lay moaning as if in acute pain, which confused me, and which I found alarming. I knew the process to be relatively painless, and his reaction to the therapy was less than usual. The leeches grew larger and larger as they engorged themselves on Eniwek's blood. I stood back, momentarily held spellbound by the dramatic nature of Eniwek's agitation, which seemed to be escalating. Muscles taut, gasping for breath, and contorting as far as his restraints would allow. He seemed a man possessed by the devil, in need of an exorcism more than a mundane letting.

This is when the sudden horrible realization struck me, that Eniwek was receiving some sort of sexual gratification from these ministrations. I cannot express how horrified I was that this might be the case. Whether specific to the Wiindigo Psychosis patient, or some other form of madness particular to Eniwek, I do not know, but it appalled me.

He gasped and cried, louder and louder, reaching a fever pitch as the first slugs removed their jaws from his flesh in satiation, leaving a bloody ring in the place where their mouths had been. Wriggling free and plump to the point of explosion. And in fact, when I stirred myself to action, and attempted to place them back into the masonware jar, the first ones I retrieved, exploded under the pressure of my tongs, much like the mosquito I had earlier killed, popping open like over-ripe fruit. Droplets of Eniwek's blood spattered across my face, my arms, my lips. It was still warm. I had delayed too long, dithering. It was much harder now to pick up the other worms, slick and fat with Eniwek's blood.

Despite my every precaution the letting had gone terribly wrong—just like Ogimaa's—and had become like some sort of nightmare. A good half of the leeches exploded under the grip of my tongs, creating a bloody mess as Eniwek thrashed and moaned about, as in an utter frenzy with every fresh explosion.

I cleaned and sterilized my tools, and my patient. Silent throughout the whole process, as I wiped up the blood from Eniwek's chest, and removed the dark blindfold from about his eyes, now half-lidded and drowsy in contentment. A small smile playing over his lips.

I came away from Drinker's cabin, thankful that I had no witnesses to my work that day, other than the half-breed Aabitiba, who had filled the role of translator. Though he looked at me queerly, upon the commencement of our return journey, and Drinker, coming up the path, upon our quitting the chamber, also noted my complexion.

"Why Harker, you look as if you've seen a ghost. You're as white as a sheet. Eniwek been giving you some trouble today has he?"

To which I mumbled some rejoinder, making the excuse that I had other patients that needed me that day, and I couldn't stay long to chat. Quickly making my departure from Drinker's encampment on the peninsula. Only feeling better when we had pushed off the shore onto Ghost Lake, though wet up to my knees from launching the boat in the shallower waters.

I have resolved that I will be performing no more bloodletting of any kind, leeching or otherwise, on any Wiindigo Psychosis patient. It does not end well.

Harker Lockwood

Rough trade

After a few hours of surveillance, Church pushed himself up off of the ground and started walking. He had been starving himself for a week, drinking only coffee and moss tea. The people on the street went around him, describing an oval sphere of empty space like the lee of a stone in The Secret of Nimh—except his lee was 360 degrees. The people parted, maybe sensing something inhuman, something predatory, something hungry.

Or maybe he was just crazy. He imagined he must have looked rather disheveled. Either was a possibility. He wasn't running anymore, he wasn't hiding. Now that his plan of starvation had been put into place, he was searching for them. He was so hungry now, that he didn't feel very human anymore. He felt that he was ready to confront the vampires, and meet them at their level, monster to monster.

But when he saw them. Ox, Hunsdfordt, and Grundel walking towards him against the flow of traffic, Church froze—for a moment—he couldn't move. Maybe he wasn't ready? When had the sun set? He hadn't even noticed it getting dark. Instead of standing his ground, he ran. His feet pounded the pavement as he cut down Tarpaulin Road, and away from the busier sections along Scrier Street.

Then Church stepped up to the curb as if it were a stage. He held his thumb over the road, eyes closed, trying to exude all the aura and mystery of a Hollywood star. Church couldn't help biting his lower lip, trying to disguise the urgency with which he performed this action; nonchalantly. Someone come. He thought, any minute a trio of vampires are going to come around that corner. He felt like a wizard trying to conjure an escape vehicle.

Church recalled all the times he had ever caught a ride, and he tried to recapture whatever it was, whatever feeling or quality it was that might have infused such moments. Arm outstretched, like the Glad Day figure in William Blake's painting, he felt naked and exposed and about to die.

All cold-blooded creatures were dependant upon external factors like the weather to moderate their body temperature. Lazing around basking in the sun to raise their body temperature, or crawling into the shade of a rock to cool down. For cold-blooded creatures transportation was the key, movement was life. Like Inri said, "If I stay still for too long, it feels like I'll die." Seeing the triplets again had jogged all his memories; Ox and Grundel disposing of his father's body by tossing it over Genosee falls; arms like a vice clamped down, and keeping him immobile as they drank from his veins.

He had made a mistake. He never should have returned to Sterling. Movement is life and stillness is death.

Scorpions

Geoff was on his way home from work when he saw the hitchhiker looking like something thrown away, crumpled and left at the side of the road. And it felt as if he were being pulled instantly in that direction. His thoughts scattered; his heart skipped and beat faster. It felt like he'd been punched in the gut.

Geoff felt sorry for the street youth, the same way he did for those guilt-inducing images of starving children on T.V. But if he was being honest with himself, he would admit that there was more to it than that. It wasn't pity that made him impulsively pull over—it was also desire. His body moving on autopilot whether he thought it was a good idea or not. He was pulled like the needle on a compass, as inevitable as gravity.

The hitchhiker was around the same age as Geoff. Like other street kids and punks, he wore a black-leather jacket studded with small metal spikes. He also wore a horizontal striped Freddy Krueger shirt, and black make-up under his eyes like some kind of predatory animal, or a baseball player trying to cut down on the glare from the sun. Geoff wondered which one he was trying to be—a predator or player? There was also something vaguely familiar about him, tugging at the corners of his memory, but the recollection refused to take form.

The hitchhiker tracked Geoff's progress, studying him with suspicion, the brown liquid depths of his irises merging with the pupils to become opaque spheres. Geoff imagined he could read the kid's mind through those eyes—windows to the soul. Densely packed crypts, contraction furrows and a running monologue of, "I've seen it all and you can't show me nothing that I haven't seen before in some other twisted fuck. I am far from being defenseless so don't even try pulling any shit. The world holds no surprises."

Church lowered his thumb as he saw the beat up Mazda truck pulling over, assessing the guy behind the wheel with calculating eyes. Church turned to look and saw Ox, Hundsfordt, and Grundel rounding the corner, making their way steadily towards him like three smiling, liquid Terminators. Church gave up on his ride, hazard lights blinking. Turning away to run instead, he realized he'd never get away now. He doubted the driver would be happy if he jumped in the car and screamed, "Go, go, go!"

The triplets, all teeth, descended upon him, grabbing him by the elbows and guiding him firmly down an alley. The alley led to a brick wall. It was a dead end.

One wiindigo. Three vampires. Church wished this were in a comic book, because then he could draw the outcome of this conflict in any way he saw fit. And the vampires would not walk away intact.

Church was outrun and outnumbered. Maybe he should have risked jumping into the escape vehicle? But it probably wasn't fair for him to drag someone else into this mess with him, certainly not an innocent bystander. He was going to have to handle this situation on his own.

Sitting in his truck, hazard light blinking, Geoff watched in confusion as the boy was reluctantly guided down the alley. Geoff sat for a moment, wondering what he should do. It wasn't his problem. He didn't even know the kid. Then again, it certainly didn't look as if the boy had gone willingly into the dark alley. Obviously, there was something wrong. He had to do something.

Getting out of the car, Geoff followed the three men to the mouth of the alley. One of the men pushed the kid; he almost tripped and fell. The three men had fanned out, converging on the boy like a pack of wolves, taking turns lunging forward to make him flinch and then laughing. Toying with their prey, they were effortlessly prompting him towards the dead end.

One man lurched forward, forcing the boy to the side of the alley while another slipped behind so that they could surround him from both sides and still block the only avenue of escape. They moved smoothly, as if they knew how to best ensnare their quarry without ever having to speak a word. They knew where they were supposed to be, and when the others were going to be where they were supposed to be, almost as if they had done this sort of thing many times before.

One of the men grabbed him. The kid bucked and struggled almost ripping one arm free, kicking and gnashing at the attacker behind him, hoofed the one in front of him as he released a stream of obscenities. But it was useless. The boy might have been able to hold his own one-on-one, but he was outnumbered, and his resistance only seemed to make his attackers more sadistic.

One of the men gut-punched the kid, doubling him over. The man who had slipped behind the boy pinned his arms behind his back, leaving him unable to defend himself, so the other two could deliver blows to his face, stomach, ribs and kidneys. Geoff winced. Some of those blows would probably leave him pissing blood for a week.

Geoff realized that if he didn't do something, the boy was going to end up in a hospital—or worse—because the kid didn't shut up. He kept on taunting his attackers, providing them with more fuel. Geoff didn't pay much attention to the words, the tone was clear.

Geoff wondered what the kid had done to deserve such
punishment—maybe he deserved it? But he couldn't stand
by and watch the scrawny little punk get torn to pieces on the
off chance he had done something to call down upon himself
such wrath. It would also give him the chance to act chivalrous.
Geoff made his decision and walked down the alleyway towards
the sounds of groans, swear words, and scuffling feet.

Geoff had spent most of his school years fighting—fighting
to let everyone know that he wasn't going to take any bullshit.
He'd graduated from schoolyard scuffles, to bar-brawls, and as
he got older he had taken up boxing and martial arts, and had
even fought semi-professionally for a few years before returning
to it as a hobby. He wasn't afraid of a fight. This, in fact, was
something that he had always been very good at.

The kid received a fist to the mouth mid-insult—but the blow
cut him off, knocking his head to the side for a moment so that
it hung limply and he had to spit out the wad of blood filling his
mouth before he could speak.

The vampires groaned, teasing each other over the "waste
of blood," and laughing like demons. It was clear they were
enjoying themselves. Maybe the scent of blood would send them
into a feeding frenzy like sharks?

Church raised his eyes and was surprised to see the driver who'd
stopped to pick him up only moments before—jeans, work
boots, and steel toes shining through worn leather—but then
he quickly turned back to his attackers, as if dismissing his
presence. Church swore at his attackers, trying to distract them
from the newcomer.

They were quick insults, Geoff thought, insults delivered with enough forcefulness and confidence to mask any fear. The three attackers looked at each other for reassurance; things weren't going as they had expected. He was putting up more of a fight than they'd expected.

One of the thugs pulled his arm back for another strike. Taking a widespread stance, Geoff anchored himself, drawing strength from the ground. Though he fought for sport, he did this naturally. It wasn't something he had to be taught. Geoff caught the guy's fist in mid-air, and punched him so hard that it sent the guy sprawling to the ground. It would take a moment for the man to get back up.

Geoff turned, planted his feet firmly on the ground, and punched the other thug, who looked almost identical to the first. The first thug recovered faster than he would have thought possible and was already back on his feet. Thug number one punched Geoff in the face. He was going to have a nasty looking bruise. While he was busy struggling with the first look-alike, the other one got back up too and tackled him, knocking him to the concrete.

. . . Geoff noticed that the sneakers on the boy's feet had staples imbedded into the rubber soles of his shoes like the claws of a cat. He was captivated for a moment by the odd detail, which he might not have noticed if he hadn't been sprawled on the ground, eye-level with the shoes. That's odd, Geoff thought, but then he was being kicked in the kidneys, too distracted to consider the metal claws.

Hundsfordt had Church restrained in a full nelson, so all he could do was watch as the fight ensued. But then a memory came to him; of his father holding one of his poker buddies in the same chokehold that he was in now. The guy had slipped his foot between Peter's legs, wrapped his ankle around Peter's heel, and threw all of his weight backwards. Peter tripped and fell onto his back, which wouldn't have been so bad—if he hadn't still been holding the other guy in a headlock. The other man was pulled down too, so that his weight was added to the force of the impact, crushing him. Church performed this same maneuver now, silently thanking the drunk who'd crushed his father.

The vampire hit the ground with a satisfying crunch. He felt the bones of Hundsfordt's ribs collapse underneath him, and the air from Hundsfordt's lungs forcefully expelled next to his ear. Church disentangled himself from the vampire and went to save his rescuer from Ox and Grundel, who were tossing the guy back and forth between them like a pinball. They laughed, elated with their new sport, and probably delighted by the prospect of fresh blood.

Geoff's nose was bleeding and he would probably have an impressive black eye tomorrow. He knocked one look-alike thug onto the ground, turned to the other, grabbed him by the front of his shirt, and slammed him up against the brick wall so hard that the back of his head made a sickening crack.

Ox got back up and came after Church, grabbing him in a bear hug and dragging him towards the mouth of the alleyway. Church struggled to get free. And while Ox's hands were full, the driver punched Ox in the face.

The boy—as Geoff continued to think of the hitchhiker— suddenly found himself free and began kicking his attackers on the ground, who had not yet recovered from Geoff's assault. The boy kicked them in the ribs and face while they were still defenseless. Geoff winced as he watched staples raking across eyes. He touched the kid's arm and had to pull the boy away, still kicking and screaming at the bloodied mass on the ground. They made their escape while the three assailants were still twitching, and picking themselves up off the ground.

"Who were those guys?" Geoff asked breathlessly, as soon as they cleared the alley.

"What the hell are you doing?" Church asked. Didn't the guy know how much danger he had placed himself in?

The boy stared at Geoff, his nostrils flaring. For a moment Geoff thought the street-kid was going to launch himself at him for lack of a better target on which to vent his anger.

"You're welcome," Geoff said, and the hitch-hiker seemed to deflate. Geoff had hurt his ankle in the fight and was limping slightly. He put his hand on the boy's shoulder to steady himself, and steer the street-kid towards his truck. Church was uncomfortably aware of the weight on his shoulder. He wasn't used to the invasion of his personal space. But the guy had been injured trying to rescue him.

While the driver unlocked the Mazda, Church examined a half-smoked cigarette that had been thrown into a puddle and stained a small cloud of water tobacco brown before freezing. Preserved like an insect in a piece of amber—an oil-slick sheen of rainbow gasoline iridizing the surface. Church turned to look back, but the three vampires had yet to emerge. They'll be back, Church thought. If they want any more of my blood, which they seem to like so much, then they will be.

Church found himself again slipping into the fantasy that his father's murderers were really vampires, and that they were after him because they wanted to drink his wiindigo blood. Like glazed vision induced by a fever, he could only sometimes see through the sick-fog to the reality beyond. Church speculated that there might be something about his wiindigo blood that the vampires found irresistible. Church knew that eventually they would find him, and he would have to be more prepared. He'd just gotten lucky—this time.

They hopped in the beat-up Mazda, and his rescuer revved the engine, making them lurch up the street. They disappeared around the corner before the vampires had emerged from the mouth of the alley.

"Do I know you?" Church asked, squinting at his rescuer, surprised that he recognized him. There was something familiar about his neck. "You're Geoff Suture, aren't you?"

"Yeah, how did you know that?" Geoff asked.

"We went to school together." Church told him, "You were in my class." Geoff looked at the kid again. There was something familiar about him.

"It's Church right?" Geoff asked, recognizing him. Geoff hadn't seen Church since they'd both been in high school together. Church had moved, or dropped out of school and disappeared.

"Why did you help me?" Church asked. He didn't like when someone did something there wasn't an obvious explanation for. There's always a price to pay, his father said. Nothing in this world comes for free.

"I saw you hitchhiking," Geoff said. "I couldn't just let you get beat up."

"Why not?" Church asked. Even generosity had its motives. Find the motive and you could settle on an appropriate strategy.

"Who were those guys?" Geoff asked again.

"Have you been drinking?" Church asked, squinting at him. He could smell the alcohol on Geoff. It made him uneasy. Peter hadn't always been predictable when he was drunk.

"Do you want a ride or not?" Geoff asked.

Church automatically slipped into his hitchhiker mode of analyzing and hypothesizing about the people who gave him rides. Church had been forced to push trash onto the floor to clear a space to sit, and the small fold-down seats in the back were similarly covered with refuse. A green, scented pine tree and a medicine wheel dangled from the rear-view mirror. The brown fabric of the interior was covered with a thousand tiny burn marks, localizing themselves about the head of the driver.

"So where are we going?" Geoff asked. He had been driving to get away, and now didn't have any particular destination.

Church settled for giving Geoff a dirty look for a moment while he thought of an answer, thinking about somewhere he could go, and when he came up with an answer he wondered why he hadn't thought of it before. The more he considered the idea the more right it felt.

"I want to go to the Ghost Lake reserve." Church said. He was certain that the vampires had now caught his scent, and they'd eventually be able to track him wherever he went. It would be better if he was on his own turf when they caught up with him again.

"Why would you want to go there? No one lives there anymore."

"One of my grandfathers still does." Church said, looking abstractedly out the window, shifting light and shadow from the streetlights passing across his face.

Geoff searched Church's face for those Anishinaabe features that were familiar to him, something about the shape of his eyes maybe, imperceptible unless you were looking for it, imperceptible unless you were used to looking for it.

"That's pretty far," Geoff said. "It'd take a couple hours to get there."

Church shrugged. "Take me as far as you wanna go, and I'll get a ride with someone else the rest of the way."

"That's crazy! It's too late to be hitchhiking. You can crash at my place tonight and set out tomorrow." It would be better than going back to the shelter, Church thought, and he needed to rest and then get back on the road.

Church knew there was more to the offer than simple hospitality; Geoff Suture might be tough, but it was also clear that the guy was quite taken with him. Church didn't know how to feel about this. It was a new experience for him. Church had always been too busy trying not to think of people as food, to worry about what else he might be able to do with them. When he looked Suture in the eye, he saw something almost like hunger.

"Okay," Church said, giving Geoff a hard look, "but only 'till tomorrow, and I'm gone first thing in the morning."

September 26th 1872, Ghost Lake,

Dear James,

Nightmares have been plaguing me these past few weeks, as if Drinker's nightmarish creatures have invaded my own dreams. The monstrous forms of extinct species that terrorize his dreams have now also found life in my own unconscious mind. I wake up in the night, saturated with sweat, and filled with all manner of childish fears and anxieties, so that it is difficult to get back to sleep. I find I am tired during the day, and have prescribed myself the treatment I have given Drinker—belladonna and a small tincture of laudanum.

The winter comes early up here.

The leaves have already turned to shades of orange and red, signaling the end of summer, as if the whole world has caught on fire and been frozen mid-blaze, shot through with jets of startling pink, crimson, and chartreuse where the flames have yet to kindle, smoulder and blaze.

Like a bouquet of flowers, the entire world seems to have turned garish in its death throes, expiring in cascades of dazzling colour. When I walk all I can hear is the scuffling of dry leaves like the wrappings on a mummified corpse, the desiccated remains crunching underfoot. When the wind blows, the whole world is filled with the sound of trees clacking: bough against bough, branch against branch, leaf against leaf, whispering their leathery words, in a secret language only the forest itself can interpret or understand.

Sssssshhhhhhhh, it says in a susurrating, sibilant speech. Sssssssshhhhhhhhhh. Like a roomful of people, all speaking to each other at the same time, in the same manner of voice.

"As soon as the leaves begin to turn," Goshko tells me, "you can soon expect to see the first snowfall." I spend increasingly more time in the wise man's company, as he instructs me in his Indian tongue, and we use our joint knowledge and his home remedies to cure the sick. When I visit the old man, Aabitiba is never anywhere to be found. I get the feeling they are not fond of each other—Aabitiba always makes some excuse for his absence.

Today, Aabitiba and I went to visit the home of the "Wiindigo's Daughter." When I questioned Goshko about his niece, he denied being related to such a person, and claimed he knew nothing of the woman.

We had to paddle by canoe for half the day before we arrived.

We entered the home, a log-cabin domicile in the style of the zhaaganash, instead of the round lodges still favoured by many of the other Indians. It is said that, the family of this 'always' wiindigo, were the first ones to convert to Christianity, and they are being punished for abandoning their gods. That is the story Aabitiba tells me. As if the light of Christianity could have turned these savage people into cannibals! Now this woman is the most confirmed pagan in the neighbourhood, and will never again turn away from the old ways. She is an outcast. Living next to—but never part of, the local tribe.

Upon entering her home, we are engulfed by the scents of cooking. A woman stands hunched over a massive cauldron. It smells like moose-meat. I found it difficult to gauge her age. She could have been fourteen or forty, probably owing to her youthful face and the grey streaks in her hair. Her lips were swollen and appeared freshly bruised. There was a tattoo of a blue line running from her lower lip to the point of her chin. She was skinny to the point of emaciation. She was also achingly lovely.

I felt my soul vibrate like the strings of a bowed violin.

I wrenched my eyes away, and scanned the rest of the room. On the edges of my vision, I had also perceived a young girl lying on her stomach on the floor at the woman's feet, making the soft mewling noises children often do, and absently playing with some small toy. But when I looked again, the child *was gone, swept away in an instant as if she were a ghost, or some fancy somehow conjured from my own mind. I don't know how the awareness of a child's presence had formed, only that it was an illusion.*

The fireplace was more than large enough to accommodate the huge pot. The stone hearth dominated the entire far side of the wall, and was big enough to spit and roast an entire pig, rotating it slowly over the dancing flames. For whom was she cooking such a large stew? I wondered. I could discern the presence of no one else living in the vicinity. And from all accounts she lives alone. Maybe she was expecting company? But she lives as a recluse. Mystery upon mystery.

The young-old woman did not look up from her pot, stirring the contents with concentration, although she could have hardly failed to notice our presence. As was the practice in the area, we entered without knocking. I am still getting accustomed to the strange customs of these people. I couldn't discern whether her ignorance of our presence was customary, or just odd. The fixity of focus with which she stirred the pot could not have been habitual, and must have owed itself to our presence.

Shyness, I thought.

My guide hung back, unwilling to step further into the home, or even to speak, leaving it up to me to make the introductions.

"Boozhoo," I said to the young-old woman, as, by this point, I had picked up some of the Anishinaabe language, offering her a small bundle of tobacco, as I had been instructed by Aabitiba, who had been very insistent that we stick with the Ojibwe protocols for entreating the spirits, an elder's knowledge, or asking for assistance.

"Mino-ishkwaa-naakwe. Ndaa gwii-gaganoozhag?" I asked, first in the Anishinaabe language, followed up by the English. "Good afternoon. I was wondering if we could speak with you? Nwii-andawenim gaganoonidiwag aajimookaanan oshki-wiindigowi-aakoziwinan. It is regarding the recent cases of wiindigo sicknesses." I felt ridiculous, holding the bundle of tobacco out to

the woman, who neither responded in any way to our presence, nor even looked up from her task of stirring the mammoth zhiisheb-kick, as the Ojibwe called it because, I've been told, it is shaped like the body of a duck. This wasn't a birch-bark pot, sewn together and smeared with bear fat to seal the leaks. This was a solid, cast-iron pot, the size of a stove.

"Gidaanis ina? Kwezens?" I couldn't help asking, looking about for the child I thought I had seen. "Do you have a daughter?"

"Nishiimenh." She whispered. Her voice seemed to carry despite how quietly she spoke. My sister. "Beshowad nishiimenh." Strangely, she used the inanimate verb, beshowad, instead of beshowizi. My sister is never far. In the Ojibwe way of seeing the world, there are only two different kinds of things, because in their language, everything is either inanimate or animate, living or dead. I wondered, into which category her sister fell? Things that one would consider non-living in English, can sometimes be considered animate in Anishinaabemoowin. The daily lessons in the Indian tongue which Goshko and, to some extent Aabitiba, have been tutoring me, have proved time and again to be infinitely useful in my interactions with the local inhabitants.

The fire burned merrily, casting a reddish-orange hue on the young woman's face, and I could perceive a slight smile in the crook of her upturned lip. She was enjoying herself. I noticed that the spoon with which she stirred the pot was not really a spoon, but more of a stick. The stick was a pale shade of greyish-white like driftwood. That's after all, what would be required to stir such a huge vat, I thought. But as she stirred, pulling up great hunks of meat from the depths so they wouldn't burn at the bottom, keeping the substance constantly mixing, I noticed that the wooden spoon wasn't wood at all. It had the characteristic texture of old bone.

From somewhere, I conceived the idea that she was stirring her pot with the femur bone of a human being, and that the contents of the pot, was not moose meat at all, but some other kind of meat I dared not let my mind think *upon. The savory aroma suddenly felt thick in the air, cloying, crowding my senses, and suffocatingly close. The appetizing scent turned my stomach, and I felt sick. I needed to get out.*

I twisted, gagging and reeling drunkenly out of the door as fast as I could. I wanted to be away from that place. The door swung open behind me and I left it that way, lurching over to a stand of trees and heaving the meal I had eaten for breakfast, breathing in great gasps. Even though, I was now, finally away from the smell of her cooking stew, I imagined that I could smell it still. Aabitiba followed, watching me from a safe distance with his characteristic calm.

Upon further reflection, I realized that the bone with which she had been stirring the pot, was too large to have come from a man, and must have been from the moose she'd been cooking, or even one of the dinosaurs Marsh and Cope were busy exhuming.

I feel like an idiot! I've let the stories and superstitions of the Indians get to me. I am a man of medical science. All this paranormal raucous is much more up your alley James, than it is mine. With your Metaphysical Club—that organization for the study of inexplicable phenomenon, and the outer limits of psychical ability—I think that you would love this place. Ghost Lake is aptly named; it has me jumping at my own shadow, as if it were truly haunted.

As for me, I felt giddy with sickness and relief. Having dispelled both my fears and my breakfast, I felt ready to carry on the task of studying this malady. Without the darkness of superstition clouding my vision, I am clearer now for having travelled through it.

Owing to the fact that I was feeling unwell, Aabitiba and I thought it best that we put off our visit to Mukade-wiiyas, or Weetikowim-O'daanisim-kwe, the Wiindigo's Daughter, as she is known. Aabitiba tells me neither Mukade-wiiyas nor Weetikowim-O'daanisim-kwe is her 'real name;' an example of the confounding Ojibwe custom of having not just one or two names, but as many as seven or eight names throughout their lifetime, and as many as four or five simultaneously! They are overly fond of these nicknames, more often than not going by a nickname rather than a given name, and only occasionally by a Christian name. If they even have one! I am surrounded by heathens.

That is the story I have to tell, and I hope it finds you in good spirits!

Always. Harker Lockwood.

October 15th 1871, Ghost Lake,

Dear James,

I feel Lost. My medicine is little better than Goshko's talismans, providing some hope, some measure of relief, but ultimately they are ineffective. I've tried bleeding my patients—using first the ivory-handled lancet that you gave me James, and when that mysteriously disappeared, resorted to leeching. I know you've always been a proponent of bloodletting, as a symbolic marker for the tools of our trade, but I've always had my misgivings.

I was at first elated. My patients seemed to improve. But letting the bad blood only provided a temporary abatement of the symptoms. Yes, these treatments eased symptoms, calmed agitation, and allowed the patients to rest, but did they cure this sickness? No. In the long-term these ministrations have had little or no effectiveness.

I do not know what other treatments to employ. And confronted by Ogimaa's increasing agitation, I have ceased my objections—I have given authorization for Goshko to attempt his last ditch cure: to pour boiling duck fat down the victim's throat in the hopes of dislodging, or melting the ice that is imagined to be the source of Ogimaa's wiindigo "transformation". The Indian chief, Mookman, is busy heating, and bringing to boil, the duck fat, and I have resolved to hang back and observe, and not interfere with the gentlemen during the application of this "cure." I will tend to the burns that will undoubtedly result, should he survive this remedy.

Though I have little faith in its effectiveness, both the patient and the Ojibwe healer, place great stock in the efficacy of this medicine, and so I hope that the element of belief—that is itself a component of the psychosis—may be put to rest. Despite my insistence, Ogimaa and Goshkǫ have also refused the use of chloroform as an anesthetic during the application of this "cure." They worry that the ice won't melt if Ogimaa cannot feel the heat of the burning oil.

It is barbaric.

Goshkǫ held the beaker in a pair of wooden tongs because the molten fat was too hot to handle. He insisted the grease simmer and boil over the course of several hours as it rendered. The smell of boiling fat filled the air like a Christmas dinner. His boy Yah-ence, who was acting as his assistant, and Chief Mookman held the man's mouth wide with leather instruments, keeping him strapped down securely so that the oil didn't spill or drip as a result of Ogimaa's inevitable thrashing.

The screams made every muscle in my body cringe, I could barely stand to listen to his agony, as the fat was slowly poured down his esophagus. The pain was such that he couldn't help but struggle, though he believed it would cure him. Despite his relative stoicism with regard to the pain of blood-letting, boiling duck-fat proved to test the limits of his endurance. His cries caused the duck-fat to spray everywhere, burning those who held him down. They continued with the forced ingestion, despite their own, no doubt, painful burns. I could only admire their determination. He was tied securely, and could only rage against the restraints, rising from the bed frame no more than an inch. They waited between each roar of misery, so the fat would not bubble and spew, and spatter those in attendance with the burning pitch.

He sounded more animal than human, for the first time seeming to me as inhuman as the wiindigo monster he feared metamorphosizing into. It reminded me of the call of a bull elk, with multiple subsonic harmonics, above and below the range of human hearing. This is what Ogimaa sounded like, as if he were screaming with more than one mechanism for vocalization; a layering of sound. Wind through a ruffled metal drainage ditch, produces such a haunting, whirling sound—and I wouldn't have thought a human throat capable of reproducing such a din—if I hadn't heard it emanating from Ogimaa myself.

At some point during the treatment, Ogimaa lost consciousness, and they were then able to pour the duck fat down his throat much more easily than when he had been awake and screaming, a leather yoke holding his jaws apart. Some measure of colour and heat returned to the patient's face almost immediately after the remedy was administered, although whether this constitutes a cessation of symptoms or a 'cure' is yet to be seen.

Mookman and Goshko retired from the room, apparently exhausted after their exertions, leaving me to care for the patient under the watchful gaze of Yah-ence. Other than blistered lips, and some swelling to tongue and cavity of the mouth, I could discern no further injuries. Most of the damage he sustained could have been internal. Counting the pulse in the radial artery at his wrist with two fingers, index and middle, I listened to his heartbeat, counting out the steady, regular beating of his heart. There were no irregularities.

As I listened with my stethoscope, Ogimaa began choking in his sleep, coughing up chunks of ice and blood onto the pillow, as if clearing a foreign object from the passageway to his lungs. With a pair of metal tongs, I carefully examined the shards. They glinted pale blue-white amidst the flower of his blood, like crystal anther stamens, just a few small flakes that quickly melted—they melted so quickly, in fact, that once they were gone, I immediately doubted that I had seen them. Was I seeing things? Could I have been imagining it? Was my mind playing tricks on me? Had the stories of his frozen heart subliminally imprinted themselves on my mind—my unconsciousness? Was I, like the child who stayed up late telling ghost stories, now feeling the full effect of nightmares—in the form of hallucinations that now afflicted my waking mind? I do not know, but I shrugged it off. A product of my troubled mind. I turned to Yah-ence, but he appeared as composed, and unaffected by this astonishing ice. Had the boy seen?

Once Ogimaa's coughing fit subsided, he relaxed once again into a serene sleep, his respiration even and regular, his cheeks flushed and ruddy, appearing as if he'd just come in to a warm room from some active exertion out in the cold. I left him to his rest, feeling relieved at the abatement to his symptoms, however transitory they may prove to be.

I will check in on my patient on the morrow.

Though they have no formal training, I do believe James, there is sometimes merit in the folk-cures and remedies of these regional practitioners.

Yours,

Harker Lockwood

Confluence, n. 1. A flowing together of two rivers, steams, or bodies of water. 2. A coming together; of people, forces or circumstances; a meeting at a specific place or point in time.

Church

From his two encounters with the 'details' men, Church had learned a few things about vampires. They were strong, but they didn't have supernatural strength. If they did, he would be dead already. They were no stronger than a strong human being. But that didn't make them any less dangerous. Humans killed. And humans didn't have super-human strength. And Church had seen what the vampires could do first hand. He had watched what they had done to his father.

They were sort of like scorpions, Church thought—the more delicate the scorpion—the more poisonous it had to be in order to survive. Ox, Hundsfordt, and Grundel didn't rely on some kind of supernatural strength; they relied on their cunning. And they hunted in a pack like wolves.

Both attacks had happened at night. Church doubted they would burst into flames on contact with the sun, but they were definitely creatures of the night. They were nocturnal.

Their only real physical advantages—their only real weapons— were their teeth, their thumbnails and maybe their eyes. When Church had looked into Hundsfordt's eyes, it had been as if he had been drawn into them somehow, but he hadn't stayed for long. And Hundsfordt had been surprised. Whatever he had been trying to do, it didn't work. Maybe Wiindigo were immune? Church would hate to find out what would happen if their fangs found a main artery—he suspected they could bleed him dry in minutes, if not seconds, if they wanted.

Church remembered what he had read about dinosaurs. There were relatively few carnivores in relation to herbivores. Even a large population of plant-eaters could only sustain a relatively small number of meat-eaters. Ox, Hundsfordt and Grundel had the teeth of carnivores, and Church supposed there were relatively few vampires preying upon the human population.

There were three of them—probably because of the safety that was found in numbers. They were after all, fragile, and no more indestructible than humans. They could be killed.

When he met them again, Church would just have to make sure that he was very hungry.

"Did you drop out of school?" Geoff asked as they drove. The last time he remembered seeing Church, they were both still in school. Smears of orange and green lights drifted across his face as he drove aimlessly, extending the length of their trip so he'd have more time to get to know the boy he used to hassle.

Church considered lying. He'd been taught never to reveal too much about himself. It was too dangerous. Church intended to lie, but found himself telling the truth. He told Geoff that he had been on the road, and living on the street, since his father died. Peter had always had official custody, and his grandmother, his primary guardian, was disabled and insane besides, and had followed his mother into Sterling Shores. Since then he had done a lot of moving around, never staying in any one place for long.

He was gripped by some kind of mania that wouldn't let him rest, a desperate need to keep moving. If he stayed still, he'd die. Church knew it was a corruption of his wiindigo nature, another method of dissolution. And Church found himself falling into the same patterns—he rode the rails, he took buses when he could afford a ticket, he hitchhiked and if no one was picking him up, he walked. It didn't matter as long as he kept moving. Momentum was the only thing that kept him going.

"I don't know why I'm telling you all this," Church said.

"It's okay, I like it," Geoff said. They pulled into the driveway of a small bungalow, and Geoff took the key out of the ignition. They sat in silence for a moment, listening to the sounds of the engine clinking softly as it cooled.

"Here, give me your hand," Church said. Geoff squinted at him, but extended his hand. Church took the hand and turned it so that he could read the lines on his palm, peering down at it as if it were a crystal ball. The lines on Geoff's hand were obscured by layers of built up calluses, hard as chunks of bone.

"Can you see the future?" Geoff asked.

"For twenty bucks," Church said.

"You're a fortune teller?" Suture asked.

"Not really," Church said, "It's more like I tell people their present. That's a lot easier to see, and also a lot more impressive because it's verifiable."

On the reverse side of Suture's hand was a pale, faded scar—as if his hand had been dipped into boiling water. The scar was old and only slightly discoloured. Scarred flesh always grew back tougher, like a callous.

"You have thick skin." Church told him, "You don't let a lot of things bother you."

Since he had learned how to read palms from a book while examining his own hand, reading anyone else felt like reading a newspaper upside-down. Though this didn't matter too much because the most important part was learning how to read people. Reading people was like an extension of what he did when he examined the interior of someone's car. Except when you were reading someone's palm, you were close enough to smell the other person, see the pores on their face.

"You have a large Mount of Jupiter," Church said pointing to a bump below Geoff's index finger, "which could mean that you have a lot of self-confidence or that you can be domineering."

As Church read Geoff's palm he interjected explanations into his process: "Reading palms is a lot like reading a horoscope," Church continued. "Anything you tell a person should be able to sound like it's very specific while at the same time being very generic—and always give people an alternative interpretation in case what you say is way off."

"But you'd still be surprised by what you can learn just from someone's hand." Church added.

"Like what?" Geoff asked.

"Well," Church said, "your hand has a lot of calluses, which means that you're a labourer—maybe into construction—a carpenter, a stonemason, something like that. You don't have a career. You just have a job. You show up, you get paid, and you work long hours. Your knuckles have been broken, more than once, and so has your nose. You like to fight, or box, or you're into martial arts. You're not married. There's no ring on your finger. You have grime under your fingernails, so I suppose you have no one to impress. You smell of alcohol, and you aren't wearing any cologne—you drink a lot . . ."

Geoff pulled his hand away. He felt uncomfortable under this level of scrutiny, and was surprised how much Church had been able to guess in the space of a few minutes. It was as if Church had been looking into his soul, and he didn't want Church to see any farther into the murk.

Fortune telling might not be magic, but Church could learn a lot about a person by being observant, making a few guesses, then watching their reactions. That's what Church had really been doing; looking at Geoff while pretending to inspect his palm.

"I do that to everyone," Church said, "whether or not I give them a reading."

"Well, it's disturbing," Geoff Said. "Let's go in."

The yard in front of his house was like a garden that had run riot; not as if it had been left to go to seed, but as if it had been encouraged to explode—the verdure had taken root like a jungle in the small plot, a profusion of flowers and plants bursting with vitality—their was order in the chaos. Geoff opened the door to his apartment and a cat ran out, rubbing itself against his legs. It was one of the most scrawny, battle-scarred cats Church had ever seen. Patches of fur were missing or growing in tufts, and it walked with a limp, holding its left fore-paw close to its body.

"That's a rough looking cat," Church said.

"Boozhence. He comes and goes as he pleases. I think he only comes back because I keep feeding him. Do you like cats?" Geoff asked him.

"I was never really allowed to have pets," Church said, looking around Geoff's home. The apartment was dimly lit and sparsely furnished with second-hand couches, and furniture made out of milk-crates. Ashtrays overflowed on the coffee table and boxes of empty two-fours were stacked up in the corners. Empty bottles of C-Six were everywhere. It reminded him of Jason's treehouse.

"He'll rub up against your legs sometimes, but Boozhence doesn't like to be touched, so don't pet him," Geoff cautioned. "Do you want a drink?" Geoff brought out a bottle of C-Six and took a swig straight from the bottle.

"No thanks," Church said, shaking his head. But when Geoff offered him the bottle, he took it, feeling the liquor burn all the way down, warming him with artificial heat.

"I shouldn't drink too much. I have to work in the morning. You can crash here if you want," Geoff said, patting one of the cushions on an orange flower-patterned couch.

"Thanks," Church said, nodding. Geoff brought him a pillow apologizing for the fact that he didn't have any extra blankets.

"It's okay, I have my own," Church said, nodding towards a tightly rolled army-surplus sleeping bag, tied to his backpack. "What kind of work do you do?"

"You don't know already?" Geoff asked, smiling. "You weren't far off. I do construction. Roofing. Landscaping." Geoff shrugged. "Whatever I can find."

"Yeah, I figured." Church said.

"My grandfather used to tell me stories," Geoff said. The conversation seemed to have swerved from one subject to another like a schizophrenic record player. Playing on one track for a while and then skipping to another song without any space between.

"He told me this one story about a woman who was pregnant, but she was sick and dying. So this old woman, this medicine woman, she took that baby and she put it into the belly of an elm tree, a birch tree or a poplar tree. Sometimes it would be a willow tree. It changed every time he told it, but it was usually one of those. Anyway, that tree carried the baby in its trunk for six months, nourishing the fetus with sap, drawing water up with its roots, converting sunlight into a sugary milk, and protecting that baby with its bark. When it was time for the baby to be born, the medicine woman returned to claim the tree's charge. The baby was born happy and healthy, but it wasn't entirely human anymore either. The baby had taken on the characteristics of his surrogate mother. He was more plant than animal, growing dormant during the winter months, and only coming alive during the summer months. He craved the sun, and he would stand for hours soaking in the rays, and taking no solid food for sustenance. He could subsist on the nourishment of light alone. He also drank—a lot—whatever happened to be at hand." At this point in the narrative, Geoff paused to take a swig from the bottle of C-Six.

"Anyway, this man was one of my ancestors from way-way back, and my grandfather used to say that as his grandchildren, we have also inherited this thirst." And here Geoff ended his story, taking another pull on the bottle of C-Six.

"Sometimes I think it's true, other times I think it's bullshit and he made the story up to make me feel better about my parents. An excuse for their alcoholism. So I wouldn't hate them. It didn't work."

"That's a fucked up story," Church said.

"Yeah. Anyway, it's time for me to go to bed. Good night," Geoff said as he retreated to his darkened room, and his own bed.

Church unrolled his army-surplus sleeping bag on the couch. He hadn't realized how tired he was, he was asleep almost the instant his head hit the pillow. Entering a deep, dreamless sleep.

Geoff watched for a moment as Church dozed off, the lines of stress and worry sliding from his face and making him look years younger. Bruises had now formed from their fight in the alleyway. He had a busted lip, and a black eye. Church still wore his shoes, so the dirt on his soles was mucking up the cushions. Geoff got up and turned off the lights, briefly considered taking Church's shoes off, but decided against it. He didn't want to risk waking him.

One of Church's elbows had rode up on his sweater and T-shirt revealing a small sliver of exposed flesh, the curve of his stomach dipping in to meet a round hipbone protruding above his jeans. Geoff took another swig of C-Six and felt the warmth spread through his chest. He took a sip of C-Six and it tasted like the best damned thing he'd ever tasted. It was so easy it was almost a mistake, as involuntary as breathing. And it felt like he was closer to something. Geoff took a sip of C-Six and it tasted like resurrection, it tasted like death.

Church felt someone nudging him gently awake.

"Are you awake?" Geoff asked softly. "Do you want to get something to eat?"

Church sat up quickly, eyes wide. For a moment he had forgotten where he was, and he was unsure what kind of situation he would find himself in. Cops hassling him for being somewhere they didn't think he should be, or someone riffling through his pockets while he was unconscious.

By the quality of the light in the window, he guessed that it was sometime around five a.m. - that dim, watery quality of the light between night and morning. He had intended to be long-gone by the time Geoff got up, but Geoff was an early riser.

Geoff flinched, taken aback by how quickly Church had sat up. "Sorry to startle you," Geoff said. "But I have to go to work soon. I thought we could go have breakfast before I leave. There's a diner around the corner that serves decent food."

The brown of Church's irises bled to black transformed by mindless hunger and something else, more incisive, measuring, suspicious. What had he said, Geoff wondered, to provoke such a reaction? The kid had a pair of weapons on him, those eyes could cut the secrets from his heart and leave what was left bleeding to death on the floor. Gone was the boy who had seconds before looked more waif-like than ever, replaced by the street-hardened punk.

"Do you want some breakfast?" Geoff asked softly. Church's shoulders relaxed and the wariness faded away as it was replaced by the hungry sharpness of an eagle's-eye, focusing on its prey.

"Yes," Church said, as hunger won out over distrust.

Church used Geoff's tiny bathroom to get washed up, and it felt as if he were washing off years of grime and stress. He borrowed some of Geoff's toothpaste to brush his teeth. It was a brand that he'd never heard of, the logo of a green and purple genii smiling out at him on the side of the tube.

Church emerged from the bathroom looking light-years better. As they left, walking out into the grey light of the dawn, Church noticed that for some reason he felt better than he had in long time.

Church wondered if vampires could walk in the sun, or whether they would burst into flames like in a John Carpenter movie. Bram Stoker's Dracula didn't burst into flames, he was simply nocturnal, but in the film Nosferatu, an unofficial adaptation of Stoker's work, the vampire is incinerated in a puff of smoke. He thought of the etching by the artist Goya, easily one of his favourite artists, El sueno de la razon produce monstrous, or "The sleep of reason produces monsters." Nightmares tended to disappear when confronted by the light of reason. Vampires did not exist, he reassured himself, and neither did wiindigowag.

But something about being in Geoff's presence seemed to have an almost anesthetic effect upon him. Church had slept better than he could last remember, and he felt better just being near him. It must have something to do with an alchemic reaction between cells, a physiological more than mental or emotional reaction. He thought of the story Geoff had told, about having ancestors in the plant-world. Willow-tree bark had traditionally been used for its medicinal qualities, maybe some of those healing properties rubbed off on him?

Terminal lunch

The diner was right next to the bus station. It was cheap, greasy and delicious. The fluorescent lights were as bright as the inside of a convenience store, and they flickered like the set of a David Lynch movie. It was a place where people stopped on their way to somewhere else. Church felt comfortable there. The waitress didn't even blink when she took in their black eyes and bruises.

Geoff raised an eyebrow when Church ordered the "Lumber-Jack special": Eggs, bacon, juice, coffee, home fries, sausage, pancakes, and toast. When the food arrived Church cleaned his plate. His busted lip kept breaking open as he ate so all of his food was flavoured with the taste of his own blood. The corner of his lips encrusted with dried blood.

Geoff watched Church eat, forgetting about his own food. He made it look so easy. When he'd finished eating, Church pushed his empty plate aside, realizing for the first time that Geoff was staring at him. "What?" he asked. "I was hungry."

"I've never seen anyone eat like that before," Geoff said, staring at him as if he was an alien.

"Well," Church said, groping around for an explanation. "Never know when I'm going to get my next meal. Have to make it last."

"I guess I'll know what to expect the next time," Geoff said. Church's eyes narrowed and his shoulders came up in unconscious posture of defence.

"Next time?" Church asked. "What do you mean?"

"I didn't mean anything," Geoff said, frowning. Church became spooked for reasons he didn't understand, and their conversation was a landscape of odd silences and hidden mines, where one word could prove to be misplaced.

"If you don't want to have dinner with me you don't have to. No one's twisting your arm." Geoff said. He saw Church surrounded by a halo of invisible thorns that stabbed out in all directions. You couldn't get too close without getting sliced.

"Dinner?" Church asked, still frowning but instantly hungry again at the thought of another meal. Church was all jagged edges, like an animal ensnared in barbed wire, struggling and only making the edges dig in deeper.

"Yeah, I'm done work at six o'clock." Geoff said, holding out the key to his apartment. "Feel free to help yourself to anything in the fridge." It felt like he was taking a bite out of a Halloween apple, and he didn't know whether or not a blade would dig into the roof of his mouth. Geoff decided he would hazard the risks.

"I know you wanted to take off, but if you're still around when I finish work we'll go out for dinner. If not, leave the key under the potted fern." Geoff said, followed by a quiet admission: "I want you to stay."

Geoff got up and left, leaving Church alone in the diner. Church rubbed the key between his thumb and index finger, examining the tarnished metal, the brass shining through the nickel plating under the flickering fluorescent lights. Geoff didn't have a lot, but everything he owned was in that apartment. There was a level of trust being extended, and Church didn't know if he as worthy of it.

When the hunger became unbearable, he dug through the cupboards and ate from canned foods which he thought Geoff wouldn't miss, hidden way in the back of the cupboard, their labels peeling off so it was a surprise when he found out what he'd be eating. Peaches, three cans of beans, a can of tomato sauce, chick peas and chunk-light tuna. He was trying to steer clear of the fridge, not wanting to noticeably decimate Geoff's collection of groceries, sticking mainly to jars of food hidden in the back. A jar of pickles, orange marmalade, olives, coleslaw, and Cheese-wiz. Church supplemented his diet with a few protein bars he always carried in his backpack. By the time Geoff returned, his stomach was growling, and he was eager for the promise of dinner.

"Oh good, you're still here," Geoff said smiling, the tension in his shoulders relaxing. "I wasn't sure if you'd still be here when I got back."

"Where are we going for dinner?" Church asked with a grin. "Terminal Lunch?"

Anatomy lesson

Geoff Suture was lying on the couch clutching his stomach in exaggerated pain, and Church was sitting in the lazy boy, Boozhence curled up in his lap. The cat purred softly, a deep, resonant, growl in the back of his throat.

Church's stomach was an empty cave ruled by the growling bear of hunger, except today Church had allowed himself to eat almost as much as he wanted—and instead of making him hungrier, it had actually taken the edge off.

"You shouldn't have eaten so much," Church said smiling.

"You did," Geoff said.

"I didn't know you were going to make dinner too," Church said. Geoff hadn't been able to keep up.

"You said you were still hungry," Geoff said groaning in pain. After they went out for dinner Geoff was full, but Church still seemed to be ravenous, so Geoff cooked his guest a meal. Geoff still didn't understand how Church could eat so much without any noticeable dent in his appetite. Church wasn't a huge guy—but he could pack it in like a line backer.

"If you get hungry later, Terminal Lunch is open twenty-four/seven," Geoff said half-jokingly. Church had eaten so much that day he couldn't possibly still be hungry. "And Pink Dot delivers," he added. He didn't want Church going hungry half-way through the night.

"Thanks," Church said, without a trace of sarcasm.

Church had intended to leave but kept putting it off; Geoff had made it clear he was welcome to stay. Geoff liked him, but he didn't want to consider whether or not that played any part in his decision.

"People can't eat as much I can." Church said.

"What do you mean by 'people'?" Geoff asked jokingly.

"You're not the only one with some mystery in your family tree," Church said.

"Oh yeah?" Geoff asked, brows drawn together.

"According to my grandmother," Church said, "we are wiindigo."

"Is it true?" Geoff asked. After seeing the way Church could eat, he could almost believe Church wasn't entirely human.

Church just shrugged.

"Come here, I want to show you something," Geoff said.

"What is it?" Church asked, squinting up at him.

"Take off your shirt," Geoff said, knowing that the request sounded like the obvious come-on that it was intended to be, "I want to show you something."

"Why?" Church asked calmly.

"Because, I want to show you something," Geoff said.

"Um. I don't know," Church said wrapping his arms around himself. He was surprised to discover that he wanted to go along with whatever Geoff had in mind, but he hesitated, afraid of revealing his scars. "I don't think so," he said, even though he wanted to—he couldn't.

He imagines the trap door of his chest swinging open to reveal his moist, beating heart, laying there like a severed tongue. Four men sit around the heart, pounding on it with drumsticks. One of the men looks up at Church with wide, surprised eyes, before the cuckoo clock of his heart retracts and the hinges snap shut again. They had made eye contact!

"Here, I'll take my shirt off first," Geoff said, pulling his t-shirt up from the bottom, his arms crossing and uncrossing as he pulled the t-shirt over his head and tossed it away. See, it's easy, there's nothing to it. Now you do it. Church watched Geoff's movements with rapt attention, unable to look away. Geoff was ripped, his muscles standing out against his skin, tanned from working out in the sun all day. Geoff was light-skinned too, but he also had a patchy complexion in places where clumps of pigmentation had globbed together, matching the boiling-water scar on his arm. Everyone had their own scars.

Geoff's hair was darker, jet black to Church's dark brown. His cheekbones and jaw cratered from where he'd once had severe acne, but his eyes were a lighter shade of grey, in contrast to Church's black-brown.

"Come on," Geoff said. He had raised his arms but they lowered now slightly in a measurement of hope. "It won't work with your shirt on."

Reluctantly, Church pulled his shirt off over his head, his longish hair sticking up everywhere in disarrangement. There was a quick movement as bared flesh was quickly covered. "What won't work?" he asked, holding the shirt in front of himself like a shield.

Why was he so scared? Geoff wondered, like a deer ready to bolt. The shirt was wrapped around his forearms, ready to be pulled back on at the slightest hint of rejection. Church lowered his arms and Geoff saw why he had hesitated. Church was afraid; he was afraid of Geoff's reaction. A sharp in-take of breath caught in his throat like the hitch in his voice, but he held it in, not letting the breath escape. Geoff could see the ribs sticking out starkly like an x-ray of what lay beneath Church's flesh, his skin almost translucent. Church was almost starvation thin—but that wasn't the most startling aspect of his physiognomy.

Scars covered Church's upper body, from his abdomen, across his chest and his shoulders. Pale, mottled patches of shiny-smooth skin arranged about his upper body in an elaborate pattern of scarification. None of the scars had been visible when he wore a t-shirt. The scars melded together with their neighbours to form large craters, like the surface of the moon, or a frozen landscape. These scars were old and long healed, but they almost seemed to bleed with their immediacy, articulating years of pain. If he were a book, the pages would bleed. Geoff could read Church's life history on the terrain of his body, and it all told the same story: a road map detailing a lifetime of pain.

Church felt goose bumps rise on his exposed flesh. There was a draft in the room. His flesh prickled like the raw-meat of a plucked bird, like the arched back of a cat ready to fight, stretched taut over his ribs like that of a starving dog.

"What happened?" Geoff asked, the air coming out in a quiet exhalation of breath as he took in the extent of the damage that lay exposed before him. "Who did this to you?"

"I was huffing gas with some kids when I was younger," Church said keeping his eyes down, staring at the floor, speaking so softly that Geoff had to strain to catch the words. "The fumes ignited and Sinunde died. I survived."

"That was you?" Geoff Said. "I remember hearing about it. I didn't realize that you were involved."

"They're ugly," Church muttered into his chest. He did kind of look the way Freddy Krueger might have looked without his shirt on. All burned and melted. Geoff had always liked those Freddy Krueger movies. The shirt Church wore with horizontal stripes, took on more meaning.

Geoff paused to think about his reply before answering, he knew he had to step carefully. If he said the wrong thing, it could make things worse. How could he say that he didn't like the scars without making Church think that he was rejecting him? How could Geoff reassure him?

"You're not ugly," Geoff said finally, settling for the truth.

"Now what?" Church asked, trying to pretend the scars didn't matter. "You wanted to show me something, remember?"

Geoff stepped forward and wrapped his arms around Church, hugging him closely to his body so that their chest were touching, Church's mottled skin against his smooth, undamaged flesh.

"What do you feel?" Geoff asked.

"You're warm," Church said, his voice muffled by the crook of Geoff's shoulder, his lips brushing up against the side of Geoff's neck, his breath tickling his skin.

"What else?" Geoff asked him.

"Your chin is resting on my shoulder."

"And what else?"

"Your hard-on," Church said thrusting his hips forward, making his jeans rub up against the bulge in Geoff's shorts. Obviously, Geoff was enjoying this. It felt good to know that he was making someone feel like that. Did this mean he was gay? Church didn't want to think too much about it. There'd be time for self-reflection later.

"No," Geoff said laughing. "Ignore that. Now tell me. What else do you feel?" Church was silent for a moment, trying to do what Geoff had asked. He closed his eyes and felt all the details of Geoff's presence, Geoff's body pressed up against his, feeling Geoff's skin against his own.

"I can feel your heart . . . "

"--Yes--" Geoff said, encouraging him. And Church could feel the deep rumbling sound of Geoff's voice, the vibrating timbre of his voice through flesh and bone.

" . . . It's beating like my own . . . "

". . . Uh-hunh? . . ." Geoff asked.

" . . . Except, it's on the other side from where my heart is. . . "

" . . . unh-hmmm . . . " Geoff mumbled.

" . . . and . . . it's almost as if I have two hearts."

"Yeah," Geoff said.

"Can you feel that?" Church asked.

"Uh-hunh . . . " Geoff said.

They held each other for a few moments, listening to the rhythm of their heartbeats almost as if they were dancing.

Geoff Suture woke up thirsty. He was always thirsty though, so it was no surprise. He reached for the bottle sitting on the bedside table and had a few swigs, wondering whether he was dehydrated from the alcohol, or whether he was dehydrated because he didn't drink enough water. It was a paradoxical chicken or the egg type scenario. It didn't matter whether he was thirsty because of something written into his DNA or because he drank too; the end results were the same. At least, when he got blind drunk, he didn't dream. Didn't have nightmares.

Downing what was left in his bottle of C-six, Geoff scrubbed at his face with his hand and looked at the alarm clock, the digital numbers glowing. He'd have to grab a quick shower and get going, if he was going to get to work on time. Standing in the doorway to his room in his boxers, Geoff froze seeing the still form of Church still asleep on his couch. He had forgotten that he had a guest staying over, and ducked into the bathroom.

Geoff's outlook for the day suddenly seemed brighter, even though the pale light filtering through the windows barely seemed to qualify as sunlight. He showered quickly, and threw on some clothes, feeling self conscious with Church's eyes on him as he slipped from the bathroom to his room wearing only a towel.

Church was now awake, his pupils large and opaque in the dimly lit room, peering at Geoff over the top of the couch like a cat. Maybe they should go get a bite to eat before he headed to work? Geoff would suggest the idea after he dressed, it would be worth being late for work if he got to spend more time with the hitch-hiker.

He had the place to himself for the day. Church spent the day reading. Geoff had made him promise he wouldn't take off. He didn't know why, but he had decided to stay—at least until Geoff returned from work. Only one freestanding lamp lit the room, filling it with shadows, even during the day. Flourishing plants crowded together vying for the light of the one large window, twining around each other in a tangled mass like a living curtain.

Church was antsy and restless. He had planned to leave—he had a destination in mind, and he felt the urge to be on the move. The vampires weren't finished with him, he was worried they would be able to track him down, and he needed to be ready. He wanted to lure the triplets to Ghost Lake where he might have an advantage—but the last thing he wanted was to bring more monsters to Geoff Suture's door.

Soon. He had to leave soon.

He read a novel called Silk, first attracted to it in a used bookstore by the dream catcher on the cover. The world the author described was oddly familiar. The slivers of light seeping in through the living-curtains shifted as the day wore on, slanting across the room like a sundial measuring out the hours of the day.

Geoff returned after six-thirty, still wearing his reflective orange vest, and steel-toed boots that he wore at work, yellow hard hat tucked beneath one arm. The late-afternoon sunlight streamed in through the door behind him like a yellow halo. Geoff sat heavily beside him on the worn couch, their legs touching. Why is he sitting so close to me? Church wondered, but he didn't mind; in fact, it felt good. It felt right somehow.

Geoff leaned forward, and when Church didn't pull away, Geoff kissed him.

Geoff's lips felt warm and dry. Faint smell of booze like cologne, mingled with the toxic tar-petroleum smell of asphalt. Soft lips, soft touch of tongue, faint prickling sensation of beard stubble.

"I'm not gay," Church said, pulling back from Geoff's kiss.

"Then why are you kissing me?" Geoff asked, and leaned forward to kiss him again. Church didn't pull away this time. Human flesh would taste as sweet, he thought.

Church had never really thought too much about his sexuality, although it wouldn't come as that much of a surprise if he was gay; he had always known that twins, homosexuality, and insanity ran in his family. Church had assumed that he wasn't gay, but now that Geoff's lips were pressed softly against his own, the idea that he might be gay didn't seem all that intimidating. There were more important things to worry about. Like monsters coming out of fairy tales to kill you.

It was hard to think about getting laid when you were always worrying about where you were going to get your next meal. Church was always hungry, no matter how much he ate, and even though he was used to it, it was still all-consuming. Hunger was a constant fixation that occupied the forefront of his mind like an addiction. Often, there wasn't any room for anything else.

Except that Geoff's lips tasted so good. The smell, taste and sensations melded together. The smoky taste of C-Six Geoff had been drinking, sneaking sips out of his flask, the smell of his sweat and the sunlight on his skin. Velvet softness of his tongue, creaking sounds of the orange plastic vest, and the rough sandpaper bristles of stubble.

Geoff kissed him and he thought, we're going to burn in Hell. And then, that's stupid, I don't even believe in Hell. He tried to push thoughts of Hell out of his mind, but for some reason they kept creeping in.

—Going-to-Hell, going-to-Hell, going-to-Hell, going-to-Hell—kept running through his brain like a freight train.

His mother and grandmother had gone to Residential School and been taught the Christian value system, but he had been spared that fate. So why was he so ashamed? Where had this guilt entered his body? Maybe it had piggybacked its way in on the air he breathed, he had been bombarded by so many subtle suggestions that this, this was wrong.

But all thoughts melted away, replaced by the sensation of Geoff's lips, Geoff's hands, Geoff's work-callused fingers holding his jaw: the sweat and booze and smell of sunlight. Church's anxiety was replaced by something else; a distinct urgency, a hunger, and it wasn't only Geoff kissing him. Church was now kissing Geoff back, and it was filling some need inside him that he hadn't even known existed. The need grew and expanded, flowering like an exploding star in fast-forward, expanding to envelope the entire universe, creating a new universe as it expanded inside him, a great empty space that suddenly needed to be filled. This sudden emptiness felt distinctly familiar, and yet subtly different.

Noondeskaade, I'm hungry. Nwii-wiisin, I want to eat.

Church kissed Geoff back, and at that exact moment every dog in the neighbourhood began to howl as if they could sense the presence of some threat, some predator, some awakened hunger.

Distantly, on the edges of his perception Church heard the sound of dogs howling, as if in harmony with his rising need. First one, then two, followed by more howls than he could differentiate.

Geoff had been pushed onto his back now, and what had started as a gentle, tentative kiss, had morphed into something else. Church was on top of him, straddling his hips, pinning Geoff's arms to either side of his head with surprising strength and kissing him with an eagerness he had never before experienced, as if some switch had been flipped inside Church's head, and there was now no turning it off.

Don't stop, Geoff thought, feels so good. Geoff couldn't help smiling into the kiss. When he'd leaned forward into that first kiss, he'd felt nauseous—not know what to expect. Would Church yell at him and call him a fag? Would Church push him away? Was he even interested? It was so hard to get a read off of him.

He didn't know if Church was gay, or straight, or indecisive. All he knew was that Church hadn't left, despite the number of times Geoff had made a pass at him, and he'd had plenty of opportunities to leave. Geoff wanted him even before he recognized Church—like someone had punched him in the gut, and he'd been out of breath ever since.

It was a rough trade when you made a move on someone who seemed straight, and you didn't know what reaction to expect, but the pay-off could be worth the risk. Church had responded with an almost violent enthusiasm. Geoff felt his cheeks flush red with heat, the nausea shifting gears as the pressure rushed to his face and endorphins flew, scattering through his dizzy, singing brain.

He's so into me, Geoff thought, reeling. He let Church take the lead, absurdly pleased. Church kissed him almost feverishly, as if he was hungry and Geoff was his meal. And he was okay with that too. More than okay, he was elated! It didn't bother him at all if Church liked to play rough.

Geoff heard dogs howling, but only distantly, dismissing them, as it did not have any relevance to what was currently distracting him. Church's tongue pushing greedily into his mouth, biting at his lips, their teeth clinking together, Church's hands digging at his clothes and tearing apart the Velcro on his reflective neon vest. He heard the fabric of his shirt tear, but found that he didn't care. Let him tear my clothes to shreds, he thought, whatever gets them off faster.

People in the neighborhood paused in their daily tasks to listen to the dogs howling, like the distant, mournful sound of a train. Like a storm that would soon pass. Something had gotten all the dogs upset, maybe there was going to be an earth-quake? Animals were supposed to be able to pick up on that sort of stuff.

And for Church too, the howling was just another part of the sensations enveloping him. He paid it no mind, too absorbed in filling this newly awakened hunger. The dog-howls hovered on the edges of his awareness like a warning, but he was enjoying this too much and felt his recklessness in dismissing them.

He vaguely wondered if he should be doing this, and remembered the words of his uncle Inri:

"You have to be careful who you sleep with, you can catch things, and I'm not just talking about diseases, although you should probably worry about those too. Things . . . good and bad . . . can rub off onto you. More than what you would expect."

Inri should know. Inri had always used sex as a distraction to satisfy his other hungers, his more monstrous cravings.

Distantly, Church wondered what kind of things might be rubbing off of him and onto Geoff, not to mention what was rubbing off of Geoff, and onto him. He quickly pushed these thoughts aside. He loved the physicality of the things they were doing. He'd never been this close to anyone, and the sudden desire that had been awakened within him wasn't giving any signs of letting up.

"Why'd you stop?" Geoff asked, a bit dazed, staring up at Church who had his head tilted to the side as he listened to the dogs howl, the pupils in his eyes shot to an almost unnatural size. They were huge in the dim light, almost engulfing the entire iris. He seemed alien and beautiful and strange. Geoff would have thought it was a drug-induced response, if he hadn't known they hadn't changed size until they'd started doing what they were doing. I am the drug, Geoff thought, and he got off big time on having this extreme effect on someone. Knowing that he'd done this, that he'd affected this change.

"Nothing," Church said, leaning down to nuzzle at Geoff's neck with his teeth, first licking then biting the sensitive flesh, making Geoff cry out in pleasure and then pain, not puncturing the skin, but leaving teeth marks. The bristles on Church's tongue like the rough bristles on a cat's, kissing and then licking the bite mark he'd made, tickling Geoff and making his toes curl inside his boots. Geoff moaned.

Church's lips moved against the pectoral muscle on Geoff's chest, sucking on the flesh, drawing the blood to the surface and creating a raised welt, like a bruise. Geoff didn't care if Church left marks on his body—like some animal marking its territory—he wanted to be marked if it meant feeling this good. Geoff cried out, and Church thought, this is what all those swear words were about, this is what everyone was so afraid of. Cocksucker. Faggot. Queer. Words he'd heard so many times, and this was what it was all about? Those words seemed unsuitable to describe this.

Geoff's hands slid across the scars on his chest, and then Church felt Geoff's lips where his hands had been and he shivered, raising goosebumps. It felt strange to have someone kiss these places, the places where the red flames had once licked his flesh. The scars he had successfully hidden from almost everyone for so many years, wearing long-sleeved shirts and never going for a swim. It felt dangerous to have them so exposed now.

It amazed him, that Geoff wasn't disgusted by his scars; they didn't even seem to bother him. His rough hands explored the dry-melted flesh with as much eagerness as the smooth. Church had always worried the scars might be a deal-breaker for anyone he might meet. But they weren't a deal-breaker, and Geoff wasn't disgusted.

It was cannibalism without death.

Church bit, sucked and kissed a trail leading to Geoff's lips. He stopped only to lick, caress and gnaw on Geoff's right nipple, while cruelly twisting the left. Church grunted. His grunts turned into moans, then low growls mixed in with his groans, crying out louder and louder, his growls growing disturbingly less human-sounding. Strange vocal sounds, unlike any sound Geoff would have thought the human voice capable of producing. Church moaned like someone possessed, producing high and low octaves simultaneously, like multiple voices overlapping, subsonic, above sonic, vibrating the air with depth, bass and high pitched whines outside the range of human hearing. Wolves, Lynx, Fox. Geoff wouldn't have been surprised if any of those animals made these sounds. It was a bit disconcerting, but he dismissed this as an exaggeration, or his imagination—besides, he was having too much fun.

Church gave one last growl, and Geoff felt all of his muscles going tense and rigid. Church lay on top of him, panting and exhausted, the tightly controlled energy that usually surrounded him faded for the moment, as his eyes slowly bled from black to brown around the edges of his irises.

"Wow," Geoff said. "Wow."

Geoff led Church to his bedroom. The room was as sparsely furnished as the living room; a bed, and some weights and a punching bag occupied one corner of the room. The wall above his bed was covered with dream catchers of every shape, size and colour. There were large hoop-sized ones made with tanned leather and gold beads, and other small medallion-sized ones, feathers dyed purple and neon green. A pair of worn red boxing gloves hanging from a peg on the wall.

"You're like a furnace," Church said.

"You're like a fridge," Geoff said.

Church stayed awake, holding Geoff in his arms, listening to the sound of his breathing, contemplating the complexity of the human body, the conglomeration of cells and blood-vessels. How fragile it was, and so easy to break. Geoff made whimpering noises in his sleep and Church wondered what nightmares haunted his dreams, and how good he would taste.

Usually, when you got drunk, you didn't dream. And Geoff had his own nightmares. In the darkness, Church quietly dressed, trying not to wake Geoff, pulling on his jeans, pulling his shirt back on, and quickly tying the laces on his sneakers. Lying on the bed, Geoff stirred in his sleep and looked up at him through blurry eyes. He became aware that Church was getting dressed, and sat upright, the blanket falling to his waist.

"Where are you going?" Geoff asked, a note in his voice quavering.

"I can't fall asleep unless I have my clothes on," Church told him, guilt stabbing through him like a fist clenching inside his gut. The only time he usually undressed was to wash or change his clothes. Oh, Geoff thought, it isn't that surprising that someone with so many scars has a few quirks. So what if he was a little bit fucked up? Everyone had their own psychological scars.

"Well, could you at least take your shoes off?" Geoff asked him. Church looked down and noticed the dirt on his shoes.

"Sorry," he said, slipping each shoe off with his heel and a toe, and letting them drop to the floor. The only concession Geoff could gain towards getting Church undressed. Church found his place next to him on the bed and Geoff wrapped his arms around him, like a praxitelean and a polykleitan youth.

Church is all-over, entirely a messed up person, Geoff thought, and held him tighter, as if his arms could shield him from things that had already happened. They fell sleep in each other's arms, going off separately into the world of dreams, miles away and only inches apart. Geoff's toes angling over the edge of the bed, as if to tempt any wayward fish.

Church's last thoughts before falling asleep were about scars. Geoff had spent so many years drinking his pain away, that he was saturated with it; like a severed limb preserved in a jar of alcohol. But the alcohol also preserved the wounds, and wouldn't let them heal. Church had a lot of experience with scars, and he was going to do everything in his power to help his new friend heal. Maybe by helping exorcize some of Geoff's demons, Church would be able to exorcize some of his own too.

Church fell asleep. And in his sleep, he was dreaming. He was dreaming of roast duck, flesh so tender it flaked off from the bone, melted in his mouth like cotton candy.Church lifted a drumstick to his mouth like the Fat Friar in Rocket Robin-Hood. Church brought the drumstick to his mouth and bit down, and he relished the sensation of his teeth sinking into the meat, ready to tear the soft tissue from bone.

—That's when the screaming started—

He didn't want to be side tracked, and for a moment he considered ignoring the sound, but the screaming was too distracting for him to continue with the feast. The noise continued, demanding attention.

Church woke to find his teeth locked like a bloodhound's, clamped down on that fleshy bit between shoulder and neck. Uh-Oh Church thought, Oh shit. He quickly loosened his grip and unlatched his jaw, the blood welling up and filling in the depressions created by his teeth. Uh-Oh, oh shit.

Geoff jumped up clutching at his neck, knocking Church to the floor in his haste to escape.

"What? What happened?" Church asked, still half-asleep. He was on the floor, blankets strewn all around him. "What's going on?"

"You bit me you fucking asshole that's what happened!" Geoff screamed, his hand pressed against the wound to staunch the flow of blood. When he removed his hand the palm came away red and the flow of blood increased, dribbling down his naked chest to his boxer shorts. Geoff looked pissed.

"What the fuck were you doing?" Geoff screamed. "You fucking bit me! What the fuck is wrong with you?"

"I'm sorry!" Church said, "I didn't mean to!"

"Fucking psycho," Geoff muttered, pacing the short space between the bed and the wall, as he held the wound. "I think I might need stitches!"

"I was dreaming," Church said, as his eyes began to water, feeling like a complete fuck-up. He knew this was a bad idea. He was a wiindigo. What the fuck had he been thinking?

"Must have been some fucking dream," Geoff said, then, "What are you doing?" as he realized Church was gathering his things.

"'I'm sorry, I should just go," Church said, stuffing some clothes into his backpack.

Geoff hopped over the bed and spun him around, hands gripping his shoulders. "No! I'm sorry. Please stay."

"But I bit you," Church said.

"And it was a mistake," Geoff said pulling Church into a hug as if to prevent him from escaping, the blood sticky between them and soaking into the fabric of his t-shirt. Church never slept naked.

"You're not mad?"

"No, I didn't mean to shout at you."

"You're still bleeding," Church said. Blood had gotten on his chin when Geoff had pulled him into a bear hug. He couldn't help flicking out his tongue to taste some of the metallic sweetness, but managed to keep himself from actually licking the wound. Cannibalism without death. "Here let me take a look at that." He took out some gauze and bandages from his backpack. Everything in the world he owned, his whole life was in that bag. Everything he might need. After the bite was dressed and cleaned, they settled back into bed.

"I think it's going to leave a scar," Geoff mumbled as he drifted to sleep. He'd known that he wasn't going to be able to get close to Church without getting hurt. Church was too messed up for things not to get messy.

Niibiishabo awasayi'iikamigoon

Geoff stared into the depths, flecks of gunk floating around in the brownish green liquid, like stirred up motes of dust suspended in light through an attic window. He took a tentative sip, and immediately regretted it. It tasted like warm dirt. He spit it back out into the cup.

"What is this?" he asked.

"I told you, you wouldn't like it," Church said.

When Geoff had asked him what kind of tea he was always drinking, and insisted on trying some, Church had made a pot of moss tea from a dried bundle he kept in a ziploc bag. He knew Geoff wouldn't like it, but made it anyway. He could finish the entire pot on his own.

Complication

Thwack, thwack, thwack. There is a muffled knock at the door. Church tenses, imagining suited goons coming to toss his corpse into a bottomless ravine. Geoff answers the door and Church hangs back, his hand twitching towards Religion strapped to his ankle in its leather sheath.

It is just the neighbour—this time—coming by to ask Geoff and his green-thumb about some small matter of gardening. Church really should have gotten around to telling Geoff about the mortal peril in which he placed his life, just by being in his presence. But it never seemed to be the right time. Oh yeah, hey, by the way, these mobster vampires are gunning for me and they want my blood, and my oil, and my land. It all seemed so crazy, and maybe that is all it was. He had run out of meds ages ago, and couldn't remember the last time he had filled a prescription. It all seemed so implausible and far away.

Complication. Church had been staying at Geoff's place for two months, when he hadn't even intended to stay two days. Geoff was just another complication, and that was the last thing Church needed in his life. His life was complicated enough without adding the complications of a human being. But he already knew it was too late. Every time Church said that it was "time to go," or mentioned that he was, "overstaying his welcome," Geoff insisted that he stay, and Church would put off his departure. Even though he knew it was an illusion, he actually felt safe here. I am being stupid. I should have left weeks ago.

It was dangerous for him to stay in one place for so long. But he had gotten distracted. No one had tracked him down yet, so he was beginning to think that it was safe, that maybe the triplets had given up on finding him. But he knew that he couldn't count on that.

October 16th 1872, Ghost Lake,

The wind howls incessantly, like a pack of wolves in perfect harmony, and the trees creak ominously under the strain, shedding branches now, the way earlier they had shed their leaves. A charcoal sky written in shades of grey, the yellow tamarack and snarls of mauve October shrubbery stand out in sharp contrast to this monochromatic world. Skeletal black boughs reach up towards a perpetually overcast sky, the autumn leaves with their bright slashes of colour, seem more dazzling for being contrasted against the infinite shades of grey and coal. The slightest bit of colour seems to vibrate with intensity against this drab backdrop, like an oil painting of red carnage on the cutting room floor. November encroaches ever closer, and I fear what will happen when the snow flies, and what the colder weather will bring.

To my bemusement, Ogimaa not only survived the cure, but he actually seems to be doing better. He is sitting up in bed, and though he appears haggard and drawn, he is no longer given to long-winded speeches about hunger, or eating human flesh; instead he accepts the wholesome food he is given, and eats his meals. We have left the restraints in place for a period of observation, should he revert back to his former derangement. Goshko and Mookman are planning on applying the same treatment to my other patient, Eniwek, and though barbaric, I can have no objections if it cures this sickness.

I do not know what to think, though I am still cautious of the efficacy of this cure, as blood-letting, and belladonna, also appeared to relieve the patients' suffering, and for a time improve their condition; I wait for the slow, inevitable back-slide to begin.

October 27th, 1872, Ghost Lake,

It is, as I feared. The 'boiling duck-fat cure,' though it offered more respite to my patient's psyche than any other, was not successful. Following another onslaught of disturbing dreams, the patient has relapsed. Ogimaa's cannibalistic ravings have begun anew, and he rejects all meals offered to him. He says that the proffered food is not fit for his consumption, and he craves only wiiyas. Meat. Though when meat is offered to him, he is unwilling to eat it. He remains chained to his bed, and not even Goshko is willing to enter the "wiindigo's" chamber now that his cure has failed. Word of Ogimaa's rehabilitation had inspired confidence amongst the Ghost Lake inhabitants, but word of his subsequent relapse has crushed that burgeoning hope, and I fear the situation here is now spiraling out of control.

The Indians believe that the spirit of the Wiindigo has taken up residence near their home on the shores of Ghost Lake, and that the monster has scared away all the game, and it is for this reason food is scarce. The young braves fear leaving camp, and have such ill-luck hunting; for fear the Wiindigo will pick them off, one by one, as they separate from the group. And it is this fear that is contributing to the general malaise in the community and the early depletion of supplies. The anxiety of food scarcity further raises the prospect of starvation, and their belief in the spirit of the Wiindigo.

Despite the tribesmen's usual proficiency and industriousness in providing for themselves and their families, an atmosphere of gloom hangs over the height of the land, where the waters flow either south to the lakes, or North to the Arctic. Ghost Lake is situated at such a height, one feels the atmospheric tumult—one feels closer to the skies—and the thunder beings who dwell here and visit this place with such frequency. The flash and boom of their presence comes with such ferocity, the low hanging clouds hover constantly; a palpable metaphor for the psychological miasma that seems to have descended over this place. Goshko is sure to put down his tobacco, his semaa, before each storm in order to appease the manitous, and keep the devil in his hole.

The bone-hunters and diggers hunker down in their shantytown of tents and makeshift structures, and the Indians take shelter in their wigwams, low-angled teepees, and log cabin homes. An eclectic mix of the old and new, some occupying both a birch-bark wigwam-style summer dwelling, and a more permanent winter cabin, simultaneously.

I too, can only hunker down and wait, to see what evil will come of this.

October 29th 1872, Ghost Lake,

Dear James,

They say a man drowned himself in Drinker's camp today. Though he had been complaining of feeling unwell, Aagamak continued to work, labouring alongside the other men, until well past noon, when he inexplicably stopped digging, and walked away. They called to him, but he didn't answer. He walked to the edge of the lake, paused for a moment, and then continued walking into the chilly waters—fully clothed.

The men stopped digging;, their shovels and tools lay forgotten where they were dropped, as they watched Aagamak walk into the lake. When he didn't respond to their calls, they grew alarmed, and climbed out of their shoulders-deep pit. The water was already above Aagamak's hips, and still he continued to walk into the depths.

"Something was wrong,.." one of the workers later told me. "He was mad!"

By the time a few of the men had run splashing into the shallows, there was nothing but rings to mark the place where Aagamak's head had gone under, like the ripples from a stone thrown into the lake. They dove into the frigid black waters, but the rough waves had whipped up particles at the bottom of the lake, and visibility was poor. They couldn't see further than an arm's length in any one direction, and Aagamak was no longer in the same place where he'd gone under. Maybe he had simply kept walking?

The men continued to search for hours, and could still find no trace of the man. It is all but certain that he is drowned, though they continue to scour for his body. It is bound to turn up, eventually.

This is another blow to the local Indians, from whom most of the labourers have been drawn, and to Cope and Marsh's mission of excavating bones. The morale in either camp is at an all time low.

We all hold our breath, and wait for a miracle, or for the body to appear, washed up along the shores like a rotting, bloated fish.

Your devoted friend,

Harker Lockwood,

More Complications

It was time for him to leave.

He didn't want to get too attached. He had enough problems without worrying about someone else. Church wished he had stayed to himself. He didn't want to get involved but for some reason Church found it difficult to pull away. All his excuses were put on hold when confronted with the solution of simply leaving.

Church pushed food around on his plate with a fork, not eating even though his stomach grumbled. He was back on the crash starvation diet again, in preparation for the day when his father's killers came for him. He was a wiindigo, and where did wiindigo get their strength, if not from hunger?

"Eat," Geoff said, "you're nothing but skin and bones." Church smiled and shoveled a mouthful of food into his mouth, but then pushed his plate away. It was as dangerous for him to eat too much as it was for him to eat nothing at all. Too much food and his hunger would grow, too little food, and his hunger would grow. His wiindigo family had long-since learned the art of balancing their hunger, like tightrope walking on the edge of a knife. They needed to eat to live, but if they over-indulged or if they pushed moderation too far—in either direction lay disaster, a fall from the precipice, and the hungry void waiting to engulf him. Some days it was difficult to maintain that delicate balance, either through a lack of food or a lack of control over his appetite.

"I'm done," Church said. Geoff quirked an eyebrow at him. First Church ate like the cookie monster, and now it was impossible to get him to eat anything. And Church liked his cooking. Maybe Church had merely come to his senses.

"Do you have an eating disorder?" Geoff asked him, piling more scrambled eggs onto Church's plate with a spatula.

"I'm not hungry," Church said.

"I don't believe you," Geoff said. For the entire length of time Church had been staying with him, he seemed to be hungry. Church had the largest appetite of anyone he'd ever met, and he was still skinny. "I know you better than that by now, you're always hungry. You're lying."

"I must have lost my appetite."

"What's wrong?" Geoff asked.

"Nothing," Church said, taking another bite to please Geoff. For his plan to work, he needed to be hungry.

–Clunk, Clunk, Clunk– There was a knock at the door.

They both looked in the direction of the door.

—CLUNK, CLUNK, CLUNK—It came again. Louder.

Geoff had already turned the doorknob when Church came barreling from across the room, slamming his shoulder into the back of the door, but it was too late. The man had wedged his foot between the door and the frame.

"What the hell are you doing?" Geoff said. Church had still not found the appropriate moment to tell Geoff the whole story, he had not yet told him that his father's killers were after him.

"Help me!" Church said, pushing his weight against the door, but then he abandoned it as a lost cause and grabbed Geoff by the collar, dragging him away from the door. He'd been expecting all three of the vampires, but only one of the suit-wearing twins pushed his way through the door. Ox stood before them with a smile on his face, canines and incisors on full display.

"Hey, what are you—what's going on?" Geoff asked.

Where were the other ones? Church wondered. I thought they only hunted in packs. Maybe I'm wrong? Had Ox come alone? Were the others coming in the back way? Church kept pulling Geoff back, too busy to answer questions. Ox caught up with them, grabbed Geoff and tossed him out of the way, his head connecting with the mantle above the fireplace with an audible thunk. Church continued backing away, for the moment leaving Geoff on the floor where he had fallen. He knew Ox wasn't really after Geoff; it was him that Ox really wanted.

Church crouched and fumbled at his ankle for Religion, the blade that had been his constant companion since Inri had given it to him. He didn't care what you were; human or vampire, being stabbed would hurt no matter what kind of monster you were. Church pulled the blade free and stabbed Ox in the stomach as he stood up. Ox reeled back, his mouth open, one hand holding his belly as he fell back against a wall. Church stabbed him again, burying Religion deep into his chest and abdomen, aiming for his heart, although he wasn't sure if he missed or not. Did the stake have to be wooden he wondered? Church couldn't imagine why it would make any difference. The movies must be wrong. Coughing blood from his mouth Ox collapsed onto the floor, canines no longer visible, eyes wide, and leaving a smear of blood as he slid down the wall behind him.

The blood formed little rivulets as it trickled down the wall, threading new paths along the plaster to where the vampire gasped and gurgled, seeming to stiffen and jerk as seizures gripped his body. Church watched as the life drained from Ox's eyes, waiting to make sure that he was dead. Number Seven, Church thought, cupping his numb fingers with his other hand. The vampire Ox, killed by Religion. The Seventh person I've seen die. And then—do vampires even count? Can vampires die? Weren't they already dead? Living-dead or undead, Ox now seemed all-around pretty much dead-dead.

Church was shocked by the amount of damage the weapon had inflicted. He had been uncertain whether his Religion would work on a vampire. All the horror movies he'd ever seen all seemed to agree; the only way to kill a vampire was a stake through the heart, decapitation, or fire. Yeah right, wooden stakes! Church thought. Consider that myth busted.

Geoff lay on the floor not too far away. Motionless.

Church crept forward hesitantly, kneeling over Geoff's unmoving form, afraid to roll him over and discover that he was dead. Church shook his shoulder. There was no reaction. A pang of fear shot through him, gripping his heart like a fist. If he had been more honest, maybe this would never have happened? But another more reasonable part of his brain argued, if you'd done that, you'd both be dead, stupid. And somewhere else in his head, a calm, flat voice added:

Number Eight. Geoff Suture. Killed by an Ox.

But then slowly Geoff stirred, and sat up on one elbow, a gash on his forehead that could probably use stitches. Church slumped as all the tension he hadn't known he'd been holding left his shoulders in rush. Geoff's expression changed as he took in the sight of the gruesome corpse, pale and sitting in a pool of blood that had drained from the body, eyes staring glassily at the ceiling.

"You killed him," Geoff said.

"He almost killed you," Church said.

"What do we do now?" Geoff asked, looking at the body lying next to them on the floor. In other words: What do we do with the body?

"I know a place." Church said.

They heaved the body over the cliff and watched as the corpse bashed off of outcroppings of rock, rolling end over end, disappearing through the rush of water exiting the rock-face from the underground source for the Genosee falls, and landing in a twisted, mangled heap forty feet below them. Around them a mixed deciduous and coniferous forest stretched out as far as the eye could see, spruce, hemlock, and pine; oak, elm, maple and beech.

Geoff's truck had barely made the climb up the old logging road, bumping wildly over the uneven terrain; the "road" really nothing more than two ruts in the ground. Somehow, they managed to make it all the way. They didn't have much of a choice. They needed to get rid of the body. The bag of bones thumped around under the tonneau cover as the flatbed shifted and bounced over rocks.

They stood overlooking the promontory of the Genosee falls, for a moment surveying the damage—Church straining to see the body of his father, which had no doubt been discovered long ago by carrion, the bones picked clean and scattered—he didn't know what Geoff's thoughts were.

Church drove on the way back down the logging road. Geoff waited until they were back on the main road and had put some distance between themselves and the corpse before he asked:

"Who the fuck was that?"

He thought he had shown real patience by waiting this long before asking any questions. Geoff knew that by helping to dispose of the body, he was now an accomplice to murder.

"The guy who killed my dad," Church said as he pressed down on the gas-pedal, passing a slower vehicle beside them. "They threw my father's body over the cliff we just threw Ox's corpse over."

"Oh," Geoff said, the lines of worry on his face softening. "Who are they? What the hell is going on?"

"They," Church told him, "are the details-men hired by a resource extraction company called Magnon Incorporated. My great-grandmother was the owner of a parcel of land that lies adjacent to Ghost Lake. And they want it for what lies underneath—oil."

"Why don't you sell it to them? —You could make a killing."

"It's not for sale," Church told him. "When they realized they couldn't buy the rights to the land legitimately, they hired Ox and his brothers to convince us; to convince me."

"Why didn't you tell me?" Geoff asked.

"I didn't think you'd believe me," Church said. "I was starting not to believe it myself. I thought I was just going crazy like my grandmother."

"Where are we going?" Geoff asked.

"I don't know yet," Church said driving aggressively through traffic. "I can't go back to your place. The others might be watching."

When they came to a rest stop, Church pulled over and killed the engine.

"I have to go," Church said.

"Where?" Geoff said, "I'll drive you."

"No, it's better if you don't come," Church told him. "They'll find me again. I'll hitch-hike." Church got out of the car and shut the door. Geoff got out too, and followed him when Church began walking away, their feet crunching on gravel.

"Well, I'll come with you." Geoff said, walking along-side him.

"No. Just go home. It'll be safer."

"Who's to say it's safe there?" Geoff said, "You said yourself that they'll be watching the place. They could be waiting for me."

"They're out for my blood, not yours." Church told him.

"I help you dispose of a body and now you're ditching me?"

"You don't understand," Church said, feeling a little as if he was kicking Old Yeller. "I don't want you to come with me. Everyone I've ever known is crazy or dead. I'm doing you a favour; trust me. You're better off without me."

"Do me a favour," Geoff said, "don't do me any favours."

"You should leave, while you still can," Church said. "Just let me go." He had lost so many people close to him. Sometimes Church felt as if death was a disease, and he was a carrier. But things didn't work like that. Did they?

Geoff was flooded with tenderness for the mad boy.

"Look," Geoff said, grabbing Church by the wrist, "I don't believe in curses Church—you are not cursed. I'm not dead and I'm not in danger of keeling over anytime soon. I'm not going anywhere, so just relax, okay?"

Church ripped his arm free and punched Geoff in the face. Geoff let go, holding his jaw, and looking up at him with wide eyes, blood and drool dripping down from his busted lip. There was no rule against hitting boys, but it felt a little like Church was now killing Old Yeller. It's for your own good, Church thought.

Geoff pulled his hand away; his fingers were red. "I'm not leaving," he said quietly. He imagined Church surrounded by a halo of invisible thorns that stabbed out in all directions. You couldn't get too close without getting hurt.

"Don't you understand?" Church said pushing him. "I don't want my boyfriend coming with me. It's too dangerous. Just go home." Doesn't Geoff understand that this is something I have to do alone?

"I'll leave if I want, not before, so stop trying to push me away. It's not your decision to make!"

"Fuuuuck!" Church screamed, looking up at the constellations in the sky, and the thousands upon thousands of stars. The constellation Bagonegiizhig, Hole-In-The-Day, was shining brightly, and easily visible; the Ojibwe cluster of stars after which Mukade-wiiyas had been named, the darkness between stars, and the doorway between worlds. He felt as if his great-grandmother was watching over him, waiting to see what he would do. But there was nothing he could do. At least he could say that he had warned Geoff of the danger and had tried to make him stay away. But Geoff was right. It wasn't his decision to make. And besides, now that he didn't have any say, he felt relieved that he wouldn't have to do this alone.

"If you get yourself killed, I'm going to be pissed off, you know that," Church said.

"Don't be so selfish," Geoff said.

"Sorry about your lip," Church said quietly, shuffling the gravel on the ground with his foot. Geoff stepped forward and raised his hand, brushing his thumb across Church's chewed up lips.

"I'm not angry at you," Geoff said, "in your own fucked up way, you were trying to protect me," and then he smiled, despite the busted lip, making it bleed even more. "You called me your boyfriend." His teeth were stained red. It hurt to smile, but he didn't care. Geoff had never had a boyfriend before. There'd been a few, drunken, fumbling encounters, but that was about it. He'd never had a real relationship before.

"So where should we go now?" Geoff asked. He tried to think of places where they could go. He thought about his few friends, and the family he'd turned his back on, and then he shook his head. He had nowhere to go.

"I know a place," Church said.

Where have I heard this before? Geoff thought.

October 31st 1872, Ghost Lake,

I begin to lose track of the days, they all run together. I know that it is the 31st of October—since it is Othniel's birthday—the same day as All Hallows' Eve, coming fast upon All Souls' Day and the anniversary of Guy Fawkes. I begin to fear for myself in this wild country. I've been run ragged, taking care of so many different patients. Going from one encampment to the other. All the Indians are boarded up in their homes, and refuse to go out to hunt or fish or engage in their usual occupations. Even the medicine man, Goshko, has boarded himself up in his home, and refuses to come out. Hunger now gnaws at everyone. There is not enough to eat.

Supplies run short.

Famine has come.

I begin to notice in myself some of the same symptoms evident in my patients. But I am too busy treating them, to look after myself. And I dismiss my symptoms as irrelevant, a figment of my imagination. I am not one of these Indians—superstitious enough to believe I could be transforming into a wiindigo—and how can one become ill with Wiindigo Sickness without belief? It is a disorder of the mind, as much as it is a disorder of the body. It can hardly be contagious.

Nevertheless, the symptoms have come. I cannot eat the wholesome food I prepare for myself. And even when I force myself to eat, I am still filled with some horrendous craving. Nothing I eat alleviates my hunger. I gnash my teeth, grinding them in my sleep, my jaw muscles ache, tight with working. There is pain in my gums, from my tongue constantly searching out some morsel in the cracks between my teeth. My lips are scabbed over with sores, from where I've worried at my own flesh like ropy worms between my teeth, though it does me harm I cannot desist. It makes me think of Mukade-wiiyas with her scarred lips, set in an achingly lovely, heart-shaped face. I am filled with a restless, motion, and insomnia that won't let me rest. I am medicating myself. I take a tincture of opium each night so that the nightmares won't come to plague my sleep, slowly increasing the dosage, as the symptoms grow worse. If I am not healthy and rested myself, I will not be able to treat my patients.

Almost all those in the encampments have now abandoned this place to its ghosts, those who have fallen ill with the Wiindigo Sickness remain. Many of the residents of Ghost Lake have taken themselves elsewhere, to their relatives, or to other seasonal campsites. Othniel and Drinker have dug into their excavation pits like soldiers on opposite sides of a battlefield, refusing to give up their treasures. They stay regardless of the casualties, and the hunger that surely must burn, and eat at them like an ember—an ember slowly being stoked by their greed and jealousy, and fed like the wind that whips a dull flame into a raging forest fire, consuming everything in it's path. They will be the victims of their own inferno if they do not stand aside, and let the fire that they started, burn out along its natural course. The lone holdouts in a personal war. Egging on their leftover men, to continue digging digging digging. Digging despite the cold wind, digging despite the driving snow, digging, despite the frozen earth—their ambitions know no bounds.

Winter is coming.

We are all starving. Famine has come.

I see Him sometimes, His quick birdlike movements, darting through the trees at the edges of my vision; a shadow, too fast to catch a good glimpse of; a creature straight out of Ojibwe legends. This is how I know the madness has taken root in my own mind. The madness is contagious, and I myself have fallen victim to this illness, that seemed to afflict only Indians, indiscriminately. Until now. Foolishly, I had believed myself immune. The winter has come. The Wiindigo has come. Starvation, famine, and death have come.

Winter has taken up residence in my heart, and now that we have invited The Wiindigo in, he will not release His grip. I can feel the chill, spreading like frost across a window pain, so my heart struggles to beat, limping haphazardly forward. Everything appears in a different light, obscured by the intricate patterns the smears of frost create. The pain is numbness. A pain that comes with a cold that numbs the pain as it causes it, so that the sting lasts only a moment as the freeze slowly advances across my heart. Small mercies.

I have determined to go again to visit Mukade-wiiyas, the Wiindigo's daughter, to see what can be learned from her. I cannot solve this mystery, and cure myself, without knowing fully all aspects of this sickness. She knows something, and Goshko will not speak to me. An atmosphere of fear afflicts everyone. It hovers over the lake, the woods, and the bones of the half-disinterred monsters, like the late autumn fog that has descended. It is a diaphanous mist that wraps itself around the islands like the sails of a ship, and makes visibility next to zero, and navigation almost impossible.

I must visit the Wiindigo's daughter. She is my last hope for finding answers, solving this riddle and curing this sickness. I will go alone. Aabitiba, my faithful Indian guide, has abandoned me to my fate. Upon discerning the symptoms of the Wiindigo Sickness within me, he deserted. I can place no blame, as—in the interests of self-preservation many have forsaken this place.

I know the route, though I will have to make the journey through the fog, which has yet to let up for these past two weeks. Hopefully, I do not lose my way amongst the cursed islands, shifting about as they do on their moorings of peat, moss and bog.

Nov. 18th? 19th? 1872, Ghost Lake,

The entire length of my forearm has become inflamed, irritated by a severe allergic reaction to the mosquito bite on my arm that has been plaguing me tirelessly with itching these past weeks—or has it been longer? I lose track of the days, and hours. It feels as if I've only just arrived, or as if I've been here for an eternity. Time warps and distorts itself to suit my deranged moods. I can only curse my own imprudence in allowing the tiny creature to feast on my blood for my own morbid satisfaction.

As my own symptoms of Wiindigo Psychosis grow worse, it seems to have exacerbated the mosquito bite on my arm. Maybe the sickness is communicable, and it is delivered to its victims by the bite of the mosquito? All I have are these wild theories. I have yet to determine a root cause, although I still believe it is a culturally mediated psychological disorder, and not a physical illness. I pray that I am not wrong in that conclusion.

Religion

Before they started on their road trip, Church had to make sure the vampires would be trailing them. He brought the serrated edge of his knife across his left wrist in one clean stroke, a stream of blood flowing, for a moment, at an alarming rate, before it clotted and slowed to a trickle.

Church wavered on his feet, his face pale in the dirty truck-stop bathroom mirror, the iron scent of his blood hanging in the air. It should draw the vampires to him like mosquitos—drawn to the pulse and beat of a living heart—that steady thrum and twitch of the vein in warm mammalian meat. Hopefully, they were close enough to catch the scent. Church had no doubt that if he splashed enough of his blood around they'd be able to smell it. When they had confronted him in the alley, they had raised their heads, nostrils flaring, sniffing the air like predators downwind, catching the scent of a deer. A Flehmen response performed by a wide range of animals—but one he'd never seen in humans before. Probably because they weren't human. They seemed to like his wiindigo blood; maybe they could taste his hunger?

Church gripped the edges of the sink, scrambles of light and darkness zigzagging across his eyeballs like popcorn amoeba. He hadn't intended to let quite so much blood. Religion was sharp. Church used a bottle of C-Six to sterilize the knife and the wound it had made on his arm. He wrapped a roll of gauze around his arm and then used a tensor bandage to apply pressure. It wasn't perfect, but it would have to do. Church pulled the sleeve of his sweater down over his wrist, covering up the spot of red soaking through the makeshift bandage. A trickle of blood slid down his pinky finger.

The wound was now as invisible as his scars.

Geoff had already finished filling up the gas tank, and was waiting for him in the car.

"Are you all right?" Geoff asked. "You don't look very good."

"I'm fine," Church said. Just a little blood loss. No big deal.

"Well, you don't look fine," Geoff said, squinting at him.

"Thanks a lot!" Church said. "Can we go?"

"Okay, okay!" Geoff said, turning the key in the ignition. He kept looking over at Church, the concern written on his face. Church felt bad for being irritable, but he didn't want Geoff to know how it was that he was insuring that they would be followed. He didn't want Geoff to think he was crazy.

Swathes of purple loosestrife grew alongside the road in abundance, splashes of beautiful violet lythrum choking out the indigenous species. Each plant the exact clone of every other, originating from the same interconnected mass of an underground root system.

Church had his thumb in his mouth while he slept. It would have made him look like a boy—eyes closed, curled up, sucking on his thumb—if it weren't for the movement of his jaw, teeth grinding, and the steady trickle of blood dribbling down from one corner of his lips.

"Hey wake up!" Geoff said.

"What? What is it?" Church asked, a little bleary eyed, unconsciously licking the bit of blood from his lips.

"Um, nothing," Geoff said, not knowing what to say. "I'm getting a bit tired. I could use a break. Maybe we should stop and get something to eat?" Church perked up a bit when he heard the prospect of food, and Geoff was relieved. Church hadn't been eating very much lately. It wasn't like him at all.

At the next truck stop, Church performed the same routine, drawing the blade of Religion across his arm, further up from the wrist and splashing as much of his blood around as he could manage without passing out. Not so deeply as he had the first time, but deep enough to let the blood well up so he could sprinkle it around, lightly perfuming the air. Sterilizing everything with C-Six, and wrapping his arm in more gauze. Church pulled the sleeve of his sweater back down over his arm. Invisible.

The thought did occur to him that he was completely fucking nuts, and that this was probably a dumb idea, but it was difficult to tell what was real, and what was delusion. It was part belief, and part hoodoo superstition that the vampires wouldn't follow unless there was blood. Guys like these—were like bloodhounds, and they needed a scent to follow, a trail of blood, left like breadcrumbs to mark the path. The scent of his blood would be unmistakable.

They stopped regularly along the route, so Church could, "go to the bathroom," and each time Church returned looking worse than ever. Sometimes he found it was easier just to re-open the old wounds instead of making new ones.

"I think you're getting sick," Geoff said. He was surprised there was anything left for Church to throw up; he hadn't been eating very much lately.

"I'm fine," Church grunted, resting his head against the window and closing his eyes. "I just need some more rest." Maybe he was bulimic? Geoff wondered if Church was making up for all those days of gorging, by starving himself? By the time he pulled back onto the road, Church was already asleep.

In his dreams, Church could see the vampires.

Hundsfordt kneeled down, examining the splash pattern of his blood on the tiled floor, Grundel standing sentry by the door. But he didn't just see them. In his dream, he was Hundsfordt, or rather he was seeing the world through the filter of the vampire's mind, like an invisible hitchhiker riding on the shoulder of his consciousness. Tasting the flavour of his own blood off of the bathroom floor—and it tasted good. So good.

Hundsfordt put his finger to the blood congealing in a puddle on the floor and then brought it to his lips, slowly tasting it, savouring it. He smiled and shuddered in pleasure like he was having a piss-shiver. It was the most exquisite blood he'd ever tasted.

"What a waste of blood!" he said, making a clicking sound with his tongue on the roof of his mouth and shaking his head.

He wasn't desperate enough to lick up blood off a dirty men's-room floor, but he was close. If he hadn't known that a source still existed for this particular vintage, he would have been lapping it up like a kitten—luckily he knew the source was still alive and kicking.

The way the blood was splattered around couldn't have been a mistake. It was obvious that this was not the result of an accidental injury as he had at first assumed, because this was the third blood soaked bathroom they'd stumbled across. The second site had been cleaned before they had a chance to examine it, but they could still smell the scent of his unique blood lingering underneath the bleach. Three blood-soaked rooms could not be coincidence. This was intentional.

What was that boy up to? he wondered.

Hundsfordt examined the bathroom like a crime scene. He stood in the ghosting where Church had stood, the shadow created by his indexical presence, and spun in a circle, examining the way the blood skewed in oblong spatters radiating outwards from this central axis point like a scattering of bloody stars, clustered closer together near the center, and growing further apart the farther the stars got from the center of this galaxy—the place where the boy had stood, rotating in place—his blood flinging as if from a centrifuge.

The blood had congealed already. That did tend to happen rather quickly. But more importantly, it hadn't yet had time to dry. Which meant that they couldn't be very far behind their quarry. Less than five hours he would guess, based on the consistency of the coagulation and the amount of drying. Hundsfordt was very familiar with blood. He'd had years and years to become quite knowledgeable on the subject, to become quite intimate with the way that blood fell, and draped itself against furnishings and walls, brushed against an ornately laid tablecloth of goblets, china and silverware, like rouge on a whore's lips, or dripping down from a chandelier. He considered himself something of an expert, much like the connoisseur of fine wine.

One thing he knew for certain, the blood of every other human tasted bland in comparison to this boy. Hundsfordt didn't yet know why. That bothered him. Magnon wanted the land—he could have it! Hundsfordt just wanted the boy. The brothers still had a job to do. There was no point pissing off their employer and making a powerful enemy when they didn't have to. He wanted to keep their prey alive for as long as humanly possible. Bleeding him slowly, over a long period of time. Allowing for the time his body would need to regenerate the blood they drank, and squirreling away every extra pint for later.

He hated the thought of diluting or adulterating the blood, but he hated the thought of not having any blood even more. He knew a recipe that called for Black-hearted Afina that did quite well as a natural anti-coagulant. The berries would preserve the blood for the future, and they wouldn't have to bleed him out all at once. As long as they kept him alive, they'd have a continual fount from which to drink. If they showed patience and restraint, they could have a supply for many, many years. If they were careful.

And Hundsfordt was very careful. He was, after all, hired to take care of the details, and the details required a certain level of dexterity, like a surgeon's steady hands, and a certain, clinical detachment.

Ox's sloppy betrayal had been his downfall. Ox had caught the scent and thought he could have the blood all to himself. Instead, he had gotten himself killed, the greedy little bastard. Hundsfordt decided to leave him dead for now, they could always resurrect him later. Vampires weren't so easy to kill, they were the cockroaches of the supernatural world. It would be a fitting punishment if they left Ox for dead until after the boy's blood ran dry. That would teach him not to be so miserly with his brothers. He should forfeit his cut of the spoils, especially if he did not participate in the capture. Besides, a resurrection would take too long.

Hundsfordt was not going to risk letting the trail grow cold again.

Hunger Pangs

The solid rock of the Canadian Shield enveloped them; stratified layers of stone rising up and falling on either side of the road. The Trans Canada highway was part of the old River Route to the west that had opened up the country to settlement, and it was along this route they now travelled to the Ghost Lake reserve. A lot of dynamite had gone into building this road, and a lot of dynamite had gone into building the country. Dynamite meant power. It said so on the back of the bottle of C-Six, the label depicting the complicated molecular structure of nitroglycerin in a latticed framework of diatomaceous earth. They passed the bottle of C-Six back and forth, taking a pull every so often as they drove. Church didn't think they'd crash; the booze was too much a part of Geoff's system. He steered with stone cold sobriety.

Church fell asleep as Geoff drove north. Geoff could feel the throbbing rumble of the engine through the stick shift as if it was a heartbeat. Nothing seemed to exist outside the circle illuminated by the range of his headlights, the dotted yellow lines flickering past, lulling him. The layers of sediment, like growth rings of a tree, detailing the history of the earth. If you knew how, you could read that history, and count the age of the earth.

Church's head rested against the window, and his lips moved in his sleep. Geoff wondered if it was a good dream. Church mumbled something and Geoff let up on the gas pedal, letting the engine quiet. Absurdly, it felt as if he were eavesdropping. Maybe it would give him some insight into what was going on inside Church's head? He was like an iceberg, and three-quarters of what was going on lay hidden beneath the surface.

Church mumbled and Geoff hunched over to listen, keeping the steering wheel steady, though the car drifted slowly over the centre line. Shnreeeeeeoonhw! A car's horn blared as it roared by, and he had to swerve to avoid a head-on collision.

Church jerked awake, looking around wide-eyed.

"Sorry," Geoff said. "You were talking in your sleep you know." Church's shoulders hunched over in an almost habitual posture of defense.

"What did I say?" Church asked.

"I'm not really sure." Geoff said, "I don't know very much Ojibwe. Mnopogwad-miskwi and . . . nbakade. You kept saying nbakade. What does that mean?" he asked.

"Nothing," Church said, resting his head against the window and going back to sleep. Delicious blood, he'd said in his sleep. Mnopogwad-miskwi. And, I'm hungry. Nbakade. But he wasn't going to tell Geoff that. He probably thought he was enough of a freak already.

"Hey!" Geoff said.

"What?" Church asked, coming back to himself.

"I don't know," Geoff said, looking back and forth, dividing his attention between Church and the road. "You were looking at me funny."

"What do you mean funny?" Church asked. A million miles away, he couldn't remember what he had been thinking.

"I don't know." Geoff said, shuddering. "Like a mountain lion was weighing me with its eyes. You know you creep me out sometimes." Oops! Church thought. I have to remember to keep the hunger under control. It would be bad if he lost control of himself in a moment of abstraction.

"Sorry, I wasn't looking at you." Church lied. "I was just thinking about what I was going to do if we run into the triplets again."

"And what is that exactly?"

"You don't believe I'm a wiindigo do you?" Church asked.

"No, I don't," Geoff said. "I think it's just a story."

"Then if I told you what I had been thinking," Church said, "you would think that I am crazy."

"Maybe." Geoff said.

They turned off the Trans-Canada onto Closest Road. They had switched seats at the last truck stop and Church was driving now. He pressed harder on the pedal, and the car lurched forward, sucking back fuel at a faster rate, burning the gasoline and releasing the souls of ancient life. Souls to burn, Church thought.

By some quirk of geologic fate, the same physical processes by which dinosaur bones had been preserved, had also preserved marine life deposited in layers of sediment, which became oil and natural gas captured in the folds and draperies of the rock, the black sludge of the modern energy economy.

Church imagined the souls of extinct species filling the sky, clogging the air and breaking down the molecules of ozone with their viscous, primordial presence; the vengeance of disturbed ghosts terraforming the world to suit their lost one—a warmer world, a world with more lizard-brained violence. They took their anger out on the fabric of the atmosphere. The spirits of animal ancestors, whose extinction made way for humanity's chance to evolve outside of their shadow.

An hour further along and they would arrive at their destination. A heavily forested area of land separated Ghost Lake from the road. From where they would have to leave the car, it was a bit of a trek over land to the river. The fastest way to the reserve lands was by boat because there were no roads out to the reserve itself. It was ironic that a reserve created to make way for a route to western Canada, itself had no roads in or out. The only way was to take the old roads, Church thought, the lakes and rivers that had once been the only roads.

"We're here!" Church said, pulling over onto a small strip of gravel on the side of the empty road.

"Where? I don't see anything," Geoff said. A two-lane highway separated a stretch of forest on either side. It looked indistinguishable from every other stretch of road they'd seen in the past hour.

"Are you sure?" Geoff asked. He'd never been to Ghost Lake before.

"I'm sure," Church said. "This is the place."

"I don't see any sign or anything," Geoff said, rubber-necking.

"Listen," Church said, "I don't want you to come with me. You've come far enough. I'm going the rest of the way alone." He hadn't planned on any of this. He had just needed a ride, and then all of this had happened. "I really appreciate everything, but you shouldn't come with me." It was possible things could go wrong, and he didn't want to drag Geoff down too.

"We've been through this already," Geoff said. "I'm coming with you."

"It's too dangerous," Church said, once again trying to dissuade him. It would be selfish of him to put them both in danger. He had to at least try to keep Geoff safe and send him away.

"You're in no condition to go anywhere. You have barely eaten anything in days, and you've been puking in every gas station we passed. You could get lost, or eaten by a wild animal. I'm not letting you go anywhere on your own," Geoff said, gesturing towards the forest.

"I'm not going to get lost," Church said, "This is my home. And, trust me, I'm likely to be the scariest thing in those woods. I'm not going to get eaten."

"I'm coming with you, whether you want me to or not," Geoff said.

"Okay, okay," Church said, feeling both relieved that he wouldn't be facing this alone, but also guilty that Geoff didn't know what he was getting himself into. Geoff didn't believe in curses, or vampires, or wiindigo.

"Are you coming out here to die? Is that why you don't want me to come?"

"No, I have a plan," Church said, "but it might not work."

"Well, it's good that I'm coming with you then. You might need my help."

Geoff left his truck parked in a small gravel parking lot at the side of the un-marked stretch of road and followed Church into the forest. There was a small footpath that wasn't visible until you took a few steps into the woods.

"Are you sure you know where you're going?" Geoff asked.

"Trust me," Church said.

Dec. 1st 1872, Ghost Lake,

Dear James,

I cannot solve this mystery, and cure myself, without knowing fully all aspects of this sickness. She knows something, and Goshko will not speak to me. I went yesterday to Goshko's cabin, set back from the lake, further inland of Drinker's excavation site.

Driven by currents of invisible air, the sleet swirls and churns, the drafts and eddies made visible by the powdery snow that is whipped up by the wind. To look upon this ice locked landscape is to feel cold, no matter how many layers of sheep's wool and animal hide one wears, appearing less and less human amongst the shapeless heaps of blankets and furs everyone wears to ward off the advancing chill.

When I arrived that morning, I could hear banging coming from within. I tried the knob, but the door was locked. The banging continued. "GOSHKO'?" I asked, yelling through the door "ARE YOU HOME?" The banging stopped, and I heard Goshko's muffled voice coming from within.

"Ningooji! Awash!" And then the banging continued. A nail punched through the wood near my face. I flinched back, the point of the barb, two inches away from my left eye.

"GOD-DAMN IT! GOSHKO! GOSHKO!" I yelled. "WHAT'S GOING ON? YOU KNOW THIS WON'T SOLVE ANYTHING!" Goshko was boarding himself up in his own home. Of all people, I thought he would have been above this sort of hysteria.

"Harker? Zhaa zhigosh! The Wiindigo has come. It's time for you to go home, there's nothing more you can accomplish here." Bang! Bang! Bang! Bang! The hammering resumed, and the door sported a few more metal teeth, growing out of the door like porcupine quills, bristling.

"Goshko! Goshko! Come now, you're being unreasonable! I just came to find out more about your niece, Mukade-wiiyas. Hole-In-The-Day." Silence. "I need to know. How is her condition different from the other cases of the Wiindigo Sickness? Why is she different?"

"Mr. Lockwood, please." The medicine man said calmly, speaking in a lower register in English, "Leave my niece alone. She has no part in this. Don't pester her with your questions. It can bring only misfortune, for you and for her."

And then Goshko resumed with his hammer, boarding himself up inside his own home, and our conversation was at an end. He would answer no more of my questions, or respond to any appeals. I had at least managed to get him to admit that the young woman is, in fact his niece, despite having previously denied any relation. Progress.

For some reason I haven't yet been able to discern, the medicine man, along with every other member of her tribe, shun this girl and barely acknowledge her existence. "Wiindigo" I have since learned, among the Ojibwe, is a word used to describe many forms of insanity, usually linked to one form of excess or another. She might not have Wiindigo Psychosis, but she could have some other form of insanity or madness. Maybe this is why they call her 'always-wiindigo'?

I have found few enough answers, and feel it is necessary to explore every avenue that lends itself towards an answer.

Your friend,

Harker Lockwood

"There is some debate as to whether there are enough documented cases to prove the existence of psychotic cannibalism, and whether it has more to do with sensationalism and prejudice on the part of Anthropologists, in the same vein as Columbus who named the 'Carib' Indians 'Cannibals' in order to justify genocide and the extraction of resources."

~Excerpt from Wiindigo Culture Amongst the Northern Ojibwe, Ph.D. Dissertation 1875, by Harker Lockwood.

Wild currents

Church led the way and Geoff Suture followed.

The forest engulfed them as if they were entering the body of some great beast; a large, living, breathing creature made up of thousands of smaller life-forms to create a larger more complex whole. The trunks rose up to the green canopy above like pillars upholding the sky, yellow light filtering down through the emergent leaves and understory to the leaf-littered floor. It was a mixed deciduous and coniferous forest, with lots of poplars and white birch, along with balsam, spruce, ash, trembling aspen, tamarack and pine. Even though he'd grown up in town, Geoff was good at recognizing different species, and remembering their names. The low-light loving shrubs and plants growing in the shadow of the large trees were a greater mystery.

The going was rough, and the footpath quickly became an unpredictable terrain of sudden slopes and narrow gullies. The path led them steadily north-west and occasionally east as they swerved around natural barriers, like swamps, and great shelves of rock sprouting green carpets.

"You see this?" Church asked, pointing at a large rock.

"It's a rock," Geoff said.

"I mean, what's growing on the rock," Church said.

"Moss!" Geoff said.

"Yeah, it's good for you."

"You can eat it?" Geoff asked.

"It's better than nothing if you're really starving," Church said, absently raising a bundle of the green gunk to his lips and chewing.

"How do you know?" Geoff asked.

"We didn't always have enough to eat," Church said. "My grandmother Day used to show me what was edible. And Mukade-wiiyas knew everything that could be eaten in the bush. It's a wiindigo thing, I guess."

"And I know about the trees," Geoff said, nodding towards a tree growing on top of the large outcropping of rock, "That's balsam fir, see how it tapers towards the top like a steeple?"

As they walked, Church pointed out the different edible plants as easily as if he was walking down the aisle of a supermarket and recognized the brand names, and Geoff catalogued the different species of trees they passed.

"That's compass-wart," Church said, pointing at a plant with yellow flowers, and picking a few of the leaves. "The leaves always point towards the sun." He pushed a few of the prickly-edged leaves into his mouth, and chewed. At least Church was eating something, Geoff thought. And plants always grow towards the light.

"Black spruce," Geoff said, nodding towards an evergreen. "They can live for up to two hundred years."

Church stopped and squatted down next to a plant growing low to the ground and fondled the leathery green leaves. "This is mshkiigimin, low-bush cranberry. But the berries are still white. They're not ready to eat."

"If we got lost on a desert island," Geoff said, "at least we wouldn't starve."

"But if it was a desert island," Church said, "there wouldn't be anything to eat." And if Geoff were stranded with me, Church thought, somewhere without a food source—he might not get the chance to starve.

"A remote-forested-area then," Geoff said.

Church paused in the middle of a clearing, looking at a plant with heart-shaped leaves that came up to his waist. "This is yellow dock," Church said. "It's a weed that followed the first settlers across the Atlantic, and now it grows everywhere, kind of like dandelions. You can use the seeds to make bread. Dandelions are edible too."

"At least the plants seem to have co-existed for 500 years," Geoff said, cynically. "Even if humans can't."

"Actually, a lot of damage is caused when foreign species are introduced into an ecosystem that can't handle them. It can create havoc. Ecosystems have evolved over thousands of years, and foreign species can disrupt that balance."

"I knew that," Geoff said. "You see that stump over there? That used to be a Chestnut tree; they've almost become extinct since the introduction of a certain fungus. They didn't have any immunity."

The root system of the chestnut tree had some resistance to the fungus, and a few green shoots grew out from the stump, like the last flickering embers of a fire that could one day become a flame, if the fungus didn't kill it first. Church supposed colonization wasn't just political or geographic; it crossed all boundaries down to the cellular level; atoms, genes, and the deadly encroachment of disease.

"You see this plant?" Church asked, fondling the red berries. "These are zhaaboomin, wild-currants." He popped a few of the berries into his mouth, sucking out the juice and spitting out the seeds. "You should always spit out the seeds, so next year, there will be more of them."

"Aren't you worried you might poison yourself?" Geoff asked.

"These aren't poisonous," Church said, brushing his hands through the currant shrub, "but this plant over here, definitely is. It's a Night-shade. Although I'm probably immune." The leaves of the vine looked like moth-eaten green lace, it had beautiful purple flower-petals with yellow pistils, and poisonous blood-red-berries. It grew only a few paces away from the wild currants.

"Immune? Why would you be immune?" Geoff asked.

"They used to be Mukade-wiiyas's favourite. They give me stomach aches, but I've eaten so many of them, I'm pretty sure they don't affect me. I've built up a tolerance, I guess."

"I don't think that's possible," Geoff said. "If you're so immune, why don't you eat one?"

"All right," Church said, and without hesitation, popped a few of the blood-red berries into his mouth, "I don't always go out of my way to eat poison berries, but sometimes I do by accident, you know?"

"No. Don't!" Geoff said, tackling him to the ground. "I was just joking!"

But it was too late.

The flavour was pleasing for such a lethal berry. In his experience, most berries that were poisonous tasted foul, but these were juicy, tart and sweet.

"Are you crazy?" Geoff asked. "You could die! We have to get you to a hospital!"

"I'm fine," Church said, smiling. "I told you. I'm immune." His pupils looked huge and dilated in the dim light that filtered down to the forest floor.

"But what if you're not immune to these ones?" Geoff asked, his voice strained by what he believed to be Church's reckless disregard for life.

"I guess we'll find out," Church said, standing up and brushing earth and dried leaves from his clothes. As they walked, Geoff kept a close eye on him, but Church just continued rambling on about the edible flora, without exhibiting any signs of distress.

 Geoff was on information overload, each plant had a name, each plant had characteristics that identified it, characteristics that distinguished it from plants with similar characteristics (possibly poisonous), and each plant had a number of separate uses and methods of preparation. Geoff was dizzy with names, including some with their Ojibwe designations, and whether they were imported, naturalized, invasive, or indigenous.

"I thought I knew a lot about plants," Geoff said.

"I only know about the ones that can be eaten," Church said.

"Are you feeling all right?" Geoff asked for almost the fifteenth time.

"Yes, I'm fine. Inri says we're like the birds and were immune to solanine because it has the molecular structure of honey." Church wouldn't have told Geoff that the Night-shade had given him a stomach ache if he had known that Geoff was going be so overprotective.

"Are you sure that your stomach ache isn't getting worse?" Geoff asked him. Church wouldn't have eaten the stupid berries in the first place if he knew how much of a hassle it would turn out to be.

"No, the stomach ache has actually gone away now," Church lied. It was only mildly discomforting, like when he ate too many hot peppers. "It's no big deal."

What Geoff didn't know was that the details-men Magnon Inc. had sent after him; were not men at all. They were vampires. If wiindigo were real, Church thought, why not vampires? Who knew what else could be real? He wondered what the details-men were up to? Had they caught his scent? Had they picked up on his trail of bread-crumb bloodstains? He tried to use some of that dream-power magic Inri claimed to have, in order to see what they were up to. Blurry at first, the brothers came into focus in his mind, but like a daydream, he couldn't really be certain it was real:

Hundsfordt and Grundel were driving, following the trail of bloodstained, gas-station bathrooms. It was possible the kid really was wounded, and his blood was leading them right to him. The right stars, Hundsfordt thought, are hanging overhead.

Grundel stuck his head out the window as he drove, like a dog enjoying the wind, trying to pick up some hint of their victim's blood on the air.

"Hurry up!" Hundsfordt said. "We want to get there while there's still some blood left in his body."

Church got first one impression, and then another as the scene shifted again. It might not be reliable, but it was better than knowing nothing; he didn't want to be caught by surprise again.

"Stop!" Hundsfordt yelled, and Grundel slammed on the brakes. "There's their car," he said. A small brown truck was pulled over on the gravel shoulder half a mile down the road.

"Maybe they ran out of gas?" Grundel said.

"There isn't gas station around for miles." Hundsfordt said, his smile glinting evil-ly in the dim light illuminating his face from the dashboard. "I can feel him. We're getting close. He's ours now."

Geoff emerged from the trees still doing up his fly, from where he'd been "going to the bathroom," and Church snapped out of his trance. The brothers had caught up with them. Good, he thought. Church hadn't been wasting his time by spilling all that blood; it had served its purpose.

Dec. 2nd 1872, Ghost Lake, the house of the Wiindigo's Daughter,

I am mortified by what I have done—and I am hesitant to put pen to paper and record the events that have transpired in this desolate, deleterious outpost. It is possible I have gone mad entirely, and everything that is written here, is but the delusional rantings of a mad man. I am not certain. How could I be, when I may be mad?

The symptoms of Wiindigo Sickness grow worse, not in any of my patients, but in myself. I can no longer stomach wholesome food, it no longer seems edible. I crave something else, something meaty and more substantial. These cravings plague me, but I refuse to let my mind think upon what that may be. My heart feels cold. I can feel the ice in my chest, in my sluggish veins, chilling me the way my heart once heated me. And with the chill I can feel an increased strength that thrills and dismays.

But enough of this; this is what I imagine to have happened:

There was something on my arm. In the dream, I was wiping some kind of black tar off my arm, a thick viscous fluid, and no matter how hard I worked to shake it off, it would not be removed. Upon rising closer to consciousness, I slowly realized that in fact, there was something on my arm, heavy and warm, like a water bottle restricting the circulation. I half sat up, but was prevented, by whatever was caught on my arm. At first I thought it was Mukade-wiiyas, resting her head on my shoulder, still fast asleep, but as the last haziness of sleep left me, I realized that wasn't what was causing the pins-and-needles sensation.

Her jaw had hinged back like a snake, and my entire arm, right up to the elbow, was entirely ingested inside the cavity of her body. Her eyes were open, and she looked up at me with a lidded, sleepy expression. It hit me with absolute certainty, that this lovely Ojibwe maiden, this creature, was, in fact, not human. I had not believed the stories of her lineage. I had dismissed them as absurd. Such things just aren't real.

But whatever this woman is, she isn't human.

Gingerly, I removed my arm, slowly, slowly. Controlling my breathing with some difficulty, as if I'd been running. Fighting the urge to scream, to rip my arm from her throat in one jerking motion, to run as I had at first run upon entering her home. She didn't fight to keep my arm inside her body, instead it slipped out easily and without resistance. My hand and arm was wet with saliva, and digestive fluids, but although damp, seemed otherwise unharmed.

Her jaw hinged back into place, as if it had never been stretched to its reptilian potential. She stretched and yawned, her perfect breasts flattening and protruding as she extended her lithe, youthful form. Salt-and-pepper-hair framed her face and body like the curtains of a theatre. I backed away from her slowly, as if from a wild animal with a hair-trigger temper, so as not to draw its ire.

Upon seeing me withdraw, she stood, and came closer. And again the full realization hit me; that this woman, though achingly lovely, wasn't human. She is some other order of creature. My head felt heavy, my insides whirling with chaotic activity. Gii-apane Wiindigowi-kwem. She was always wiindigo, an entirely different order of species from the madness that afflicted the diggers. I turned and fled. Leaving her home, the same way that I'd left the place when we first met, leaving the door open behind me in my haste to escape.

I am done researching Wiindigo Psychosis. I no longer know which parts of my account are truth and which are the product of the madness that I came to study, which in turn has afflicted me. I have learned all that I care to know about this Wiindigo Sickness, and this forsaken country, so far away from the light of god. The damned place attracts nothing but madmen, and deranged dinosaur hunters digging up demons from the mantles of hell.

The Double Slit Experiment: When electrons
are shot through two slits, they create an
interference pattern like a wave, but when an
observation device is used to measure which
slit the electron actually passes through, the
electron then acts like a particle, creating a
pattern in a band, in line with the slit. The act
of observation changes the way that the smallest
particles in the universe behave in quantum
events. Matter can behave as both a particle,
and a wave. This is known as the wave-particle
duality.

The road of all souls

An hour later they came to the Jiibay River, fast-moving and twenty paces across. Church led them in the direction of the current, following the course of the water as it carved through the terrain. Water always took the path of least resistance.

"We follow this river for another thirty minutes," Church said, "and then we'll reach Ghost Lake."

Church was getting tired and he began to lag behind, letting Geoff lead the way along the path that ran parallel to the river. Church felt the 'day-dream' continue even as he was awake, except the details were murkier and more opaque, like looking through a window at night; all you could see was darkness.

When he was blinded by the lit interior of their kitchen, he couldn't see any details, but he knew the yard was still there; their small victory garden, the chicken coop, Godzilla's abandoned dog-house, all overshadowed by the soaring, skeletal boughs of the cherry tree—they were all still there, even when he couldn't see them. Because things that are real, didn't need you to believe in them, did they? Real is real, regardless of whether you can see it or not.

Like one of Inri's Buddhist koans: if a tree falls in the forest does it make a sound? Church's answer to this question was yes. He could feel the dream continue on without him, even though he was awake, like dull beacons throbbing dimly somewhere in the back of his awareness. The dream continued even without his dream-self observation of the events, which made him think they were not dreams at all, but actual events taking place in real-time.

They paused for a moment as the sound of a distant tree falling reverberated through the forest, making a racket as it crashed through branches on the way down. The sound radiated outwards like the waves from a stone thrown into the lake, the percussion slowly dissipating, until it was imperceptible. Things that are real, don't need you to believe in them, Church thought, they'll kill you just the same.

The dream was more opaque than ever. He couldn't seem to make it come into focus anymore. But he could feel it—feel them. The two triplet twins were getting closer. He knew it, even if he couldn't exactly see it as clearly as he would have liked. They weren't far now.

Hundsfordt and Grundel stopped to listen.

The muffled sounds of voices carried over the traffic of the river, and they smiled at each other. They'd located their target. Hundsfordt whispered his plan into Grundel's ear, "Let's loop around in front before they reach the lake. They won't be expecting an attack from ahead." And if they split-up, and converged from the South and west, the two boys would also be trapped with the river at their back. It made sound tactical sense. "They won't have anywhere to run." And then they smiled, their teeth glinting like the serrated edge of a knife.

"We've got him now," Grundel said, "but his friend, that fighter, he's a threat." Grundel always did have more sense than their triplet brother Ox.

"You take the boxer," Hundfordt said, "Keep him distracted while I go after Church. He's already lost a lot of blood, and he's probably weak. He shouldn't be too much of a problem. But remember, whatever happens: don't kill the boy! I want him alive! And don't forget we still have a job to do for Magnon."

Church stopped in the path. Listening.

Geoff paused after a few steps when he realized that Church had lagged behind and was no longer following behind him. "What's wrong?" he asked.

"Did you hear something?" Church asked.

"No, why?"

"No reason. I think we should hurry, the sun's going down soon, and we don't want to be caught out on the water after dark."

"Okay," Geoff said, again taking the lead.

A large shape jumped out of the bushes beside Church and grabbed him in a headlock, holding a forearm against his throat, choking him. Church tried to scream, to warn Geoff, but only a gurgling sound escaped. Ohfuckohfuck-ohfuckohfuck, Church thought, ohfuckohfuckohfuck.

"Did you hear something?" Geoff said, right before he too was jumped by a black shape that appeared fluidly out of the forest like a shadow. Arms restraining him like bands of iron, Church could only watch as Grundel kicked the shit out of Geoff.

If Geoff died, it would be his fault. He had allowed Geoff to walk unknowingly into this without convincing him of the dangers he could face. Stupid! Stupid! Now he was going to get both of them killed.

Church closed his eyes and let the hunger rise, relaxing the defensive walls that he always held between himself and the emptiness inside, letting the black cloud of darkness devour him. His jaws closed around the forearm that was pressed to his throat. His teeth sank into the marshmallow meat like a lynx sinking its fangs into the vulnerable flesh of a rabbit. Church felt his teeth grind against bone and the attacker behind him cried out.

Hundsfordt's victim was taking a bite out of him! But the vampire was not in a position to appreciate the irony. Church locked his jaw and tore away with a vicious sideways wrench of his head like a dog, which wrent free a chunk of flesh, veins, tendons, and muscle. And then he went back for more, taking another bite, he gritted his teeth and pulled, in his mind picturing a gorging lion devouring a zebra. Hundsfordt screamed in pain, and Grundel looked up sharply, distracted from his own attack, his eyes lit up like a feeding hyena caught in the sudden flash-bulb of a camera's glare.

And then, smiling, Church began to chew.

His mouth was ringed with blood, like a child caught eating an entire cake, any denials refuted by the evidence on his lips. Geoff and the vampire Grundel stood for a moment and watched as he chewed, both of them caught—rapt, in frozen-tableaux with expressions of shock. Hundsfordt clutched at the gaping wound on his forearm where the white of his bone could be seen glinting through his fingers, and the blackish-red blood sluggishly flowed, more black-brown than red in the dim light under the trees.

Now free of Hundsfordt's grasp, Church stepped forward, walking purposely towards Grundel, the blood now dripping down his neck as he chewed. He strode forward without fear, ignoring all doubts, as if to say: you're next. The two vampires stared at him, as if their lamb had suddenly morphed into a wolf staring hungrily at its prey. A mask had been dropped, revealing the monster that had been hiding behind the disguise.

It happened fast. Broken from the spell of his initial shock, Grundel finally reacted, charging forward like an enraged rhinoceros, he barreled into Church like a battering ram. Church went down like a bowling pin. He found himself falling, rolling, and then falling again, crashing head first like a lead-weighted dummy backwards into the river. Immediately, the current of the river snatched him up in its grasp, carrying him swiftly downstream. He found that his only task now, was to try to keep his head above water.

Geoff

Their attackers had emerged so silently from the trees, it was as if the shadows had taken on substance and form. Church claimed that these "details-men," had been hired by Magnon Inc., and that they had murdered his father. He knew that Church thought these men were vampires. Church talked in his sleep. But Geoff didn't believe that Church was actually a wiindigo, anymore than he thought that these men were vampires; however, he did believe that they meant business. It was a good thing they weren't

vampires—as they were only as strong as strong humans—
otherwise, he and Church would have been screwed. Church's
vampire theory also overlooked the fact that it was clearly still
daylight—though the sun was going down—in all the movies
he'd ever seen, vampires burst into flames when touched by
sunlight. Still, these men were dangerous, even if they didn't have
any sort of vampire super-strength.

Geoff felt his stomach drop when he saw Church falling down
the steep embankment and down to the rapids below. He stood
rooted to the spot for a moment before he took action and
moved, diving head first into the river. He hoped fleetingly, mid-
dive, that there wouldn't be any rocks to knock him unconscious
when he broke the surface. He wouldn't be doing anyone a favour
if he got himself drowned. But he wasn't sure if Church would
still be conscious after his fall. Geoff had to do something.

Geoff dove, and thankfully, when he pierced the icy surface,
there were no rocks, only cold, cold water. Geoff swam with
quick strokes in the same direction as the current trying to add
what little speed he could to the already powerful force of the
river. Church had already been carried far from his position,
and then he lost sight of his boyfriend when he saw Church's
head went underwater.

Church

The current was swift and violent, dragging him far downstream
in a matter of minutes. It was all that he could do to keep his
head above water, let alone fight the current. Church had never
been a strong swimmer, and his reluctance to bare his scars
had kept him from getting any better. Even a strong swimmer
wouldn't want to go swimming in this stretch of river.

There is a classification system for rivers, which are rated for their severity. Class I are considered easy with a clear path, Class II is considered moderate with an obvious route to take, Class III is considered moderate-to-difficult and still maintains a visible route, Class IV is more difficult and requires prior scouting to maneuvre a path through the rapids, and Class V is extremely difficult and requires advanced paddling skills, precise maneuvering, and a hell of a lot of practice. After a certain point, rivers are merely classified as un-navigable, or suicide. This does not mean that a river with a rating above Class V can't be navigated, it just means that it isn't recommended.

In the Anishinaabek language, there are a ridiculous number of words to describe the word "canoe." This is because the rivers and waterways are also a transit system. But a transit system that required portage routes, to circumvent impediments, such as Class V rapids.

It felt as if Church were on a very fast, wet roller coaster, except that this ride had no seat belts. He was bashed against rocks, and he knew that if he survived, he would have bruises. He inhaled and swallowed, water. He was pulled under and he held his breath, his lungs burning. Murky green water with suspended debris, and air bubbles clogged his vision. His hopes for survival dimmed.

The water twisted and turned, buffeting him, tossing him about like a paper-boat sent over Niagara Falls. He felt like he was in the wash cycle of a washing machine. He surfaced briefly and then went under again breathing in more water when he inhaled, then coming back up choking, gasping for breath, trying to pull as much oxygen into his lungs as he could. He gasped the way he imagined a man dying of dehydration drinks in the desert; he drank the air in—greedily. It hurt when he inhaled. His ribs must have been broken or bruised in the fall, or maybe when he was bashed up against one of the rocks. It hurt to breathe. He still couldn't get enough air. He was grateful for air in a way that he never had been until it became a scarce resource.

Church knew he couldn't keep his head above water for much longer. He tried to see land but was blinded by the spray. All he could see of the shore was a blur of green, passing like the scenery outside a car window. He caught a quick glimpse of trees and then he was sucked down by an undertow, and then caught in a whirlpool for a moment, he was spun around, before he was spit out at twice the speed. He popped up again thirty metres down the river from where he had last taken a breath. He had inhaled great reams of water, and only had time to come up coughing before being dragged back down again, where his head came briefly into contact with a rock, and everything went to black.

When Church opened his eyes again he was underwater. Bubbles foamed and frothed in all directions like a shook-up bottle of coca-cola, and the water was just as black. He floated along with the current, and the river became like a tunnel he travelled through as it burrowed its way west on a fast-paced trajectory through the rough terrain. He understood why rivers were the transportation system of the country: they were wide, flat, exposed, and free of trees, just like roads, except rivers always chose the path of least resistance—no dynamite needed—and they leveled their way through mountains, trees, and plains just as easily.

For some reason, Church no longer seemed to have any problem combating the competing currents, or limply avoiding the dangerous rocks. The underwater landscape scenery flew by. It was quieter and more peaceful fully submerged than on the surface. He seemed to travel almost undisturbed, and he wondered what had changed. He wondered why he didn't seem to have any problem breathing.

Then he noticed that he wasn't breathing.

Some people said that The Road of All Souls was in the stars, and that the road itself was our galaxy, the Milky-way continuing on into the rest of creation through the constellation Bagone-giizhig, Hole-In-The-Day. He was going to see his great-grandmother in the sky. But maybe it was different for every person. On the Road of Souls—all the dead travel west. And, he realized, he was headed in that direction more quickly now, than ever before.

Geoff

The muscles in his arms burned from exertion, but he couldn't stop now, he was so close. He could see Church's head bobbing above the water, struggling and splashing, and occasionally going under, but he always reappeared, spluttering. Geoff had always been a strong swimmer. It had been part of his cardio training when he was still boxing. He could make it. He knew he could.

Church went under again, and Geoff scanned the surface, waiting for Church to re-emerge, but he didn't come back up again. He kept praying that he would re-surface, but he never did. Holding his breath, Geoff dove, keeping his eyes open so he could see what little there was to see in the murky waters, but it was useless. Visibility was almost non-existent.

Church

The neon, black-light scenery passed by serenely, and he began to become lethargic, despite the initial alarm he felt over the discovery that he was no longer breathing. When nothing impending seemed to happen, he relaxed. The water no longer felt cold. Strange presences seemed to accompany him on his journey, glowing like pale bio-luminescent jelly-fish swimming along-side him, as distant and aloof as the stars. Shimmering coldly in the darkness.

But then the pain returned. He fought against it, not wanting to leave the peaceful flow of the river, and his sparkling neighbours who were following the path of souls. But he wasn't given a choice. The quiet calm was ripped away, replaced by a deep, bone-freezing cold. He was on his side barfing up a seemingly never-ending stream of water. It came in waves, and with each new wave his stomach muscles knotted like a dish-rag twisting out the contents of his belly. Then he was shivering violently, and someone was holding him. Geoff was holding him, hugging him as if he were a rock in the white-water-rapids that threatened to sweep them away and he was the only thing to hold onto.

Geoff

In late August it wasn't really swimming weather anymore. Church's lips had turned blue. Geoff's teeth clattered. It was now late enough in the year that the water was almost hypothermia-cold.

Church's brown eyes stared glassily at nothing like a dying steer as the last few electromagnetic particles fired off in his brain, and within their depths, the shadow of his spirit departing from this world.

As soon as Geoff had dragged him ashore, he placed Church on his back, tilted his head back to open the passageway, held his ear to his mouth to listen for a breath, and tried to recall the details from a long-ago First Aid course, checking his wrist for a pulse. He felt no breath against his skin. Church wasn't breathing! He tried to quell the rising panic. He couldn't fuck this up! But then he found a pulse, a weak pulse, but it was still there. A weak pulse was better than no pulse.

He was slick, grey, clammy, and wet . . . but he was alive.

How long had he been under? Once the oxygen in his blood was used up, there would no longer be a supply to the brain. Five minutes? Maybe Ten? If he didn't start breathing again soon, he could have serious brain damage, and not long after, brain death. Geoff would have to breathe for him. Air is 21% oxygen, air that is exhaled has about 16% Oxygen, which is more than enough to keep someone alive, since every breath only extracts the 5% it needs.

Geoff placed the heel of his palm on Church's chest and began chest compressions, thirty in quick succession. Then pinching Church's nose shut, Geoff began blowing into Church's mouth in a macabre parody of a kiss, two full breaths, watching the chest rise with air like an inflated balloon, then checking his wrist again for a pulse—weak but still there—and continuing to breathe for him, counting one breath for every five seconds. Then alternating between chest compressions and breaths. Two breaths for every thirty chest compressions.

One one-thousand, two one-thousand, three one-thousand, four one-thousand, five one-thousand. Breath.

One one-thousand, two one-thousand, three one-thousand, four one-thousand, five one-thousand. Breath.

--Thirty quick chest compressions--

One one-thousand, two one-thousand, three one-thousand, four one-thousand, five one-thousand. Breath.

One one-thousand, two one-thousand, three one-thousand, four one-thousand, five one-thousand. Breath.

--Thirty quick chest compressions--

One one-thousand, two one-thousand, three one-thousand, four one-thousand, five one-thousand. Breath.

One one-thousand, two one-thousand, three one-thousand, four one-thousand, five one-thousand. Breath.

Geoff didn't know how long he repeated this process. It felt like an eternity, though he knew it couldn't have been more than a few minutes. At twelve-breaths /minute, Church started breathing on his own. He sat up like Frankenstein's monster, like the girl in Pulp Fiction who OD'ed, then Church coughed violently, puking out water onto the forest floor.

His plan had worked. Sort of.

The two surviving triplets had followed them out to the Ghost Lake reserve, where, Church had believed, the tables would be turned. The vampires would follow the scent of his blood, drawn to him like a hummingbird drawn to the pollen of a brightly coloured flower—only to discover this flower was carnivorous. And then, the hunter would become the hunted. It sounded like the tag-line to an action-horror movie like Predator, maybe his brain had been fried from watching too much television, but at the time it had seemed to make sense, and he didn't have a hell-of-a-lot of options. The last part of the plan hadn't worked out so great.

But all wiindigo nonsense aside, Geoff thought, it wasn't that surprising that Church created this fantasy in which he could get revenge on the men who had killed his father. Geoff hadn't believed Magnon's goons would actually come after them, but vampires or not, these men were extremely dangerous. Geoff had gone along with Church, because he couldn't let him go alone. And because, he was already implicated in the murder. He had helped to dispose of the body.

"We need to get you to a hospital!" Geoff said, hugging Church's body to him for warmth. Church usually felt cool to the touch, now he felt like ice.

"I'm fine," Church said, even as great shivers wracked his body. Wiindigo didn't need doctors. And the closest hospital was way too far away to be of any help now.

"If by fine you mean almost died, then yes, you're fine," Geoff said. He had already learned once that day that it was impossible to convince Church to go to the hospital, even after eating poisonous berries.

Church pulled his shirt over his head. The shirt was sopping wet and clung clammily to his skin, revealing first the scars on his chest, and then the bandages he had kept hidden on his arms. Geoff's eyes grew wide as he took in the extent of the new damage that now lay exposed. White bandages washed to pink.

"What are those?" Geoff demanded. Church looked at him in a way that Geoff was beginning to recognize—he had seen that look before—Church looked hungry, the water dripping out of his hair carved rivulets down his flesh. "What? Now?" Geoff asked incredulously. Why would he want to do that, now?

"Yes, now," Church said hoarsely through gritted teeth, and then lunged forward, as if he were trying to rekindle the heat lost from his body. Firewood licked by flames. Maybe this wasn't Church? Maybe Church had drowned, and all that he had rescued was a hungry spirit inhabiting his body? If he resisted, it might snap his bones like dry twigs, drink his blood, and suck the marrow from his bones. Fie Fie fo Fum. I'll grind his bones to make my bread!

Then he remembered that Church was supposed to be a wiindigo. And that wiindigo, were cannibal monsters. Maybe Church wasn't completely human after all?

He was a wall, hit by a storm, and it was hard to remain intact. Despite himself, Geoff found himself getting drawn in. He was a kite unfettered, pushed and pulled and taken wherever the winds would take him. By the time they were done they had both stopped shivering. And Church seemed better—less inhuman.

It seemed to have taken the edge off his hunger.

"Come on." Church said, sitting up and pulling his wet shirt back on, covering up the old scars on his chest, and the new bandages on his arms. "We have to get out of here."

"You're fucking crazy, you know that right?" Geoff asked, looking a bit dazed. "We're being chased, we almost drown, and then all of a sudden you want to fuck! What is wrong with you?" Maybe the proximity to his own death made him crave life and warmth, and all that he had almost lost?

"And what happened to your wrists?" Geoff asked again, gesturing to his bandaged arms.

"You ever heard of Hansel and Gretel?" Church asked.

"The fairy tale?" Geoff asked, forehead scrunched.

"I wanted to leave a trail of bread-crumbs for them to follow."

"You tried to lure them with your blood—by slitting your wrists?" Geoff asked, raising his voice. It dawned on him how truly messed up Church was. "Why would you even want to do that?"

"I told you I had a plan," Church said.

"You could have been killed!"

"I didn't say it was going to work. I shouldn't have let you come."

"You're lucky I did," Geoff said. "Otherwise you'd be dead."

"I could have told you," Church said, "but you wouldn't have let me do what I needed to. I never wanted to get you involved in any of this."

"Okay, you might be crazy," Geoff said, "but those guys still want to kill us—whether they're vampires or not—so let's get the fuck out of here!"

Church stood up, took a couple of steps, then cried out in pain and crumpled to the ground as his ankle gave out.

"Are you okay?" Geoff asked, rushing to his side.

"I must have twisted it." Church said.

"Here," Geoff said, hoisting one of Church's arms over his shoulder, helping him stand up. Church leaned on Geoff, and held one foot off the ground so he wouldn't put any pressure on the sore ankle.

They hobbled along slowly, Church nodding with his chin in the direction they were to go, hopping on one foot and trying not to lean too much of his weight onto Geoff. They made painfully slow progress, and Geoff couldn't understand why the details-men hadn't caught up with them yet.

"I thought these guys were supposed to be vampires," Geoff said, "don't vampires only come out at night?" The sun was going down but they still had a few hours of light before full dark. Geoff didn't suppose that this would be enough to convince Church that they were dealing with people, not monsters.

"I guess not," Church said, "they must have lost our scent in the river. Maybe they think we drowned?" By the time they emerged from the trees onto the shores of Ghost Lake, they were both panting. The river had carried them further downstream than he had thought. Church considered all the monster-movie myths he'd heard, including the one about vampires not being able to cross running water. Whatever the reason, he was grateful the two triplets hadn't caught up with them yet. The lake stretched out before them, strangely still, with barely a ripple to mar the mirrored surface.

"Which way now?" Geoff asked.

"Down there," Church said, nodding in the direction with his chin. Further along the shoreline was a small cinder block building, a dock floating on black tire-treads lashed to the sides, and a concrete boat launch descending into the waters. Geoff hefted Church's arm like a backpack and they hobbled towards the shed, feet slipping on loose stones.

Church disentangled himself and produced a key for the cinder-block building, then Geoff helped Church drag out one of the old metal boats, before selecting a small outboard motor, paddles, life-jackets and a red gas can with a yellow bendy-straw nozzle. A smaller concrete bunker held storage and paraphernalia for Ski-doos and all-terrain vehicles, serving as a garage, although it was currently empty.

The method of choice for reaching this service site were Ski-doos in the winter, and all-terrain vehicles during the summer; the Jiibay River being too rough for the purposes of transportation. Church had made this trek countless times, from the Closest Road, following the path parallel to the Chee'bye, with Day driving, and Mukade-wiiyas and Marie crowded onto the back of their all-terrain. Church was usually left to hike it out to the lake on foot, sometimes accompanied by Inri.

The boats looked ancient.

"The band council doesn't spring for new gear too often," Church said.

Geoff affixed the motor with clamps, helped Church into the boat, and walked into the water up to his knees before casting off, the bottom of the boat scraping on rocks before it got into deeper waters. Church paddled farther out onto the lake before starting the engine.

He pulled on the draw-cord like a lawn mower to get the engine to turn over—pulling and pulling—but he had difficulty getting enough leverage on his sore ankle. The engine would rumble, sputter, and then die. Church stood up on his one good leg, pulled with all his might and finally got the engine roaring to life, cutting through the silence like a chainsaw, echoing off the trees and bouncing back seemingly amplified. Geoff cringed, thinking that everyone in a thirty–five mile radius must have heard the saw of the engine, but knowing it was just his imagination. Sound might travel well over open water, but it was another thing once you took a few steps into the forest.

Church tilted the tiller, raising the motor up until they got out into deeper waters; he didn't want to damage the propeller. Church seemed to know how to steer the tub, his left arm resting casually on the throttle, two jets of water flying past in their wake. When he pivoted the till right, they went left, and when he pivoted the till left, they went right. Sitting in the prow, Geoff noticed that the bow lifted out off the water as they gathered speed, faster than he would have believed possible for such an antique vessel. Conditions changed quickly out on the water, the wind had picked up, and it started to drizzle. They skidded like a skipping stone across the surface, launching off of the crest of each wave, becoming almost airborne for a moment before crashing back down into the spray, only the rudder staying in contact with the lake. Damnit, Geoff thought, boats are supposed to stay in the water! The trees at the edge of the lake whipped by like a green smear.

Geoff yelled something over the grind of the engine that sounded like, "Stop grandstanding," so Church let up on the throttle, but then on impulse did a 360, coming around in a

circle to catch the waves from their own wake. Geoff gripped
the sides of the boat as they caught some air, white knuckles
showing, and Church laughed over the sounds of the engine.

In the distance Osedjig's cabin stood on a slowly ascending rise
among sparsely distributed spruce. Church shut off the engine,
raised the out-bound motor, and let them coast the rest of the
way to shore. It was quiet now, and all they could hear was
the lapping of waves. The sun was dying a bloody death on the
horizon behind them, crepuscular rays shooting up like golden
pillars, and the light reflected blindingly off of the windows of
the cabins; a warm place of wood and light.

They docked, tied off, and scrambled onto ashore. Osedjig's
cabin was somewhat more dilapidated than the last time
Church had laid eyes on it. The snow had been piled up on the
ground three feet deep, stars had been twinkling in the night
sky like diamonds against black felt, smoke had been curling out
of the chimney, and a trail of footsteps had led up to the door.
But that had been years ago. Now it stood empty.

It was still good to be home.

The building was a sturdy, four-walled log-and-daub structure
that had stood for over a century. When Gaawiin and her
husband had been converted to Christianity, they had built a
log cabin style home, emulating the newcomers to the land,
instead of living in a traditional roundhouse or tepee. The log
house had then sat empty after Gaawiin's tragedy, the murder-
cannibalism of Osedjig, and her subsequent pregnancy.

Mukade-wiiyas later took up residence in Osedjig's cabin, rather
than returning to her uncle's family and her human relatives.
When the hunger threatened to spill out of control, Mukade-
wiiyas had run away to live as a recluse, returning to take up

residence in the log house after her hunger had been tamed. She no longer felt she belonged—she didn't belong anywhere—not in the human world, nor in the inhuman world. She wasn't far-gone enough to want to join Bakade-winan, Hunger—her father. She had enough hunger on her own without becoming hunger itself. The vacant log house provided shelter from temptation, because it had been constructed at some distance from the rest of the Ghost Lake Anishinaabe. No one wanted to live near the wiindigo house; it might as well have been haunted. But she was wiindigo, so she lived in the house, with her sister Tough-meat and the other ghosts of the past to keep her company.

They called it 'Nshoomis's cabin,' even though the man who had constructed it probably wasn't Day's grandfather; he had been Gaawiin's husband, but they were not likely his descendants. The truth was supposed to be much crueler: they were descendants of his wife, and his murderer, the monster, Bakade-winan. The Wiindigo. Or so the story goes . . .

By the time they reached the door, the sun had already sunk below the horizon. Church unlocked the door, and they pushed into the dim interior—there was no electricity out here—and no light switches, so Church lit an old William-Coffin-Coleman lantern. There was a tchssshhcht! sound, and a flare of brightness as he struck a wooden match and fiddled with kerosene knobs, producing a high-pitched hissing as he held the flame to the silk mantle, illuminating his face cherry-red for an instant before it was washed out by an intense, white, incandescent light, pushing back the darkness and producing shadows about the room.

White sheets had been draped over the furniture, and cobwebs lay everywhere. In the family's absence, the spiders had taken up residence and reigned supreme. A gigantic stone fireplace dominated one entire wall, large enough to spit and roast an entire moose, and occupied by a large cast-iron pot that could only rightfully be called a cauldron. It was clear that the hearth had been the kitchen when the building had first been constructed, and that for all intents and purposes, it still was, being the focal point and center of the entire structure.

Geoff collapsed onto an old couch and a plume of dust shot into the air making Church cough. Geoff rested as he watched Church limp around, pulling down sheets, and knocking down the worst of the spider-webs with a broom. He didn't know how Church could come so close to death and still have so much energy. He acted as if nothing happened. Geoff was so exhausted, he could barely move.

"What are we supposed to do now?" Geoff asked staring at the exposed raw beams above his head like the ribs of some immense creature, "Do we just wait here until they come for us? What were you planning to do out here?"

"I had a plan," Church said. "But I'm not so sure about that now."

"What were you planning to do?" Geoff asked. "Eat them?"

"Well actually . . ." Church trailed off.

"You can't be serious," Geoff said.

"You saw me take a bite out of the Hound! They'll be much more cautious next time," Church said. "We'll stay here tonight; I don't think they'd set foot inside this cabin." Did vampires need to be invited in? Geoff wondered, Or was that another myth? Church set about smudging everything, wafting the smoke onto the furniture, the windows and the walls.

"Do you really think that'll help?" Geoff asked.

"Crosses and holy water are supposed to keep them away," Church said as he went about affixing cedar branches above the windows and doors like lucky-horse shoes. "I don't see how it could hurt."

"No garlic?" Geoff asked. Between the two of them, their only knowledge of vampire lore had been gleaned from pop-culture and horror movies. So far, none of the myths were proving to be accurate. But that was probably because vampires aren't real, Geoff thought.

"Sunlight doesn't kill them, who knows what the movies got right," Church said. Geoff didn't believe Magnon's men were vampires, but if Church insisted on believing it, Geoff wasn't going to dissuade him. That was probably his way of coping. Geoff still had trouble believing any of this was real.

"So now what?" Geoff asked.

"I have another idea," Church said slowly, as if the words were being dragged out of him and he was reluctant to voice the ideas aloud. "There's a place where the may-may-gwezhiuk are supposed to live . . . and other things—the Burnt Grounds— it's a place where people have seen things—the little people, ooghouls—everyone avoids the place if they can help it. We'll go there tomorrow."

"And what are the little people going to do for us?" Geoff asked, playing along. Church had been counting on his familiarity with the reserve to guide them past pitfalls that the vampires wouldn't know about. The Burnt Grounds could only be considered a pitfall.

"Well," Church said, taking the question seriously, "Long ago there were two boys who went off in a canoe together. They never came back. A few days after they went missing, someone found the drawing of two figures sitting in a canoe carved into a rock near the Burnt Grounds. The may-may-gwezhiuk stole them, brought them into the rock, and turned them into an image."

"There are lots of carving like that around here," Geoff said, "How would they even know the carving had anything to do with those boys?"

"Because they were found—or at least parts of them. All that was left of them was their heads. Their bodies were missing. And both of the figures carved into the rock are headless."

"Have you seen these drawings?" Geoff asked.

"Yeah, it's creepy," Church said.

"Sounds like a ghost story to me," Geoff said.

"What other kinds of stories are there?" Church asked. "The Burnt Grounds are dangerous." Church said. It will be the perfect place to lie in wait.

They stayed up to dawn. Neither one of them was able to fall asleep while it was still full dark. Church spent the night throwing around wild strategies for a plan of attack, or an ambush, while Geoff tried to interject some reality into the discussion. At dawn they climbed into the barn-style overhead loft that was divided into a four separate quarters. This time even Geoff didn't bother undressing before they fell asleep; he was almost too freaked out to sleep, but he was too exhausted to stay awake any longer. They could only hope that vampires needed to sleep as well. Even monsters needed to rest sometimes.

crystallofolia, n. Frost formations, that usually manifest from certain species of plants following a sudden cold snap, but can also develop on trees, logs, decaying organic matter, or even out of the ground. As the plants freeze, the stems crack and the moisture inside is extruded, producing a variety of shapes, from ribbons to the appearance of flowers. Hence the name 'frost flowers', and 'frost freaks'.

Dec. 5th 1872, Ghost Lake,

We woke early.

"Are you sure you want to go through with this?" I asked. "It's not too late to change your mind."

"It's not exactly the cliffs of Weehawken, but it will do." Othniel said, pulling on his long coat. "This is Indian Territory, outside the reach of British law. The whole area is remote enough that any given spot could be a field of honour."

Brennen, one of Othniel's former Yale students followed at our side. Brennen would be acting as his second. What was left of the labourers fell into step behind us as we left the encampment. We made a grim procession as we trudged, as if to an execution, through the forest. The sun had not yet risen, and stars could still be seen glittering through the black boughs of the trees. The sky was just beginning to lighten in the east.

I kept seeing quick snatches of movement out of the corner of my eye, my imagination plaguing me with peculiar thoughts on this strange morning. Paired with the same pervasive feeling of being watched that I've felt for days, it made for an uncomfortable trek.

The temperature had dropped radically overnight, bringing with it a sub zero frost, and an oddly incongruous fog. It was so cold, one would think that it wasn't possible for water to exist as a vapour in order to create the conditions necessary for mist—and maybe this was the case—as the mist seemed to hover in a most unusual way. It gave me the impression that if I just reached out, I could gather the fog in the palm of my hands like solid ice crystals, suspended in space like the stars hanging in the ether of the sky.

As we made our way to the appointed field of honour, I noticed frost freak formations—also known as frost flowers—scattered here and there about the ground. These frost freaks are elongated strands of ice that grow from the cracked stems of frostweed like pipes that freeze and burst in the winter. When there is a sudden drop in temperature sap is drawn up to the surface, where the moisture freezes on contact with the air, creating beautiful filaments in ornate configurations. The arrangements are as intricate and fanciful as the patterns of hoarfrost on a window—impossible, whimsical shapes that defy logic and the imagination.

"Nigigwashkadin." Mookman, the old Ojibwe Indian Chief called them. Not raising his voice above that of a whisper.

Some are thin and delicate, like the neck of a swan, others are jagged stalagmite spikes, tall knee length columns, or folded ribbons, feathers and cones and snail-like curls, fractals growing infinitesimally smaller, branching out, each one an exact replica of the whole, bulbous rounded mushrooms; streamers, ruffles and lace; a diverse multiplicity of forms. Even some of the trees seem to be effected, in a way that is most disconcerting, with threads of ice sprouting from the sides of the trees like hair. It looks like they are growing white beards!

We stepped on the frost flowers, audibly crunching the queer little things underfoot as we walked. Given the sombreer nature of our expedition, no one was brave enough to comment upon them, even in passing. This was a life-or-death situation, not a birding tour.

When we entered the clearing, Drinker was already there, waiting for our arrival, and to my surprise, and considerable confusion, it appeared that Aabitiba was to be acting as his second! I could have sworn that Othniel had laid claim to his allegiances. Apparently I was mistaken.

Marsh and Cope took up positions on opposite sides of the field, a few frost flowers flourished in the intervening space. Everyone except their seconds, stayed back, giving both men plenty of room to maneuvre. I took up a middling position at the edge of the clearing, not wanting to appear to be taking sides. I was only here in a medical capacity. Each time they exhaled, *puffs of their breath were visible in the cold air. Both men breathed heavily, their breath emerging in great streams of smoke. They seemed unaffected by the cold.*

Both men wore their best clothes, as if they were going together to have their images preserved forever in the black glass of an ambrotype, instead of meeting in a forest clearing at dawn. Light reflects off the black backing of the negative silver nitrate and collodian plate, to create a positive image; light is dark, and dark is light. They wore neckties, and long overcoats with wide lapels and contrasting collars, waistcoats and watch-chains, as if it were a formal occasion. And I suppose that it was. They were dressed for their own funeral, as it was entirely possible only one, or possibly neither, would be walking away from this engagement without injury, let alone walking away at all.

The observers were comprised of what was left of the workers from the opposing digger encampments, and a few curious Indian braves who'd come out to watch the spectacle of two white men fighting to the death. All were dressed in thick furs. It was extremely cold. We could have been animals, instead of men, drawn out of the woods by the prospect of fresh blood.

"Those were my bones, and you know it." Drinker said quietly. His voice carried easily in the early morning hush. A dense fog still clung to the ground, making the clearing, and the trees immediately surrounding us, seem like the entire universe, obscured. The world had retreated and shrunk to this small circle of our surroundings, and the drama being played out here.

"That thing with Vorhees?" Othniel scoffed. "That was business. Don't become a soldier if you don't want blood on your hands."

"THOSE WERE MY BONES!" Drinker raged, his voice pitched harsh, and guttural, filling the silence of the forest. "MINE! I introduced you to Vorhees. You went behind my back and made a deal, you snake." I was shocked. I'd never seen Drinker display any amount of anger, he had always been perfectly civil. And now his voice sounded almost demonic. "Money can't bail you out, this time Charles. You should crawl on the ground like the legless creature you are!"

Twenty yards apart, they pointed pistols at each other. Each man aimed for the head or heart; shots to kill, not wound, though any wound could prove fatal, as I well knew. Given the rate of infections, even a grazing wound could be deadly. Drinker raised his pistol first, and Othniel's followed, matching his stance and trajectory.

I felt powerless. Waiting for the blood to flow, so I could patch up the injuries. Both Marsh and Cope had asked me to stand in as their second. And I had refused. I am a medical doctor and I cannot be party to such barbarity. I will sew up their wounds, because my Hippocratic oath demands it, but I resent doing even this much. I am a healer, not a seamstress. I should have stayed home and let someone else stitch them up after they'd willingly participated in such violence.

"I see Aabitiba is acting as your second," Othniel said, his voice warm as a summer's day. "You know he sold me the information."

"What information?" Drinker's voice was flat, and devoid of emotion.

"Why this dig site, of course," Othniel said, pleasantly. "How did you think I found out? He soooold me the location of these bones." Aabitiba took a few steps back, retreating into the trees. As if to absent himself, or prevent himself from being drawn into their quarrel. But it was already far, far too late for that.

"LIAR!" Drinker screamed.

"Oh? I thought you knew." Othniel said mildly, "And here I was thinking Aabitiba was just in my employ because you hired him to spy on me."

Drinker's face turned purple, veins appearing on his forehead, a teakettle with a plugged nose, and no whistle. Aabitiba reacted by hunching in on himself, as if to make himself a smaller target for their wrath.

"How many paces? To first blood, or a la outrance?" Drinker asked with a sneer, "You are the injured party in this matter." Sarcasm threatening to trade in for stupid blows.

"I don't know," Othniel said with a smile, knowing that only his enemy, Cope, would likely catch the insult he volleyed, "maybe we should we flip a coin to decide the matter. Heads, or tails?"

If it was possible, Drinker's face seemed to darken even further.

"Did dear Uncle Peabody buy you another teaching position at Yale?" Drinker asked. "How about your digging crew, does he pay their salary too? Oh wait, that's right. He's dead. Did he know how you were going to fritter away all your inheritance?"

"Oh, go cobble together more skulls onto rectums." Othniel responded. "Call it a new species—maybe you can name it after yourself! Wouldn't that be appropriate?"

"You always had it in for me, waiting for the first slip up so you could publicize my errors!"

"Oh come off, Drinker! Even Leidy, your professor, took my side in the matter. You can't buy up all the mistakes that hit the shelves when they're published, you'd go bankrupt! Everyone already knows what a hack you are!"

They argued, yelling over top of each other, their voices overlapping, like separate waves trying to drown out the other so they could be heard over the crest and crash. But they were made of the same material. I couldn't ascertain who said what, anger and blame pouring out in a stream of vitriol. They were venting years of bitterness, jealousy, avarice, and greed. Fears, insecurity, and hostility, it all crashed down.

The depth and complexity of their hatred for each other was much deeper than I had realized. I had never guessed that they knew each other so intimately. They spoke about past grudges they held against one another, and events of which I have no knowledge. In their passion, they seemed cut from the same cloth.

"You destroyed my bones!" Cope responded. "In Dreamland, remember? The Badlands. Come on now. Don't deny that you did it. I know it was you! Did you smash them yourself, or did you have someone else do your dirty work? I know you don't like to get your hands dirty. That's probably why you turned to dynamite!!!"

"Your bones? Your bones? You're the one who smashed my fossil! You knew how rare of a find that osteichthyes was! Ichthyology is one of your areas of expertise. You couldn't stand that I had found such a valuable creature! You'd rather destroy it than let me get any credit!"

"Oh, come off! I bet you collected the algae and set the charges yourself! You wouldn't want anyone else to have the pleasure of destroying my finds!"

"You know, I really didn't think you'd have it in you, to put your own career ahead of the discovery. You're a traitor to our field!"

"I'm the traitor? I'm the traitor? You utterly destroyed my excavation site in Dreamland. There was nothing left except shrapnel."

"Coward! I'm surprised you even showed up. I thought maybe you would flee to Europe again like you did during the Civil War. I would have thought the prospect of getting shot in a fair duel would have struck too much fear into your heart."

"And you were in Berlin for purely scientific reasons, you self righteous bastard! Not all of us have rich uncles to buy their way through life, some people have to actually work for their achievements!"

"I staked my claim in Wyoming before you ever stepped foot in Hell's Half Acre! I warned you to stop poaching on my territory!"

"Survival of the fittest old chum."

They shouted their recriminations at each other, each man holding his gun steady, trained on the other, but neither man pulled the trigger, so intent were they on getting the last word, as if mere words could settle their arguments. I got the sense this was the first time they'd spoken to each other face to face in some time, and they were not going to give up this opportunity to air their grievances. Only then would they attempt to kill each other.

'You've done me wrong!' And, 'No, you've done me wrong!' They screamed the various wrongs committed, one against the other, variations on the same theme. There was no resolution to the list of resentments they'd accumulated.

--Craaack!--

The sound of a gunshot echoes widely across the clearing in the early morning light.

Both men flinch, expecting a bullet to punch through their rage. Both men open their eyes, a matching look of surprise on their faces that would have been comical in another situation. When they realize that neither one of them has pulled the trigger, and neither one of them has been shot, they turned to look, actively scanning the forest for signs of movement, some indication for what has caused the noise. Could it be some sniper hiding in the trees? And to what purpose?

Craaaack! The sound of a gunshot.

Both men flinch, again expecting a bullet. The sound is from outside the clearing, and from another direction this time. Both men turn to look, their eyes wide, faces scrunched in confusion.

Bang! Bang! Bang! Bang! Bang!

Everyone ducks, and takes cover. Hunching close to the ground, looking wildly in all directions for the stray bullet that might be making a bee line for the nectar of their heart.

More explosions, as of bullets ricocheting. Some closer, and some further away. Pistols trained on the forest now. A Cacophony of phantom bullets ripping through the trees, though both men remain unscathed. They whip their heads around franticly, looking for a sniper. It is as if their own limbs, acting independently of their thoughts, had betrayed them, instead of the forest, which seemed to be misbehaving, and mocking them.

Ghosts. I couldn't help thinking. The forest is full of ghosts.

For a moment, I thought I saw some movement out of the corner of my eye; a swift moving predator, so well suited to its environment, it blended seamlessly into the trees. Horns, like those on the head of an elk, elongated face like the bleached skull of a deer, but with the body of a man, naked and emaciated. But whatever I saw; some spirit, or trick of the mind, it is gone when I turn my head to look. My imagination still haunting me with strange thoughts, and I can't help thinking of the pervasive feeling of being watched that I've felt for days.

A tree explodes right next to the clearing with a loud bang! The trunk of the great tree is riven in two, and shards of ice and splinters explode outwards in every direction. Aabitiba, who is closest to the tree, holds his hands over his ears and screams, positively deafened by the blast as debris rains down upon him. His face is a pincushion of wooden darts where the splinters have imbedded themselves into his soft flesh. He falls to his knees, holding his jaw-line where blood has begun to dam up above his fingers, and flood onto the frozen ground.

The sound of trees exploding echoes hauntingly through the forest, like gunshots. Some close, like the one near poor Aabitiba, and others far away, as if a war were being waged in the forest all around us. The sudden cold snap had caused the sap to freeze and expand inside the capillary vessels of the trees, producing a sound exactly like a gunshot. Bark bursting, branches snapping, trees exploding.

With evidence that no weapons had been fired, both men lower their pistols. Evidently, their thirst for death quenched.

Shivering, I am convinced that the Wiindigo out of legend has shown up at this friendly crash. He came in the form of a flickering shadow at the corners of my vision, too quick to be seen, melting away and gone before I can catch but a glimpse; and in the form of hard bodies being broken, and ice cracking in violent percussion, impossible to separate sound from the action. His presence fills the forest all around us, surrounding us.

I suspected that I am being watched, and this is confirmation. Whatever this creature is, we are not alone in this remote situation, so completely removed from the stir of civilized society. The wiindigo is real. And it brought the early Winter, flash freezing the frost-weed, and the trees alike.

As all those in attendance stood in awe and terror, silent except, for the explosion of the trees ringing through the clearing, and absorbing this unexpected turn of events, a new sound emerged from the forest. The snapping of branches and twigs as something crashed through the underbrush in a conflagration of sound, something larger than a hare, and less quicksilver than a deer; unlike any wild animal that I could think of, except maybe for a rhinoceros, suddenly transported to this northern waste, and charging through the woods and bog in fear and confusion, ready to trample and impale anything in its path. No wild animal that I knew of, not a moose or bear, would make this much noise. The two men turned, weapons raised to face this new threat, possibly expecting some beast enraged by the cold explosion of the trees?

The shape of a man appeared, bursting from the trees and into the clearing, bare feet numb and blue from the cold, crunching through the delicate frost freak formations, slicing through tender flesh, the ice as sharp as shards of broken glass, staining the blue ice a slick crimson and leaving a trail of bloody footprints. The man was naked, marked by the welts and lacerations of branches from his mad dash through the forest, and his expression quite mad, pupils large and dilated, all thought and awareness blasted from his mind, as if replaced by some other, alien presence. His lips looked as if they were ringed with black tar, as if he'd been eating the soil from an exposed section of the dinosaur excavation sites. And it was with some shock that I recognized this figure as my own patient, Ogimaa; somehow escaped from the locked chamber of his sickbed, the shackles and ropes, which had been used to bind him to his bed, still clinging to his wrists and ankles, trailing behind him like ghostly raiment. During the period of his thrashing derangement, it had been necessary to restrain him, so that he could not injure himself or anyone else. Upon realizing that this was not some rabid creature of the northern wilds, but the culmination of a disturbed mind, both Drinker and Othniel put up their pistols.

Ogimaa came to a stop at the edges of the clearing, his head pivoting from side to side, tilted as if he were having trouble seeing through his murky eyes, or as if he were seeing from a long distance away. He took in the tableau of the two men placed at opposite ends of the clearing like two rooks on a chessboard, and the cluster of wide-eyed spectators.

"--NOON-DES-KAA-TAAY--" Ogimaa whispered, his voice gravelly, and yet somehow managing to fill the entire clearing with its insinuating vibrations, maybe due to some quirk of acoustics, as if he were standing at the center of a Roman coliseum constructed to amplify sound. Sounds torn awkwardly from his throat, as if something else was speaking by proxy through him, like a puppet on a string, or as if he were speaking through unfamiliar vocal chords, each syllable emerging slowly, drawn out, and pulled excruciatingly from his chest. Noondeskade. I'm hungry.

Ogimaa taking in first the cluster of spectators, "WAA-BEEE-SEEAAK," and then the two combatants on the 'Field of Honour', "MOOOOZ-OOOOWN-ZAAAAACK," he seemed to come to a decision. All those in attendance cringed, as Ogimaa's voice scraped chalkboard scratches across our eardrums. The audience huddling closer together in obvious fear. Moozoonsag. Young moose. Waabiseg. Ptarmigan.

Ogimaa charged forward, having selected his closest target, Othniel. He closed the distance between himself and the paleontologist in short order, and grabbed the man about the neck in a stranglehold and began squeezing, ringing his neck like a duck, intent on snuffing out his life with a strength only the truly mad can fully harness. It was this that finally snapped us into action, smashing apart the stunned paralysis of those in attendance—a few Yale-men and Ojibwe stepped forward to intervene and prevent Ogimaa from killing the man. Even Cope stepped forward to intervene, though he himself had come to the clearing this very morning to kill the man.

There was a jumble of limbs as we sought to remove Ogimaa's iron grip from Othniel's neck watching as the strangled man's face turned first red, and then a darker shade of purple. We frantically pried Ogimaa's cold fingers from Othniel's throat, bending them back, one by one like frozen sticks. Some of them had to be broken, so intent was he on strangling the other man, and in order to save the paleontologist's life. It ultimately took five of us to subdue and restrain the rabid creature who appeared more monster than man, leaving a darkening welt of bruises ringing Othniel's throat like a hangman's knotted rope. He was lucky that his windpipe hadn't been crushed, or he would have required an emergency tracheostomy. I had come prepared to treat gunshot wounds, not the injuries resulting from hand-to-hand combat.

Othniel gasped for breath, like a fish out of water, while the grunts and curses continued as we struggled to subdue his attacker, and his face slowly returned to its natural shade. From black-purple, to red-beige. The duel was abandoned, and Ogimaa's sudden, unexpected appearance on the field of honour, brought an end to all thoughts of any further violence, at least for this day.

Dec. 17th? 18th? 1872, Ghost Lake,

I think I have gone mad; I am mad. I no longer trust my own reasoning, or my ability to think rationally. Even my thoughts and experiences are untrustworthy. All is suspect. I can be certain of nothing when my own powers of observation and deduction are themselves compromised. Nothing is solid or certain in this state. I can barely distinguish between my dreams, and when I am awake. My life has become a waking nightmare. From the corner of my eye, I see the creature, stalking me and dodging out of sight before I can catch a solid glimpse of his form, which appears in all his solid glory in my dreams, where I am plagued by an intense hunger, and the promise of the cessation of my cravings, if only I eat from the ice fashioned into the shape of a bowl. I know better than to eat, and end up like my patients, or like Persephone, forced to spend eternity in Hades. I know this: Do not eat the fruits of hell!

Still, he terrorizes me even during the day, a shadowy figure flitting through the trees, the howling wind picking at the kinks in my shelter, trying tirelessly to find a way in with his cold fingers. Quietly, quietly, on the edge of my hearing, I faintly hear the high -pitched whine of the saa-geh-menh. Is it inside my head, or outside of it? I do not know. It is much too cold for mosquitos now, so I suspect it is my mind, playing tricks.

I step outside. The chill, dry air freezes the moisture inside my lungs. The shock of it makes me sputter and choke. I've decided to take the last ditch cure. The boiling oil. I feel there are no other avenues of treatment left to me, and I am desperate. I would try anything if I thought it would disperse the darkness that has been clouding my mind.

First I collected kindling, trudging through the calf-deep snow plunging over the lip of my boots to melt into my socks. My feet would be damp for the rest of the day if I didn't replace them with dry ones. I didn't go far from my camp, not wanting to go more than a few steps into the trees. The second I stepped into the bush, I could feel it waiting out there for me, catching snatches of movement, too quick for me to see directly. I knew he was there.

I took my time, despite the pinching cold, steepling the kindling so the sticks leaned against each other like an Indian teepee, drawing out the process, I placed a few scraps of parchment underneath, carefully lighting the paper with a match cupped between my palms as shelter from the wind. I am not delaying, I told himself, I'm just doing things right. The parchment caught, and I could see the flames slowly eating up some of my words, spidery script advancing across the crumpled pages.

I set the duck fat to boiling on the cook-fire outside my tent. I had no fear of being interrupted. The snow-swept landscape has now been abandoned by all but the heartiest of men who are digging for Drinker. The Indians have boarded themselves up in their homes. The encampment is almost deserted. Occupied only by the dirt devils that form out of sleet whipped up by the wind, zephyrs spinning about like mini tornadoes on the barren, frozen-surface of the lake. Snow devils.

As the duck-fat simmers, it gives off steam like a hot pot of coffee. The smell is not unpleasant. I wait patiently for the fat to render. I am in no rush. Like a man walking towards his own execution, I luxuriate in each individual task, drawing it out, as if to ward off the inevitable. When the fat is ready, I spoon it out into a tin can with a ladle, cupping it in my palms and feeling the heat radiate outwards. The liquid still bubbles, chunks of white, glistening lard rotating in the churning mess. I steel myself as best I can to the pain. I know it is coming, all I can do is accept it. Drink it while it's still hot. Not just hot, boiling. I raise the can to my lips and drink, my lips burn, sticking to the hot can like a wet tongue pressed to cold metal, except my flesh sticks, burning, and the grease hits my tongue scalding, burning, I swallow, trying to down it as fast as I can like a shot of Rust, like a bandage pulled off too quick, I almost gag, the spray sending the blazing oil back up, burning the roof of my mouth worse, I almost falter, but I tell myself, the quicker I drink, the sooner the pain will subside, I swallow, swallow, swallow. Three long gulps and I've emptied the tin can, and the warmth is seeping into my lungs, my throat, my chest, my arms, burning, burning, burning, burning. I fall on my side onto the hard packed snow, gagging, struggling to draw in breath, too shocked to inhale. It takes a moment for me to recover enough to draw in air to even scream, inhaling, the passage of air through my windpipe is like torture, I scream, and though it hurts to scream, I can't help myself, I have to let some of the pain out, as if to eject some of the agony with the scream that rips its way from my ragged throat. My scream goes on and on, reverberating against the trees, and extending out for miles in all directions, scaring away a few crows, who flap away startled, cawing their displeasure. If a man screams in the forest, does anyone hear him scream?

My insides are burning, and I know not what damage the oil is wreaking, burning me from the inside out, a warmth spreading outward from my chest, my esophagus, my limbs, all the way down to the space where I can feel my frozen heart aching to beat. I curl up in a ball on the frozen tundra, fetal, waiting for the pain to recede. I am in agony. The warmth spreads outward, with so much pain, more pain than I could have ever prepared for, spreading outward from my chest. Warmth. Pain. Warmth. Pain. Warmth.

And then it happened. I could feel something beginning to stir, come loose in my chest, as if someone had cracked open my rib cage and reached down my throat, into my chest, held my beating heart in their fist, and began to pull, pull, pull, ripping my frozen-razor-sharp heart, all jagged edges, back up the way they'd entered, slicing me apart all the way. I began retching, coughing up frozen, bloody shards of ice like crimson flowers on a pure white bed of snow.

Raised up on my arms, I examined the ice below me, like cool blue shards of lapis lazuli, and I smiled. That is the last thing I remember, before the darkness of oblivion came to wrap me up in her arms, ensconced in nothingness, and far far away, where nothing exists, and there is no pain, only the darkness.

I was happy to be welcomed into her embrace.

```
Time Dilation*: As you approach the speed of
light, time slows down. The classic example is one
where a twin goes on a journey into space at high
speeds, while the other stays on earth, and then
returns to discover the twin on earth has aged
more.

  *(The result of an actual difference in elapsed
time between two events as measured by an
observer.)
```

The night air had a bite to it.

Geoff shivered and wondered why they had to do whatever it was they came out here to do at night. "Everyone knows that night is the time when vampires are at their most powerful." Geoff had tried to reason with Church, "We should have come out here when it was still light out."

But vampires, Church thought, aren't the only ones more powerful at night.

"This is a trap remember, and we want them to fall into it."

"Yeah, with us as the bait." Geoff said, "Are you sure this is going to work?" He kept remembering the story Church had told, of the two boys who had gone off in a canoe and never returned.

"No," Church said, "I'm not."

Geoff was almost certain that the sudden drop in temperature wasn't his imagination, there was a definite chill to the air, and it was getting colder. It felt more like a winter's night in December than it did a late summer's night in August. He could see his breath when he exhaled. He got the impression that whatever Church was leading them towards, was as dangerous as what they were running away from. Maybe they'd be better off turning around and taking their chances with the details-men. The devil you know.

"We're here," Church said. The ground under their feet had turned to gravel and the trees made way for pulverized stone. Church had insisted they paddle all the way across the bay instead of using the motor, and once they dragged their boat onto shore, hadn't spoken a word. They used hand gestures instead, as if there was a camp of enemy soldiers over the next rise and the slightest whisper might give away their presence. Church's paranoia was infectious, and Geoff found himself following Church's lead, taking directions wordlessly.

In front of them lay a clearing of black rocks, lit by a clear sky littered with stars and a waxing quarter moon that bathed everything in a bluish cast—and Geoff understood why people called this the Burnt Grounds. Why didn't anything grow here? Geoff wondered. What could happen to a place that was so bad that it had never recovered? Then he changed his mind, deciding that he didn't want to know. Even a few days after a forest fire, there would be a few green shoots sprouting up out of the destruction—some species depended on wildfire for reproduction. But there were no green shoots sprouting up out of these blasted rocks.

"Why doesn't anything grow here?" Geoff asked.

"Why doesn't a tree grow in the middle of a river?" Church asked, and shrugged in response.

The current, Geoff thought, imagining a vast, invisible river of darkness flowing through the Burnt Grounds, bathing everything in a noxious radiation. The rocks here were volcanic, almost as if they had been brought from somewhere else.

"What do we do now?" Geoff asked in a hushed voice. Even though this place was creepy as hell didn't necessarily mean that it was haunted, or that the ghosts would care if a little blood was shed.

"We wait," Church said.

Geoff felt, more than he actually saw, strange rushing movements, like the squiggly blue-and-white dance of a head-rush. "What is that?" he asked.

"It's the may-may-gwezhiuk," Church said barely above a whisper.

"What are they?" Geoff asked, eyes wide. Are they real? In the distance he could hear the leaves in the trees rustling, as if by a breeze, except that the air was perfectly still here—too still. Except for the strange sounds, which he figured were probably just his imagination. The place was creepy as fuck all.

"I don't think they like us being here," Church said.

"Great," Geoff said. He didn't ask Church who he meant by 'they'. Wait, and the predators would come to them.

Time passed and the sky became more overcast, shrouding the moon and blocking the light of the stars. In the darkness, the shape of the rocks looked like the refuse of a scrap-metal yard, shadows of all different shapes and sizes, from the gravel under his feet to monolithic boulders. He kept catching movement out of the corner of his eye, a flicker here, and he would turn his head only to find the immobile rocks. The place wore on his nerves, forcing him into a state of constant alertness, like those moments of hypertension caused by lack of sleep, when he imagined hearing sounds and voices at the edge of his hearing. The crunch of gravel beneath his feet, every sniff and cough seemed supernaturally amplified in this unnaturally quiet place, as if it were constructed like an ancient Roman coliseum, to carry sound. High above, fast-moving clouds scudded past the moon, while the Burnt Grounds were shielded from the vagaries of the weather as if it were inside the invisible dome of a fish bowl, untouched by any hint of a breeze.

Geoff hugged himself, feeling the chill eat its way into his bones. Church didn't seem to show any response to the cold. But hell, I'm cold even if Church isn't, so he huddled next to Church for warmth, and Church adjusted to Geoff's presence without resistance. The hunger enveloped Church in its numb embrace so the cold didn't really feel like anything. The warmth radiating from Geoff's body was a blanket against the numbness.

At some point Geoff fell asleep, because he woke up to find himself stretched out on the rocky soil. It was still dark but the sky was beginning to lighten in the east. His ribs felt sore from lying on the stones, and when he sat up, his right cheek was covered with grit imbedded into his flesh.

—The vampires had not come for them—

"Maybe they gave up," Geoff suggested. Maybe they had thought better of it, and had gone off to find some easier prey. Church wasn't convinced.

"They're not going to give up," Church insisted. "They'll come." And so they waited, with the rocks, and the flitting presences of the may-may-gwezhiuk.

"I'm hungry," Geoff said.

"That's the idea," Church told him, "And there's nothing to eat around here except rocks."

"I thought you told me you aren't allowed to fast," Geoff said. "You're not still planning on trying to eat them are you?"

"Better to be prepared," Church said.

Prepared for what? Geoff wanted to ask.

"The boundary between this world and the next is thin here, like a higher altitude. Nothing grows here. If you transplant something here, it will die. During the summer, the rocks here are cold, and during the winter the ground is hot, and it radiates heat. This place is like the after-world, where everything broken and destroyed is made whole, and everything burnt and wrecked is alive. This is a place that is closer to the spirit world."

"And that's important?" Geoff asked.

"The boundary between this world and the next is thinner here, which means it's easier for spirits to manifest."

Geoff was about to ask if Church had brought his Ouija board and what spirits he was hoping to 'manifest' when they heard the sound of a snapping branch in the murky woods. The two triplets, like bullies-in-business-suits, emerged from the trees looking around themselves at the rocky clearing, weapons drawn.

—They both carried handguns—

Oh fuck, Geoff thought, this is not good this is not good...

Things happened fast.

The air seemed to bristle with shadows, thicken and condense like a storm cloud massing, blocking the progress of Magnon's goonies. Like the brown cross-hatching you see before passing out, Geoff thought, when someone strangles you. It looked like a swarm of bees, enveloping them, and Church was relieved. The may-may-gwezhiuk were not happy. The details-men frowned at the strange atmospheric disturbances, but pushed their way through the brown cross-hatchings clogging the air. It wasn't slowing them down any. Hundsfordt and Grundel were still coming towards them, weapons drawn.

"Um, Church. Who is that?" Geoff asked.

Two new figures emerged from the shadowed undergrowth of the forest. Church made out the almost identical figures of Inri and Marie, differentiated only by their respective sex.

"Inri . . . mom?" Church asked, his jaw hanging open. He knew he wasn't hallucinating, but he had trouble making sense of what his eyes were telling him. What were Inri and his mother doing here? And she was awake!

There was no mistaking the look in Marie's eyes. She was actually there, not asleep, not away, not lost in a trancelike state while physically present. She was here, in the moment, looking at Church, and actually seeing him. He had only rarely seen the fleeting glint of awareness in her eye, a mere glimmer letting him know she was still alive, still inside there somewhere. This brief glimmer was now clear, and strong, and unmistakable, shining from within her like a nuclear generator radiating power. The appearance of any emotion on her normally placid face seemed like an exaggeration. She looked hungry. And she looked royally pissed!

Uh-oh, Church thought. He'd never seen his mother awake before, let alone angry. Something must have finally gotten through to her. She was as beautiful as the model on the cover of a magazine, but this wasn't a fairy tale, Marie wasn't Sleeping Beauty, and Church was pretty sure it wasn't a kiss that had woken her—more like a dragon awoken to find his gold stolen. Something had roused her, and that something made her angry.

"I thought you said she was locked up in some mental institution?" Geoff asked.

"She was," Church said, his voice hushed.

"Maybe she is like Akasha. Who knows who will play Enkil, or rather—Lestat—to her Akasha?"—Inri's words came back to him. Church figured Inri would know better than anyone else what went on beneath the calm visage of Marie's face, like the undisturbed surface of Ghost Lake.

It turned out that Church didn't have to play the violin like a demon to disturb her sleep, all he had to do as put himself in enough harm's way to awaken her maternal instincts. She was one ticked-off wiindigo.

"Mom?" Church said again, captured by the sight of his mother, captured like the flashbulb explosion of a camera's glare, he was frozen to the spot. She stalked onto the burnt grounds with a determined step.

"Get down!" Geoff screamed, tugging on Church's arm as a shot rang out. A loud POP! ricocheted through the clearing. Grundel had pulled out a gun and aimed it in their direction. No, not in their direction, the barrel was aimed at Geoff! They wouldn't want to waste Church's wiindigo blood by spilling it out onto the ground. But the bullet must have gone wide, because Geoff was still standing.

Time seemed to thicken and slow down. Or maybe Church's reaction times sped up? He had time to see everything in exquisite detail, down to the slight tensing of muscles in Grundel's index finger as he re-took aim and began to squeeze the trigger.

Church pushed Geoff, slamming his body into the other boy and knocking him to the ground. Church was now standing where Geoff had been a moment before. POP! Another shot rang out, and time seemed to return to normal, rushing forward in a blur as if to make up for the brief delay in action.

A quick flash of brown flesh—streak of quicksilver movement—and the glassy sightless eyes of a deer lay dead at his feet, staring at nothingness. The entry point of the bullet hole was smoking slightly and blood leaked out, pooling beneath the animal. The slug had hit a carotid artery and severed its spinal chord so that it was dead before it hit the ground. An impressive shot—and nearly improbable.

That bullet had been meant for him—the white-tail had bolted from the nearby trees, streaking across the space at the perfect time to intercept the bullet aimed at his heart. It was too unlikely to be a coincidence. Maybe Waabitii, or one of his ancestors, had sacrificed themselves again? Church had another reason to be thankful. But he had only a moment to consider the unlikely sacrifice, before returning his attention to what was taking place on the Burnt Grounds.

Another form appeared, loping out of the wilderness like a dangerous and graceful animal, except that it was the form of a man who seemed to be wearing the skull and antlers of a deer. A long, narrow, wrinkled face, great, massive, gnarled pieces of bone, reaching for the sky like the skeletal branches of a tree. Church's grandfather perched on a granite rock with his head tilted to the side, almost the exact same angle at which a bird of prey tilts its head to examine its kill, pupils contracting like laser beams focusing in on its victim.

His Grandfather's lips were all black where they were not already eaten, exposing teeth like perpetually drawn curtains in a rictus grin. He looked hungry. Starved in fact. Skin stretched taut over bone, protruding like that of a starving dog's. Bakade-winaan saw the wavering guns and his smile grew larger. His smile grew larger, because his teeth were always barred, so he always smiled.

Grundel let out a surprised cry when he saw the creature, took aim and fired. It sounded like a cannon in the silence, echoing and re-echoing off the multiple granite edifices, so that the sound of the gunshot became multiplied, receding and becoming quieter and quieter with every reverberation, growing more distorted as it bounced back and forth across the quarry. Fun-house thunder. The Wiindigo didn't flinch, the shot must have gone wide.

"What are you shooting at?" Hundsfordt asked, his gaze sweeping the clearing, but he didn't see the source of Grundel's alarm. Had he gone mad? Hundsfordt saw Inri and Marie standing at the far edge of the clearing, but Grundel's firearm was pointed in the opposite direction, into the trees.

Before Grundel had a chance to fire another round, the creature was already upon him. One minute he had been crouched on a rock twenty feet away, and the next it was at his throat, without any space between, as if the frames for that particular sequence of time had been deleted, and it was ripping out his carotid artery with its teeth and catching the spurt of blood that escaped.

Hundsfordt turned to see the spurt of blood, and his brother on the ground, but still couldn't see what had done the damage. What the fuck?

For Church, his grandfather looked like a lion barreling down on a gazelle and feasting on its flesh while it was still alive, too hungry to be bothered with making sure that it was properly dead before he began wolfing down great hunks of living meat. Ripping open the rib cage to get at the still beating heart, like a rare delicacy, forgetting about the rest of the meat as he cupped the heart to his lips; hands and face smeared with blood and gore.

Hunh, Geoff thought, a vampire's heart does beat—another strike against Church's vampire theory, another myth busted. Geoff wasn't sure what he was seeing, or whether he was hallucinating, maybe he was finally falling into Church's delusions, for the moment seeing things the way Church viewed them. Nature is not humane, Geoff thought, nature is cruel.

Grundel's screams were short-lived, and Hundsfordt turned back to Church and Geoff, aimed and pulled the trigger. Church supposed Hundsfordt thought he could always resurrect his brother later if he needed to. The bullet caught Geoff on the side of his neck and a spray of arterial blood exploded as he fell to the ground grasping at his throat, blood gurgling and bubbling up between his fingers like a three year-old blowing bubbles in his milk with a straw. Red bubbles.

Bakade-winan looked up at the sound of another shot reverberating through the clearing, the grey cross-hatchings of the may-may-gwezhiuk like a swarm of angry zagimek clouding the air between Bakade-winan and his next meal.

Church saw his grandfather look up at the crack of Hundfordt's gun, pupils contracting as he focused on the source of the disturbance. At this point Hundsfordt must have decided that he and his brother were in over their heads because he turned to run, but didn't get very far. He found his exit blocked by Inri and Marie. He was surrounded. Church's grandfather caught up with Hundsfordt before he could raise the gun again, twisting and tearing off his head like the twist-off cap on a bottle of soda and letting the rest of the meat fall. The three wiindigo converged on their meal.

Church knelt down beside Geoff and applied pressure to the wound, thankful for once that he had seen so many people die that he didn't immediately panic. It's just a flesh wound, he tried to convince himself, but he knew that wasn't true. Geoff looked up at Church, his lips working but no sound emerged. Geoff knew that if his carotid artery had been hit, he'd pass out from the drop in blood pressure, and he'd be dead within minutes.

"Don't worry I'll take care of you," Church said, squeezing the wound shut as hard as he could, trying to keep the blood inside Geoff's body from spilling out onto the hungry ground.

The details-men were dead and gone, and Church barely had time to register their deaths as they fell. Eight, and Nine, he counted, as he listened to the sound of his family feasting, flesh tearing, meat rending, crunch of cartilage and bone. Everyone he knew seemed to die. A frightening amount of blood had leaked down the front of Geoff's shirt. Geoff mouthed words Church couldn't hear, and his face had gone deathly pale.

"I'm cold," Geoff said, mouthing the words. Then his eyes went glassy as he lost consciousness. Church watched helplessly, holding the wound as tightly as he could to keep what little blood Geoff still had, inside his body, as if the harder he applied pressure, the longer he could hold off the inevitable.

"Don't go," Church said, as the fire of life died. Church crouched over Geoff, cradling him. He sat alone with the bodies, and the sounds of his uncle, his mother, and his grandfather, eating.

Miisaa'i minik. The End.

Bakade

Bakade. Hunger. He had no name. He was Bakade-winan—Hunger—this was not his name, hunger was who he was, hunger was what he was. There was no room for anything else. There was nothing else. Only Bakade.

Bakade-winan watched as the two men picked their way carefully through the dense underbrush, bulky backpacks jammed with all sorts of gear, strange instruments dangling from the loop straps, twill bucket hats providing shade from the sun, slathered in mosquito repellant and sun-block they could be scented from a mile down-wind, cursing every time they became caught on briar or thorn, cursing every time a black-fly took a pound of flesh, or a mosquito stuck in her proboscis, despite the deterrent of poison. Meaty calves sticking from khaki cargo shorts—they followed a slight deer path until the way became impassable due to the increasing ambiguity of the terrain as the path skirted the edges of a bog, and their shoes became mired in the muck so that it was impossible to continue, and it was as difficult to retreat, as it was to go forward. The ground itself was hungry here, and if they had been walking unaware, easily could have been swallowed by the earth itself. There were many of these swallowing places—and Bakade was slightly saddened that he didn't get to watch the two men being devoured—maybe they would yet fall victim to another swallowing place, as treacherous as quick-sand. The thought made Bakade's smile widen—widen, because his lipless mouth always revealed his teeth, and so he was always smiling. Bakade's smile widened as he imagined the two men crying out to each other as the marshy earth slowly ate them alive—a little bit at a time as they squirmed, their panic worming them deeper into her suffocating arms. But the men turned back from the slough, trudging through the mud, past their ankles, sucking at their heavy boots, describing the arch of a circle as they went wide around the hazard—yet another obstacle encountered on their trek.

Given the number of times they had needed to back track, it would be easy to get lost here, even for experienced surveyors. The men marched on, a cluster of mosquitos following the warmth of the blood thrumming through their veins like the beat of a drum, drawing them on—though they were largely held at bay by the poison—and Bakade followed the cloud of whining mosquitoes, their high-pitched voices almost outside the range of human hearing, but clustered so numerously together, they formed a palpable presence, blotting out, and darkening the sky, their smaller hungers amassed like a chorus of bullfrogs singing along to the rhythm of his own thoughts.

The two humans encroached further and further, coming at last to the foot of a cliff-face bluff, rising up forty feet into the air above and revealing the stratified layers of sediment built up over the millennia, as the detritus of each age fell, sandwiched between that which had come before, and that which would come after. From this outcropping of rock, a black, viscous bile extruded from between the sandwiched layers of sedimentary rock, flowing like the gummy sap from the injured bark of a tree, thicker and darker than blood, sticky as honey, though far from sweet, this nectar reeked of oil and bitumen and the fermented remains of ancient life—Bakade thought for sure they would go around, describing again the wide arch of a circle, or turn around, back-tracking as they had done many times already on encountering other such natural obstructions, in order to find a more passable route—but this was not the case.

This out-cropping of rock was not treated as merely another obstacle in their path—like the badlands, the swamps, and the nearly impenetrable undergrowth—instead they dropped their heavy packs, whooping with laughter and excitement. It was clear, that they had found whatever it was they were after. And whatever the men had come to take—Bakade didn't want them to have—if they wanted the black bile—he would do his best to make sure they would never have it. One of the men pulled out a small pick-axe and dug into the cliff face to remove a chunk of rock and examine the crumbling compacted soil between his fingers.

"Jackpot," the man said, smiling. He dropped the black rock and wiped his hand on his shorts—now black with sticky tar.

Bakade-winaan knew—if he allowed the men to leave with news of their discovery—more men would come—many men—and maybe they'd start digging again—dragging whatever it was they were after this time from the depths of the black soil. Maybe even the sludge they seemed so elated to have found. They'd be stamping through his forests—and though the mosquitoes would feast—Bakade's refuge would be invaded, cluttered with the stinking meat of human bodies, they would despoil everything they touched—and he had a special place in his frozen heart for the Jiibay Zaa'iganing. He would protect it.

Bakade-winan descended upon the men quickly—and though he was hungry—not only hungry, but hunger itself—he allowed his teeth to sink in only far enough to hold his prey still, while he tore through the man's chest, cracking open the rib-bones like tent-flaps to dig out his still-beating heart. The man's screams did not last long, and the other man didn't get far—though his boots pounded the earth, and his breath came quickly in excited terror. Bakade-winan descended upon the second surveyor with as much speed as he had the first; the man took one look back at his attacker as he ran—which was a mistake—he lost his footing on the uncertain terrain, for the first time catching a glimpse of what monster stalked them.

Bakade cut off his victim's cries with quick efficiency of movement, wrending flesh from bone, and wrending cartilage from flesh, devouring a few mouthfuls of the still-quivering meat; in his haste, biting off two of his fingers, and feeling the crunch and shatter of the bones between his teeth, and yet still he chewed. Dropping the corpse to go back to collect the body of the first surveyor, he returned to pick up the second, carrying both men now, flopped over his shoulder like limp ducks, he walked towards a ravine where he knew a hungry predator—bizhew—had been stalking her prey. The mountain lion was expecting, and she would soon have hungry lion-cubs to feed.

More men would come. They'd come looking for the men he'd preyed upon—and partially consumed—and Hunger didn't want them to discover the tar-like substance oozing from the rock-shelf like congealed blood—so he carried the dead men, their arms swinging limply as he paced towards the valley where bizhew would soon have her cubs.

A note on the Anishinaabe-mowin in this text:

I am not a fluent speaker of the language. I learned many of the words used in this novel from my grandmother, Anishinaabe was her first language, which is the language of this land—and it was my mom's second language while attending Residential School, and it is now my language, third-hand. Miigwetch to my mom and Grandma!

I also learned many of the Anishinaabe words in this book from Ojibwe language teachers: from Shirly Ida Williams, while attending Trent University, and Isadore Toulouse, through his online Anishinaabe language teaching platforms. Chi-Miigwetch Isadore and Shirly!

I also used many different Ojibwe language dictionaries, both online and in print, to construct my sentences. I hope I have not made too many mistakes. Shirly taught me to use the language I have, whatever my skill level, and this is what I've done. All errors in spelling and grammar are my own. Miigwetch!